**W9-ACK-838**

# The Sirens of Oak Creek

by
**Robert Louis DeMayo**

*11 /21 /23*

This book can be ordered on: Amazon, Ingram,
B&N Press, Kindle and other retailers.

Available in print, eBook and audiobook.

Edited by: **Nina Rehfeld**
Nina@txture.com

Cover Design: **Andrew Holman**
www.andrewholman.com

Interior Maps: **Tom Fish**
tfishart@yahoo.com

Interior Illustrations: **Jan Marc Quisumbing**
holla@the janimal.com

Audiobook Narrator: **Lindsey Ross**
www.greenandclover.com

Drawing of woman: **Sharolyn Maleport**

Interior Photos: **Robert Louis DeMayo**

# *This is a work of fiction.*

This book is filled with historical facts and many accurate geographic details, but they are interwoven with local myths and legends. The story is my creation, and I had my own agenda in writing it. It is not a proper history. If you would like to learn more about Oak Creek Canyon and the Verde Valley, and the people who populated it over the years, I have some suggestions:

The Verde Valley has well-preserved ruins, including the Honanki and Palatki ruins, Tuzigoot and Montezuma Castle national monuments, and the largest petroglyph site in the area, the V-Bar-V Heritage Site. To understand the early cultures better, visit the Verde Valley Archaeological Center, located in Camp Verde. Its curator, Kenneth Zoll, has published two books on the rock art of V-Bar-V and the Verde Valley and some of the astrological calculations made there by the ancients.

The pioneers in my story are all based on real people, but I'll let you decide where the facts end and the story begins. At the end of the book is a Pioneer Lineage page to help reduce confusion. Even better, the Sedona Heritage Museum offers great exhibits on what used to be a pioneer homestead and lets the visitor glimpse into the lives of Sedona's pioneers and the town's early days.

In Flagstaff, the Museum of Northern Arizona has an impressive collection of Native American artifacts and natural history specimens collected on the Colorado Plateau. A notable ruin that is well worth a visit is Walnut Canyon. Located ten miles east of Flagstaff, off I-40, the Sinaguans lived here in 25 cliff dwellings from 1100-1250 CE.

*for*

# Diana Lee DeMayo

"When I walk beside her, I am the better man."
(*Eddie Vedder – Hard Sun*)

Writing this book required feet on the ground, and I'm indebted to my hiking friends who helped me reach the far corners of Oak Creek Canyon, the plateau above it, and the West Fork: Steve Donovan, Lincoln Fiske, Raef Lillesve, Mark Patton and Saydrin DeMayo. Jason Wesley took it a step further, exploring the plateau in his Polaris Razon and then flying over it all in a small Piper Archer. Brian Rosenberg gave me an unforgettable flight in a helicopter, up Oak Creek Canyon and then down the length of the West Fork, all the way to Sycamore Canyon.

My editor, Nina Rehfeld, returned for this novel, and I feel it is better having survived her talented eye. Drew Holman created the cover using one of his own images. The illustrations were drawn by Jan Marc Quisumbing and Sharolyn Maleport, and the maps and the box canyon sketch by Tom Fish.

For this novel, I was also proud to have my family close to me. My intern—and daughter—Tavish Lee DeMayo, was a great help with production and created the eBook. Pat DeMayo still has an eagle eye for proofreading. And Ronald DeMayo assisted in straightening out the firearms used in the story.

3

Delving into the past was another challenge, and my Sedona friends helped with their recollections, including: Tracey Dunbar & Chris Lockett, John Bradshaw, Bob Brill, Eric Henkels and David Cushman Holton III. Chris Hilt from the Junipine Inn, and Daniel & Monica Garland (Indian Gardens), helped paint a picture of their locations in 1987, as did Eric & Gayle Glomski from Page Springs (Winery). Jeff Goebel educated me on mining in this area, and Mike and Sherri O'Neil helped me make sense of the land up on the plateau and a few forest service policies. Thank you, Sensei Rick Koehler, of the Sedona Karate Academy, for a few defensive insights, and Betty Ruiz for telling me of the Legend of La Llorona.

Special thanks to Jut Wynne and Kenneth Dall for schooling me on specific aspects of the area's natural history and early tribal history. And Martin Gray for allowing me to use some of his material from a lecture he gave at the Flicker Shack in 1987.

Being an introvert, it took a few musician friends to help me appreciate how music and song has always moved us—humanity—toward something higher. Thank you: P.K. Gregory, Eric Kerns and Chris Fitzpatrick.

A writer has a tough battle ahead if he doesn't have good support, and my wife, Diana, and three daughters: Tavish, Saydrin and Martika, have always encouraged me and helped me keep the act of storytelling fun.

I hope you enjoy reading this story as much as I did writing it.

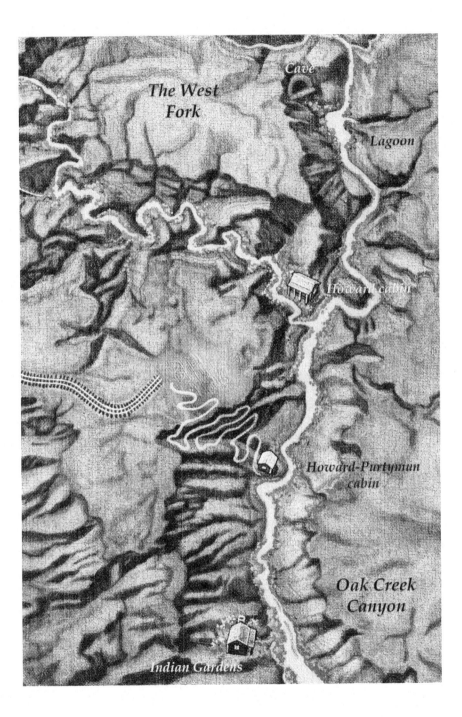

*Drawing by Sharolyn Maleport.*

# *Prologue*

### 2,000 B.C.
### (September)

**W**ater trickling. A murmuring brook. Ancient pale-barked trees. Moss and rock. The rich scent of earth. Lingering wisps of morning mist. Shade and glinting sunlight. Endless cobalt sky.

The canyon in the fall is marvelous. Mellifluous.

The first frost has come and gone, leaving wilted brown ferns in its wake. Fiery red maples blend with the crimson sandstone. Yellow cottonwood leaves shiver in the breeze, not quite ready to drop.

By a quiet dell, the creek widens to form a small lagoon. Several mule deer — all does — graze alongside in the emerald grass. Their flanks wet from dew. Their large, innocent eyes occasionally drifting to the lagoon.

By the edge of the water, a buckskin-clad man paces nervously.

He stops and rests his hand on a tall flat rock. The face of the sandstone pillar is covered with a dark red patina, and someone has begun to etch a spiral into its center. Spinning from a midpoint, a few dozen dots have been pecked into the rock.

The man glances at the water, where a woman — his wife — lies on a flat rock in the middle of the lagoon. The rock is moss-covered and dry and can be accessed only by hopping from stone to stone.

The woman is half-covered with a soft deer hide.

A large raven perches on a nearby rock, watching closely.

The woman looks over at the man and smiles.

And then another contraction seizes her, and she winces.

The man begins to pace again.

He attempts to calm his nerves by building several piles of stones.

Across the creek, nestled amongst a dense patch of sugar sumac, a large bear also watches.

He's more interested in the red sumac berries, but as the afternoon wanes, he drops his head and stares at the woman on the rock.

She cries out again.

Suddenly the wind ceases. The trees no longer sway. The vegetation seems ready to wilt. And the browning leaves look prepared to finally succumb to the pressures of fall and drop.

All is pending.

It feels like time has stopped…

Until another cry burst through the canyon, echoing off the high walls.

But it's not the woman — this time, it's her child. Loud and vibrant.

The man is the first to sigh with relief. And then the winds picks up and a warm breeze blows through the lagoon, skimming over the water.

The child wails again. And this beautiful sound makes the mother smile.

The bear drops his head and rubs a paw over his ear. After another moment he ambles downstream, heading for his den.

The woman sits up. She wraps the child in the doe skin and holds her close to her bosom.

She nods to her husband that it is okay. No complications.

He smiles as he watches them. Happy. Overjoyed.

Using a pointed piece of basalt and a round rock as a hammer, he etches another dot into the spiral.

The woman sighs as well, now that it is over. Of course, there is still a lot that must be done, but for a little while, she will rest — and let the child rest.

She will listen to the birds and the insects.

She slides to the edge of the rock, wincing slightly until she can drop one of her feet into the water.

And then, the other.

It looks impossibly deep below her, and the mystery of this special place — and the cool water flowing around her bare feet — fills her with life.

She lifts her head slightly and begins to sing.

And the forest sways around her, flowing with the wind and her cadence.

And the man sways as well, staring at the trees as if he sees the world anew.

And further down the creek, the bear pauses and listens, too.

And the water continues to trickle by...

# BOOK ONE

## THE ANCIENT ONES

# *Chapter One*

Act I

**800 A.D.**
*(October)*

*A* Hohokam runner came through with news of the visitors two days before the small procession arrived. He had talked briefly to Tokori, the headman of our Sinaguan pueblo, and soon, rumors of strangers from the south spread like wildfire.

At once, everyone was tidying up their dwellings: sweeping floors, watering plants, putting away food bowls, and dusting off fabrics and pelts.

We lived on the edge of a sinkhole: a dark and mysterious place—but also one with permanent water. Behind our pueblo ran a creek that flowed to other settlements further downstream. From our elevated perch on the rim of the sinkhole, we could look down at our fields and hear the gurgling water just beyond them.

My mother, Kayah, walked over to Itzel, an ancient parrot missing most of his feathers, and did her best to clean his cage and perch.

He squawked, outraged, and then shouted his one word, "Itzel!"

"Settle," said Kayah soothingly.

I watched all the commotion from the shadows, trying to stay out of the way, and hoping I wouldn't be assigned many chores. Young girls in our pueblo aren't often allowed to remain idle.

And having seen only ten summers, I didn't understand the fuss: I thought they should have been happy and excited, not nervous cleaners; and I was surprised that of all the things my mother could do to ready for the visitors, she would waste time on the ancient, molty bird.

But then again, I didn't always understand my mother. Her name meant Elder Sister, and she was that to all the females in our community. There were always many women in our dwelling, and often late at night, I would hear my mother whispering consolation to some distraught woman in the process of baring her soul.

She was the female counterpart to Tokori and was consulted for important events, like plantings, births, or matrimonial ceremonies.

Yet, she was very different from Tokori, whose name meant Screeching Owl. I'm sure he would like to think his name might inspire fear, but when the women were alone, they referred to him by his nickname: "Gossiping Chicken."


I was up before dawn the morning the strangers arrived— everyone was up! These would be the first visitors from the southern people we'd had in many years.

My mother was very busy, and I quickly hurried out of her way. She barely acknowledged my departure because she knew I'd be with everyone else, crowded along the creek where the southern trail passed, hoping to get a glimpse of the visitors when they arrived. They called themselves the People of the Corn, although, in later days, they were known as the Mayans.

On my way through our courtyard, where some of our best fabrics were now on display, I overheard some gossip about problems the last time the People of the Corn had visited. None of it interested me until I heard them mention a bear attack, and my blood froze.

I was terrified of bears.

I rushed along, checking every dark shadow on the descent down to the creek. In the verdant coolness along the water's edge, I finally shook off the image.

Long before most of the villagers arrived, I climbed an old sycamore whose thick pale limbs stretched over the path along the creek.

And then I waited with the birds.

Above me, a black and white flicker pecked his way into a dead branch, looking for insects. And below, a quail called out mournfully, alarmed when other spectators arrived, settling too close to its nest.

As the first golden rays of the sun crested the rim of our valley, the strangers appeared in the distance along the riverbank. They came from the west with the rising sun lighting their faces.

I counted eight in the group: five men who seemed to act as guards and porters, two female retainers, and a high-ranking woman. Two of the men led the way. Wearing mantles decorated with bones and exotic feathers, they hefted their shields high but smiled as they marched, making it known that they came as friends.

The men were covered with tattoos and piercings, and their dress was so outlandish—so otherworldly—that for a few brief moments, all I could do was peer through the green foliage and gawk.

Behind the two in the front walked a mountain of a man with bulging muscles, a stout spear, and a severe and untrusting stare. He wore a spotted pelt over his shoulders, and later the men— having never seen a jaguar—argued about what kind of animal it came from.

Even the porters, who wore only loincloths, had strange piercings and sported ornaments made from jade or obsidian.

When they passed underneath me, I saw the important, white-haired woman whose stately gait and regal expression seemed to underscore her importance.

Vibrant quetzal feathers bounced in tight circles over her head, seemingly floating above her. Beautiful blue flowers decorated her dress. Her entire appearance took my breath away.

I was always around the women, and in our tribe, they took great pride in the fashioning of textiles. They made beautiful cloth, and our designs were sought after; but the craftsmanship and colors of *her* clothing were so exotic, so brilliant, they seemed to be plucked from a dream.

There flashed at me reds and blues and greens that were so vivid I had never seen them captured in cloth or on pottery before. It was like a cardinal had given up its secret and handed over its red color, or maybe it was the blue from the belly of an insect, or all the colors of the sunset. They were all there, and in the quick glimpse I got from the tree, I felt all the colors I'd known up to that point slowly fading.

They dulled even the reds in Itzel's feathers—back when he had feathers.

The woman seemed to have to balance her head ornaments carefully but still somehow managed to glimpse me above her.

Ever-so-slightly, she tilted her head up and winked at me.

I almost fell out of the tree, and she seemed to suppress a smile.


Tokori greeted them with my mother at his side and led the visitors to the rim of the sinkhole, where they were seated and given refreshments. I climbed down from my perch and followed silently, all ears and eyes.

The white-haired woman took small sips of water while she shook off her journey. Her eyes kept straying to the sinkhole and the dark water that filled it, about a hundred feet below. The other members of her party all looked tired, and I guessed they'd come a long way.

My mother asked her if she wanted to rest, and she nodded.

Her name was Ts'aak, and surprisingly she spoke our language, although haltingly. She seemed determined to become fluent again and steadily engaged in conversation with my mother.

After a few brief formalities with Tokori, Kayah led her and her companions to the courtyard in front of our dwelling.

They talked of trivial things, but there seemed to be some urgency to her visit, some unknown motive, and it appeared she would not tackle it before she could communicate clearly.

The others in her group only occasionally whispered to each other, all their attention focused on Ts'aak and her needs. None appeared to know any of our language.

"What you name?" asked Ts'aak.

I replied, "Totsi," and she laughed.

"This mean moccasin? Yes?"

I nodded. "When I was a baby, I was so small that my father could set me inside his moccasin."

She chuckled, and I spent the rest of the afternoon helping her learn the names of people, some plants, and household items.

Tokori came around the next day, hoping to acquire some knowledge of his guest, but Ts'aak gave him a few gifts and then politely bid him farewell. I knew then that whatever quest had led her to our pueblo would be for the women to discover.

The bird squawked again, loudly, "Itzel!"

Ts'aak looked at the bird and blushed slightly.

"Itzel. Do you know what this word mean?" she asked.

I shook my head, "He just yells it when he's excited. I didn't think it was a real word."

There was a mischievous glint in her eyes as she leaned closer and said, "It is not just word — it is name. My father was Itzel."

My mother approached just then, and I asked, "Did you know the bird can say someone's name?" Kayah rubbed my hair and said, "Of course I do. Itzel gave me this bird a long time ago."

Ts'aak nodded. "It must be thirty years since he made the journey north."

"And why would he give you a bird?" I asked.

My mother hesitated for a moment, and Ts'aak answered for her. "Your mother saved my father's life, that is why."

My mind was flooded with questions while I watched this strange, white-haired woman, but the one that stumbled out first was, "Will he come back for his bird?"

Ts'aak frowned slightly, "No, child. He has moved on. He is in Xibalba now, or hopefully, beyond it."

I tried to get in another quick question, but instead, I was rushed off to bed.

Kayah handed me my doll, Ila, a corncob husk wrapped in a piece of soft, yellow leather, with reeds for arms and legs. I pulled Ila close and then snuggled against my mother.

She said, "Ts'aak and I are going on an adventure tomorrow — she wants me to bring her someplace."

"Can I go with you?" I pleaded hopefully.

Kayah nodded, solemn. "Ts'aak requested it."

Now I hesitated, feeling I was missing something.

"Why?"

My mother peered into my eyes, and I could feel her weighing me, trying to decide how much to tell.

She said, "You're the same age I was when I found her father. So maybe she feels a connection. I don't know — it'll be fun."

We were up with the sun. The birds sang around us, their chatter floating over the rumbling of the water. Looking down at the creek, I could see the cottonwoods stretching off as a crooked line of light green that was beginning to yellow. Summer was ending, and the first traces of fall were in the air.

Ts'aak was dressed plainly, with a long skirt, sturdy sandals, and a shawl that wrapped around her upper body and covered her hair. This seemed to be her travel outfit, and her entourage also wore sturdy, practical clothing.

The ornaments and feathered headdresses of the day before were left in the care of Tokori, who appeared flustered at not knowing what was going on. He also seemed slightly anxious. He was one of the few people in our settlement who was old enough to remember the last tragic visit from the People of the Corn, and he didn't want this encounter marred by tragedy, too.

Before we left, Ts'aak introduced me to her large bodyguard.

"Totsi, this is Sotz," she said. "He has been taking care of me since I was a baby."

I tried to pronounce his name and failed miserably.

She laughed. "In your language it means *Bat*, so call him Bat."

I had noticed how Bat apprehensively scanned the face of anyone approaching his mistress, and he usually wore a formidable scowl. But when I hesitantly nodded at him, his face broke into a warm smile.

I greeted him, and he looked to Ts'aak, who said, "Bat cannot speak." He shrugged and smirked, then went back to preparing for our trip. With my mother and me accompanying the group, there were now ten of us.

We left our village by the sinkhole and followed the creek southward. Red cliffs lined the way, rising about one hundred feet on either side. The clifftops were burned black by the sun, but their shaded faces were covered with pale green and mustard-colored lichen. On several flat sections, I glimpsed rock art panels.

First traveling southwest, and then northeast when we forked off onto a dry creek, we walked quietly, the sounds and sights of the morning coloring our day.

Beyond the cool gully the high desert ruled. The ground was hard and cracked, and mesquite, prickly pear, and creosote bushes dotted the land to the distant mesas.

Ts'aak sent one of the guards ahead to scout the way, and one followed behind, making sure we weren't being pursued. Bat, she kept near, with the two female servants; and the two porters trailed at her heels.

One time, Bat caught my eye and winked, but otherwise he was on full alert, keenly aware that he was moving through a strange land with unknown dangers.

I walked with my mother next to Ts'aak and marveled where this mysterious journey would take us.

21

# Chapter Two

We continued to follow the dry creek, stepping over rounded red and gray rocks in the riverbed, and over piles of driftwood. Sometimes we walked along the bank when the thorny catclaw wasn't too thick. The tall cottonwood trees continued to shade us, their leaves flashing with the sunny breeze.

Other shrubs had taken advantage of the seasonal deluges that roared down the wash during the monsoons, and sugar sumac, mountain mahogany, and manzanita grew along the banks.

My mother—always on the lookout for herbs or medicinal plants—stopped a few times to harvest.

When I accompanied my mother on her wanderings, I often held the basket where she stored what was collected, and I knew most of the plants we passed.

She scraped some sap off a creosote bush and then collected a few dried mesquite leaves that I knew she used as a powder on cuts and scrapes or in a tea to soothe sunburn, rashes and insect bites.

It was a glorious fall day, but all I saw was the end of summer. The prickly pear pads lay withered and faded, there were only a few light blue berries left on the junipers, and the snakeweed through which we trudged had been burnt tan and brittle.

Ts'aak marveled at this strange landscape through which we passed. Whenever we paused for my mother to collect herbs, she stared off at the distant buttes layered in red, pink, yellow and white, or she examined the microscopic lichen clinging to a boulder.

Soon my mother began to probe Ts'aak with questions about her father and his visit to their valley thirty years before.

"I remember very little about him," said Kayah, "it was so long ago, and I was young. Would you tell me what he was doing here, so far from your home?"

A slow smile spread across Ts'aak's face as she thought of her father. "I assisted him since I was very young, but even though I am older than you, I was too young to come on that journey."

She took a sip of water and said, "My people have a tradition of traveling and recording what we encounter on the fringes of our world — we have always looked for a better place."

A large tree that lay fallen across the trail momentarily stopped our progress. The brush on both creek banks was thick with the red-barked manzanita, and the guards hacked a path for us, beating the bushes down with sturdy clubs.

Ts'aak said, "My father, Itzel, was the nephew of Nuun Ujol K'inich, the glorious ruler and thirtieth king of the city of Tikal. Itzel was a learned man. He knew how to read and write the holy symbols, and with the king's permission, he ventured into unknown lands and recorded what he saw."

Kayah seemed intrigued. "How did he do this?"

The older woman nodded and gave a short whistle for one of her attendants to come to her. I had a hard time telling the two female retainers apart. Neither spoke, both had straight black hair, chopped at the neck, and they wore similar plain, practical outfits like the rest of Ts'aak's group.

Ts'aak sat down on a rock, and the attendant knelt before her. She reached inside a small backpack and pulled out a cloth-wrapped package. She opened it to reveal a thick piece of parchment that had been folded into a stack. A thin wooden cover protected it.

"This is a Codex."

Kayah gingerly accepted the Codex and gently ran her fingers across the gold-stitched designs on the cover. Ts'aak waited a moment and then showed her how it could be opened.

My mother squinted at the symbols etched on the parchment pages. I peered over her shoulder, just as confused.

"What is it?" asked Kayah.

"It is a story," replied Ts'aak.

I gazed hard at the images but didn't understand.

"And this is a map," she said and turned to a page with a detailed drawing of our valley and the plateau. I didn't understand the map either. The squiggly lines and symbols made no sense to me.

The men had cleared a way, and Ts'aak carefully put away the Codex. "We will talk as we continue," she said. "And I will begin with Itzel's first visit to see your people."

"His first visit?" asked my mother.

"Yes, this was thirty summers past, and he had about a dozen people with him. He stayed with your people for a few days, by the sinkhole, and then continued north, following a large canyon until he emerged on a plateau. For many days after that, they trekked until they came across an enormous canyon."

Ts'aak turned her gaze north. I imagined her father telling her of his stunning discovery.

She drifted back and continued, "There, my father turned back, but when he reached the southern end of the plateau, he had difficulty locating the canyon he'd previously ascended. He left the group and scouted ahead, and that's when a great bear attacked him."

I looked up, my heart pounding at the nightmarish images welling up in my mind. I'd only ever seen one bear, and it was one of the smaller black ones, not the fearful brown bears whose tracks were occasionally seen along the creeks. But I knew about the great bears and dreaded nothing so much as encountering them.

I glanced at Ts'aak. Maybe she was just trying to scare me. But her face was pale, her expression grave.

"My father buried his blade in the bear, but to little effect. He fled and barely escaped by jumping off a cliff into a box canyon. An old juniper broke his fall. But the bear wasn't done with him and somehow found him again."

She faltered. For a moment, she was silent. Then she looked around to see who might have been listening. I sat there confused.

She remained silent and walked on with her head down. I suddenly felt like I had to run to keep pace.

Eventually, we left the dry creek bed behind and walked across an open plain with massive crimson buttes in the distance and one large, mound-shaped rock directly ahead of us. A herd of antelope drifted by, and I watched their dust cloud until it faded into a side canyon to the west.

We walked all day, and I grew tired. It had been months since the last rain, and we left no tracks on the hard, cracked earth. I stumbled along, through an endless field of creosote bush, clumps of high desert grass, and scrub oak, trying not to trip on the heads of soap-root yuccas that crept up on me if I closed my eyes.

In the afternoon the heat picked up, and for a while, it didn't feel like fall at all. But by the time we reached the mound-shaped rock, the shadows were lengthening, and Kayah decided to make camp.

I was ready to drop.

Bat made a fire on the shaded side of the rock, in an alcove where it could not be seen from afar. I imagined his home, far to the south, and I wondered why he was constantly on guard, always scanning both ahead and behind us for danger.

Shortly after dark, Bat slipped away with a bow slung over his shoulder. I wondered if he was hunting man or beast.

I slept fitfully with nightmares of bears. My mother had told me to travel lightly, but I had snuck my doll, Ila, along. And that night, I kept her close.

Most of my people fear strangers, but I don't mind them—people like me, especially when I sing. What I fear are the wild animals: mountain lions, wolves and coyotes, and of course, bears. I'm small, and they see me as prey—and what ten-year-old wants to be eaten?

I woke to the sun, cuddled up close against my mother. In the night, Bat had returned with the haunches of an antelope. He had skinned them, carved out the choice cuts, and was now smoking strips of the meat over a low fire.

The men cooked several manioc tubers, scraping off the skin, boiling the vegetables until they softened, and then sharing the food. Soon we all had something in our bellies, and we were on our way.

We hiked through the morning until the sun was directly overhead when we came across another creek, this one flowing strongly. I heard my mother tell Ts'aak that we called it Oak Creek.

A robust and bitter wind flowed down the canyon, hovering over the water, and when it hit my face, I was reminded once again that fall was upon us.

We followed the sparkling water upstream and north, and by and by, many of the desert plants disappeared. Instead, riparian greenery now surrounded us.

Beyond the leafy edge of the creek, I could see that we were entering a deep canyon carved out of the plateau which loomed above us.

We continued up this canyon. The creek had cut a deep trench here, and the rock walls that lined it were dark red and ancient. They rose two hundred feet, and beyond, wooded cliffs of piñon pine and juniper slanted up to the rim of the plateau, thousands of feet above.

The land rose slightly as we pushed upstream, walking along game trails that followed the banks. The stream flowed at us gently, gliding over the rocks in its cascading tumble downstream.

A few times, I glimpsed mule deer bounding away, their white tails flagging at us above the shrubs. And once, we came upon a family of five javelinas that grunted amongst themselves, unconcerned.

Soon we passed a large, steep-walled canyon on our left, with a small stream exiting it, and then one on our right. My mother had often warned me not to get caught in such places during the summer monsoon storms, and I instinctively glanced up, relieved to see blue sky.

We continued, slow and steady, but never stopping. Once, we paused, taking a standing break, while Ts'aak shared more of their manioc. But then we were on the move again and didn't take another break until we had ascended quite a way up the canyon.

At one point we passed a small tributary on our left side; I saw Kayah take a long look at it, but then she kept moving upstream.

Finally, she slowed her pace when the nature of the creek began to change; it was at this point that I also started to recognize things.

Here, the creek meandered through high grass, dividing and reuniting, but always only a few feet deep. We followed it, each finding our way, the long grass whispering as it brushed our legs.

And even though the water was shallow, it moved along in a hurry, and mixed in with the water's gurgling was the muffled tumble of round rocks, clacking and scraping.

It sounded like they were talking to each other, but the cascading water was clipping their words, and the urge of its flow silenced them further.

But I felt that if I sat there long enough, I might understand what they were saying. I caught Ts'aak's eye, and there was a twinkle that seemed to say: Yes, indeed.

We came upon a mossy glade where the water appeared to barely move by. The wind was now gone, and the only sounds were the gurgle of the water, the song of the birds, and the hum of the insects. Suddenly the heat of the previous day felt far away.

On the shore stood a tall rock, covered in large parts by a dark patina. A spiral had been etched into this black canvas, and several hundred dots flowed out from its center.

Below it was a large pictograph that had been split in two by a crack in the rock. On one side was a bear paw print, with a bear claw necklace hoovering over it. On the other, I recognized the symbol for a woman in childbirth, suspended over a rippled line of waves.

The soft, green banks of the creek were covered with small piles of rocks—or cairns—and Ts'aak marveled at them when we first appeared. Some were ancient, covered with lichens.

There were several boulders by the water's edge that could be used as stepping stones to get to a large flat boulder that lay in the middle of the creek.

My mother and I stone-stepped our way to the flat rock in the middle. She giggled when she slipped a little, and I chuckled too.

"Do you remember this place?" asked Kayah.

I looked around. "Yes—I do!"

She nodded. "Every fall, we come here to pick berries. Sometimes we go further up the canyon or into one of the side canyons. There's a cave nearby, too."

I glanced around, and suddenly a memory floated to the surface. "I remember you taught me a song here."

My mother nodded, pleased. "Do you remember it?"

I began to hum the wordless melody. My mother beamed and softly began to accompany me. A light breeze swept through, yellow sunshine pouring down on us from above. It almost was as if the creek and the moss-covered rocks knew the song as well.

From about twenty paces away, Ts'aak stared at us. Slowly she maneuvered across the water toward us, and she seemed to be straining to hear our song.

She joined us on the rock, silently.

Eventually we finished, and the three of us sat listening to the water flowing around us.

"What is this place?" asked Ts'aak.

"My people have been coming here for a long time," said Kayah. "It is a place to say *please* and *thank you*."

The older woman processed this silently.

Kayah had a pensive look in her eyes while she glanced over Ts'aak, like she was deciding what to tell her.

"I wanted you to see this place," Kayah finally said. "We will have to backtrack a little to get to our destination—but this is an important location because Itzel left something for us here."

She nodded at the water. "Beneath this rock is a hole in the river, and in that hole lives a river spirit. What Itzel left us is with that spirit."

Ts'aak peered into the water. It looked impossibly deep. Far below, there did seem to be a light—a glow—that emanated up.

The old woman looked startled when my mother slipped into the water and disappeared. We both leaned forward, observing Kayah's form as she propelled herself down and then under the rock we sat on.

She returned a long moment later, clutching an object close to her chest. She smiled and said, "My mother told me about this, but I never had a reason to fetch it."

With that, she handed over a perfectly white stone. It was round and somewhat flattened, and embedded in its circumference was a gold band etched with Mayan symbols. I would imagine after all this time it would have been caked in mud or covered with slime, but it shone a brilliant white.

Ts'aak held it in awe. "Yes," she mumbled, "we can use this—but we should return it when we are done."

She whistled for one of her retainers and then gave the stone to the woman for her to store in her pack.

She handled it tenderly, lost in thought.

Kayah pulled her from her reverie with a question. "Would you tell me how Itzel came to visit the Sinagua for a second time?"

Ts'aak nodded. "Of course," she said as she sat back on the rock and turned her gaze inward.

She began, "The story is written in the Codex, but I remember it well as Itzel told it to me several times. After my father had escaped from the bear, he stumbled down a steep ravine and found himself in a serpentine canyon.

"He didn't know which direction to go and feared the bear was still in the area. In his distress, the sky seemed to spin, and he was on the verge of losing his mind when he heard a beautiful song floating on the wind."

I looked at my mother, and I knew it was the song we'd just been singing. I said, "It was you singing, wasn't it?"

She smiled shyly. "I think it must have been. I know that year we had been camping some ways into the West Fork."

She roughed up my hair. "I was adventurous, like you, and on our way back to Oak Creek, I'd lagged behind—probably off exploring some side canyon."

"That's right," said Ts'aak. "Itzel told me you were some distance away, and by the time he'd followed the song to you, you were almost back to the others who waited by the confluence of the two creeks. When they saw Itzel stagger in their direction, they quickly assisted him. The rest of his party had since stumbled into the Sinagua and had organized search parties but had found nothing."

"Itzel was in terrible shape. He scared me," said Kayah.

"Yes, he barely survived."

"But what had happened with Itzel and the bear?" I asked. "You left that out." As much as it scared me, I had to know.

"You have to finish the story," I pleaded. "You said he fell into a box canyon. Did the bear find him there?"

Ts'aak seemed to close up at the mention of the box canyon, and Kayah quickly changed the subject. "I don't think now is the time."

I was crestfallen but strangely, also relieved not to hear the story.

My mother and I left the rock and together made a cairn on the shore. Ts'aak remained, staring down into the depths below. Eventually I heard her whisper, "If only you had found something beautiful, like this place, not the dark one I'm returning to."

She must have thought she was out of earshot, but I heard her clearly. I glanced at her from the shadows of the shrubbery on the creek's bank, waiting to see if she would say more. Instead, Ts'aak quickly took out a flint knife and nicked her hand.

She held her hand over the water, squeezed her fist, and a drop of blood fell into the water. Then, she whispered, "If only you hadn't gone into that cave."

I withdrew into the shadows, afraid she might realize I had witnessed all this. But she just hopped back to shore as the drop of her blood slowly sank into the depths.

# *Chapter Three*

We walked back downstream to the small confluence. Another creek flowed out of a twisting pass on the right. This was the West Fork, and I'd heard my mother say the canyon continued for a day´s walk before finally ascending the plateau.

Four willows marked the entrance. Their foliage had turned a perfect gold. As I watched a cold breeze rushed down the canyon and took a great flutter of the leaves in one violent swoop.

The steep red and yellow walls around us were the last refuges of the desert plants like manzanita and agave, but once we turned that first bend into the West Fork, these gave way to tall pines. Soon we were walking beneath a green canopy. These weren't the stunted piñons of the high desert but mighty ponderosas that stretched skyward to the clouds.

Interspersed were oaks, their light tan leaves littering the floor. Dead reeds lay bent on the water's edge.

A light rain picked up, and the drops tap-tapped on the crisp leaves. I raised my head to greet it. I had not felt rain since the monsoons, but now we were nearing weather that had spilled down off the plateau.

We continued, always surrounded by the gurgling of water. The immediate canyon walls were red with streaks of black.

Not too far from the confluence, we made camp at a shadowed point where the walls seemed to close in on us. The sun had disappeared early, and the darkness in that canyon was as thick as smoke.

The guards collected a pile of dead logs and lit a fire, ringing it with stones. Bat plucked some green branches, impaled a few strips of antelope on them, and set the skewers to sizzle over the coals.

The fire was nice, and my stomach was growling, but the steep ravine felt confined and a little spooky. And just as I had the thought that this would be a bad place to come upon a bear, Ts'aak said, "I suppose you want to hear what happened with Itzel and the bear?"

I almost shook my head, thinking this was the worst place to finish that story, but I was also curious. I desperately wanted to know how Itzel got away.

We settled by a low fire, and she began, "Well, I told you already that the bear had attacked my father, and as he was fleeing for his life, he fell into a box canyon."

"Was it a big canyon? Did he hurt himself when he fell in? How bad was he wounded? How badly did he injure the bear?"

She laughed. "One question at a time. From his Codex, I know the canyon was narrow, maybe thirty paces wide and twice as long. One end tilted down to a small pond, its bottom cluttered with dull oak leaves that had fallen from the plateau.

"And even though he'd survived a mighty drop, he was more worried about his shoulder, where the bear had mauled him. He could find no exit from the canyon as he staggered around, only a cave in the back."

As she talked, I pictured the scene in my mind and kept Ila pinned to my chest for courage.

Eventually, she continued, Itzel entered the cave:

To the left was a dark chamber, and straight ahead, a low-ceilinged room with several wide puddles and a mound in the middle. The puddles reflected the soft sunshine outside and gave a dim light.

He limped to a puddle, collapsed to his knees, and drank deeply. As he leaned forward, blood from his mangled shoulder dripped into the clear water. Suddenly he picked up the trace of a sinister breeze on his wet face. It felt like the fetid breath of a carnivore. He strained to make out what might lurk beyond the pools of water and glimpsed a low, dark tunnel.

His hair stood on end as he sensed an ominous hum coming from it. He thought that if he were smart, he would turn and run, but the low hum and the strange breeze had a numinous grip on him.

My mother looked up, and the two women held each other's stare for a moment, then Ts´aak described how at this very moment, a noise from outside drew Itzel´s attention. To his horror, an ominous shadow darkened the entrance. He could make out a large bear lumbering forward, limping and grunting.

It shook its massive head and then turned left into the small dark recess. Itzel realized he had stumbled right into the bear's den.

With no other option, he slowly backed into the dark tunnel.

"What was at the other end of the tunnel, Ts'aak?" asked Totsi.

Ts'aak glanced at Bat, her retainers, and the two remaining guards. Bat was mute, and his loyalty was unquestionable, but she could not chance the others. Suddenly there seemed to be too many ears about.

She caught my mother's eye. "We will talk about that at the proper time."

"But how did he get away from the bear?" I pleaded.

Ts'aak's eyes widened. "That you won't believe."

I leaned forward eagerly, and she continued. "Eventually, Itzel had to sneak past the bear," she said. "He could tell he'd wounded it terribly and hoped it would die, but it just lay in the shadows panting.

Itzel waited until the soft glow reflecting off the water had faded entirely and then tip-toed past the beast, praying that he could pass unnoticed.

But when he had safely emerged from the cave, he still couldn't find a way out of the box canyon. A bloated, pale moon had risen, and its reflection in the small pond of water lit up the canyon. He was surrounded by enormous walls that shot up toward the night sky. He looked toward a growth of ancient alligator-bark junipers that crept up the wall, but their uppermost branches were far short of the rim of the plateau.

He looked at the pond. Its bottom lay thick with rotting leaves and broken sticks. Something about the water soothed him, but he had to find a way out and get away from the bear.

The evening was serene, and he felt enchanted as he looked around the moonlit canyon."

Ts´aak looked up. "He told me later that he didn't know how long he stood there taking it in. The strange experience was timeless, and he was overcome with a peaceful sensation — not thinking of the bear at all — feeling benevolent and happy when he turned and saw the bear standing not five paces away.

It shocked him to his core. He hadn't heard a thing.

Horrified, he stepped backward into the water and felt his feet sink into the muck.

The bear roared and lumbered forward. Itzel took another step away from it, and just as the bear looked ready to attack, there was a mighty crack.

Itzel's feet broke through a rotted leaf barricade, and he was sucked down. For one quick moment, his momentum stopped his eyes just above water-level, the bear staring at him coldly.

And then he was tumbling through the earth, choking and gasping in the torrent of dark water, banging violently against rocks and debris, until finally, he came to a stop, sprawled on the ground outside the box canyon.

He felt like he'd been swallowed and spat out by a giant.

What Itzel did not know was that the debris had filled in the only exit chute from the box canyon, and it was packed so tightly that even the water couldn't drain out until his weight broke it.

He got up and stumbled down a narrow, steep canyon, battered and half-drowned."

I leaned closer, knowing this was close to when my mother found him — and the white-haired woman soon confirmed it.

"At the bottom of that canyon," said Ts´aak, looking at me, "where it flowed into the West Fork, he heard your mother singing.

He didn't know she was Sinaguan, only that her song was beautiful, and after his experience in the sinister cavern, he was drawn to her like a moth to a candle."

Ts'aak looked up at Kayah, and I could tell this was a burning question that had been on the tip of her tongue since she'd first arrived. She asked, "Do you know where that canyon is?"

My mother sat up a little straighter, "Yes, I do. Since the time your father visited us, we have called it Itzel canyon. It is close."

At these words Ts'aak smiled. But even my child's eyes could see that something was still troubling her.

# *Chapter Four*

*T*he first rays of the sun took longer to reach us as we followed the twisting path of the West Fork. Soon the upper reaches of the canyon, above us, were bathed in gold. But I shivered in the canyon's shadows, waiting, as the sunshine slowly slid down the vertical walls, lighting up ghostly slabs of pale sandstone and grey stains of desert varnish.

When daylight finally peaked over the far-off rim of the canyon, winking from above, we'd already been walking for an hour.

The party was smaller now; Ts'aak had ordered the porters and retainers to remain behind at the confluence of the main canyon and the West Fork. This left us with Bat and another guard, Ts'aak, my mother and myself.

Before we left, I had watched Bat fill a backpack with rope and enough food for about a day. In the evening he'd finished drying the antelope meat and had packed some of that away, too.

We walked over the smooth, worn red rock, occasionally stepping through shallow water where the game trails we followed meandered across the small creek. Eons of waterflow had carved into the side of the sandstone cliffs, and now the banks seemed to be leaning out over the water, undercut, like giant frozen waves.

As we got deeper into the canyon, the cliffs closed in, and we had to wade through waist-deep water several times.

Soon the walls were only twenty paces apart. The water crept over the bedrock here, collecting in pools, and all that impeded its slow flow were clumps of grass that had sprouted in patches of sandy gravel.

Fall already had its grip here, too, and the ferns were brown and folded. Yellow-leafed willows and alders grew wherever they could find purchase, their dry leaves rustling when I brushed against them, some already crunching under my step.

Occasionally a cold blast descended from above, where the higher altitude welcomed winter with open arms. Lightning-struck trunks of pines lay across the trail, blackened and bald, and we crawled over them.

Thick red and black-barked pines reached for the heavens, desperate for the sunlight that filtered down to us as it penetrated their branches, glinting off their needles and dangling tendrils of moss.

A few insects were still buzzing around in the cool morning air, zipping ahead of us as they flew in and out of the light.

Finally, a large, steep canyon appeared on our left. "This is Itzel's canyon," said my mother.

Ts'aak stared up at it and all color left her face.

This canyon was nothing like the flat and navigable one we had been following. After a short approach, it rose steeply into massive boulder fields and precipitous steps. Near the top I spied an enormous wall. How would we climb that?

I was about to say something to my mother when I saw Bat and the one remaining guard unpacking several coils of rope.

"We've never gone up," said my mother. "I only know that it is where Itzel came from."

Ts'aak nodded.

We proceeded up the trail for the next few minutes with no obstacles other than a tangle of briars that choked the canyon, but I dreaded the climb that surely lay ahead. The rock towered before us, daunting and full of shadows.

Bat went ahead now, scouting the trail, leaving the other guard by Ts'aak's side. It was rough going. Finally, he found a game trail that we could follow—until we reached the first step.

Here, Bat shouldered the rope and somehow scurried up to a ledge. I was surprised at how nimble he was, considering his size. He tied the rope to a massive juniper with roots deep in the rock and then continued up the trail while the other guard helped Ts'aak, my mother and me ascend.

I was the last to go up. They tied the rope around my waist and pulled me as I scrambled up the rock.

We ascended several cliffs in this fashion.

Now we were higher up the canyon, and the depths below scared me. The sandstone had changed from crimson to a soft yellow, and high above, I could now make out the blue-black rock that capped the plateau.

As I looked ahead again, a black-eared squirrel blocked my way. It chattered loudly at me but quickly retreated when Bat approached.

We paused and ate a lunch of manioc while Bat scouted ahead again. Upon returning, he told Ts'aak what he had found with a series of hand signals.

She said, "There is a long, slanted rise ahead of us. Bat has set a rope. Beyond that is a very high cliff. My father would not have survived a fall that high. So his hidden canyon must be close."


As we finished eating and got on our feet again, she sent the remaining guard down the canyon to wait at the confluence of Itzel canyon and the West Fork.

We continued, now a party of four. The long, slanted rise wasn't as scary as the steps, but we would never have made it without the rope. I wondered how Bat had scrambled up it in the first place.

We paused at the top of the rise and looked around.

On our right, towering yellow sandstone walls rose straight up; on the left, a long, steep slope of pines loomed; high above I could see tall trees swaying along the edge of the plateau rim. But I could not see anywhere that Itzel's canyon might be tucked.

I walked along, my mother beside me. A steep scree leaned against the base of the cliff. It was cluttered with massive boulders that had toppled down from above over the ages.

On one sat a large raven.

I imitated his gurgled clicking, and he danced around.

Then he hopped down into a shadow beneath a rectangular-shaped boulder and disappeared.

Curious, I climbed across the talus slope, my feet slipping in the loose earth until I reached the place.

I looked around the boulder where the raven had disappeared, and underneath it found a slanted chute. It was a long, narrow tunnel, and at the far end I could see blue sky. I crawled inside. It was cool in there, the rocks covered with moss and ferns.

"Hey!" I shouted over my shoulder. "Come look."

I scurried up the tunnel and could hear my mother following behind, calling for me.

We paused at the exit, and I peered back and watched Ts'aak turn to Bat and point at the ground before the chute. She looked nervous. I couldn't understand her words, but it was clear she was telling him to remain there, and under no circumstances was he to follow.

When I emerged from the chute, the first thing I saw was the raven hopping in place ahead of me. He ogled me expectantly, but as more and more people appeared behind me, he fidgeted and soon flew away.

The box canyon was almost perfectly aligned east-west. We had entered from the eastern wall, and aside from a level area to the left of the chute, the land tilted uphill to the west.

A grove of old alligator-bark junipers appeared to lean against the yellow cliff at the far end. I'd seen some big ones, usually up on the rim or in higher elevations, but none as large as these. Not far above their uppermost branches was the plateau's rim.

It had taken us the better part of the day to reach the box canyon, and the sun hovered over the western wall. Although it would not be nightfall for a few hours, we would be cast in shadow soon.

My mother started a fire on the flat area to the left of the chute. Ts'aak sent me down to Bat to obtain some supplies. He would stay where he was.

When I came back into the box canyon, I explored around a bit.

Ts'aak seemed nervous and kept glancing at the junipers at the back of the canyon. She stood up when she saw me approaching them and was about to call out when I shouted.

"There's a cave here!"

She quickly scrambled after me and yanked me away.

"Stay by the fire!" she commanded.

Then my mother was at my side, alarmed by the tone of Ts'aak's voice and the look of worry now on her face.

She walked us back to the fire. "We will explore the cave in the morning," was all the older woman said.

I was a little sore at being yelled at, and that's when it hit me that we were in the actual place where Itzel had confronted the bear.

And why wouldn't there be other bears here now? With Bat stationed outside, what if a bear somehow showed up undetected? Or could there be one living in the cave right now? I did stay close to the fire for the remainder of the day—and nobody had to tell me to do so again.


That night we stared up at a perfectly framed window of the sky that was dense with stars. The fire was banked, and I lay on a soft blanket next to it.

When I noticed my mother and Ts'aak glancing at me, I knew they were waiting for me to fall asleep. I was painfully curious about what was so important and pretended to drift off, clutching Ila and keeping my ears perked up as a hunter's moon crept into the night sky.

They began a casual conversation, discussing the route we had taken up the canyon and which part might prove difficult on the descent. Ts'aak also had some questions about the weather and how much colder it could get.

Eventually, they must have figured I was asleep and moved on to the topic I was pining to hear about.

Ts'aak said, "Tomorrow we will enter the cave — only you and I." My sharp intake of breath almost gave me away.

Kayah said, "You spoke of your father being attacked by a bear here — are you afraid there is a bear in the cave?"

She shook her head. "No, that bear should be long dead — and I've searched carefully, and there are no tracks."

A silence followed, and in it, I breathed a quiet sigh of relief. I opened my eye just a slit. Kayah patiently looked at the Mayan woman until she began to speak.

"What my father found in the cave he did not record. The only hint was a symbol which he scribbled on the map."

Kayah nodded and waited.

Eventually Ts'aak continued, "But as he grew older, he confided in me. I don't believe he ever told another what I'm about to relate."

I listened, feeling young and like I wasn't ready for such a story but unable to close my ears.

"When Itzel crawled into the tunnel, his only fear was the bear, but soon the passage got so small that he knew the beast could not possibly follow. He crept along and could feel the walls change from sandstone to hard, cold volcanic rock.

At first it was pitch black, but as his eyes adjusted, he could make out something luminescent in the cracks of the rock. His fingers told him it was a fungus or lichen. A glowing powder from the same plant covered the ground, dimly lighting the way.

It was then that he began to sense something strange again: a darkness and timelessness, enhanced by the low hum he had felt back in the chamber where the water dripped.

In the dim glow, he felt his way further into the tunnel.

The gloom seemed to thicken around him, as did his fear.

But then the tunnel got wider again, and he was able to turn around and move along on hands and knees.

He saw another soft glow in the distance. As he crawled closer, he realized that the same luminescent growth from the tunnel was spread over the rock, comprising a high domed ceiling.

He could barely make out the chamber floor, which was covered with water. In the middle of a small pond lay a large pyramid-shaped mound that rose to the ceiling as if it had once been a platform where a pedestal supported the black dome far above.

He wanted to inspect it, but a terrible sense of dark, unrestrained potential seemed to emanate from the cave. He cowered and cringed in fear.

An unquenchable desire for power crept over him, surged through him. His mind suddenly raced. He was thinking about becoming king, about toppling his uncle. And even though he loved his uncle and had never yearned for power, here he was, plotting and scheming with a sinister energy."

I shivered and pulled Ila close.

Ts'aak threw a few twigs on the fire and sat up.

"If anyone in Tikal ever heard me say those words, my entire family would be killed."

She sighed. "Somehow, he realized he was bewitched and pulled himself out of the trance by retreating. So powerful was this energy that he would rather face the bear. Well, as you know, he escaped."

Kayah watched as Ts'aak retrieved the Codex from her belongings and opened a page with a map.

Kayah stared at the map as Ts'aak made sense of it by pointing out landmarks. "This is where you live, by the sinkhole, and here is the creek we followed to get to the special place for thanking the spirits that you showed me."

Kayah nodded, the drawing slowly coming to life.

"Oak Creek, yes."

"And here," continued Ts'aak, "is where we turned off into the West Fork and then again up Itzel's canyon."

About two-thirds of the way up Itzel's canyon was a symbol, and Kayah pointed at it.'

"This is where we are, true?" she asked.

Ts'aak nodded, and she pushed for further explanation. "And what does this mean?"

"The word is Xibalba, and it means *Place of Fear*. Xibalba is where we go after death to be judged by twelve angry gods, or demons."

"And your father thought this was Xibalba?" my mother asked.

Ts'aak's eyes were fearful. "He said he thought he might have found a door to the place—a backdoor if you will—to our afterworld."

The two women then fell silent. I lay there thinking for a long time, somehow wishing I hadn't listened to all this. But now I knew that such places might exist.

How much simpler it would have been to just fear a bear.

# Chapter Five

*I* woke to see Ts'aak standing before the junipers at the far end of the canyon. Her back was to the cave, and she appeared to be looking east, in the direction the sun would rise. From her vantage point at the far end of the canyon, she could see over its eastern wall, but the soft pink horizon was only now lighting up, and sunrise would still be a ways off.

When I walked up to her, she said, "Venus" and nodded at a white dot, low above the rim in the eastern sky.

My mother joined us and smiled knowingly at the planet.

"It is good that Venus is in its morning phase," said Ts'aak. "Now, we will just wait for the sun before entering the cave."

After listening to Ts'aak and my mother last night, I was very nervous about what we might encounter, and I kept glancing behind us at the cave entrance.

Ts'aak walked down to the chute and made sure Bat was still in position; he stood like a statue, with his back to the entrance, munching on a piece of his smoked antelope.

Then she instructed me that I could not enter the cave under any conditions. "I know you are adventurous," she said, "like your mother was, but you must not follow us."

I nodded sheepishly.

We stood next to the thick-trunked trees and peered into the darkness. The ground around us was littered with little light-blue berries.

Eventually, the sun crept over the edge of the cliffs and shone directly into the cave. The trees were ancient and crowed together closely against the wall. The roots of two of them had grown around the entrance, framing it.

I gazed beyond the trunks, trying to get a glimpse of Kayah and Ts'aak as they entered the cave.

"Remember," warned Ts'aak, "do not enter. Stay there."

I nodded. Afraid and not at all eager to follow.


The two women disappeared into the cave. They stepped gingerly, frightened of what they might awaken. The cavern's ceiling was low, and the further they went into it, the lower it got. Ahead, water dripped down through the ceiling and formed puddles on the ground, and beyond that was the shadowed entrance to a tunnel.

To the left of the entrance was a dark chamber.

Kayah peered into it and saw a skeleton.

"What is that?" she asked.

Ts'aak examined the bleached bones more closely and then said, "It's a bear."

Kayah looked around fearfully. She asked, "Do you think it could be the same one that attacked your father?"

Ts'aak shook her head. "I don't know."

Kayah moved a few of the bones and then lifted an obsidian dagger with a jade hilt. A skeleton wearing a crown and brandishing two knives was carved into the handle.

"My father's dagger," Ts'aak said in disbelief.

"Leave it," she said quickly, and Kayah dropped it. "It was given to him by our King, and it has great power—it should stay with the bear."

Next, they entered the chamber where the water dripped, delving deeper into the cave, away from the light.

There was a mound in the middle, about ten paces from the tunnel, and they paused there.

"I don't feel anything strange here," said Ts'aak.

"No," replied Kayah, but the words had scarcely left her mouth when a dark breeze blew through the shaft, making the hair on her arms stand on end.

They both looked at the forbidding hole in the wall.

"I don't know what we will find," said Ts'aak. "My father speculated that a direct door to the afterlife might allow one to bypass the trials of Xibalba — or, even, to return from the dead."

She looked up at Kayah and added, "Thanks to my father, we do have some protection."

She produced a cloth bundle, unwrapped it, and soon held the white stone. She added, "We will only use it if necessary."

From my place by the entrance, I felt as if time was standing still, like I was an ancient tree, slowly taking it all in: I watched Ts'aak lift the white stone. I watched my mother, looking at it with hope, and listened to their mumbled conversation. And I watched them both turn and stare at the tunnel.

After what felt like an eternity, the air left my lungs as they hunched over and began to crawl out of sight.

And I tried to be like that ancient tree and see things in terms of years, or generations even, and be detached and unconcerned. But I was only ten, and the anguish that gripped my heart like the twisted-iron roots of the ancient juniper was that my mother might never return.

Ts'aak led the way, bent forward with the white stone clenched tightly in her hands before her. When the tunnel dropped lower, she held it against her heart and crawled with one hand.

My mother followed after throwing one last glance at me over her shoulder.

A dim luminescence escorted them, reflected off the rock and the ground they crawled over.

When they emerged into another chamber at the far end of the tunnel, the dull hum enveloped them.

They stood and looked over a flooded cavern with an island in the middle. The ceiling and walls were carved out of the black volcanic rock in such straight lines that it almost looked man-made.

A great dome stretched above them.
Kayah was awed by the vastness of the chamber.


Ts'aak said, "We should stay near the tunnel," but then her eyes became unfocused, and she began walking forward.

Kayah wanted to stop her but was suddenly short of breath. Her mind raced with images of wealth and suffering. Disturbing pictures of naked bodies flared up. Emotions washed over her: All the bad that had ever happened to her seemed to creep up her spine.

She thought of Tokori, who appeared suddenly incompetent, and in need of replacement. She thought of Ts'aak and the Mayans and wondered what the knowledge of this place would be worth to them.

She looked up and saw Ts'aak standing thigh-deep in the water.

She was halfway to the island. Kayah called to her, but the words felt muffled before they even left her mouth.

Ts'aak was battling with her own mind. She thought of her uncle, Nuun Ujol K'inich, the great Lord of Tikal, and how she might wield his power.

Ts'aak made it to the island and reached out a hand, but the sharp volcanic rock cut into her finger. Her blood dripped steadily into the water.

This pulled her out of her reverie for just a moment.

She shook herself and looked around in panic.

She saw Kayah on the shore calling over but couldn't hear the words. But even as she stared at her, dark thoughts flooded her mind — thoughts of distrust and violence.

And then she heard his voice.

Her father's voice.

And in front of her, she glimpsed an image moving toward her. It shimmered, and the more she tried to focus on it, the more it seemed to dissipate.

Yet, she could see him drifting her way.

The spirit reached out his hand and touched hers and then pushed her bleeding hand lower onto the white stone.

When her blood touched the stone, it flared up, bright and powerful, and for a moment, the voices and images in her head abated.

In its place came a memory of her father holding her, whispering softly to her as she fell asleep. She felt loved.

And at peace. The ill sensations around her swung positive, and she felt overcome with joy. Her breath quickened as she thought, "I could teach this — I could share it."

And then, just as quickly, she found herself standing thigh-deep in the murky, dark water.

The vision was gone.

Ts'aak waded to shore and found Kayah slumped on the ground. She tried to help her up, but the woman was lost in the turmoil of her mind, cringing and cowering on the hard rock.

Suddenly Ts'aak, too, felt the voices taking over again.

She gripped the white stone tightly, but it wasn't strong enough. She sank to her knees.

She fought with all her might but couldn't shake the oncoming darkness of the mind. She was about to give in when she heard the singing.

It was faint, emanating softly from the tunnel, but she could hear it clearly.


The song came from me, and I sang it out of love and fear for my mother. It was the same wordless melody we'd sung by Kayah's special place along the creek, and I sang with all my heart.

The melody flowed out of me like the water of the creek, meandering and peaceful, and it seemed even the ancient junipers swayed with my song.


Slowly, Ts'aak managed to stand, and a moment later, she had Kayah upright as well.

Kayah's ears, too, picked up the song, and the darkness around her faded away as images of her daughter´s birth flooded her mind. They were followed by the times they'd had — we'd had — and that we shared: the two of us laughing and dancing and playing and loving each other through the years.

Ts'aak and Kayah gripped each other's hands and stumbled toward the tunnel, and without looking back, they crawled through the blackness until the light of day shimmered between the tree trunks by the entrance of the cave, where I waited.

# Chapter Six

*T*s'aak remained silent when we were all back in the box canyon. She returned to our camping spot by the chute, rekindled the fire, and made tea using some herbs she traveled with.

My mother followed like a ghost.

"Totsi, check on Bat," Ts'aak ordered when the tea was ready.

I found him staring down the canyon, observing two red-tailed hawks that were spiraling past. He was blissfully unaware of what had happened in the cave.

I returned and found the women still locked in silence.

"He's fine."

Finally, my mother snapped out of it. "Shouldn't we get out of here?" she asked, her voice trembling.

Ts'aak shook her head. "No, we cannot leave this place for another to stumble upon."

Kayah was dumbfounded. "But what can we do? We barely made it out."

The older woman looked frail and tired, but her voice was still strong. She glanced at her hand, which the stone had somehow healed.

She nodded. "Yes, but we did make it out. And I believe we would have eventually escaped. The danger I sensed in that cave is a lust for power."

"And I think that lust for power is what that place feeds on," said Ts'aak. "I crave knowledge more than power. But it gripped even me so.

Kayah stood and faced the cave and asked, "What do we do?"

Ts'aak sipped her tea and pondered the question. This canyon was remote, but it wasn't very difficult to get to. If a grown woman and a ten-year-old girl could make it—albeit with Bat's help—others could.

She stood and walked back to the cave and my mother followed, and I trailed her.

She noticed me and tried to send me back to the fire, but Ts'aak intervened. "Totsi should come with us," she said. "She has proven herself, and someday she will be the future."

Reluctantly, I stepped past the junipers and entered the first chamber.

In the cave, we crouched on the mound in the middle of the chamber where the water dripped. The only sound was our breathing and the occasional drop hitting a puddle.

Both Ts'aak and Kayah could not take their eyes off the tunnel.

I hadn't heard the full tale of what they'd encountered, but one look at their faces when they'd escaped, and I knew it had been terrible.

"We have to seal it," said Ts'aak.

The three of us sat silently, breathing in the damp air, listening to the water drop. It was a peaceful place, except for the tunnel.

Ts'aak spoke. "This needs to be guarded against the greed of men. It has to be a place for women only."

Kayah nodded. Ts'aak sat up a little straighter and said, "You will make the box canyon a place for women only and use it rarely. Keep the men away. We will seal the tunnel and only allow those you choose to enter the cave where the water drips."

Over the next few hours they meticulously blocked the tunnel while I waited in the dark chamber near the bear skeleton, watching.

First, they collected rocks and built a wall.

By the cave entrance, there was a seep and a small pool where the freshwater collected, and they mixed water with the clayish soil to place a layer of mud over the rock wall.

I collected the bear's claws and began boring holes into them for a necklace—anything to keep me from thinking about the dark tunnel.

Before they left the cavern, Ts'aak handed over the white stone. It was wrapped in the cloth again, and my mother hefted its weight but didn't unwrap it.

"Bury it in the sand of the mound, between the puddles—that way, when you return, it will be here to aid you."

Before we left the cave, I took my precious doll, Ila, and set her on the mound above the white stone. Something inside me had changed on this journey, and I no longer felt like a child.

When we left, both women lingered by the cave entrance. Kayah's mind raced with thoughts of how to keep an eye on the box canyon while also trying to keep it a secret.

Ts'aak wondered again just what she had found in the cave. Was it a place that amplified certain emotions? Or was it a portal like her father had suggested? And how had she seen her father in the cave?

She could never tell another Mayan about this. If the wrong person found that evil place, disaster would surely ensue. It could bring about the end of the Sinagua in this area—and the consequences could be even greater.

With a chill, she realized she would have to destroy the Codex her father had made. It could lead others to the cave. It saddened her, as the book represented her father's life's work—she hoped she could do it.

She still needed the Codex for the return journey, but before she reached Tikal, she would burn it.

There were so many questions, and she planned to talk to Kayah at length before returning home.

Bat awaited us when we left the box canyon. The weather had turned, and a cold, cutting wind blew through Itzel's canyon. In the box canyon, we'd been sheltered from the wind, but now it assaulted us.

Ts'aak glanced at the grey sky, not at all accustomed to the weather. Her home was in the tropics, and this was the furthest north she'd ever been.

I could tell from her expression that she feared it was connected to the cave as if the dark weather was an extension of it, but I knew it was just winter. We were not far below the rim of the plateau, and up there, winter was setting in.

Bat had a little difficulty on the descent because Ts'aak didn't want to leave any ropes in place, so after we'd descended, he had to untie the rope and scramble down on his own. Other than that, we were down in no time.

The other guard had observed our descent and had prepared a light meal for us.

We ate while we walked through the West Fork and eventually joined the others who were waiting at the confluence of Oak Creek.

By early afternoon we were back at my mother's place in Oak Creek, sitting on the flat rock in the river, with our feet dangling in the water.

My mother and I sat side by side, and for once, we didn't sing our song. It had been a long day, and it didn't feel right.

Ts'aak joined us, but before she'd even sat down, we saw a man trotting up the trail along the creek, heading our way.

He was Mayan and looked exhausted.

He relaxed slightly when he saw Ts'aak and knelt on the shore until she stone-stepped to him. Then he whispered into her ear, and her eyes shot open.

She quickly returned to our side and said to my mother, "I'm sorry, but I have to leave now. Right now."

My mother nodded silently; she had hoped they would have more time to talk about the tunnel and the dark cavern.

Ts'aak stared into her eyes and said, "I'm sorry," then turned and hurried down the trail. Quickly, they fell into the same formation: one guard up front, one behind, Bat by Ts'aak's side, and the porters and retainers surrounding her.

Within a minute, they were out of sight, and I never saw them again. I never found out what urgent event pulled them away so quickly.

All I knew was there was now a secret place, and my young brain knew even back then that I couldn't tell my friends about it.

On that day, I was forced to become an adult. Or at least to bear an adult burden. But I followed my mother's lead, and we never let a single man into that canyon.

# Chapter Seven

## Act II

### 1395
*(November)*

The sun rising over the dark line of the horizon, radiating forth, and then warming tired old bones is something you live for as you get older. In November, the month of the beaver moon, the first frost sets in, and after that, the rocks are too cold to lean against, and my feeble fire is too small.

So, I must wait for the sun to warm me.

But I am used to waiting. There are no sons or daughters here to fetch me water, start a fire, or even mend my worn blanket. There are no young braves to kill a beast and bring me back a fur.

There is only the sun. And he is a fickle partner.

The days are shorter, too, and the distant sun seems to arc quickly overhead, never pausing in its quest to slumber again.

Some days I do nothing but lay on my side and watch the sun.

The rim of the plateau is not far above me, and I can see the mighty ponderosas there, bathed in gold as they sway in the wind.

It looks warmer up there, although I know it's not.

Maybe I'm yearning for the sun's forgotten summer heat, wishing it could singe my skin and make me feel alive again.

It's been many years since I felt alive—too many.

In my home, deep in a hidden canyon, I only get a few hours of direct sunlight. The high walls block out the world.

The lower walls are painted and etched with many stories, all created by the ancient ones. I know a few of the symbols, but most remain a mystery even after all these years alone here.

The old ones—you know them as Sinaguans—built a dwelling in a corner of the lower end of my canyon. It's right next to a narrow chute I use to leave when hunger drives me. Over the years, I've tried to maintain the roof, but when it rains hard, I still get wet.

There is a cave in the back of the canyon, and even though it would be drier and warmer there, I stay in the crumbling dwelling.

In all my time here, I never slept in the cave.

And why would I, after *she* told me what it hid.

Maybe if I'd listened, things would have turned out differently. Perhaps if we hadn't stumbled upon Itzel canyon and then smelled smoke, we wouldn't have explored further.

Who can say? The old woman believed our fate was set the moment we ascended the chute. All I know is that before that horrible day was done, my life had changed forever.

And before the next sunrise, no one had to warn me about that cave—never again.

But on that day, when we first came across Itzel canyon so many years ago, all seemed so innocent. I remember basking in the glow of the sun. It was this time of the year, but it seemed to have been warmer.

# *Chapter Eight*

*T*hree figures slowly made their way up the West Fork, moving like shadows: Two were men, up front, scouting for game, the third was a woman who checked the deep pools for trout.

They had been following Oak Creek, heading downstream after scrambling down from the plateau, when one of them had spotted bear tracks.

The tracks had led into the West Fork but then disappeared.

The deep canyon proved to be a refuge from the wind that had been battering them, and they decided to push on.

From the moment they left the confluence, the canyon had changed. Oak Creek was shaded by cottonwoods and sycamores that grew along the waterway, but now they were surrounded by a canopy of towering pines, and the tall, green-leafed trees had disappeared.

It was quiet. All morning they'd only heard the occasional bird and the crunch of leaves underfoot. The man in the lead stepped on a stick, and the crack echoed off the encroaching walls and underlined a feeling that they didn't belong here.

Soon, the cliff walls were only twenty paces apart, and then ten. Above, the sun reflected off the cliffs, illuminating their crimson crests, and beyond that, fading in the distance, the rim of the plateau extended higher still.

They had to wade through thigh-deep water and later traverse a long, flooded tunnel. Eventually, the creek retreated into still pools of water, no longer flowing, with gaps of worn sandstone between them.

The walls seemed to fall away then, and they grasped they were deep in the heart of the West Fork.

Around mid-day, the woman lay down to rest on a flat rock near a glittering pond where the water reflected the sunshine hypnotically.

I remember that morning like it was yesterday, and I would give anything to go back and tell that woman not to fall asleep, not to drift off in the sun's warm embrace.

But we cannot change our past, so I'm forced to remember laying there, sleeping in the sunshine, until one of the men returned and found me in slumber.

"Hey," he said as he gently woke me.

I opened my eyes to see his face smiling at me.

And I can still see him in my mind. Beautiful. Young. Strong. I won't tell you his name, only that he was my husband. He had seen eighteen summers and me, two short of that.

I giggled. "It was so warm and peaceful that I must have drifted off."

He lightly patted my stomach where a slight rise indicated our unborn child, which I hoped to greet in the spring.

He lay next to me, on his back, with our shoulders touching.

We watched several red-tailed hawks spiral along the surrounding canyons, seemingly flying right up the walls to where the canyon greeted the sky. Wispy white clouds stretched across its perfect egg-shell blue, and a gentle breeze floated over us on the floor of the canyon.

Far above us, I could faintly hear the wind howling, and this made the warmth and sunshine all the sweeter.

And even on that day, I wanted time to stand still.

We were young and in love, and we both enjoyed these explorations into some of the more remote parts of the land. We were Indeh, or as you might know us, Apache, and although we didn't settle in permanent homes like the Sinaguans, we loved the sacred earth. I welcomed any chance to explore it.

"Where is Bodaway?" I asked. He was my husband's best friend and our traveling companion. He had no living relatives then, so nobody living now knows his name, and I can tell it.

He nodded. "He's not far behind."

Then he laughed and added, "He really didn't want to give up on that bear."

I sat up reluctantly, and my husband tickled the small of my back. We were a half day's walk into the West Fork, and on our left, a steep canyon had just opened. It was sheer in places, cluttered with fallen logs and brush, and held little appeal.

Now, as we rested on the rock, we looked up at it.

My husband sat up suddenly. "I smell smoke."

I glanced around, perplexed. None of our people were in the West Fork or by Oak Creek. And Bodaway had no reason to kindle a fire.

I sniffed the air and could faintly pick out the scent.

"I smell it, too—who could it be?"

It had been more than ten summers since my people had attacked the Sinaguan dwelling by the sinkhole and another cliff dwelling downstream from it.

Some of them had remained in other settlements in the valley, but many had left and traveled north and east. The rest would follow in the coming years. All that remained were their empty homes along the cliffs.

At a few locations, we grew corn and squash in their abandoned gardens, but otherwise, we just let nature reclaim the land.

"I don't know," he said, "there's been no lightning, so someone must have ignited a fire."

He pondered for a moment. "Maybe one of the ancients never left."


That moment Bodaway appeared and grinned when he saw us sitting in the sun. Strapped to his back was a large elk antler.

He said, "I hunt the bear while you two loaf." He set down the antler and added, "Those were big tracks."

"You only want a bear because you think its pelt will impress the women," teased my husband.

"And what woman wouldn't want a warm fur for the winter?" I asked, raising an eyebrow.

My husband put on a stern expression. "Well, there's only one woman here, and she's taken," he said and laughed.

Bodaway looked around seriously. "I smell smoke."

"Yes," said my husband and twitched his lips in the direction of the steep canyon before us.

"Let's go," said Bodaway after a moment.

Before I could stand and brush myself off, they were off.


The men were only a short way into the steep canyon when I caught up with them. They were scanning the bush.

"We found the bear's tracks again," said Bodaway.

I glanced at the steep rock walls before us. It didn't seem like we would be able to ascend this canyon to the plateau.

"Not much up there to hide in," said my husband. "You might have a pelt soon."

We reached a rocky step, as high as four men. Bodaway scampered up it easily.

He waited as my husband helped me up, and we continued up a game trail to soon come across another track.

A few minutes later we came to a second step, and beyond, more bear tracks.

Bodaway began to glance over his shoulder from time to time.

Then we found ourselves staring up a long, slanted slab of weatherworn sandstone.

Bodaway grinned at us and then stared up the slope. I knew him well enough to know this was false bravado, and he was troubled.

We looked around, and there was simply nowhere else to go. The rock around us was no longer vermillion up here but instead the soft yellow of a cougar's pelt.

"I think your bear has disappeared," I said.

Bodaway frowned and slowly scanned the steep ravine.

"The bear may have, but the smoke has not."

Stealthily, the men took out their bows, notched arrows, and crept along the right wall of the canyon. Then, Bodaway spied a chute leading up into blue sky.

"Here," he whispered.

He crept forward, my husband a step behind.

# *Chapter Nine*

We emerged into a box canyon with high sandstone walls. The land slanted up into it towards a row of old junipers that leaned against the far wall.

On our left was a dwelling: A decrepit, two-walled ruin that was tucked into the corner of the canyon, and next to it, an old woman slept by a low, barely-smoldering fire. Her clothes were in tatters, and her hands and feet were filthy.

My husband laughed and pointed at her. "Here's your bear."

Bodaway didn't think this was funny. "I know a bear track."

He stepped beside her to examine a necklace of bear claws she wore and wrinkled his nose at the pungent stench of leather and old furs that hovered around her.

The woman woke. Startled, she screamed and scrambled to her feet and pushed herself back against the wall, as if it would give and let her get away.

She was feeble, her teeth worn down to brown stubs, and her eyes were red-rimmed with brown veins in the whites.

Her angry cries were interrupted by hacks and coughs.

I had the gift of tongues and often helped my husband negotiate trade when we came upon other tribes. I recognized a few of her words and said, "calm" in her language.

She glanced at me, wild-eyed, and then her gaze darted to the men with distrust.

"This place is only for women," she screeched, "men are not allowed."

"She is one of the old people," I said to my husband.

He shrugged and looked away. "She should have left with her kinsmen — this is our land now."

I moved closer, and the old woman glanced at my stomach and said, "You are with child."

I nodded, and that seemed to bring her around a little. Slowly, she slid into a seated position, and after a few moments, motioned for me to sit next to her.

"This place has seen a few births," she said with a gesture that encompassed the box canyon. I looked around and made out fertility symbols among the various pictographs covering the walls.

"So, you are not alone here?" I asked.

She chuckled. "No, I am not alone. Someone is with me. Someone watches over me."

I pointed to our supplies, and I asked if she was hungry.

Again, she chuckled dryly, a mischievous glint now in her eyes.

"I barely eat — maybe once a month," she said.

She coughed again and nodded at some herbs hanging from a peg on the outside wall of the shelter. I saw the purple leaves of yerba santa.

"Tea," she croaked and cleared her throat, "...helps me breathe."

I nodded. I bade the men to gather some wood for a fire, and as they went off, I prepared the leaves and added a few herbs I carried with me, grinding them in an old Sinaguan metate.

She silently watched my every move.

The dwelling was well-stocked with bowls and pots, decorated with intricate brown and red designs. One large basin was filled with rainwater. I dipped a cooking pot in it and then set it on the fire to boil.

We decided to remain in the box canyon for the evening, but it was still early afternoon, and the sun was making its brief appearance overhead, so I found a nice sunny spot and took a nap.

I woke to find Bodaway restlessly pacing the canyon, examining the ground for tracks and the cliffs for another way in or out. He paused for a while by a mortared wall with a sealed door—most likely a granary built by the ancients—and then his exploration drifted toward the row of junipers along the back wall.

The old woman silently stood, watching him.

The late afternoon rays lit up the uppermost rocks for a while, but soon we were plunged into cold shadows. Through the gloom, Bodaway could make out a dark recess between two of the alligator-barked trunks.

The old woman shuffled his way, limping along with the help of a walking stick. She banged it on the ground and shouted at Bodaway.

My husband sat down next to me and began some minor repairs to his bow and a few arrows.

He glanced at me. "What's she going on about?"

I watched her slowly close the distance until she was just behind Bodaway. "I don't know," I replied.

"Hey!" called Bodaway. "There's a cave here."

The old woman shouted and gestured madly, and when Bodaway ignored her and bent to enter the cave, she began whacking him on the back with her stick.

He fended her off easily and then turned and stared into the dark chamber. "You don't want me to go in there?" he asked. "What are you hiding?"

She began hitting him again, and Bodaway turned his back on her, laughing, and entered the cave.

From our position by the fire, we could see the old woman reach into a fold in her clothing and pull out an ancient Mayan blade; the black obsidian glinted below its jade handle.

I yelled out a warning.

The old woman raised the blade and was about to plunge it into Bodaway when my husband's arrow whistled through the air and buried itself deep in her lower back.

She screamed and sank to the ground.

Both of us jumped up and hurried toward the far end of the canyon, where Bodaway was shaking his head. "Crazy old witch."

The old woman lay there writhing in pain. The arrow had lodged itself deeply. My husband picked up the knife, and after examining it for a minute, stuck it in his belt.

I helped her move from her stomach onto her side, and then I half-dragged her to the entrance of the cave.

Her eyes were weak, but I could see her desperately watching Bodaway's movements as he again turned to enter the cave.

"We need a torch," he said, and my husband quickly returned to the fire and came back with two burning sticks.

Inside, they explored a small alcove on the left first. This room had a low ceiling and was about three paces wide. Along its back wall, five bear skulls were propped up, glaring at them in the flickering light. They had been decorated with many of the same symbols I'd seen on the walls.

My husband joined him and asked, "Who killed these bears?"

Bodaway glanced at the old woman who watched weakly. "Not her."

My husband lifted one of the skulls and whistled softly.

"This must have been one big bear," he said. "And look how yellowed the bone is. I think this is very old."

The men ventured into the main part of the cave, where water was dripping down from the ceiling and forming puddles on the ground. Several pots were placed to collect the water.

They bent low under the ceiling and made their way to a dry mound in the middle of this chamber.

I waited by the entrance with the dying woman and watched her eyes, trying to understand what motivated her. Why had protecting the cave been worth her life?

Bodaway looked over the walls and noticed a section that seemed plastered over. He walked to it and tapped it with a rock.

The old woman sat up, screamed, and collapsed.

Bodaway began hammering at the plaster until it crumbled before him.

A dry blast of stale air flooded the chamber.

My husband peered into the darkness ahead, which was lit by a soft green glow, and I could see a look of fear creep over his face.

We all sensed a dull hum.

"There's a tunnel," he said.

"Let's see where it goes," said Bodaway.

The old woman looked at me miserably. "They will never leave that cave if they enter."

Neither man understood her words, and they wouldn't have heeded her warning if they did. They were young and cocky and turned to push ahead into the darkness.

"Take this," said my husband and handed me the Mayan blade. "Just in case." Then he bent forward to follow Bodaway.

Before he vanished in the darkness ahead, my husband turned to me one last time and smiled. It was the last I saw of him as I knew him.

# Chapter Ten

As the men disappeared with the torches, I was left in the dark. I realized that the sun had now set, and it was cooling rapidly. I had to get warm; I had my child to think off.

I grabbed a few embers from our fire, transporting them in one of the bowls left behind by the old people. In front of the smaller chamber with the bear skulls, I scooped up some earth to make a depression and soon had a small blaze whose smoke flowed lazily out the cave to rise into the old juniper branches.

The old woman was pale and shivering by the cave entrance. I didn't think she'd survive the night. I knew if I pulled out the arrow, she would bleed out.

"I'm sorry," I said, ashamed of the terrible consequences of simply smelling her fire.

She peered into my eyes, and something in hers softened.

"We are sisters, you and I," she said. "You are not to blame."

I glanced at the tunnel. "And my husband and Bodaway?"

Her face sank. "They will pay for their actions."

I added a handful of twigs to the fire, and we sat there silently, listening to them take to flame.

"Is there anything I can do to ease your suffering?" I asked.

She moaned and gave a weak half-smile. "I would like to see the sun again, but I am not sure I will make it."

With some difficulty, I moved her inside, dragging her backward. In the cave with the bear skulls, I broke off the arrow's shaft, so she could lean back, propped up between two skulls.

She must have been in great pain, but she barely winced, and her only concern seemed to be the tunnel where the men had disappeared.

A distant shout emerged from the passage, and instinctively I moved toward it, but she raised her arm and feebly gripped my shoulder.

"No," she whispered. "Your child will not survive."

She labored greatly to lift one of the bear skulls and reveal a white stone encircled by a gold band. Her hand was covered with blood from when she first had tried to extract the arrow, and as soon as it touched the stone, it began to glow.

I stepped back in alarm.

She could barely lift the glowing stone, and I stood transfixed as she placed it against her lower back. For a moment, she appeared to relax, but then she slumped.

"It is too much for even the stone," she said.

The muddled sound of angry shouting emerged from the tunnel, a dark rage echoing off the walls.

The old woman didn't look surprised at all, like she'd been expecting it.

I picked up the Mayan blade and crept toward the tunnel. She stopped me once more. "Wait," she pleaded. The desperate tone in her voice made me pause, and I stared at her.

She said, "Take the stone. And do not set foot in the chamber at the far end of the tunnel, or you will doom your child."

And then she tried to take the blade from me.

She said, "This will not help you in there."

I wanted to keep it. She was weak and could barely lift her hand, but her warning made my blood run cold, and I reluctantly let the blade go.

The frantic screams continued to echo in the tunnel, and I couldn't remain and listen. I grabbed the stone and quickly scrambled into the long darkness.

It wasn't easy to fit through the narrow shaft in my current state. I prayed for my child's safety as I held the stone against my belly. A dull luminescence lit my way, emanating from the lichen that grew in the cracks, and I seemed to be crawling through a fine powder.

I passed their abandoned torches, extinguished on the ground.

The tunnel seemed to be buzzing, and I was overcome with a feeling of dread as I neared the opening on its far side. The closer I got, the louder the screams, and by the time I reached the end, I was frantic.

In the dim light of the chamber, I could vaguely make out a small pond circling a steep little island. On the island, the men were fighting. I couldn't tell which one was which. They each held stones in their fists, and they were smashing them against each other while trying to climb to the top of the island.

All breath seemed to escape me as I watched, desperately trying to make out my husband among the two raging fighters. Their screams were so terrible that I couldn't match them with either of the men. Not the men I knew.

Horrible, dark feelings were overcoming me, but I couldn't turn away. The men were on their knees now, pummeling each other with the last of their energy. One went down under a savage blow to the head, and then the other collapsed on top of him.

A sudden silence descended on the chamber.

I stared, transfixed. Were they dead? Was my husband dead?

Why had Bodaway betrayed him? Why had he betrayed me?

As I edged closer into the dark chamber, I was suddenly overcome with a mighty lust for vengeance.

My mind was darkening. All fear for my child faded when suddenly I heard the song. Through the tunnel, and barely discernable, a wordless melody was floating toward me. The song was almost a whisper, but it spoke of trickling water, fresh wind, sunshine, and love.

And as I listened, I could not help but slowly back up.

# *Chapter Eleven*

*B*ack in the cave where the water dripped, the old woman watched me return. There was a radiance coming from outside, and as I stepped out, gasping for air, a full moon stared at me from just above the eastern wall of the canyon.

"You see the moon?" she whispered to me.

I nodded, lost in grief. I collapsed beside her.

We sat there quietly as our little fire dwindled.

Eventually, she nodded at the tunnel.

"Men must never go in there."

I stared at her, wishing we'd heeded her warning.

"Someone must be here," she said. "Someone must watch."

I didn't really hear her words. I just wanted to sleep.

Draped over one of the skulls was her necklace of bear claws. More than twenty claws adorned it.

She dragged it to her lap and then held it up to me.

"You will wear this tonight," she said.

She slid the necklace my way, and I accepted it. Tough leather thongs held it together, and it had some weight to it — like it was a collar more than a necklace.

I slipped it over my head. With that, she seemed to relax, and she only watched the fire. I slumped to my side, and within minutes was asleep.


And in that slumber from which I hoped never to awaken, I dreamed I was a large bear. I dreamed I left the cave and the box canyon, and I wandered through the West Fork looking for something to eat.

In the dream, I was not heartbroken—I was only a bear.

And I relished this dream, where I could simply be a bear, not a woman of barely sixteen summers who was pregnant with a dead man's child.


I woke on the cold stone floor of the box canyon as the day broke. My hands and feet were filthy, and my face was covered with blood—not my blood.

I staggered to the cave where the old woman sat against the entrance, bathed in the morning sunlight.

She was dead. She had a slight smile on her face, and I wondered if she'd seen the sunrise. I also wondered how she'd found the strength to move her wounded old body.

I entered the cave and placed the bear claw necklace on top of one of the bear skulls.

Then, before I could think about it, I made my way to the tunnel and began to rebuild the wall that had concealed it.

# *Chapter Twelve*

*T*his is how I came to be alone here in this canyon. I won't leave it. My husband is here, close. On some nights, I can hear him whispering to me, begging me to break the rock wall that seals him inside.

Is it him? I don't know.

The old woman said someone must stay and hold watch, and it might as well be me.

In the coming years, I would learn that others knew about the box canyon with the cave and the dark chamber beyond it.

They would visit alone, or maybe there might be two of them — never more.

They were always older women.

They would enter my box canyon timidly. They seemed afraid of me, and I liked that.

It's best that they remain afraid, or better yet, stay away.

When they noticed I was with child, and then later, when I held a baby girl, they asked who the father was.

I wouldn't give them his name any more than I gave it to you. He was my husband. That's all you need to know.

I also refused to give my name, and they took to calling me Cocheta, the Unknown.

I later learned that they believed there was no father, that I'd become pregnant when a drop of water in the first cave fell on me.

Let them believe what they want.

When my daughter had seen her second summer, they talked me into allowing her to live with the rest of our people. It broke my heart to let her go, but I was glad to get her away from the evil cave.

I have no desire to raise a child here, and any love that was inside of me died inside the cave.

So, I remain.

# *Chapter Thirteen*

### Act III

### 1521
*(December)*

**Y**aotl stood on the edge of a small mesa and looked at an abandoned pueblo in the near distance. It was perched on the edge of a sinkhole, just as he'd been told. He had come a long way to reach the pueblo, and the fact that it was uninhabited left him perplexed.

He was a Mexica, although history would know his people by the name Aztec. Yaotl was solidly built, in his prime at thirty-five, and his stern expression was supported by a prominent nose and strong jaw.

He wore a lightweight, close-fitting breastplate, which left his battle-scarred arms exposed, and his legs were protected by leather strips that served as shin guards.

The moon had not yet risen, and he held a torch to light his way. The reports from his scouts suggested that not a soul resided in the crumbling adobe structures on the next mesa, but he still felt a presence out there in the darkness.

Another scout appeared out of the gloom and knelt before him. "Speak," ordered Yaotl.

"We located a camp, not far from here," said the man, his eyes cast to the ground. "There are about twenty women and children — it looks like the men are away hunting."

"Make sure no one leaves," ordered Yaotl, and the man hurried off.

Yaotl turned away from the ruin and looked down at the valley below him, peering through the darkness, at a long line of men bent down under heavy burdens. By the dim starlight of the early evening he couldn't make out much, but he could hear their moaning and the snap of the lashes of the men who drove the line forward.

They had left the capital, Tenochtitlán, nearly two months earlier, just as the Spaniards were closing in on the city. Initially, more than two hundred slaves had accompanied Yaotl on his mission, but they had died like flies over the grueling march. His soldiers — of which there were only twenty — had captured new slaves along the way, but most were in shock or wounded, and they didn't fare well.

He'd decided to push forward with those he had rather than taking a chance of being caught from behind by the Spanish soldiers. The foreigners had great magic, and cast disease upon the land wherever they appeared, so he threw caution to the wind and drove his procession north, relentlessly.

Whatever the human cost, he thought, it will be worth it.

He had left Tenochtitlán as the battle between Montezuma and Cortez had only begun. He hoped his king would prevail, and he knew of the gravity of the orders he had been given: The sacred mission he was on would turn the tide of the war, after all.

But now, as they neared their destination, he feared they would stall. He had made this last push with over one hundred and fifty slaves, and they were down to half that.

He still had the Blue Men, he thought: Twenty-five hand-picked slaves who had been tortured and beaten into submission and then trained to do whatever he needed.

They were merciless and inured to hardship.

On the outset of the journey, still on the outskirts of the capital, they had come upon a Spanish supply train, and his men captured a true treasure: weapons, chains, and other apparatuses, made from what the foreigners called *steel*. These were far superior to Aztec tools.

And the chains came in very handy with the slaves.


Yaotl left the mesa and walked down to the line where his soldiers were busy unloading the crates and bundles carried by the slaves. A dozen torches on poles lit up the area.

The slaves each wore metal collars on their necks. These were connected by chains, whose bights clinked rhythmically as they stumbled forward with a deathlike indifference.

The burdens they carried were of various shapes and sizes, wrapped in thick canvas and then bound with ropes. There was no way for an observer to tell what mysterious items lay within—but they were clearly heavy.

Yaotl watched one man approach. He was gaunt and utterly exhausted; the joints of his limbs stood out like knots in a rope. His legs were bare and scratched raw by the acacia and catclaw he'd marched through. They shook unsteadily with each step.

His back and shoulders were crisscrossed with welts, and his hollow eyes were bereft of hope.

As the slave limped forward, two of his soldiers grabbed what he was carrying and stacked it.

Suddenly unburdened, he staggered backward until another soldier snatched his arm and led him, stumbling, into a makeshift enclosure.

The pen used a rock wall and several sprawling stands of prickly pear to contain the slaves. A guard stood facing the miserable humans.

Yaotl was relieved to see none carried disease. He didn't know how far the wrath of the Spaniards might extend.

In one quick glance, he knew none of the slaves had the energy to try to escape. But he could take no chances.

"Let them sleep in their chains," he told the guard.

To the side, several Blue Men were cleaning and organizing the heavy Spanish tools. Each morning they applied a blue powder to their bodies, but it had become faded after this day's exertions.

Now, through the smeared powder, Yaotl could see cuts and scrapes on their legs; and one man had a particularly nasty gash on his shin.

He was glad to see the man had attended to the steel before his own injuries.

He approached him, and the man sprang to his feet.

Yaotl nodded at his leg. "You are injured," he said.

The man shrugged. "It is nothing."

"Have it tended to after you are through with the steel," said Yaotl.

The man nodded, and when Yaotl turned his gaze away, his comrade threw a handful of blue powder on his injury — as if that were medical attention enough — and they both laughed.

Several more Blue Men approached, carrying caged and tied-up sacrificial animals, including a jaguar suspended from a long pole. The cat hung limply, and Yaotl nervously approached it and nudged the feline with the tip of his foot.

The cat growled in irritation, and Yaotl exhaled.

The men lowered the jaguar, and Yaotl stepped forward and smacked one of them in the face.

"If he dies, I will have your skins," he warned the porters. "He needs to be alive for the sacrifice — give him water." One of them scurried off to find water, afraid now that they'd been warned.

Another carried a cage with a golden eagle. And behind him, a man held a basket that he knew contained a large viper. There would also be a human sacrifice, which Yaotl would determine in time.

There was a bear, too, an old Mexican grizzly. Four stout Blue Men were holding him by long rods attached to a metal collar, and although they'd kept him moving forward, the bear could lift them off their feet with a lunge.

This great beast wasn't meant for the sacrificial ceremony Yaotl planned. But when he'd first seen it in the mountains far to the south, a sense of raw power had gripped Yaotl, and he felt they were somehow connected.

Soon his captain, Coatl, approached: his name meant Snake, and Yaotl thought it a good omen considering where they were going.

Snakes, after all, had access to the underworld.

Coatl wasn't tall and muscular, like the Blue Men, but he radiated a fierceness, and an unflinching, uncaring attitude toward anything that stood in his lord's way.

He wore a white scar on his face that ran from his now blind left eye to his chin, and he had a way of shifting his head from side to side regardless of where his one good eye wandered that had unsettled many of Yaotl's more civilized relations in the capitol.

"It will take some time still for the last of the slaves to arrive, my Lord," he said in a whisper while bowing his head and avoiding Yaotl's gaze.

Yaotl watched a bat circle in the sky before him, hunting the few insects still buzzing this late in the year.

"And this new camp your men located?"

Coatl nodded, bobbing his head. "As you know, the men are away, but I took precautions. Our warriors are surrounding them and will soon have everyone rounded up."

Yaotl smiled with filed, pointed teeth.

"There should be one there who knows about Itzel Canyon," he said. "If they don't give up this person, enslave all of them."

Coatl gave an evil grin and slipped back into the shadows.


Yaotl walked beyond the unloading area to a temporary camp his men had set up. A low fire burned in front of a small, round shelter with a sparsely thatched roof. His was the only structure. Everyone else slept in the open.

Inside, a burning tallow lamp illuminated a chair, and a blanket was spread out for him to sleep on.

He stepped to the chair and sat down by the small flickering flame. Beside it lay a pile of his personal belongings. Reaching inside a leather satchel, he pulled out a handful of tiny, brown, oval seeds—Ololiúqui—from the morning glory plant.

He silently chewed the seeds, which contained psychedelic properties, and felt the spirit world opening around him.

He picked up a yellowed piece of parchment and held it before the soft light.

Before him glowed the only remaining page of Itzel's Codex: It was the map. The edges were burnt, and the bottom of the image was missing altogether.

What was left showed the upper half of Oak Creek, the turn up the West Fork, and then Itzel Canyon.

Yaotl had no way of knowing that this parchment was more than seven hundred years old. But he did know it was valuable, for it pointed to a sacred place. More precisely, to a location which he hoped was a shortcut to that holy place. His stomach churned with excitement when he thought of the potential.

The dark lord lifted his hand, gently touched the symbol that hovered over the location of the box canyon, and said, "Xibalba."

# Chapter Fourteen

*I* have always preferred the soft sounds of the morning to those of night or even sunset. There's something about the freshness of a new day: the leaves dripping with dew, the deeply soothing scent of the earth, the twittering birds as they flutter about, and the golden, glinting rays of sunshine that spill into our valley.

Maybe it's the potential: knowing all the things that need to be done—both fun and menial—that add up to more than just the end of something.

I don't know why people like sunsets so much.

And night reminds me of my betrothed, Elan.

That's why I'm alone tonight, away from the others—all the women and children. In the darkness, I'm barely visible as I sit inside the sinkhole, down by the water, missing my love.

I, Imala, would count my heartbeats if it would make time pass quicker. Having seen eighteen summers, I am ready to wed. My sisters tease me that I'll soon be too old, and Elan won't want me.

But I know that's not true—he professes his love all the time.

These are challenging times. The lands are awash in sickness, and the happy times are far and few between. I would like to be married now, but my grandmother tells me that we must wait until spring. So, I must be patient.

She is a strong woman, as were all the women in our line. They would only be defied at a high cost. My grandmother is the great-great-granddaughter of Cocheta, the Unknown, whose own mysterious daughter was born in the secret canyon one-hundred-and-twenty-six years ago.

When grandmother sets her mind to something, you just have to go along. So... I'll be getting married in the spring.

In the mornings, that doesn't bother me so much. I lay there listening to the birds, trying to identify them from their song.

Sometimes I even sing back.

But when it is dark—especially on nights like this when my beloved is away—then all I do is yearn.

On this night, there were no sounds in the sinkhole. No frogs. No insects. No people chatting in the distance, or even dogs barking. It was dead silent.

I barely noticed it as I sobbed a few times, missing Elan, and then I began to sing, my voice cutting through the darkness like rays of sunshine on a chilly day.

Yaotl stepped out of his tent when he heard the song. It was faint, but he knew it came from the ruined pueblo by the sinkhole. He grabbed a torch and walked that way, leaving his guards hurrying to catch up.

Down in the sinkhole, I sang, unaware of Yaotl or even his procession. All other sounds were eclipsed, and I'd been alone there for hours.

When I walked up the stone steps to the rim of the sinkhole, I was startled to hear the crack of whips and people crying. I gaped, bewildered, and nearly jumped out of my skin when I heard a voice behind me.

"Seize her," said a demon-like man with filed teeth.

If only I had remained quiet and grieved in silence.

They grabbed me and dragged me back to his shelter, where two of his guards tied my wrists behind my back and threw me on the ground.

An hour later, they yanked me to my feet and led me down the path to our camp. My heart sank when I realized they knew where my people lived. I was in the company of the leader and about a half-dozen warriors, who walked silently with a determined step.

The ancient ones had dug canals and channeled the water that flowed out of the sinkhole, and some of them were still in use. The path we followed ran along one of these canals, lined by ancient trees, as it flowed away from the abandoned pueblo.

Before long we came to a clearing where the land slowly slanted down to meet the creek. A big cottonwood grew right where the canal terminated, and the water fanned out over its roots and onto the field.

Although the Sinagua were long gone, their fields remained, and we used them when convenient. We were not farmers, like the ancient ones, but we took advantage of fields like this when we could.

In the darkness, I could make out the harvested stalks of corn and withered vines from where we'd grown our squash. We grew what we could, harvested other plants when we traveled, and hunted for game wherever we went.

Our current home consisted of five wickiups. These circular, dome-shaped homes were made from a wooden frame held together with yucca fibers and then covered with brush. After our union, Elan and I would build our own wickiup, and I often daydreamed about it.

But today, the sight of my family's wickiup filled me with terror. In front of it, everyone was cowering in the dirt.

My mother saw me approach and ran to me, but a soldier stepped forward, a club in hand, and knocked her on the head so hard she sank to the ground, unconscious.

I knelt beside her and leaned into her body, sobbing, unable to comfort her with my arms tied.

They dragged us to the others and tossed us in the dirt.

And then the leader began shouting at us as he held a piece of parchment in his hand.

He kept shouting one word.

"Xibalba! Xibalba! Xibalba!"

None of us grasped the meaning of it.

I caught my grandmother's eye and suddenly knew exactly what he wanted. And she knew it, too.

It was the place of power, and bad energy, that I had known about all my life.

We never talked about it openly, only on special occasions, but it was a part of our family knowledge, just like the blood in our veins that came to us from Cocheta. Generation after generation, we learned about the hidden box canyon with the cave in the back, and the concealed tunnel there—and what it led to.

My mother always said it was a place that veered away from peace, not toward it. It was a place to be avoided.

The leader—whom I heard referred to as Yaotl—barked an order at his men, who began to drag people out of the crowd to beat them. I saw my cousin get clubbed in the back and sink to the ground, and then one of my sisters was backhanded.

And then they took my poor old grandmother and began to beat her—and it was too much for me. I watched as a savage blow knocked her to her knees, and when the warrior raised his club, I screamed, "Stop!"

Everyone froze and stared at me.

My grandmother collapsed to the ground, unconscious or dead, I didn't know. In a weaker voice, I said, "stop," again.

It suddenly dawned on me that they would kill us all unless one of us took them there.

I stood and faced the leader and said, "Xibalba."

I had been there only once, but I knew I could find it.

He peered at me intently, and with a flick of his hand, the beatings stopped.

# Chapter Fifteen

*I* lay in the dirt, arms bound, in front of Yaotl's tent. The remnants of a fire smoldered beside me but gave no warmth. Sunrise was still an hour away, and in the dull, cold pre-dawn gloom, I shivered, despite my efforts not to.

I will feel no pain, I told myself. I will feel no emotion. I will give them nothing. From now on, I am discipline. From now on, I am vengeance.

Eventually, the horizon began to lighten, and I could make out the desert brush around me. The first living thing that entered my field of vision was a tarantula.

The spider should have been deep in a nest, riding out the winter, but it must have been unearthed when the soldiers made camp, tearing up shrubs, roots and all.

The spider twitched.

I barely took note. I had no other thoughts in my mind but the revenge I now plotted. I seethed with it.

But then the tarantula's odd spasms got my attention.

I realized it had fallen victim to a tarantula hawk, or spider wasp. The wasp would have stung and paralyzed the spider weeks ago and then dragged it to a brood nest and deposited an egg on it. Over the coming weeks, the egg would hatch into a larva, which would feast on the still-living, but paralyzed spider.

A few days ago, the twitching spider would have filled me with disgust. I would have been tempted to kill the spider and put it out of its misery — something my grandmother would have forbidden because all life was precious to her.

But now, I don't care what lives or dies. I have decided to lead the invaders to the evil place, and I doubt I will live beyond it, which makes me cold inside, unfeeling.

No longer will I eagerly await the return of Elan or make plans for our spring matrimonial. No longer will I spend my mornings following the cool, shaded creek banks with my mother, searching for food and medicine while we sing softly to the coming day.

Instead, I will be death.

Death for those who follow me.

For I know that once I lead the men there, none can ever leave. I will not allow the poison to spread.

A ray of sunshine touched the spider, and suddenly the wasp larva emerged from the abdomen of the tarantula.

And when the slick creature began to crawl out of the tarantula's body, I turned away.


With the first light, Yaotl stepped out of his shelter. He glanced at the sky and ignored me crouched before him. Coatl, his captain, almost stumbled over me in his haste to kneel to his commander.

"Great lord," he said, "The men are ready to begin loading the slaves."

Yaotl nodded. "And what are our numbers?"

The captain's gaze slid over me, and he swallowed before he spoke. "Of the one hundred and fifty slaves, there are only fifty-five left. We lost five of the Blue Men, too. Twenty remain."

Yaotl flashed his pointed teeth, and Coatl quickly added, "We can continue with these numbers—you yourself said it is not much further. We will bring what we can and then send the slaves back to get the rest. I'll leave five men to guard everything until we return."

Yaotl's eyes simmered like hot coals. "No, we will take it all. Have my soldiers and the Blue Men divide whatever cannot be carried by the slaves. "

The Aztec lord paused then, his cold mind calculating their diminishing odds of success.

"And how are my soldiers?" he asked.

Again, the captain hesitated for a quick second.

He said, "We lost three yesterday, leaving seventeen. The bear killed two, and one was lame."

Yaotl glanced at the bear, who slept in the shadows, impressed that it still had the energy to kill. He didn't ask about the lame man: He had standing orders that anyone who couldn't keep up would be put to death. He would take no chances of someone revealing their location or what they were carrying.

Then he walked up to me and pulled out the map.

"You know this place?" he asked.

I didn't understand his words, and the parchment he held in front of me made no sense, but I knew where he wanted to go. My grandmother had told me it was the place where all weak men were drawn.

He pointed at the Mayan symbol near the top of Itzel Canyon.

"Xibalba," he said.

I held his gaze and nodded.

"Xibalba," I said.


I stood by Yaotl, at the head of the long line. He had cut my bonds, but after only a few moments, he had my hands retied in front of me. When I looked back, all I saw were the forlorn, hopeless faces of the slaves.

Beside the loading area, there was now a pile of about twenty bodies. While I watched, several soldiers started a fire beside them, threw a dozen logs on top of it, and then hefted the bodies into the flames.

As we began marching, the acrid smoke floated toward us, and I sucked it in. This was death, and I would accustom myself to it.

In the distance, toward the far southern end of our valley, I could see a long tendril of smoke reaching skyward — the last pile of burning bodies.

I saw in my mind the line of such fires stretching south, all the way to the hot tropics where these invaders came from.

When we left my wickiup, I didn't glance up to see if anyone was watching. I did not want to meet anyone's gaze.

I concentrated instead on the turkey vultures circling above. They were here for the burning flesh and rotting bodies.

I led them north, along the creeks and then the open plain. Heads down, in silence, we continued — accompanied only by the cursing from Yaotl's men and the crack of their lashes.

Coatl the Snake continuously marched up and down the line of slaves, shouting orders to lash those not moving fast enough.

He seemed to take joy in pestering both me and, for some reason, the poor bear. He carried a stout staff with him, and whenever he passed the bear he would whack it hard, sending the beast into a rage with men scurrying to control him.

A cold winter breeze blew at us, coming hard from upstream. The slaves were barefoot, and barely clad, and shivered helplessly.

Every now and then I'd hear a slave cry out in terror as he was pulled from the line. Then, moments later, his shrieks would grow as the guards beat him.

They cried in despair as much as the pain because they knew whoever failed to redouble his pace under the heavy loads would be beaten again and again until death was the only reward.

And when one of them died, his load would then be redistributed to the others who were also struggling fiercely to survive the ordeal.

I forced myself to blot out the cries and not look back.

By noon we had passed a bell-shaped rock, and by late afternoon we were on the banks of Oak Creek. Here we paused.

We had walked a long, hard day, and I collapsed as soon as Yaotl gave orders to make camp.

Over the next few hours, I watched the long line of slaves slowly catch up with us, and with each wretched face that passed before me, I strengthened my resolve to destroy these evil people.

Coatl supervised the unloading of the cargo, and when everything was stacked and the slaves in a newly constructed pen, the head count revealed that another twenty slaves had perished. They were down to thirty-five slaves, but they still had seventeen soldiers and about that number in Blue Men.

Before Coatl allowed the soldiers and Blue Men to relax, he made them collect and burn the newly dead. Only then would he let them sit and eat and tend to their injuries. Most had feet that were cut and blistered.

Yaotl inspected his camp before retiring, with Coatl a half-step behind him, watching everything with a cunning look in his eyes.

"The men are fine," warned Yaotl, "but the slaves will not hold much longer."

Coatl chanced a short laugh. "What does it matter if they live or die?" he asked. "You yourself said none will be left breathing when we are finished here."

"Don't be a fool," berated Yaotl. "If any more slaves die, you will have to start bearing a load."

The shocked expression that took over Coatl's face sent Yaotl chuckling as he retired to his shelter.


We set out the following day with ten guards and the remaining fifteen Blue Men. The Blue Men were loaded with the Spanish steel but no other cargo.

Coatl remained with the slaves and a half-dozen soldiers who were transporting the cargo. Through gestures, I had told Yaotl that we were a day's journey from Itzel Canyon.

There was no way the battered slaves could carry all the freight that distance in one trip, so they planned to make several. Most wouldn't survive another day.

We left another pyre of burning bodies behind us as we entered Oak Creek Canyon. A cold wind blew down the canyon, and we had to lean into it as we progressed upstream.

For the next six hours, we trudged up the creek. The trees had all shed their leaves and did little to break the wind. Sometimes I led Yaotl´s people along game trails that followed the water. Other times I hopped from stone to stone. Ice had formed in shady spots along the shore and around the rocks that stuck up out of the flow.

I steered toward routes with treacherous or slippery footing, hoping that Yaotl´s men would slip and fall—and some did.

But it was difficult with my hands tied. My head spun. Several times I scooped up a handful of water, but I hadn't eaten in twenty-four hours. Most likely, Yaotl and his men expected me to be dead long before I starved.

When the day was half spent, we turned left into the West Fork.

Yaotl left two guards there to make sure the slaves could follow.


The smaller canyon lay forlorn and devoid of life, twisting before us like an immense uncoiled snake. There was no splash of color or trace of an animal. Even the birds were silent.

We pushed on, frigid step after step. Soon most of the water lay trapped in cold black puddles covered with a thin layer of ice.

As the walls closed in and rose higher, we were forced to break the ice and march straight through water that was sometimes waist-deep. The men shivered and occasionally cursed under their breath—even the Blue Men seemed to be moving in a stupor.

When we passed through a flooded tunnel, some of the men began to panic, glancing at each other with eyes full of dread, as if they sensed we were moving deeper into some forbidden place.

In the cold, dark tunnel, their heavy breathing echoed and reverberated. It seemed to whisper all around them, reaffirming the fear that they were entering a realm controlled by the spirits.

Nevertheless, they had no choice but to continue until finally, we reached a fork where a steep canyon appeared on the left.

I nodded at it and said, "Itzel Canyon."

Yaotl had his men set up camp right there, by a bend in the creek where a small pond reflected the remaining daylight. While they were clearing brush and lighting several fires, he sent two scouts up the canyon to see what terrain awaited.

When they returned and reported what they had found, he sent Coatl and the Blue Men up the ravine. They carried with them steel mallets and wedges and the saws.

Over the next few hours, the canyon was filled with the sounds of hammering and trees being felled.

Night came early that deep into the West Fork, and I slunk off to a corner to sleep.

# *Chapter Sixteen*

*T*he sun was high overhead when I woke the next day. How I'd slept so long was a mystery. I was still bound, my wrists raw and swollen, and my back and limbs ached from the previous day's journey and sleeping on the hard rock of the canyon floor.

Much of the strangers' cargo had been hauled up the canyon in the interim and lay stacked twenty paces away. One of the bundles had torn, and I could see several yellow pieces of metal on the ground.

I picked one up, surprised at its weight. My people had little use for the metal, but clearly, it had value to the invaders. We were transporting a treasure—for what use I still didn't know.

A man coughed behind me, and I turned to see Yaotl watching me. He was seated in the shade of a juniper, a few paces away.

I dropped the coin, which had begun to burn warmly in my hand.

He laughed, grinning, and walked to me and picked it up.

He held it before me. Do you know this metal? his eyes implored.

I nodded. I'd seen the yellow metal before.

Yaotl pointed at the sky and then swept his arm down in an arc until he pointed at a rock by his feet. He picked up the rock and then touched the stone and the gold coin together and smiled.

Was he telling me there were stars in the metal?

He shook his head at my blank expression, grabbed my elbow, and escorted me to the mouth of Itzel Canyon, where we gazed up its length.

All the low shrubs had been cleared, and the fallen trees and logs removed. Using the hammers and chisels, the Blue Men had removed any boulders that blocked the way and carved steps out of the canyon's sandstone walls.

They had built a trail leading up the canyon, and steep sections that previously had to be climbed were now traversable. Near the top was a lengthy, slanted ascent with a long series of steps.

Suddenly, I was roughly grabbed by my hair and then pushed forward toward Yaotl. I glanced back quickly to see Coatl the Snake, watching me with a grin.

He had caught up with us in the night.

I glimpsed another gruesome stack of dead slaves behind him. Piled by the side were their discarded chains and collars.

Shackled to a cottonwood was the old Mexican grizzly. He was lying down when I had observed him before, but now he paced restlessly. He was a head taller than a man and must have weighed as much a four.

And his coloring was different than any bear I'd ever seen; not brown or black, but silver, with darker, yellowish underfur. He'd injured one of his paws but still watched his captors intently.

When one of the soldiers passed too close to the bear, it swiped at him and almost took his head off.

The man cursed, then threw a rock at the bear, hitting him solidly in the shoulder.

The bear roared defiantly, and the man chuckled.

Suddenly, through my hardened resolve that knew nothing but revenge, I felt pity for the bear.

So intently had I been watching the bear that I didn't see Coatl walk up. He cuffed me on the side of the head to get my attention.

"Come!" he commanded.

I joined Yaotl and waited while he instructed Coatl and his men to haul the treasure up the newly constructed canyon trail.

Robert Louis DeMayo

It didn't take us long to ascend to the highest accessible point in the canyon, where four guards were blocking the entrance to the chute that led to the hidden box canyon.

I climbed up through the dark, damp entrance and took in the canyon. It had been years since I'd been here, but it felt like not a second had passed.

I was again surprised at how big it was and how high the walls were. Numerous paintings on the lower walls documented the time of the ancients here and reminded me of the long line of women who had kept the place hidden.

I had been warned about this location for as long as I could remember. And yet, it was connected to my mother, grandmother, and tribe, and something was comforting about it.

But I shut off the emotions that tried to take over.

Soon Yaotl was next to me, surveying the box canyon.

He gave me a questioning glance, and I nodded toward the cave in the back. The morning sun had risen high enough to glint over the eastern wall, and it shone straight into the entrance. The roots of the junipers flanking the entryway gripped the sides of the ingress as if trying to stretch them wider.

The Snake's eyes eagerly darted in that direction.


At the mouth of the cave, Yaotl ordered his guards to stay back.

Only Yaotl, Coatl and I entered.

Inside, we could dimly see by the sunlight coming from behind. The ceiling sloped down toward the back, and water dripped from it into clear puddles. The ancient ones had left clay pots under a few of the drips, and the water in them rippled darkly.

On a dry mound in the middle of the cave, I noticed a mano and metate next to several bowls of powder.

I tried not to look at the section of the wall where the evil tunnel lay concealed. The plaster hiding it had been painted with symbols, and some old baskets were placed before it.

Instead, I lingered by a small chamber to the left of the entrance, choking down the fear that was slowly taking over my senses.

Several old bear skulls were lined up on the floor, and a necklace of bear claws hung from a peg above them.

From behind me, I heard the Snake whistle.

I turned and saw him nod at the wall in front of the tunnel.

After a word from Yaotl, he stepped outside and returned with a hammer and a torch. He gave the torch to Yaotl and began smashing down the barrier to the tunnel's entrance.

My heart was beating wildly.

With the first blow, a hole opened, and the air rushed by with a sucking sound as if the tunnel led to a place devoid of oxygen.

Despite my pledge to remain cold and impassive, I lost control of myself and turned and fled. I made it out of the cave and halfway to the exit before one of the soldiers tackled me. He grabbed me roughly by the arm and led me to Coatl, who smacked me in the face and then dragged me back into the cave.

The tunnel's entrance had now been opened. Yaotl stood before it, the flickering light from the torch illuminating only the first few feet. He was sweating and pale, but his eyes glowed with exhilaration as he peered into the dark passageway ahead.

He observed Coatl staring into the tunnel also and grabbed him roughly. "You are not to enter under any circumstances," he commanded.

The Snake said, "Yes, my..." but was cut off when Yaotl gripped him by the throat and squeezed.

"Do you understand?" asked Yaotl threateningly.

Coatl tried to speak but couldn't. He couldn't breathe.

He managed a weak nod, and Yaotl let go.

The Snake quickly retreated, bowing submissively as he backed away. "I swear, my lord," he whimpered, "I will never go in."

The Snake saw that I'd been watching and roughly shoved me into the room with the bear skulls. Then he pointed at the dark recess where I sat, held up his knife and fingered the sharp obsidian edge. The message was clear: If I left the chamber, he'd kill me. We both watched silently as Yaotl disappeared into the tunnel.

Coatl left the cave for the box canyon when he could no longer hear his lord scampering through the tunnel, and it became apparent that Yaotl would not be returning right away.

I searched around me, then the cave where the water drips, and eventually found a small shard of black, volcanic rock. It was about the same shape that I would have used to skin an animal — or cut someone.

And I also paused by the clay bowl and quenched my thirst.

Then I crept back into the recess with the bear skulls and cut the rope binding my hands. I retied them loosely before laying my head down to rest in case the Snake noticed.

Sleep swept over me like a shadow, and I knew not how long I'd been unconscious when I woke later.

I crawled to the cave's mouth and peered past the junipers to see what was happening in the box canyon.

The sun had passed over the rim of our canyon and left us in shadow, and I guessed nightfall wasn't far away.

Blue Men and Yaotl's soldiers were hauling up the crates and stacking them in the box canyon. I saw very few slaves.

Some men came my way, and I slipped back in the recess with the bear skulls. On the other side of the cave, on the dry patch between puddles where the metate lay, they placed the bound jaguar, the basket with the snake, and the caged bird.

The eagle screeched raucously as they set it down.

There was a commotion outside. Then the bear was led into the cave, ruthlessly encouraged by several Blue Men with lashes. Somehow, they had shackled his front and back feet, and he had to shuffle forward awkwardly.

He still roared defiantly. His screams were terrifying in the small cave, and the men were anxious to be rid of the bear.

One man carried a spear, and he stabbed the bear in the side when he wouldn't move next to the other caged animals.

The bear lunged forward and bit the man in the throat, killing him instantly.

Coatl sounded an alarm, and soon the cave was filled with men carrying spears, but the bear would not go any nearer to the sacrificial animals — or the tunnel behind them.

The best they could do was drive the bear into the small recess where I sat, right next to me.

Coatl laughed uproariously when he saw me scamper to the far wall. But the bear seemed to have no anger toward me and instead snarled at his captors.

When the men left the cave again, the bear turned away from me and curled up against the wall.

I sat there listening to it breathing and panting and realized how badly it was injured.

I scampered to the clay pot filled with water, retrieved it, and placed it before the bear.

Its eyes opened just a fraction, and then slowly, the bear leaned forward and drank.

For one brief moment my spirit soared, but then I realized that most likely neither of us would survive, and my cold heart broke in two.


Yaotl emerged from the tunnel. His body was tense, every muscle flexed. He was covered in an orange powder that appeared luminescent. His pupils were dilated and seemed to have a yellow glow to them.

Coatl knelt before him, almost giddy with the power in his lord's eyes. They'd found Xibalba, the entrance to the other world.

"I need ten Blue Men," said Yaotl. "Put them in chains."

Coatl nodded at this unusual request. After all, they prided themselves on being more than mere slaves.

Yaotl rubbed his chin, "And I want five of my best soldiers. Give each man a lash, but no weapons."

He grabbed Coatl by his chest plate. "You are to make sure I am the only one ever to enter the tunnel with a weapon — understand?"

Coatl whimpered. "Yes lord, of course," he said and backed away.

Soon he returned with ten Blue Men, all wearing steel collars and chained to each other. Although the men were cut and bruised and exhausted from the ordeal of opening the canyon, their pride had not been broken. Some were glaring at Coatl for chaining them—but none dared to look Yaotl in the eye. They feared him and seemed to sense his newfound power.

Yaotl ordered them to widen the tunnel. Five soldiers with lashes were to supervise their work. But before any of them entered the tunnel, Yaotl had them fill their ears with wax.

I watched. The men worked hard while Yaotl stood back and observed, one hand on the hilt of a dagger, the other holding a club that rested on his shoulder.

As they moved deeper and deeper into the tunnel, and the shouting and the crack of lashes intensified. The Blue Men screamed in agony, but the steady pounding of steel on rock continued.


In the box canyon, Coatl was supervising the shuttling of the rest of the treasure. He still had ten warriors, a half-dozen Blue Men, and some remaining slaves.

It was dark by the time they finished, and they'd only been laying down for thirty minutes when Yaotl emerged from the tunnel with his soldiers and the chained Blue Men.

The Snake had been waiting by the tunnel entrance, drawn there by horrid screams and shouting from within. Of the ten Blue Men, only six were still alive. They hauled their dead, chained comrades out of the tunnel and collapsed.

Coatl examined the body of one of the dead. He was also covered in orange powder. Dark bruises hinted that he'd been beaten with a mallet. His face was a gruesome mask of frozen terror.

Yaotl's soldiers all looked like they were in shock. They were each bloodied and bruised, and it was apparent they'd been in fights with either the Blue Men or each other.

Yaotl glared at everyone around him.

He shouted, "Teōnanācatl!" and within a minute, a soldier was kneeling in front of him, holding a clay bowl above his head.

He saw me watching from the shadows and called out, "Mushrooms—the flesh of the Gods!"

He offered me some and then laughed raucously when I refused.

He stuffed several mushroom caps in his mouth and shredded them.

"Do you know about these?" he asked, his pupils zeroing in on me. "They are wondrous—they carry you to where God is."

I slid back toward the bear, and Yaotl jumped, noticing the beast for the first time. He laughed and stared at me anew.

Yaotl was feeling benevolent and ordered all the Blue Men to be fed, but no sooner had they eaten than he rounded them up again and sent them back into the tunnel.

Maybe a dozen wretched souls slipped into the passageway that night. It was hard to tell in the shadows, and I never saw any of them again.

All had wax in their ears and no weapons.

Before he turned away, Yaotl glared at Coatl and some of the other soldiers who had gathered around.

He said, "Nine hell cycles of fifty-two years each," and then he was gone, leaving them perplexed.


I woke with a start, early the next morning, when I realized I was lying against the bear. There was little room in the small recess, and the beast had shifted toward me in the night.

I felt no fear of the bear. The night had been cold, and I welcomed the warmth that radiated from the rich, silver fur. Its deep, earthy scent pulled me from the awful reality of our situation—if only for a moment.

We were left alone for most of that day, and time seemed to stretch. I stayed in the small recess, always within a few feet of the bear who slept most of the time, his breathing becoming more labored.

From the other end of the tunnel, in the dark chamber beyond, I could always hear the hammering of mallets and the howls of the men.

It never stopped.

Yaotl had the remaining soldiers and slaves transporting the treasure through the tunnel into the dark chamber.

Around mid-day, Coatl entered the cave and perched himself where he could see me and watch the men coming and going from the tunnel.

He had a steaming bowl of food, and the scent of it floated toward me, causing my stomach to rumble. The bear lifted his head, too, and when he saw the Snake, he growled.

Coatl stood nervously, but after a moment, realized the bear didn't have the energy to stand. He laughed weakly and then sat again.

But his eyes didn't leave the bear for a long time.

Eventually, he tried to catch my eye, waving the bowl before me to torture me. But I simply retreated into my coldness, which seemed to madden him.

He suddenly glanced at his food as if it had lost its taste and then dumped it in the dirt.

When he was gone, the bear gazed at the pile of food, and so did I, but neither made a move to get it. The thought of eating it made me sick, like biting into something rotten would.


The morning of my third day in the box canyon, I awoke when Coatl dragged the last remaining slave into the cave and threw him next to the sacrificial animals on the mound.

The man was a wretch: His limbs were shredded with cuts and scrapes, his body covered with bruises, and his eyes were filled with fear and confusion.

The last vestiges of his sanity had left him, and he shrieked like a wild creature until one of the men clubbed him unconscious.

Coatl glared at the soldier and then relaxed when he saw the unconscious slave was still breathing.

He gave the soldier an evil smile. "You almost replaced him."

Later, the slave woke and watched me for a long time. But he didn't try to speak or even sit up.


He remained like that for hours until the hammering in the tunnel suddenly stopped.

At this, he looked up fearfully.

Moments later, the soldiers emerged from the tunnel and grabbed the jaguar, the eagle, and the snake; as they disappeared into the passageway again, the cat let out a roar that made me tremble.

Then they returned for the slave.

The man shrieked and fought, but it was a useless effort.

Coatl seemed to enjoy the show. He was the only foreigner who hadn't entered the tunnel at this point.

But just before the slave was hauled into the tunnel, Coatl glanced at me, and an evil thought bled through his mind.

His face twisted into a half-sided smirk as he commanded, "Halt!"

The soldiers paused, and when he said, "Take her instead," they dropped the slave and started in my direction.

The soldiers had all but forgotten the bear, assuming it was near death.

I backed against the wall, with nowhere to run or hide.

One man reached forward for my bound hands.

But suddenly the bear was between us, rising as much as the small space would allow.

It swiped at the soldier, sending him crashing into the wall.

The Snake screamed at his men. "Kill it!"

Another man went down under a savage blow, but from behind, a soldier buried his spear into the bear.

The old grizzly roared in pain and agony.

And then another spear sank home.

"No!" I screamed as the bear collapsed.

Coatl stepped over him and snatched my arm.

Quickly, I pulled one of my hands from the loose ropes.

With the shard of rock in my hand, I struck for his face.

I cut him under his good eye, and he staggered backward.

A half-dozen soldiers stood behind him as the Snake felt the cut and blood on his face.

He backed away from me, uncertain.

And when he noticed the men watching him, he nodded at the slave in the dirt.

"Take him into the tunnel," he said and stormed off.

They hauled him away, and the slave's screams echoed through the tunnel for a long time after that.

I was left with a handful of soldiers. They'd each had their time in the dark chamber and looked fearfully at the tunnel. Soon they left for the box canyon, leaving me alone with the dying bear.

I threw off the rope dangling from my wrist and hugged the bear, fighting back the tears. It took in a painful breath, and when the bear exhaled, I felt its body slump and knew the great beast had died.

I hadn't moved when sometime later the Snake approached me again.

I was surprised to find I still gripped the stone shard tightly.

He glimpsed it, and his hand reflexively moved to the fresh cut below his good eye.

If only I had blinded him, I thought.

The sun had long since passed over the western wall of the box canyon, and the shadows were thickening. Usually, this period when the day embraced the night would be filled with bird song and the sporadic cries of coyotes. But on this night, the box canyon lay as still and quiet as the dead.

I could see the Snake sensed the strange silence as well.

And then, from the tunnel, a crazy chorus of screaming filled the chilled night air. It rose in crescendo — as if every man in the dark chamber was screaming at once — and then it suddenly stopped.

Coatl stood there listening with a confused expression.

I sat in the small cavity, leaning against the dead bear, and began chanting. Coatl turned away from the tunnel and leaned against the wall, watching me.

I stared into his one good eye, no longer afraid.

I fingered the stone shard, gripping it with the sharp edge facing out.

With my other hand, I lifted one of the bear's paws and grabbed a claw where the skin started and felt for the joint. Using the stone shard, I cut into the knuckle and separated the claw.

Coatl's eyes were full of a new fear as he watched.

I continued to chant, and when I finished with the paw, I stood and grabbed the ancient claw necklace, lifting it off the peg.

My eyes barely left the Snake as I tied each claw into the necklace.

One of his men approached, saw me cutting off the claws on the next paw, whispered something that sounded like a prayer, then slowly backed away.

Outside, the full moon was just peeking over the rim of the horizon.

# *Chapter Seventeen*

*F*rom the east, a luminous full moon crept over the horizon and lit up the silent canyons in a shiny grey hue. This was the moon of the long night, the cold moon. The moon that frigidly reminded one that the warm days of summer were far off, for only after its passing would the nights begin to shorten.

The remaining soldiers who paced around the box canyon barely noticed it at first. They'd become anxious after their leader had vanished into a dark tunnel that now lay silent, and their eyes were constantly darting to the cave entrance.

They had a fire burning by the exit chute, but none stood around it for warmth or comfort because it was still consuming the bodies of the last slaves.

The acrid smoke from the burning bodies hung heavily in the box canyon, looking ghostly in the moonlight.

Coatl was restless. Could his dark lord have failed in his mission? He had lurked into the cave just after dark, carrying a torch. In the flickering light, his one white eye hideously glared.

I stood and faced him.

He took out his knife and fingered the sharp, obsidian blade, trying to scare me, but I spat on the dirt by his feet.

Several times he leaned into the tunnel, but he did not dare set foot in it. Nor did he chance calling out the sinister lord's name for fear of disturbing the heavy silence that lingered here.

He glanced at me when he passed the chamber where the bear now lay dead. Harvesting the claws had been a difficult job, and I'd finished it covered in bear blood and hair.

The other men crept in and looked me over, and I heard them whispering a word I'd come to recognize, "Witch."

Soon they began collecting their weapons and the few provisions left in the box canyon.

Regardless of what riches may now have lain unguarded in the dark chamber, they didn't want to go back into there. They were ready to flee if only Coatl would give the word.

I doubted they would leave me alive, but the thought didn't bother me. It was as if I were another person, watching myself suffer as a stranger would. Seeing but not feeling the actual pain.

Outside, I could hear them arguing. The moonlight had begun to shine into the cave, slipping around the barbed bark of the junipers.

I knew they would come for me.

I didn't care. I had known this would be the place of my death ever since I'd agreed to lead them here.

I came from a long line of strong women, and I wouldn't let them down.

I would end this.

I took the necklace of bear claws and placed it over my head and then sat back and waited.

Coatl and the remaining soldiers — nine of them — approached the cave. An owl screeched from somewhere nearby, and they froze.

And then suddenly, standing before them, was the grizzly bear.

The moonlight reflected ghostlike off its silvery pelt, and it seemed bigger than before, taller, and more powerful. It roared, and its angry cry reverberated through the men, shaking them to the core.

The bear rose on his hind legs and towered before them.

The men gawked, paralyzed with terror, until Coatl screamed, "What are you waiting for? Kill it!"

They tried to encircle the bear, but its wrath would not be contained. Finally, one man got too close, and the bear lunged at him and swatted him into the canyon wall.

Another soldier threw his spear at the bear.

It stuck in its shoulder, but the bear continued its rampage undeterred. The soldier's weapons seemed to have no effect on it.

In two heartbeats, the bear killed as many men.

When the bear's gaze fell on Coatl, it charged straight at him.

It stopped just a pace away and rose above the terrified man, roaring.

Coatl hefted his spear, but the bear was upon him already. With one mighty swipe of the paw, the bear disemboweled the Aztec before he could even utter a scream.

Coatl stood there in shock, staring at his intestines dangling out of his abdomen.

Chaos ensued. The men turned to flee in vain. None escaped the beast's wrath. In Itzel Canyon, terrible screams echoed off the walls and faded into the West Fork below.

# Chapter Eighteen

Soft morning sunshine was pouring over me, urging me to sleep longer. My body felt rested and warmed from the smooth rock beneath me. It was mid-day, and an old raven clucked by my head, hopping in place as it watched me.

Other birds called out in the fresh morning air: A mountain bluebird twittered expectantly for its mate; a scrub jay bellowed its harsh screech, and from nearby, a red flash of color alerted me to the presence of a cardinal, who soon enchanted me with its long, clear, whistle, "*Wheet, wheet, wheet...*"

Although the canyon was still gripped by winter, for a few hours each day, the creatures at home here embraced the sun.

As did I.

My head swirled with dreams from the previous night, and I moved slowly, in a daydream if you will, as I sat up and took the first deep breath of the day.

Scattered about the box canyon were the bodies of Yaotl's soldiers. They'd been disfigured most horribly. Their blood had pooled, and a small trickle of it had flowed down the box canyon and into the chute.

I wondered briefly if any of them had gotten away.

The Snake's body was worst of all. His intestines spread out around him. From the smeared blood beneath it, it looked like he'd been dragged all over.

A fleeting memory of his evil sneer crossed my mind, and I spat on the ground.

I glanced up at the sun, which only moments before had caressed me, and now seemed to mock me. The day had seemed so peaceful, but as I regained my senses, I knew I had work to do.

So, I turned away from the sun, away from the box canyon littered with bloodied corpses, and headed back toward the cave.

Creeping past the junipers, I peeked into the small chamber on the left and saw the bear's carcass, unchanged. The bear claw necklace hung from the peg on the wall behind it.

I crouched there for a few minutes, staring across the cave where the water dripped, into the tunnel. I strained to hear with all my might, but no sounds emerged.

I felt trapped, just as Coatl must have. I didn't think I possessed the nerve to enter the tunnel — but I couldn't walk away.

I didn't care what had happened in the dark chamber, but what if someone was still alive in there? Would they eventually escape and tell others?

I had to make sure nobody discovered the tunnel again.

My hesitation seemed to last an eternity, but eventually, I stood and stepped outside. By the exit chute, embers from a fire were still smoking. I kindled a flame and made a torch out of some fabric that I ripped from the tunic of a dead soldier.

With the torch, I entered the tunnel. Thanks to the Blue Men's work, there was no need to crawl or even crouch.

After twenty paces, I came to a mid-point where a clearing with a wooden framework had been made. A massive stone block had been set into the sandstone floor.

I held the light over it and noticed a head-sized hole in the center, and when I knelt on the slab to peer into it, I heard a *whoosh* over my head and dove to the side. The torch dropped to the ground.

The wooden framework was a trap, and my weight on the slab had triggered it. A log with a spike on the end had shot out from the side and barely missed my head.

Before I could take a good look at the trap, my attention was drawn away by a low growl. It was close. My blood froze.

Slowly I picked up the torch and looked around. All I could see was the exit back to the cave where the water dripped, and the tunnel leading to the forbidden place.

And then I realized the growling was coming from the hole in the slab beneath me. I held the torch over the hole and what I saw made me suck in my breath. Since leaving my pueblo, I had witnessed many horrors, but none like this.

The slab of rock I knelt on sealed a room, about as long and wide as a man and at least that high. In the pit, I saw a man — the last slave I'd seen alive — and with him were the jaguar, the snake and the eagle.

They had all been bound, but it appeared the snake basket had been tipped over, and the eagle had escaped. The snake was coiled and hissing, and the jaguar was growling with his yellow eyes flashing.

There wasn't much room in the pit, and they were almost touching each other. One of the eagle's wings looked broken, but it flapped the other wildly, creating chaos.

The man was sweating and pale, and I thought he'd been bit by the snake.

He saw my face through the hole and pleaded with me to help him. I didn't need to understand his language to feel the anguish in his words.

I looked down at the large capstone that covered the pit and realized that even with a half-dozen strong men, I wouldn't be able to move it.

I tried to communicate with him, but each time I held the light over the pit, the eagle would begin beating his wing, and the jaguar started screeching. In the darkness, they may have come to some form of truce or acceptance of their plight, but soon as visibility returned, they attacked each other.

And it was here that I almost broke. I suddenly felt useless, utterly unable to fight the great evil around me. I looked at the tunnel ahead of me and wondered if I dared to continue.

The man below me pleaded, but he knew his fate was sealed. When I stood and moved the light away, he became silent.

His terrible plight angered me, and I used that emotion to take the first step toward the dark chamber. I no longer needed the torch as the luminous powder now showed the way clearly.

It was then that the first trace of a shadowy force came over me.

I stopped and opened my ears.

I could hear no sound from the forbidden chamber ahead.

Somehow, I knew everyone there was dead.

But I had to make sure. I began to creep forward.

And it was then that my grandmother´s words returned to me. Words passed down to her from her mother and her mother´s mother, leading back to Cocheta, the Unknown.

"Don't go into the dark chamber," the mothers from my past chanted, and I stopped.

I closed my eyes and whispered to myself, "I will not, and neither will anyone else. If that is your will, then I will enforce it."


The first thing I did was reset the trap. If another made it this far, there would be a failsafe. Then I returned to the box canyon, and one by one, dragged the bodies of the soldiers into the tunnel where I stacked them just inside the entrance. I made sure to include their weapons and other belongings.

I also hauled the chains and steel tools into the tunnel.

The last thing I tossed in was Yaotl's bowl of mushrooms.

I then collected stones and walled up the passageway. With dirt and water from the puddles, I made mortar to set the rocks. It was a poor job, but in the end, the tunnel was sealed.

I left the box canyon. I stepped over blood-stained rocks, but otherwise, the canyon and the cave where the water drips were devoid of evidence of the invaders.

The dead bear I left where it lay after silently saying goodbye.

I descended Itzel Canyon, walking quietly over the stone steps. Now that the arduous task of hiding the bodies and resealing the tunnel had been completed, I fell back into the dream state I'd awoken to. My mind wanted to shut down.

At the confluence of Itzel Canyon and the West Fork, I lay back on a flat rock by the small glittering pond.

I intended to rest for only a moment, but I fell into a deep sleep.

And in that sleep, I dreamt I was a silver bear, running through the forest under a glowing moon, free and unconcerned.


I opened my eyes to the golden light of the late afternoon, thirsty and aware of my hunger. I continued my journey to the confluence of the West Fork and Oak Creek, and when I reached it, I turned north, upstream, rather than heading in the direction of my home.

I wasn't ready to return there yet.

A short walk brought me to a quiet place where the water slowed as it flowed around a large flat rock whose surface was just above the water. Behind this stood a tall stone with a swirling design etched into the stone, and on both shores of this quiet lagoon, small stacks of rocks had been built.

I sat on the flat rock and let the water swirl around my feet.

The events of the last few days raced through my mind like a biting wind.

My grandmother would tell me there was no use trying to run from my fears, so I faced them. I closed my eyes, letting the flowing water soothe my nerves, and began to relive the last few days from start to finish. I thought of the attack on our wickiup and the long march here. I thought of the piles of burning bodies and the crack of lashes.

And I thought of the silver bear, dragged all this way just to die an ignoble death in chains. I wept for the bear and only stopped when I remembered my dream.

Finally, when all the horror and pain and sorrow had flowed out of me, my breathing slowed down. I felt the trees and high grass swaying around me, and I swayed in the breeze as well, and I smelled the rich earth and sensed the living things that still lived in this beautiful forest.

I opened my eyes and took in my surroundings: I was in my mother's place, the sacred place.

As much as the wickiup was my home, something told me this place was where I was from. I felt my former self return—and I began to sing.

The song came out timidly at first, but soon the forest around me responded and embraced me, and my voice grew as it reverberated in the canyon.

I thought of my mother and my grandmother, and although for days I'd convinced myself that they might be dead, I knew now—somehow—that they were both well.

I would begin the long walk back in the morning, but I would take my time. I would return casually, not like one who just survived an ordeal. The dark chamber must remain a secret.

I will tell my mother and grandmother the truth, but to everyone else, I will simply say they continued north, and I escaped.

Because I did escape. Somehow, I had lived. And I was determined now to have a good life and to leave that dark place behind.

And while I sang, I thought of my husband-to-be, and for the first time in what felt like an eternity, became excited about our matrimonial. My heart picked up pace as I thought of seeing him again.

I thought I would collect some firewood, or maybe find something edible, but as soon as I laid my head on the soft green moss covering that rock in the creek, I fell into another deep slumber that cradled me all the way to the birds announcing the next day's sunrise.

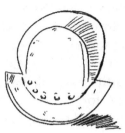

# Chapter Nineteen

## Act I

### 1705
### (January)

$A$ white haze floated through the desert brush, banishing shadows and hovering over the desiccated landscape. The sun was low in the southwest sky, radiating more light than heat, but that glare was penetrating, and the bleached limestone that capped the low mesas reflected it back to the sky-blue void with an equal intensity.

The mesquite and creosote bushes that dotted the land appeared immune to it, as did the prickly-pear and agave. Here at the southern fringe of the canyon country — the end of the known world to most people — the desert rambled on with no end.

Most of the critters were smart enough to lay low; the sky was free of birds, mule deer and coyotes lay secluded in the thickets, and even the lizards kept to the shadows.

In the distance glimmered the hope of coolness.

At the other end of the valley — to the north — the Colorado Plateau rose into the clouds in a brilliant ribbon of colored sandstone, and there, winter had an icy grip on the land. Beyond the edge of the plateau, there extended several snow-capped peaks.

Two Spaniards cut through the desolate landscape, riding mules single file, moving toward the peaks. They were Cristóbal de Niza, a tall, bearded man in his late twenties, and his younger brother, Alonso. Their outfits resembled a cross between those of a conquistador and a prospector.

They both wore helmets and breastplates and were armed with black powder rifles and pistols. They also carried small miner's picks and headlamps. Tethered to the second rider was a pair of stout Sonoran burros, which were loaded with shovels, coils of rope, gold pans and other mining gear, and cooking supplies.

Cristóbal rode lead with a determined stare. He was letting his mind drift over the last few months of travel, of the endless ravines and plains and waterless mountains, and the twisting, lifeless canyons, always bordered by distant faded mountains that never grew closer.

Part of him still felt he was traveling through that desolate land of stony, barren hills and endless slopes of cholla cactus. This desert in winter was void of color, and so monotonous were the faded olive shrubbery and worn auburn cliffs that he believed his party contained some of the only living people in the land.

To make matters worse, he felt like he was chasing ghosts.

It had been one hundred and eighty-four years since Cortez had attacked Tenochtitlán, and aside from that treasure and the gold Pizarro took from the Incas, what else had been found?

Nothing. Copper rattles. Trinkets in comparison.

Then Cabeza de Vaca had stumbled out of the Americas, half-mad with stories of Cibola and the Seven Cities of Gold, and everyone thought it was the beginning of another era of enormous riches.

My ancestor tried his hand at finding that treasure, thought Cristóbal. In 1536, Marcos de Niza attempted to locate those fabled cities with Esteban—a black slave who'd accompanied Cabeza de Vaca. De Niza should have found it; he'd been with Pizarro fighting the Inca, and by all accounts, he was a competent man. But he came home empty-handed, leaving Esteban for dead on the open plain.

And even the last of the great expeditions came up empty. In 1541, Don Francisco Vasquez de Coronado led a small army into the north: two hundred armored knights, seventy crossbowmen, eight hundred *Indios*, and a long pack train of mules loaded with baggage and supplies.

And in the end, they too limped home unrewarded.

But Cristóbal could not let it go. The more he heard of the rumors and legends of these undiscovered riches, the more he believed there was vast treasure yet to be found. And the magnificent riches of the Mayans and Incas were fabulous precedents. Noblemen and peasants alike were aroused by tales of Quivira, and Cibola, and other such places yet to be discovered, and they believed a *new* Mexico could be won through military conquest and exploration.

If he closed his eyes, he could see it: Cities with streets paved with gold, turquoise-studded walls, treasure piled before him — unimaginable wealth.

And then two days ago, when they'd entered this valley, he had stumbled into the old woman, and what she had told him had confirmed his wildest suspicions.

Now it is all within my grasp, he thought.

He lingered there, content that with this new information, he might finally locate his prize, but then the murmur of running water pulled him away.

Solitude invites daydreaming, he warned himself. And daydreamers lose their focus and die.

When the creek came into view, he hopped off his mule, walked to one of the burros to retrieve a Mexican cask, and brought it to the water to fill it.

The little stream gurgled through a grove of towering cottonwoods, tumbling over the exposed roots along the bank. The trees formed a canopy overhead, casting the Spaniards in lucent green shadows. In the coolness, two canyon wrens chased a screeching jay until it finally flew off.

Alonso pulled his mule to a stop, smiled as he took off his helmet, and looked around. His face was youthful and untried as he sat there listening to the birds and the gentle, clear water gurgling over the pebbles.

Cristóbal gave him a menacing glare from where he knelt by the water and ordered, "Keep it on, little brother — there are things worse than a sore head."

Alonso pleaded with him. "Come on, Cristóbal! We've been riding since the port of Guaymas — I feel like I've spent a year underneath this helmet."

"It has barely been two months. We have traveled far because what we search for is great. It is hidden in one of these canyons, so keep your eyes open," warned Cristóbal.

Alonso laughed while putting his helmet on again.

"You are too serious, *Hermano* — you should relax."

"I will not!" spat Cristóbal. "And you should not either. Your casual attitude will someday cost you your life."

Then he scoffed and added, "With my luck, it will cost my life as well."

Cristóbal walked to his mule and took a leather-bound journal out of his saddlebag. Then, using a quill he kept in the book, he scribbled a few notes before putting it back.

Then he took out his pistol and checked it while Alonso let his eyes sweep over the horizon. They were much closer to the glowing cliffs and buttes now, and in the afternoon sun, the rocks lit up in vibrant reds and yellows; in the soft light, they seemed close enough to touch.

Behind them, on their left, the sun glared from the horizon, casting their shadows far ahead, to the northeast.

Alonso wondered how they would get around these cliffs, as there seemed no way to penetrate their secret depths.

Cristóbal said, "What we search for is well protected. Of that, I have been warned."

He stared at several scalps dangling on the side of his saddle. When they first entered the valley, they had come across several indios, and Cristóbal had shot them from afar.

When he got closer, he saw that one was a young girl.

He took her scalp anyway, knowing he could still get a few pesos for it.

And then they had come across a small band of *indios* living near an old sinkhole. Cristóbal had bound and tortured an elderly female to get the information he had been searching for.

He wasn't unafraid of reprisal because the large pueblos they'd passed along the way were all empty and looked to have been abandoned a long time ago. But Alonso had been sickened by watching his brother torture and maim, and he'd vomited at the first sign of blood.

Now Alonso felt another sick pang in his stomach. "What do you mean, protected?"

Cristóbal cupped his hands in the water and drank deeply, and then once more as his brother anxiously awaited his reply.

Eventually, he said, "They say a witch guards the treasure — *una bruja!*"

Alonso hastily crossed himself and muttered, "*Sangre de Cristo,* what next?"

Cristóbal laughed as he climbed back on his mule.

He said, "We are modern men, and we do not fear witches."

His brother gawked at him.

Cristóbal continued, "It might work in our favor. The witch lives by the treasure, and the local *indios* consider the place to be taboo."

"How is that good for us?" asked Alonso.

"Maybe their primitive superstition will keep them away. The witch's canyon could be our sanctuary."

Alonso rubbed the back of his neck and said, "Could've mentioned all that earlier."

Cristóbal stared him down, "If you had learned some *indio* like I told you too, you would have heard."

Alonso shivered. His brother had already spent years in the *new* world and had a working knowledge of several dialects.

"Do you think knowing *indio* will make me safer?" he asked hesitantly.

Cristóbal snickered and glanced at the scalps. "It didn't help them."

He scanned the high cliffs before him and then nudged his mule along the creek, following the upstream flow. His shadow wobbled ahead of him, ten times as long as he was.

"Just keep your helmet on," he shouted over his shoulder.

Alonso scurried to untangle the burros' lead and catch up with his brother.


At the far end of the valley, the rocks enclosed them on three sides. In the late afternoon sun, the cliffs above glowed majestically in radiant shades of crimson and tangerine, and Alonso momentarily forgot his trepidation.

Enormous crags around them appeared to soar upward, layers upon layers of sandstone and limestone, all of it capped with basalt. The lofty pines on the ridges seemed like blades of grass.

But then, the first shadows overtook them, and Alonso let his gaze sink down.

Directly in front of them, one dark canyon penetrated the cliffs, skirting to the right. The creek they were following seemed to originate in that ravine. The walls here were a deep red, like dried blood, and in the shadows, the water rippled darkly.

Alonso sucked in his breath as if he might hold it until they emerged out of the canyon and up onto the plateau.

Cristóbal didn't say a word. Instead, he nudged his burro forward into the dark canyon. A chilling wind now buffeted Alonso's face, and he leaned into it and forced his mule forward as he began to pray.

\* \* \*

One week later, a white-haired Apache sat in a cave about two-thirds of the way up Oak Creek Canyon. He was called Kuruk, and though he was old, his eyes were still sharp as he surveyed the canyon below.

The cave lay tucked in the cliffs, high above the river's west bank. It had been a difficult scramble, and the man thought how easily he would have climbed up here when he was younger.

He had a low fire burning and was watching the two Spaniards below, who were also sitting by a fire.

He barely moved, although he doubted they would notice him even if he did. These strangers seemed unaware of their surroundings as they stumbled aimlessly up and down the canyon. Any one of his people would have detected his fire long ago.

Kuruk sighed. He knew he should have them killed and be done with it, but still, he hesitated. Too many men die young these days, he thought. He wished his wife was still alive. The years since her passing had been dark, and he missed both her friendship and her counsel.

Soon he was joined by his grandson, Aditsan, who was in his twenties but looked younger. The young man shuffled to the fire, moving with a dreamy air, totally unconcerned about whether the Spaniards might see him or not.

Kuruk motioned for him to sit down, out of sight.

Aditsan glanced around to make sure there was nobody nearby that could hear him and then leaned over and said, "I saw a girl today."

The old Apache's eyes twinkled. "Tell me about her."

Aditsan had come to a confluence earlier, where the canyon walls melted away, giving the distant sun an unobstructed view. There he had found a clearing with tufts of grass and a partially thawed pool of water.

It felt like spring, and he'd napped luxuriantly on a large flat rock by the edge of the water, the light reflecting off its ripples hypnotically.

Eventually, he had sat up, stretched, and then leaned over the creek to get a drink.

When he lifted his head, he saw her for the first time.

She had stayed in the shadows, perfectly still, like a nervous doe. They held each other's gaze for what seemed a long time.

And when her face moved through a shaft of sunlight, he saw she was beautiful. She was disheveled and in need of a wash, but her smile took his breath away.

He forgot to breathe, and she gave him an awkward expression when he gasped.

Her clothes were made of buckskin, but the craftsmanship was average, and they needed repair. And the embellishments that he could see didn't resemble those of any local bands.

"I wanted to ask her name," explained Aditsan to Kuruk, "but she was skittish, and a crack of a branch not far away sent her scurrying."

Before the old man could say anything, they were joined by two warriors, Bidzill and Tarak. Both wore stern expressions. Bidzill was a large man with a strong jaw. Tarak was taller and lanky and closer to Kuruk's age. They bent low when they approached and seated themselves, so they were out of view and could also watch the Spaniards below.

Bidzill gestured at them with his chin.

"Tarak just returned from the valley," said Bidzill. "He said those two have been causing trouble."

"They are strange men," said Kuruk. "What were they up to?"

A darkness descended over Tarak's features. "They tortured an old woman — and several people are missing."

"An old woman?" asked Kuruk, not believing his ears. "Why would they do that?"

Tarak shrugged and placed a log on the fire.

"And who is missing?" asked Kuruk.

Bidzill held the old man's eyes. "My niece and a young man."

Kuruk nodded, "See what they're here for," said Kuruk. "But do not engage."

Bidzill was about to protest, but Kuruk held up his hand and said, "When we rush into things, only death comes of it."

# Chapter Twenty

The brothers followed Oak Creek, now heading downstream, again. For the last few days, Cristóbal had marched them back and forth as he tried to orientate himself and apply what the old woman had told him.

Her information puzzled him. At first, she had refused to say anything, even when beaten. But then her eyes had changed, and she began talking, as if, for some inexplicable reason, she suddenly *wanted* him to find the treasure.

Her gaze haunted him; it was as if she knew something important that he didn't. And that feeling stayed with him as he led his mule along a game trail that skirted the creek.

Both Cristóbal and Alonso moved cautiously now, solemnly scanning the cliff tops, which seemed to lean inward, their steep slopes now covered with ponderosa pines in place of the stunted piñons of the lower desert. The desert plants had all vanished, and the icy blast of wind that occasionally roared down the canyon had them yearning for the hot temperatures further south.

"Cristóbal... *Hermano*," pleaded Alonso, "why are we dragging ourselves through this wilderness? We should be where there are active mines—I heard two fugitives discovered an incredible lode near Chihuahua City."

"*Si*," sighed Cristóbal, "I am aware of that find."

"And in Sinaloa, there are many Spaniards! If we stayed there, we would have protection," continued Alonso. He remembered their last stay in a Spanish home upon first arriving in Mexico: The soft lights over the long table, maids baking tortillas on the charcoal stoves and dealing them out, dogs under the table, hoping to score some scraps.

But Cristóbal's mind was somewhere else. He spat as he thought of a yellowish roll of parchment, wrapped in buckskin, that he had purchased from a servant in Mexico City. It contained official correspondence between the Jesuits and their headquarters.

"Sure," he said patiently, "there are thousands of Spaniards in Sinaloa, but the Jesuits there send their disciples to seek out the minerals in the area. So much of the gold panned from placers in that watershed is made into candelabras and other religious ornaments for the churches."

"Still," said Alonso, "they say there are a lot of gold nuggets there — *mucho oro bruto!*"

Cristóbal spat again. A vast treasure had been described in the parchment: Six muleloads of minted silver reales, three chandeliers of beaten gold, several crates of silver chalices, a gold baptismal urn... the list went on and on. It was treasure! *Tesoro!* And the church simply claimed most of it.

"I will not let those *bastardos* get this treasure!" he hissed. "Not my treasure. Not this time."

What made him equally angry was how treasures also ended up in the hands of the noble Spanish families who had never lifted a shovel or feared for their lives in the hunt for it.

He had seen their heirlooms: silver mugs, spoons and platters, and washbasins, all made of solid silver. He'd even heard of one man who owned his own hand-press for coining silver reales.

Someday he would be so rich that he need not care what they thought or did. Even nobility would then be beneath him.

A rock skipped down the east wall of the canyon, and its echo filled the morning.

"Not so anxious to take off your helmet now, eh?" Cristóbal teased.

Alonso looked scared. "We are not alone."

Cristóbal nodded in response; they continued in silence.

Soon, they stopped at a fork in the creek. The main stream continued, but a smaller tributary flowed in from the right, emerging from an even narrower, high-walled canyon.

Cristóbal surveyed the confluence and squinted his eyes, trying to see what lay beyond the narrow entry.

He said, "We separate here."

He began to divide their gear, leaving the two burros and most of the supplies with Alonso. "I will explore this fork. You follow the main creek, going upstream until you summit on the plateau."

Alonso began to protest, but his older brother cut him off. "Obey me, Alonso. Go to the top of the canyon. Search any side canyons you encounter on the way — and then return to this point. You will be fine."

"But how do we meet up again?" Alonso asked. "What if you're not here?"

Cristóbal scratched his chin. "Be here for the next full moon."

Alonso furrowed his brow, "I don't like this place. "

Cristóbal chuckled at his uneasiness.

"Don't laugh at me!" Alonso shouted. "I hear things all around us!"

"It is all in your mind," said Cristóbal.

"No," Alonso insisted. "I hear singing."

Cristóbal lifted the string of scalps and said, "Do you want to take these? Maybe they'll scare away these sirens you keep hearing?"

He tossed the scalps at his brother. They landed by his feet, where he gaped at them. "I think it's been too long since you bedded a woman," chided Cristóbal.

"Don't play with me, *Hermano*! I know you feel something, too," cried Alonso.

Cristóbal stared at his brother, hard, without uttering a word.

Finally, he said, "What you sense is my treasure, and I will not leave without it."

Then he reassured his brother. "You'll be fine."

He slapped Alonso's mule, and it moved upstream.

He shouted after him, "You will wait for me here, by this fork. If I'm not here for the full moon, stick around for a few days, then come back in a month."

Alonso's face rippled with dread. "In another month?" he whispered in disbelief.

As he rode away, he heard his brother yell, "Keep your powder dry and your breastplate on!"

Reluctantly, Alonso continued up the main canyon. His eyes darted across the cliff tops, and when a raven cawed near him, he jerked and sent his mule hopping forward.

\* \* \*

Bidzill watched the two Spaniards separate by the confluence, and when they were barely out of sight, he inspected their campsite. Tarak was with him, and he whistled low when he discovered the scalps.

"Indeh," said Tarak. "Our people—looks like they did more than just hurt an old woman."

One of the scalps had beadwork woven into a braid, and after inspecting it, Bidzill sank to the ground. His eyes teared up. This was his niece's braid.

He screamed, not caring whether the Spaniards heard him.

Kuruk listened to the two braves when they returned to his fire.

"The mean one has turned off into the West Fork," he said. "He cannot leave that way this time of year—there is too much ice and snow at the other end."

Kuruk exhaled. "That is true—follow him from the high trail. When he returns to Oak Creek, you can kill him."

A silence descended over Bidzill and Tarak. Bidzill stared at the fire for a long moment before lifting the scalp and holding it before Kuruk.

"I will have vengeance," he said.

The old man nodded. "Yes," he began, "you will. But the Spaniard heads into the land of the witch. If you see her, you will die soon."

Bidzill scoffed. "I am not afraid of witches."

Kuruk lowered his gaze. He could not share with Bidzill what his wife had told him just before her passing. A warning was all he could give.

"Be patient," he said, "follow him and observe — your time will come. But do not descend to the canyon floor."

Bidzill nodded obediently, but as his eyes peered deep into the fire's coals, he was shaking.

\* \* \*

Cristóbal walked up a slender canyon, a frozen creek cutting through its floor. Far above, dense gray clouds heralded a change in the weather.

The canyon wended its way ever deeper into the plateau, and it seemed colder here than Oak Creek. No sunshine reached the icy ground.

The serpentine trail beneath them led along walls rising steeply to long slopes which climbed all the way to the plateau's edge.

From side canyons and drainages, a steady flow of ice clung to the rocks. A few times he came across a frozen pool and wondered if there would be fish lurking in the cold darkness below the ice.

The footing was treacherous, so he walked in front of the mule, wondering if he should have left the animal behind. But of course, without the mule, he'd be carrying the load now fastened to the saddle.

It was only mid-afternoon, but the sun had left the sky overhead, and a sharp coldness had descended. His footsteps, and those of the mule, echoed in the crisp, cold air.

And then he heard more footsteps. They seemed to come from just around the bend ahead.

He stopped. "Show yourself!" he shouted. No answer came.

As he stood listening, he could clearly hear steps echoing and then distant singing.

He turned the bend, but there was nothing there.

He yelled, "Coward!" and the word echoed right back at him.

By his feet something sparkled. He bent down to pick up what looked like a gold coin, frozen under the ice.

He grabbed his pick and was about to strike when he heard a hissing sound.

Cristóbal stood and scanned the canyon. But there was no one. The high walls were only twenty paces apart now, and there was nowhere a person could hide.

He took off his helmet and pricked up his ears. Faintly, he heard it again, coming from below. He knelt and placed his ear close to the icy ground—and heard whispering.

And then the dark sandstone walls wailed as if they were in terrible pain. He jumped to his feet, then shook his head to snap out of this mad hallucination. Was he losing his sanity?

Suddenly the sky was black. A wet snow came down, soaking the red walls and giving them a deep crimson color.

He put his helmet on and quickly headed deeper into the canyon, forgetting the gold coin.

* * *

From a trail that followed the higher ground, Bidzill observed Cristóbal's progress. Tarak crouched beside him with a young warrior, Nitis, who fidgeted in place, eager to prove himself.

Below, the Spaniard advanced slowly, picking his way through the icy landscape. His armor was impractical here, and when he slipped and fell, the clang of steel on ice reverberated throughout the canyon.

The Apaches on the high trail had the sun on their side. They were out of the shadows and welcomed the warm rays that had already melted the snow around them.

But Bidzill was still anxious to reap his vengeance. He watched Cristóbal, hoping at every turn that he would finally turn around and return to Oak Creek.

And then a young warrior approached on the high trail, coming from deeper in the West Fork, and Bidzill feared the man's presence would alert the Spaniard below.

He motioned for him to crouch and stay out of sight.

When the man got closer, Bidzill wasn't surprised to see it was Aditsan. A quick glance showed that while Bidzill had been distracted, the Spaniard had moved out of sight.

Bidzill ordered Nitis to scout ahead and see what the Spaniard was up to.

"What are you doing here?" he snapped at Aditsan.

Aditsan squirmed but held his tongue.

Bidzill looked into Aditsan's eyes. "The old man doesn't like anyone going into the West Fork."

Aditsan shook his head. "Only the canyon where the witch lives is taboo, and nobody even knows if she is real. I saw no witch — only a beautiful girl. She smiled at me."

Bidzill shook his head. "You better not mess this up for me — the Spaniard must die."

# Chapter Twenty-one

*A* narrow tunnel blocked his way. Well, not entirely. Cristóbal laid on the ice, staring down it. There was just enough space for a man to crawl between the ice and the passage ceiling. When the water wasn't frozen, he imagined one could just wade through, but now he would have to scramble if he wanted to explore the canyon further.

The mule would have to remain behind. He would reconnoiter the canyon on the other side of the tunnel, then return to the mule and make camp for the night.

A cold wind rushed at him across the ice.

Cristóbal paused to make a torch using materials from the mule's saddlebag, and then lit it with his flint. Then he grabbed his pistol, rifle and powder horn and began sliding up the tunnel on his back, propelling himself along by kicking off the ceiling.

This was awkward and slow, especially with the torch, but at least in the darkness of the tunnel, the flickering flame provided just enough light to see.

It was spooky in here. Every sound echoed loudly around him, and each movement seemed to create enough noise to wake the dead.

About halfway through, the lambent light illuminated a hole in the tunnel's ceiling: the entrance to a small cave, it seemed. Unfortunately, the opening was too small for even a small man without armor to fit through. Cristóbal stuck his torch into the hole and could see that the cave ceiling was filled with hibernating bats.

He continued and was almost out of the tunnel when he heard the ice crack. Cristóbal knew he was going to get wet. He held the torch up in one hand, and his rifle in the other, and the ice gave way.

The frigid water seemed to suck all the oxygen out of his lungs, and he gasped for air. He frantically kicked and twisted, trying to keep torch and gun above water.

The water wasn't deep; nevertheless, all but his head and hands went under before he found his feet.

He staggered through the broken ice, out of the creek, lifting the torch and gun above him.

Shivering violently, he stuck the torch into a snowbank and desperately looked around for dry tinder. He grabbed an armful of debris left by monsoon floods in the bushes around him, set it on a flat rock, and then put fire to it.

His body was going numb as the dry faggots took and began to crackle. He rubbed his pale hands over it. The armor had been cold before it got wet, but now it chilled him to the bone, and he reluctantly took off his breastplate.

Lying next to the fire, he praised his luck on having a torch with him. He didn't know if he would have survived the crawl back to the mule, and then making a fire, if he hadn't.

The sun made a rare appearance, and he lay back, trying to control his breathing as his body slowly warmed.

He closed his eyes. The wind rushed above him, and on its wings, he thought he could hear someone singing, very softly.

He opened his eyes slightly and looked around, but he saw nobody and closed them again.

Suddenly, a dull thud hit his shoulder, immediately followed by a sharp pain. An arrow pierced his flesh, and he screamed. His eyes scanned the cliff tops in panic. He could see a man scampering to get a better shot and others behind him.

Up top, Bidzill announced proudly that it was his arrow that hit the Spaniard.

Arrows landed all around Cristóbal as he scurried for cover.

He stumbled and almost fell when another penetrated his leg.

"*Puta!*" he screamed.

He huddled behind a jumble of boulders. He ignored the arrows protruding from him and checked his guns. The black powder rifle was still dry, but the pistol was soaked. He stuffed it inside his belt, where he wouldn't lose it.

Thankfully, the powder horn, which hung from a cord around his neck, was sealed.

He began loading the rifle with shaking hands and stiff fingers.


At first Bidzill had only intended to harass Cristóbal from above, but when his arrow struck home, he found himself unable to hold back. He would have his revenge.

Tarak and Nitis were just as anxious and followed him without a second thought. Moving like goats down the canyon slopes, the braves closed in quickly.

Bidzill taunted Aditsan, "This is your chance to be a man, Aditsan."

Aditsan reluctantly followed but looked miserable. When Bidzill teased him again, Nitis sprinted past them and took the lead.

Bidzill glared at Aditsan. "If you cost me his scalp, I will beat you," he threatened. Aditsan stepped up his pace.

Cristóbal had barely finished loading as they were upon him.

He shot Tarak in the stomach, and the warrior staggered backward.

Then he turned to locate Nitis coming from behind. He smashed him in the head with the butt of the rifle, and the young man crumbled. There was smoke everywhere.

Bidzill and Aditsan retreated, fading into the rocks.

Cristóbal took two quick steps toward Tarak, pulling his knife out on the way, and quickly finished him off.

He grinned fiercely, turned, and hastily limped up the canyon towards cover. On the ice, he left a trail of blood drops.

# Chapter Twenty-two

The sun stayed hidden the next day as snow fell on the plateau above the canyons to the north. Every now and then, a grey-bellied cloud spilled over the plateau´s edge and drifted through the narrow canyon with a trail of flurries.

The canyon floor lay in shadows, dark and cold, and Cristóbal hid under a low, overhanging rock.

On the high trail, up over the West Fork, several braves watched, looking for signs of the Spaniard.

He observed them pass, shivering, and lost consciousness.

\* \* \*

At the cave on Oak Creek, Kuruk sat by a fire, warming himself, chanting softly as he tended to a chunk of meat roasting over the coals.

Bidzill had returned and informed him of the death of Tarak and that the Spaniard had for now escaped. He had kept to himself the fact that Nitis had been knocked out; he took this as an insult.

He then stormed off, intent on revenge.

Kuruk had sent men to butcher the mule carcass, and they'd returned with a few of the Spaniard's possessions. The old man now sat with Cristóbal´s breastplate by his side, which he'd been working with his knife, trying to take it apart. Aditsan arrived and seated himself while Kuruk tinkered with it some more.

Eventually, he looked up at his grandson and noticed a welt over one eye. "Did the Spaniard do that?"

Aditsan looked away. "No, this was a punishment."

Kuruk nodded, but he didn't look pleased.

He looked over his grandson, who always seemed to live in a different place—one without greed or envy. When he was with the boy, he felt the world was a better place.

"So," said Kuruk, "you met a girl."

Aditsan beamed. "I did."

Kuruk pried a panel on the breastplate loose and peeked under it as he asked. "Who are her parents?"

"I don't know," replied Aditsan. "I only saw her once, the other day, in the West Fork."

Kuruk's eyes became serious upon hearing these words, but he acted relaxed. He poked at the roasting meat and tossed a few small sticks on the fire. "You know you were near the witch's canyon," he said casually.

Aditsan grinned. This was an old argument between them. "No one knows where this witch lives, so how can I fear her? Or her secret canyon?"

The old man looked up very seriously. "It is not a place for men. Stay away from there."

He cut a piece off the cooking mule meat and handed it to Aditsan. "Eat some meat. If the Spaniard does leave the canyon, he will have to walk."

Bidzill walked up, hearing Kuruk's words, and stated, "He will not leave—and I will not eat again until he is dead."

"You should not make vows where the witch can hear you," Kuruk replied, but once the words were out, he wished he'd held his tongue.

"I'm not afraid of your witch," said Bidzill. "I have said I will kill her as well."

Kuruk turned away. "You should have heeded my warning."

Bidzill was offended. "How can we let the Spaniard dishonor us? He has killed three of our people. For this, he must die."

"You should have waited for him to return to Oak Creek. From the beginning, I advised you to stay away from the witch's canyon," stated Kuruk.

Bidzill said, "He killed my niece," and then looked away.

Kuruk reached forward and gently grabbed Bidzill's wrist. "I see you are ruled by anger now," he said, "but there will come a time when that ends." Bidzill seemed to listen for once.

"The witch has not harmed you," continued Kuruk. "Forget the witch. Go for the Spaniard, for he has proven to be an enemy. Leave the witch alone."

Confused emotions clouded Bidzill's face. He'd heard Kuruk's warnings about this witch many times, yet he knew no one who had seen her. Then why was the old man so obsessed with her, he asked himself. What was *he* hiding?

He grabbed his bow. "I will return for the Spaniard." Before he stormed off, he glared at Aditsan. "And you will come with me."

Kuruk felt a great weight descend on him. He didn't want any of his people venturing further into the West Fork, but to allow the Spaniard to do so was just as bad.

He tried to shake off the ill feelings, knowing he would ponder it all later in the quiet of the night.

He turned back to Aditsan, and with a slight glimmer in his eye, said, "So you want to impress this girl you met?"

Aditsan nodded shyly. Kuruk grew solemn. "You must leave an offering. There is no other way."

The old Apache then leaned over the Spaniard's breastplate. On it was a pile of tiny wires that he had extracted from the plate and bent into hooks. He poured them into a soft leather pouch.

"Leave this bag where the girl will find it," said Kuruk and handed the pouch to Aditsan.

Aditsan took the pouch and tied it to his waist. Then the old chief added, "And you must be near water if you hope not to fall under her spell."

# Chapter Twenty-three

*H*idden in a dark recess at the base of a cliff, Cristóbal watched Bidzill passing on the high trail. He figured they were staying high until they could corner him and attack from multiple sides.

The arrow was still lodged in his shoulder, but he had broken off most of the protruding shaft. His calf injury had not been severe. The arrow had just grazed the muscle, and he'd tied the wound off with cloth he'd ripped from his shirt.

But Cristóbal was shivering, and he was pale. His guns were laid out beside him. He had dried the pistol, and now both weapons were loaded.

From his hiding spot, he could see a bend in the canyon, cluttered by a pileup of large dead logs, no more than twenty paces away.

Nothing moved.

He felt nauseous; pain and fatigue overwhelmed him.

He woke from the swish of a large raven's wings cutting through the air as it landed on one of the logs on the pileup.

The raven did a strange dance and cried out. "Awk! Awk!"

The sound echoed absurdly in the silence.

Then he heard something moving out there.

He sat up as much as the small space would allow, swallowing his pain silently.

Suddenly, a large piece of bark slid off the top of one of the logs, and a woman wearing ragged buckskins appeared from within. She looked about twenty and moved with caution. There was something oddly childlike about her.

A small, circular abalone shell was tied to a strand of the young woman's hair, suspended on her forehead, the concave side facing out.

She smiled as she looked directly at Cristóbal. Then she motioned for him to remain hidden while she looked around suspiciously.

Cristóbal noticed that she carried a cord with two trout dangling from it. Quietly, like a cat, she stepped forward when a whistle pierced the silence.

Suddenly, the canyon filled with the broken clatter of rocks tumbling off the cliff and crashing down into the shadows.

She quickly withdrew into the log again and covered the opening with the bark.

The Spaniard pressed himself deeper into the shadows.


Bidzill descended to the canyon floor, Aditsan twenty paces behind him. He walked straight toward the log and pulled out an arrow.

He flipped a piece of bark away, exposing the young woman.

But he had not yet tightened the bowstring when a raven dove from the sky and attacked him.

It swooped repeatedly, claws extended. Bidzill fought it off, trying to smack it with his bow, gasping in surprise at the bird's persistence, and finally watched it fly away.

Then he turned once more to face the woman who observed him without fear. Her beauty bewitched him, and for one long, confused moment, he stood frozen.

The raven returned and landed on her shoulder, where it watched him. He stared in disbelief.

"Witch!" he finally hissed.

Aditsan finally caught up with him, and when he saw the young woman, his eyes widened, too.

"No!" he shrieked when he saw Bidzill about to kill her.

Aditsan grabbed Bidzill's arm to stop him from raising his bow. Bidzill spun with a vicious punch that knocked Aditsan out. Turning to the woman again, he notched his arrow.

Suddenly, the thunderous "bam!" of a muzzleloader echoed through the canyon. Bidzill's expression dropped, and he fell forward.

In the ice-covered world, the repercussion felt otherworldly.

From where Bidzill had dropped like a wet sack, a line of smoke led to Cristóbal, who stood a short distance away, the sun reflecting off his helmet.

He appeared feverish and swayed unsteadily.

He fumbled with his pistol and pulled his knife out, then lunged forward toward the unconscious Aditsan, ready for the kill.

But in a heartbeat, the buckskin-clad young woman was standing between them.

He squinted at her, confused, and then collapsed at her feet.

From the high trail, shouting resounded in the canyon.

She knelt, lay Cristóbal's arm around her neck to take up his weight, and dragged him to the shadows.

His rifle was left behind.


Out of sight, under a high wall of the narrow canyon, the woman observed the unconscious Spaniard. His shoulder was swollen, and his skin was burning hot.

"I could not let you kill him," she said. It seemed that she was used to talking to herself.

She removed his helmet and examined it, amazed by how it reflected light.

Laughing quietly, she touched his face and said, "He will be your undoing. You don't belong here."

She heard something, scanned the crags overhead, and then held her breath.

A moment later, a man appeared running along a trail on the edge of the canyon rim. The morning sun highlighted his hurry, and she could clearly see him watching the canyon floor.

As quick as a mule deer, he was gone.

The woman continued to drag Cristóbal further up the canyon, always staying close to the wall or under the cover of the low shrubs and trees that filled the canyon floor.

But their progress was slow.

"They will not find us where we go," she said. "But you must help us get there."

Finally, Cristóbal came around.

He couldn't understand many of her words, but it was clear she couldn't carry him. He struggled to his feet and staggered along with her help, his focus coming and going.

After what seemed an eternity, they turned into a steep canyon. Here the brush was thick, and they had to maneuver through it. She darted ahead, knowing each turn like a fox knows its run.

Cristóbal struggled behind her up the canyon. The way was steep, but at one point, it almost looked like steps had been carved into the soft sandstone.

They made it to the top of the canyon, and then the woman led him to a tunnel under a large rock. They ascended.

She returned not long after to cover up their trail and then disappeared into the tunnel again.

The raven was also there. He sat perched on the rock for a moment, like a sentinel, and then vanished as well.

# Chapter Twenty-four

**W**hen I had the stranger in my hidden canyon, sleeping by a low fire, I found my thoughts returning to the two bodies I'd left motionless in the canyon below.

I wondered which one was sleeping and which one dead.

The thunderous roar that caused the angry one to drop was a mystery to me, but it seemed the other man — the one that smiled — should still be alive. He was the one I saw the other day, sleeping on the flat rock, and my heart warmed.

So, I left the stranger in my box canyon, and did the foolish thing and returned.

They both may be dead. Or maybe he lives. Maybe. I will see.

On the way back it began to snow, which was good because it covered my tracks. The canyon was silent as I moved along in a world that had turned ghostly white.


A faint scent of gunpowder still hung in the air, mixing with the smell of the pines, when I arrived back at the hollow log. There were no new tracks in the snow, but I still moved with stealth and kept to the shadows.

I spotted my two trout on the ground, picked up the cord, and tied them to my belt.

The snow covering the angry one was soaked with blood, and I knew he was dead. Where his anger — or fear — came from, I didn't know.

I paused next by the one who had smiled at me, and when I saw he was alive, my heart filled with joy. Kneeling by him, I melted some snow in my mouth and then dribbled it into his.

He spat it up and began to stir.

I raised his head and softly brushed some snow off his face.

His forehead was swollen where he'd been punched.

He groaned in pain.

He seemed so beautiful with the snow on his eyelashes. But there were others, even if I didn't see them. It wasn't safe.

I took a single eagle down-feather from the back of my hair and tied it to a strand of his, soothing him.

He was barely aware, and then he tried to open his eyes, blinking confusedly.

I smiled at him and said, "I remember you."

He gazed at me, struggling to come to fully.

I said, "I knew I would see you again."

A clump of snow fell from his hair into his eyes, and again he blinked and swept his gaze around us, trying to figure what was real.

"By the creek, in the morning light," I said softly, "you seemed so beautiful that it frightened me, and I ran away. I have been alone too long."

Then I kissed him, long, until I sensed he was truly awakening; as his eyes started moving, I jumped up, giggling.

"And I will not forget that you tried to save me," I said with a departing smile.

Aditsan lifted himself on his elbows and stared after me, shaken. I walked toward the canyon wall and disappeared into a grove of junipers. I was glad it was snowing; within no time, it would cover my tracks and I would be safe.

Not even an Apache would be able to follow me. Oh, how I yearn for him to join me, but my canyon is no place for him — or any man for that matter.

# Chapter Twenty-five

## Act II

### 1705
*(February)*

*I*n the cold predawn, Cristóbal awoke in a small, steep-walled canyon, with no apparent exit. He was shivering uncontrollably. He sat up painfully, wincing from a piercing pain in his shoulder.

The ashy remnants of a fire smoldered before him.

He looked around in the gloom and estimated the canyon to be about thirty paces wide and at least twice that long, rising and narrowing near the back wall where a grove of old junipers buffered the cliff.

The young woman who had rescued him stood further back in the canyon, looking east to greet the sun.

She now wore a spectacularly fringed buckskin dress, very different from the dirty, worn outfit he'd first seen her in. This new one was decorated with bells and beads, all set in beautiful designs.

Her appearance confused him. She was younger than him. But there was also something ancient about her.

He observed her standing there, motionless; her eyes closed until a shaft of light plunged over the canyon rim and struck the abalone shell on her forehead.

Then she began to dance in place softly, occasionally jumping as if to see the sun better. The small bells on her dress tinkled.

She started to chant.

He could not follow her words but saw her point to herself and repeat something over and over as she chanted,

*"Kamalapukwia… Kamalapukwia… Kamalapukwia…"*

He called out to her then, believing the strange word to be her name, "Kamala, *por favor.*"

She stopped and smirked at this and walked to him.

Kneeling and standing three times, she sprinkled pollen on his head.

He was still feverish and now began to fade.

She produced a straight yellow drinking tube and sucked up some liquid from an old Sinaguan bowl.

She then leaned forward, opened his mouth, and spat the liquid into it.

He passed out.

A day later, the Spaniard came to again. He tried to sit up, panicked at a sudden sharp pain in his shoulder, and started clawing at some bandages there.

I rushed to his side and eased him back.

He looked at me, and slowly recognition flowed over him like a gentle rain.

I had on my old worn buckskins again, and I could see he remembered them. I let him swim in the memory of how we met while I added some small twigs to the fire and set a bowl on it to heat water.

"Kamala?" he finally asked.

I smiled at that.

"You are safe here. They will not find us," I said, but he didn't understand my words.

He touched the cloth bandages that covered his shoulder curiously. His probing fingers told him there was something heavy inside, but he couldn't get to it.

I knew from experience that it created a buzzing—a warm glow that was hard to ignore—and it would heal him.

He tried to sit up again and winced.

I laughed, and my childish giggle echoed off the surrounding walls.

The Spaniard spun his head around, afraid the Apaches would hear me. He tried to hush me with an *indio* word for "quiet," but his accent was strange, and I only stared at him, uncomprehending.

I chuckled lightly once more and then began to sing.

A wordless melody rose through the surrounding canyons, echoing. The Spaniard seemed torn between peace and panic: I could see my song moved him—but he was convinced it would lead to our discovery.

He tried to stop me again, "*Do dah Ha'do'aal*," he whispered urgently. "Don't sing!"

It did stop me. I gazed at him, started to laugh, and then repeated his words, "*Do dah Ha'do'aal?*"

He nodded.

I giggled and started singing again—this time louder.

\* \* \*

Far up on the canyon rim, Kuruk lifted his head to a song he thought he heard. It was impossible to tell where it originated, the melody coming and going with the wind.

One of the younger warriors closed his eyes and began to sway to Kamala's melody, then jerked himself conscious, afraid, as if he had just been bewitched.

Kuruk listened, and as the tune meandered, he grew sad. His wife had also known this melody.

* * *

A bit further away, Aditsan heard it as well and became desperate to know its source. He walked through the frozen canyon, and when he passed a long pool of ice, he lowered his ear to listen.

What came to him was a clearer sound but no direction.

Turning his head, he caught his reflection in the ice, and for the first time, saw the eagle-down feather tied there.

* * *

I squatted next to the strange man to feed him fish stew from a small clay bowl.

As I leaned close, I said, "Fish."

He repeated the word, "Fish."

He knew my language, although we had to work at even the most basic conversations. Still, it felt so good to have company; I yearned to talk with someone — anyone — like a thirsty man craves water. I gave him another mouthful and said, "It is worth leaving my canyon for fish — although usually there is no one out there. I was lucky to catch these before I found you, but I shouldn't try again for a while."

He gazed at me, understanding little of what I'd said.

He said, "Talk... slow... please."

The raven landed between us and cried out loudly.

I brushed him away and said, "He is jealous. Before you came, he was my only friend. "

I stirred the soup and offered him more.

"I have been alone," I muttered.

The raven cawed as if insulted.

Cristóbal eyed him with distrust.

Then he tossed a small rock at the bird, making it hop out of the way with an "Awk!"

I said, "Earlier, I thought you were a God. Now I don't know."

The raven cried out again.

"He doesn't think you are," I said. "We will see. If you're only a man, then you're in a bad place—at least for men."

I had set the Spaniard up next to the old ruin, by the fire. Since we'd arrived—a few days ago now—he hadn't moved more than a few short steps from the spot.

The morning was well on its way before the sun reached us there, but when it did, I sat near him, our backs against the canyon wall, and worked on some artwork.

On my knees I held a soft piece of leather, on which I was painting a circular design. In several bowls by my feet was a powder that I mixed to make paint. I used a frayed yucca leaf for a brush.

I stabbed my finger with a thorn and added a drop of blood to the mix.

Cristóbal glanced over at the symbol, watching me curiously. The design was broken into two halves. On the left, a bear print with a bear claw necklace suspended above it. On the right, a woman crouched on a rock above running water.

I showed it to him and said, "I make this for you."

He stood awkwardly and hobbled over to me.

"Is beautiful," he said as his eyes swept over to the chute.

He had missed the exit chute at first because a stone wall hid it on three sides—most likely built to prevent debris from falling into it. But once he began moving around, he was bound to see it.

And now he finally had.

Twice, when I thought he was sleeping, I slipped out, unobserved. The first time I returned to where I had found him. Someone had butchered his mule and collected the meat and hide, and the coyotes and wolves had finished the job.

I did find his helmet where I had set it down and a leather-bound book by the few remaining bones of the mule.

I brought both items back to my canyon.

Aside from a few pieces of trout in a soup, I had no other food, and I'd hoped I would find something to eat.

But it was the middle of winter, and I returned empty-handed.

Cristóbal approached the chute and stared down into it. But he went no further.

One morning, he watched me place a clay container full of water on the glowing coals and then check his bandages.

"Thank you, Kamala," he said in his strange accent, "I don't know how to show gratitude for saving me—for helping me escape."

There was genuine affection in his eyes.

He pointed at his chest and said, "Cristóbal."

I nodded slightly and said, "Cristóbal."

He beamed confidently. "I am your friend—you can trust me."

He tried again to see what was bundled over his wound, inside his shirt.

As I had done earlier, I pushed his hand away firmly.

"That medicine is the only reason you're still alive!" I chastised, "But if you even look at it, you will be doomed."

Cristóbal leaned back. I figured he understood my warning, but when I turned to tend the fire, he dug into the bandages again. I whacked him with a wooden cooking spoon and moved away, laughing.

Cristóbal chuckled as well, but I could tell he didn't like being told what not to do. I thought of removing the special object by his wound before he discovered what it was, but he still needed it badly.

Soundlessly, I made my way down Itzel canyon and onto the floor of the West Fork. A heavy chill lay over the land, and I would have preferred to wait for winter to soften its grip, but we were out of food, so I had to go.

I can go a long time without sustenance, but I know Cristóbal cannot, and if he grows hungry enough, he will begin to search around.

More snow had fallen, and it lay thick on the branches of the trees and shrubs I crept under. I was grateful I'd lined my moccasins with rabbit fur. Normally I enjoyed how my toes gripped the ground through their soft soles—but not in this weather.

In the early-morning light, I moved like a doe, stepping carefully, as I tried to leave as little evidence of my passing as possible.

At the confluence of Itzel Canyon and the West Fork, I came to the ice-covered pool by the large, flat rock. This was where I had first seen the young man who smiled so much. I remember he watched the birds around him, and in my mind, I called him the Listener. That day had been warm and full of sunshine—so different from now, a little over a month later.

I searched for a rock, and after listening for any signs of human presence, I broke the ice.

I sat on the flat rock by the water's edge, very quietly, listening again—just to be safe—and then retrieved a small leather pouch tied to my side. I opened it to reveal two small ears of corn, no longer than my fingers.

I broke off the tip of one of the dried ears and crumbled the corn over the water. Then I waited.

Soon the water stirred, and a trout rose slowly to eat the corn.

Slowly, I placed my hand, and then forearm, in the water.

My hand went numb, but I still held it motionless, and only after an eternity did I slide it under the fish and begin tickling its belly.

When my hand was finally completely under the fish, I flicked it forward and launched the fish out of the water onto the shore.

I retrieved it and then caught one more fish in the same manner. I dropped them into a leather bag, took one quick look around, and departed.

Twenty paces away, Aditsan stood; he'd been lying flat behind a boulder. He moved to where she had sat and examined the spot. The flat rock where she lay still held some of her warmth.

He took the small bundle Kuruk had given him and opened it to reveal the fish hooks made from the Spanish wire.

With reverence, he placed the package in the open, on the rock by the water's edge, and walked off in the direction she took — searching the ground for tracks as he went.

\* \* \*

Cristóbal was sleeping. Kamala was nowhere in sight. The raven hopped over to him until it was very close to his face.

It put its beak forward, all but touching his eye, and glared at him, clacking angrily, seemingly daring the Spaniard to wake up.

\* \* \*

One week later, I was back at the frozen pool of water. The Spaniard had grown restless with his hunger and watched my every move but seemed hesitant to leave my box canyon.

So on my excursions to find food, I relaxed, glad to be away from him. I found a rock and smashed a hole in the ice, but this time, rather than sticking my hand in the water, I opened a leather pouch and took out a length of string made from yucca fiber. Attached to its end was a hook made by Kuruk from the Spanish wire.

I felt pleased as I put a small piece of corn on the hook and dropped it in the water — no more freezing hands for me.

I waited patiently, enjoying the morning, sure I was alone — until suddenly the Listener gently grabbed my wrist from the other side of the flat rock, where he'd been concealed since sunrise as if he were waiting to capture an eagle.

I shrieked, but he had already dipped his hand in the hole in the ice and flicked some water in my face.

Surprised, I found myself lost in his eyes, my vision blurred — just as his had been the day I'd found him unconscious. He had a soft sunburned smell of sage smoke and woodfires.

"I won't harm you," he said with a smile. "I am Aditsan."

I moved closer and gently touched his forehead, where the faintest signs of his injury remained. He smelled my hair when I came near. He said, "I saw you before, by the creek..."

I nodded and put my fingers over his lips to silence him.

Slowly he crawled up to me on the flat rock where the sun had burned away the ice and snow. We lay back on the warm rocks and embraced, and I felt like I was in a dream.

* * *

I hurried up Itzel Canyon about an hour before sunset. A storm was moving in, and I didn't want to get caught in the open.

I emerged up out the chute, a string of trout in my hand.

Cristóbal was upright with his bandages loosely strung around him. In his hands, he held the object that I had packed against his wound.

I glared at him, "I guess it was to be expected."

Cristóbal didn't hear me. His eyes were riveted to the heavy stone that he had just pulled from his bandages.

The stone was the shape of a flattened ball. It was pure white, with a band of gold inlaid. Hammered into the gold were Mayan glyphs and symbols.

Cristóbal was shaking and breathing heavily as he coarsely demanded, "Where did you get this?"

He stood, menacing and red-faced.

"It comes from a place that will bring you no good," I warned.

He reached for his gun and belted out, "Bring me there!"

I tried to calm him, but he backhanded me.

Almost immediately there was a flash of lightning and the crash of thunder. It echoed over and over throughout the surrounding canyons. Cristóbal stepped back in fear and looked around.

The raven landed next to me and watched him, and then started to caw loudly and repeatedly. The echoes of the raven´s call mixed strangely with the thunder.

The sky had darkened, and rain-laden clouds were now circling above us.

I said, "Do something wrong, and the rains come."

Cristóbal whispered, "Great mother of God."

# Chapter Twenty-six

At first, Cristóbal searched every corner of the box canyon, running excitedly from point to point, almost hysterical in the hope that his treasure—his *tesoro*—would just be piled up somewhere.

He seemed to find it ironic that he had been brought to the very canyon where his treasure lay. But after several long moments of unsuccessful searching, he slowly realized that it must still be hidden.

I watched as he flipped a few large stones and crept into several dark cracks in the wall. But he was running out of places and was growing irritated.

He came to the sealed doorway of the granary. Here, the ancients had taken advantage of a gap in the cliff wall and created a small room to store their corn.

He grabbed a rock and began smashing his way into it. The old plaster crumbled before him, and a blast of decrepit air floated out.

He staggered backward, choking, but only paused a moment before he was poking his head inside the granary, looking around.

The space inside was filled with small cobs of red and yellow maize, all desiccated and no longer edible. The location was not a good one for a granary because water had seeped in from the back, and most of the cobs on the top were covered with mold.

Next, he dug through the sheltered area near a fire pit, tossing old digging sticks and wooden bowls out of his way. Some of the discarded items were things I had collected, like feathers, sinew and shafts for arrows, and others I had put a lot of work into—like a yucca cordage net.

He treated it all like it was worthless.

Inside the crumbling ruin, he found only a basket with material for creating snares.

I waited silently, the raven on my shoulder.

Slowly he accepted the fact that the treasure was not here.

He shot an angry glare at me, and I smiled back, but I was fed up with my guest. I now wished I had never brought him here.

Cristóbal pulled out his pistol and walked up to me. He pointed it at my face and screamed, "Where is it?"

I touched the gun barrel curiously and asked, "Will you make the thunder now?"

He shouted, "Will you not be serious?"

My laughter, even just a giggle, seemed to drive him insane.

I caught his eye and warned him. "Your gun won't save you."

His gaze slid past me and fixed on the grove of trees at the far end of the canyon. He ran that way, limping slightly still where the arrow had notched his calf.

I followed a few paces behind.

Between two large trunks of ancient alligator juniper was the entrance to a cave. The trees grew so close to the wall that their roots framed the entrance.

Beyond, there was just enough daylight to show a dim chamber.

I wiggled past Cristóbal and stood in the cave entrance, blocking his way. "This cave is not for men — only women go here."

He pushed me out of the way.

I warned him again. "People who go beyond these trees must have a pure heart — not everyone can enter."

He just laughed.

"Do not go inside, Cristóbal." I pleaded, but I knew it was futile.

* * *

On the Colorado Plateau above the canyons, a crackling fire burned in a ponderosa pine forest. Several feet of snow blanketed the land, but under the cover of the trees, it was sparse, and here Alonso had made camp.

The haunch of an elk sizzled on a spit over the fire; behind Alonso on the ground lay the rest of the animal's carcass.

Alonso grinned as he cut off a chunk of meat.

"Cristóbal," he said, "if you could see how well I live now."

He chewed with relish until a sharp snap of a branch startled him. He thought he saw movement in the shadows and grabbed his rifle with shaking hands.

A cold breeze came through the camp.

He waited. Heart pounding. Not breathing. Only listening.

A lone coyote came into view. It was limping.

Alonso puffed out his breath and relaxed.

"You won't make it long with that leg," he said to the coyote and tossed him a piece of meat.

It sniffed the meat, hesitating only briefly, before snatching it up and quickly disappearing.

\* \* \*

Kuruk watched the scene from the darkness. He observed Alonso feeding the coyote with amusement, but when he saw the elk carcass on the ground behind him, he shook his head.

He backed away and said to a brave who accompanied him, "This one will be lucky to survive at all. We will leave him."

# Chapter Twenty-seven

The cave was low, damp and full of shadows. Cristóbal, being a large man, had to crouch and shuffle forward as he moved further in. I stood by the entrance watching him.

The walls had been plastered, then painted over with symbols, by the ancient ones. Some may have been curses or protective spells, but they did nothing to stop him.

He explored a smaller chamber on the immediate left but seemed uninterested when all it revealed was three old bear skulls and a necklace made from bear claws.

He moved back to the central part of the cave.

In the center of the cave was a small, sandy rise covered with a pile of offerings, several bowls with cornmeal and pollen, and one with brown seeds. An old metate lay against the cave wall, its flat surface covered with an orange powder.

The water did not drip here, and it was dry.

Cristóbal started pawing through the pile. I grabbed him from behind to stop him.

"Those things are to be respected," I said.

His eyes were all over the cave as he dug into the sand mound. "I know the treasure is near!"

He held up a doll made from a corn cob and a piece of soft leather in disbelief, "What is this rubbish?" The doll was ancient, and some of it crumbled away in his hand.

I grabbed it from him and tried to steer him away.

He turned and smacked me.

A drop of blood flew from my face onto the sand.

I dropped the doll.

He peered deeper into the cave, not seeing anywhere else to go.

But still, he headed to the low, far corner, toward the sealed entrance to the tunnel.

I couldn't let him go there, and I gripped his leg desperately.

We wrestled, and he rolled on top of me, trying to pin me.

And then I sensed his anger turning to lust, and he began tearing at my buckskins, trying to remove them.

It started to pour outside.

I screamed, but the sound of my voice was lost in the booming of thunder. "Is this what I saved you for?" I asked between clenched teeth.

The lightning beyond the cave entrance was blinding.

I fought him with all my strength, biting and punching at every opportunity. I had a small knife at my waist, but he held one wrist, and I couldn't get to it. He was determined to have me.

But I wouldn't allow it, and I somehow fought him off.

Bleeding and scratched, he eventually gave up, retreated a few paces, and sat back staring at me.

I sat up, facing him, and pulled my small knife out and held it between us.

He stared at me, shaking with adrenaline and lust, but he didn't dare come closer.

Eventually, he cursed and left.

For the moment the dark tunnel still lay undiscovered.

I lay back, sobbing and staring at the cave ceiling not far above me. Eventually, I wiped my bloody face.

Slowly my emotions hardened.

I looked at my hand and noticed it was smeared with blood. Looking up at the ceiling, I reached up and made a red handprint.

Then I placed the doll upright, where it had been.

The raven landed next to me.

I addressed it. "His days are numbered. He will be gone soon."

The raven cocked its head; it didn't seem to need to blink.

"He will bring it upon himself," I added, "This is not a place for men."

***

The next day I avoided the Spaniard as best I could in the small box canyon, and he ignored me as well. I tried for fish again, but the pool was empty, and the others I checked were all frozen solid.

When I returned, Cristóbal was pacing the box canyon with a wild, starved look in his eyes but was not willing to leave—even to find food—because he now believed without a doubt that his treasure was close.

I wished again that I'd never brought him back to my canyon.

He took up the leather-bound book I'd brought back, and using a feather he found as a pen, began furiously scribbling notes in it.

He pricked his finger and used his blood as ink.

He made me nervous. His hunger was making him unpredictable.

When the full moon crept over the yellow sandstone walls that night, I knew what I had to do.

Silently, I went into the cave and grabbed the bear claw necklace. While Cristóbal was busy trying to flip a large, flat rock over in the back of the canyon, I slipped down the chute, and once clear, I put the necklace on.

* * *

Later that night, Alonso leaned back and crossed his arms behind his head. This was the first night of the full moon, and in the morning, he would check the confluence in Oak Creek Canyon and hopefully connect with his brother and leave.

The moon was high overhead now, brightly lighting up the forest.

Suddenly a dark shadow hovered before him. He spun around to see the massive head of a silver grizzly as it sank its teeth into the elk carcass.

The bear stared at Alonso for at least five heartbeats, close enough to touch. Then the beast clenched the carcass in his teeth and disappeared with it into the pines.

Alonso realized he was shaking.

He cried softly, "Brother, where are you?"

* * *

Cristóbal lay there watching me hang strips of meat on a rack made of green willow branches. Underneath it, a low fire of mostly coals smoldered.

By the exit chute lay the hind half of an elk which I'd been butchering with a sharp shard of basalt.

Guilt hung off him like day-before smoke.

He limped to the carcass and scratched his head. It was more than twice my weight, and I could see him wondering how I'd managed to kill the elk, partition it, and drag this massive chunk back here.

"How did you...?" he began but faltered when I turned away, ignoring him, to collect a few sticks for the fire.

Let him wonder.

As confounded as he was, his hunger took over, and he shuffled to the drying rack to snatch a piece of the meat.

I watched him, pensively, as he gnawed on it.

# Chapter Twenty-eight

*I* ignored the Spaniard as he slowly moved to the fire and squatted. The raven sat nearby, but unlike me, it watched his every move. Cristóbal gazed at me with the same eyes as when he'd first arrived, injured and scared, but now there was also desperation in his look.

But I no longer cared if he lived or died, and I didn't return his gaze. I found it strange that he didn't see my hatred when he looked at me, but he didn't.

The scratches covering his face were a testament to what had happened—one that couldn't be ignored. They stung, I bet. He gingerly touched them when he thought I wasn't watching.

I hoped they would get infected.

I was weaving a basket from a pile of yucca leaves, beginning my preparations for the spring, when I would forage through the West Fork, collecting what I could. How I longed for the days when my basket would be filled with black walnuts, acorns, and acacia pods.

He looked up at the sky. Pure blue glowed above us, with not a cloud in sight. He said, "Finally, a clear day. We should see the sun soon."

I said nothing.

He held out his hands, palms up. "I'm sorry about what happened in the cave. I should not have taken liberties with you."

I got up and filled a bowl with some elk stew. I handed it to him and then strode away.

"I am of noble blood, pure Spanish," said Cristóbal. "In Mexico City, I am allowed such privileges — with any woman."

I glared at him with barely concealed hatred. I could understand his attempts at my language well enough now, but even without words, it was written clearly on his face: He was important, it was his right, I should be grateful.

But my heart held only one truth: He will regret what he did to me before our time together is done. In all my time in the hidden canyon, he was the only one I ever brought back. I could see now that it had been a mistake, but I had been so lonely.

The raven hopped over and stood by me. Cristóbal was uncomfortable with the silence.

He asked, "How did you come to live here alone?"

I stared at the raven before replying.

"When I was young, I was brought here for the Changing Woman ceremony," I said. "I was blindfolded and fetched here in the presence of five elderly women."

Cristóbal moved closer. "Did they tell you of the treasure?" he asked.

"No," I said gravely, "they told me of greater things."


I leaned against the wall, feeling sickly. Cristóbal lay in the sun with his shirt off, on the other side of the fire, his body a mass of scars and bruises.

He tried to get me to relax — to forget — but I would not.

"Would you leave this canyon, Kamala?" asked Cristóbal. "Would you go away with me?"

I didn't respond, only peered at him angrily. Did he think I would soften to him now?

I could see his wounds were healing, but I no longer checked them. He watched me all the time, convinced I was hiding something.

"What did the elderly women tell you?" he asked. "Were they medicine people? Can your women hold that position?" he asked.

I threw a few sticks on the fire and looked into his eyes.

"They were wise — that's all I know," I said. "One knew herbs, one the body, one the blood, one the proper food to eat... and one the heart and soul."

I added, "The one that taught matters of the heart said I would one day find love — do you love me, Cristóbal?"

Cristóbal looked away and would not meet my eyes.

I continued, "When they had finished, another old woman appeared and told me the legend of White Painted Woman."

"She spoke of what life would be like, how to cope with hardships and depression, how to be happy, and how and where to find guidance and protection."

I refrained from telling him the stories she had shared about the forbidden cavern at the other end of the dark tunnel. That was the reason I didn't dare bring Aditsan back here. I had never been into the tunnel or the dark chamber beyond it, but the old stories had put a deep fear in me.

I should have kept the Spaniard away out of duty to those women.

I turned away to fetch something from my supplies and from the corner of my eye saw Cristóbal reaching behind his back to grab the pistol and stick it inside his shirt.

I giggled. He really believed that the gun would help him here.


Cristóbal approached me while I was harvesting a few withered pods still clinging to a mesquite bush on the far side of the box canyon. He was covered in mud and grinning.

I stepped back in apprehension and dropped my basket. Quickly he knelt and started collecting the spilled contents.

When he had picked up all the pods, he said, "Kamala, come with me," and took my hand and led me to the sheltered area.

I stepped behind him reluctantly, and my eyes stayed on his hand like it was a limb that needed to be chopped off.

Cristóbal had been repairing the old Sinaguan ruin by the fire. Using water from a seep by the cave entrance and dried mud that he had collected near the chute, he had made clay; and he'd used it as mortar to hold what stones he could collect in place.

He'd even constructed a new ceiling from branches and twigs.

It was only one room, with two walls closing off a corner in the canyon. Seeing as I avoided the cave, he seemed to hope that the new shelter would please me.

I stepped forward, and Cristóbal proudly nodded and said, "I hope this makes you happy — I want you to be dry when it rains."

I entered the structure alone.

Inside, I dug down in the soft earth of a back corner. Soon I lifted a sharp knife — an ancient obsidian blade.

As quick as a ferret, I reburied it.

When I came out, I awkwardly nodded a thank you.

Cristóbal put a withered red flower from last year in my hair.

I tried to step back, confused when he hugged me.

I stood as still as a heron as he placed his arms around my waist, and then I stepped back and eyed him with mistrust.

The raven flew in and landed on my shoulder.


I emerged from the box canyon's exit tunnel with a basket of sacred datura; the white blossoms looked alive they were so vibrant, but in fact, they were from last season.

Cristóbal sat by the fire. He looked exhausted. I glanced around and saw he had destroyed most of my possessions in one of his fits.

He pleaded with me, "I'm sorry, Kamala. I can feel that I am near. It haunts me."

I gave a weak smile and started processing the sacred datura. As I prepared the tea for Cristóbal, I recalled the warnings I had been given about the poisonous properties of the plant. I said, "I will make you a drink to relax."

Before he could reply, I turned, knelt, and got sick. He moved to help me.

I resisted him initially but gave in and allowed him to help me to the fire. The tea would have to wait.

I leaned against the wall, my eyes unfocused. I didn't feel good; something was wrong. I was too weak to ignore him and allowed Cristóbal to make me a bowl of stew.

When he saw I was in a congenial mood, he asked, "Can you tell me more about the women you met when you first came here?"

I shrugged, "When the women left, they said they would return in the morning, but they did not."

Cristóbal sat down next to me, a puzzled expression on his face. "That was it? They left you here alone?"

I said, "A few times over the years, I awoke to see one of them standing over me. They looked aged and defeated. In the morning, they were always gone. Sometimes they left food."

After some thought, Cristóbal said, "Maybe something bad happened to your tribe." He thought some more, then added, "It could have been disease, or they could have been attacked."

I shrugged, "I don't know. It was long ago that they visited last. The year must come and go—it is still like that."

He asked, "So you have been alone here all this time?"

I smiled and said, "Not at all. Somebody watches me. Somebody hears me. I am not alone."

# Chapter Twenty-nine

Cristóbal tended to me, worried now about my health. While I slept, he brushed my hair out of my eyes, and he adjusted my clothing so that I would be more comfortable. And when I woke, he offered water.

The evening was cold and silent. He collected wood and stoked the fire when it burned low. A bright three-quarter moon lingered behind dark clouds, casting a silver silhouette over them.

Caring for me temporarily took his mind off the treasure. He seemed at peace, for the moment, although he still scribbled in his journal.

He said, "I will never forget that you saved me — and I will take care of *you* now."

I opened my eyes weakly and said, "You will forget me when you are tempted."

He smiled affectionately and said, "No, I am a man of honor."

Then he took his knife, pricked his thumb, and said, "I make a vow to stay by your side."

Ever since he had first discovered the white stone under his bandages, Cristóbal had kept it by his side. He went to move it aside now, and when he touched it with the finger he had just pricked, the white stone began to glow in a magical, otherworldly light.

His eyes opened wide as he stared at it.

The sky overhead clouded up and darkened.

I cried out, "What are you doing?"

I sat up and reached for the stone.

He pushed me away, and I fell. At that instant, a bolt of lightning hit one of the trees at the back of the canyon.

He stood over me and shouted, "I will be denied no longer — where is my treasure?"

Cristóbal held the stone over his head. It pulsed with light. The wind blew in furious gusts. I screamed, "No!"

Cristóbal stepped closer to me and shouted. "I will smash it if you don't tell me!"

I stood up on wobbly feet and reached for it, but he held it higher. "I will break it," he warned.

Panic pulsed through my veins, but then a change came over me. I relaxed.

I looked in the direction of the cave and said, "What you seek is in the cave."

Cristóbal stared at me in disbelief. Then he set the white stone on the ground and moved toward the back of the canyon.

As much as I hated him now, I dreaded what he might become if he entered the cave. I had been warned.

One last time I called to him. "Cristóbal."

He turned.

I said, "The old women told me that men who enter the cave do not return the same."

He nodded. "I am not afraid."

I said, "You saved me once, so I will warn you. It is protected."

He laughed. "I will kill anyone in my way."

I let my gaze fall to the ground, then slowly raised it and met his eyes.

He turned and marched to the back of the box canyon.

# Chapter Thirty

At the cave's entrance, the lightning had set the ancient junipers on fire. The heavy rain barely did anything to dampen the flames because the overhanging rock sheltered them. Through the thick smoke, the interior of the cave was barely visible.

Cristóbal grabbed a burning branch and ran through a corridor of fire and into the cave. I followed several paces behind. The dancing flames were reflecting in the puddles and made it seem like the cave itself was on fire.

Holding the torch in front of him, he walked the chamber's perimeter. He leaned forward under the low ceiling.

"I pray you are not lying to me, Kamala," he hissed as he splashed through the puddles.

The smoke was slowly filling the cave. Cristóbal took out his pistol and checked it.

"You *indios* may fear witches," he said. "But you will soon learn to fear lead."

As he passed a dark recess, where the top of an adobe wall had crumbled away, the flame from his torch got sucked away with a howl.

"There!" he shouted.

He kicked at the wall, and it fell away before him, revealing a low tunnel lined with blue-tinted bones and rusty chains.

He stepped into it, bending slightly, and kicked a gaping skull out of his way. There were skeletons everywhere, all covered with little brown mushrooms.

As he proceeded, bones below his feet gave way with a sickening crunch. The walls held a luminous green glow.

He took several strides forward, and as his torchlight began to fade from sight, there was a whipping sound and then a thud.

Cristóbal screamed.

After a long silence, his weak voice whispered from the tunnel, "Blood of Christ."

# Chapter Thirty-one

## Act III

### 1705
*(March)*

*T*he Spaniard dropped and knelt, a log pinned against him, a stake piercing his thigh. He'd walked into a trap. Through the dim light, he could see that he'd stepped on a stone trigger that somehow set off the ancient device.

He grinned despite the pain and cursed, *"Puta!"* A trickle of blood flowed down his leg and onto the cold stone floor.

His torch sputtered on the ground where he had dropped it.

He wrenched the stake out of his thigh, howling in pain.

The darkness swallowed his cries, muffling them as if the walls of the tunnel were a giant throat

He grabbed the torch and held it over a cut hole in the floor with a shaking hand: In the dark cavity lay a pile of scattered bones, and a horrid stench emanated from it. He swallowed dryly and looked away.

He painfully got up and limped down the tunnel, leaving a trail of blood. The walls were of black volcanic rock and were sharp-edged. It looked like they had been cut and hammered to make the tunnel. He noticed a sprawling lichen growing in the cracks that glowed softly.

Soon he emerged into a large cavern. The walls and ceiling were also covered with lichen, but the lighting was barely enough to see by. He took a few tentative steps and soon found himself standing in cold water.

He heard whispering in the shadows and thought he'd caught sight of a flicker of movement by the cavern wall. He no longer felt like he was alone.

He stopped and hollered, *"Hola?"* but all that came back was his own weak echo, which seemed to fight for existence.

This seemed to be a big place, but it was difficult to tell. The ceiling high above him seemed to expand and contract.

The whispering grew louder, and he held up the torch and shouted, "Show yourself!"

To his left a large metal bowl reflected the flames. It sat on the edge of what looked like a pond. He peered inside it and saw a murky liquid filling the bowl.

It smelled like blood.

He quickly stepped away.

But then curiosity overcame him. He returned, touched his torch to the bowl, and the liquid ignited: A burst of flame fire-balled up into the air with a deafening boom.

He staggered backward and covered his ears in pain; there was a dribble of blood coming out of one.

To his horror, flames were shooting out of the bowl and racing along a track into the darkness. An instant later, more fireballs burst into the air as the fire reached other metal bowls hidden in the gloom.

The detonations were overwhelming in the chamber, shaking him to the core. Cristóbal cowered behind the large metal bowl until the last explosion had faded.

Then all was silent, while the smoke cleared, except for Cristóbal's moans of pain.

As the smoke dissipated, the light from the flaming bowls and the glow coming off the lichen on the ceiling combined and flooded the entire cavern with light.

The first thing visible in this new light was the flaming metal bowl next to him: It was made of solid gold.

Then he saw an island in the middle of a dark and shimmering pond. Other flaming bowls outlined its perimeter — and there was a stone causeway leading across the water to it.

The walkway was wide enough for two men, and it sat just above the water. It seemed like the builders had used the quarried rock from the tunnel to make it.

And then, on the island, a huge object slowly emerged from the rising smoke. He could make out a pyramid: Aztec in design, stepped, and what appeared to be a temple sitting on the flat area at the top.

Cristóbal fought through the haze that the pain had enveloped him in and stood.

Everything was muted.

He yelled again, "*Hola!*" but could not hear it; his voice had been silenced.

He limped forward, across the causeway to the pyramid, where the main staircase led to the top. The entire structure had been carved out of the hard basalt that also formed the floor and ceiling.

And there it was before him. The uppermost steps were covered with gold that had spilled over — lots of gold. There were masks, chains, coins, bars: all made of precious yellow metal. There seemed to be no end to the treasures!

Suddenly, Cristóbal shrugged off his pain. His injuries were nothing compared to this treasure, he told himself. He took a first painful step toward the treasures and chuckled at his wounded thigh.

I will hire a thousand nurses when the time is right, he thought.

On his ascent to the top of the structure, Cristóbal stopped to pick up a gold coin and was surprised to find it warm to the touch.

He whispered, "It is mine!"

Below, the golden bowls glowed with a sinister light, their reflection skimming off the dark water. Cristóbal's pupils were dilated and glossy, and at this moment, his eyes were equally dark and shimmering.

He slowly climbed the staircase until he reached the golden treasure spilling off the platform on top; it was piled so thickly that the uppermost steps were not visible. Several wooden crates had burst over the years, causing the mess.

He eased himself onto his knees in the gold and ran his hands through it, his eyes wild with excitement.


Near the pyramid base, I caught my first glimpse of him at the top, almost swaying with glee. He was giddy in his triumph and didn't seem dangerous at the moment.

But I knew better than to be careless here.

I'd taken the precautions the old women had suggested, pausing just long enough in the cave where the water dripped to get prepared. I had covered my naked body with grey paint and had added black spots and spirals.

I had also filled my ears with wax, as I had been told.

But it had all done little to prepare me for the assault on my senses that hit me after I'd passed through the tunnel. Even with my ears plugged, I could hear whispers and chanting, and I saw movement in the shadows around us.

I pointed at the pyramid and shouted, "Does the treasure still haunt you, Cristóbal? Now that you've found it, will you let it go?"

Cristóbal looked around.

He saw me but seemed to be unable to make out my words.

I mouthed the words, "This is a bad place."

Cristóbal waved his hand in the air and shouted, "This treasure no longer concerns you!"

I stood where I was and watched him. Even though I'd been abandoned by the women who first brought me to the box canyon, I still feared their warnings. They believed that the evil that lived in the dark chamber could spread, and it was their duty to prevent that. And mine.

I wondered how I could stop the Spaniard. He glared at me, but my new appearance seemed to unnerve him.

"Stay there!" he ordered, not able to shake my stare.

Then he turned and dug his boots into the gold like he was climbing through ice to get to the pyramid´s top.

He giggled when some loose coins caused him to slip.

"Too much wealth to climb!" he shrieked.

The level area on the top was occupied by a square temple with framed doorways on three sides. Its walls were adorned with scenes of human sacrifice.

He stumbled through the piles of gold and approached the temple reverently. I started to follow.

A golden throne marked the place of honor, facing the main staircase, but what lay sprawled before it was a scene of horror.

A desiccated corpse lay clinging to one leg of the throne. The skeleton was covered with chains of gold and precious stones, but the skull was frozen in a horrible grimace of filed, pointed teeth.

Cristóbal walked towards the skeleton and said, "You're not Montezuma—I heard what happened to him."

He had stumbled upon Yaotl, whose body had lain undisturbed for almost two hundred years.

He fingered the tattered tunic which the dead man was wearing. He inspected a piece of jewelry and slipped it into his pocket. "You had good taste," I heard him say as I approached, "I'll give you that much."

I took the last stair and slowly advanced. Cristóbal was oblivious to me.

He said to the skeleton, "You must be someone Montezuma trusted. He didn't want many people to know about this."

He broke off a fingerbone to extract a ring, and the whole hand crumbled under his touch. He glanced over the vast pile of riches and asked, "Why would he send such a treasure to this remote place?"

A few steps away was a pile of rags, bones and chains.

Cristóbal cautiously moved closer, momentarily distracted. Over his shoulder, I saw that it was a mound of chained bodies. The remains of fifteen men—Yaotl's soldiers and the last of his blue men—formed a heap of bones, metal collars, and leathery skin, all seemingly pointed at Yaotl laying before the throne.

Cristóbal said, "Those must be your helpers."

I walked up behind him and said, "You will end as they did."

Cristóbal turned in surprise; his hearing was returning.

He said, "This man deserves the treasure no more than you or I. And he's certainly not guarding it now."

He turned back to the skeleton and shouted, "I am no more afraid of this man's evil magic than I am of the *indio* witch they warned me of!"

He grabbed Yaotl´s skeleton by the ribcage and tore off his tunic, then stepped back, surprised and said, "Well, look at that."

Under the tunic, a dozen sharp shards of basalt lay imbedded in the mummified flesh still clinging to the Aztec's bones.

When he beheld the pile of bodies again, Cristóbal could now see that the chained and dying men had been crawling after Yaotl, eventually pulling close enough to bury their weapons in him before they died.

With the last of his lifeforce, he had crawled to the throne.

I glanced at the bodies, unmoved.

I said, "Leave this place, Cristóbal."

"Kamala, we could share this," he said.

I insisted, "This is a bad place."

And then he began to hear the whispers again, and something changed in his eyes. I knew then that I could never allow him to leave the box canyon.

He smiled disarmingly and said, "We could live like royalty, you and I," but he didn't fool me, and I was prepared when he lunged for me. I screamed and met his attack head-on, with a ferociousness that came from I knew not where. Suddenly I was full of rage, my only desire to stop him from ever leaving the cave.

Cristóbal fought me off, surprised, with fear in his eyes.

With difficulty, he finally shoved me to the ground. As I attempted to stand, he threatened me with his pistol.

He shouted, "Obey me."

# Chapter Thirty-two

$A$lonso sat on a ridge of blue-black rock, watching the sun set far off to the west. He was on the edge of the plateau, and the soft, distant mountains were bluish with haze. The cliffs below him were slowly fading into mist and shadows.

Behind him, his mule and the two burros tore at some grass that a patch of melted snow had revealed. The weather had turned warmer, but he still looked forward to getting back to the desert where there would be no snow at all.

When the sun disappeared and darkness claimed the land, he lit a fire. He would descend into Oak Creek Canyon in the morning, and with luck, find his brother, but he wouldn't relish the journey.

He had returned once, for the last full moon, and waited by the confluence for four days. But Cristóbal had remained absent, and the canyon filled Alonso with dread. So, he'd returned to the colder weather of the plateau to wait.

In the oncoming gloom, the outcrops and boulders of basalt no longer looked like rocks but more like demons or gargoyles that were watching him, waiting to bear witness to his cowardly actions.

Suddenly the night air reverberated with the wild whoop of a pack of coyotes. They sounded very close. He searched the pine forest around him with wide eyes while they yipped and barked and howled.

He stepped over to his animals to ensure they were hobbled, then crouched by his fire. The yipping stopped. This early in the spring, there were no insects—especially up on the plateau. And aside from an occasional crack from the fire, he heard no sounds at all.

He walked back to the ridge again and listened, now hoping to hear a little more of them crying down the sun, but they were gone.

In their place was a stillness which felt unnatural—contrived.

It was a silence so complete that any sounds he made were instantly absorbed into it.

The temperatures had plummeted with the coming darkness, and he shivered as he stared into the dimness below him.

He thought, "*Dios*, how I hate the north."

\* \* \*

Cristóbal sat on the throne, rubbing its golden armrest. His eyes darted around, occasionally focusing on imaginary people as he rambled out loud about his plans. The fuel in the flaming gold bowls was running low, and now he sat bathed in the eerie emerald glow cast by the lichen.

I knelt by his feet; my eyes fixed on the ground submissively.

"With this wealth, I will start an empire," declared Cristóbal.

He began collecting items and piling them on the tunic.

He admired the workmanship on a golden goblet as he paused in his work. He breathed on it and rubbed it to a shine.

"I will have power," he said to his reflection in the gold, "and my name will echo through history."

Off to the side was Yaotl's skeleton and Cristóbal beheld it, frowning disdainfully. He got up and kicked the skull with his heavy boot, laughing as it rolled away.

"Your time here is over," he said, "It is now mine."

He lifted what was left of the skeleton and tossed it on top of the pile of bones. He was light-headed.

"Out with the old!" he exclaimed. "Go visit your amigos."

Then, for a long time, he stared at the pile of human remains, peering at Yaotl's headless body as if it might somehow offer advice.

He finally said, "You were a smart one. If one of these men had escaped, this treasure would be gone now. There'd be nothing left but an ugly black pyramid."

He glanced down at me. I didn't want to enrage him and remained passive. I had well caught the madness in his eyes, and now I had to bide my time.

Cristóbal mumbled, "It really would be stupid for me not to follow your example."

The look that came into his eyes then was enough, and I stood and stepped backward. I unconsciously placed a hand over my belly as I moved.

Cristóbal took a step toward me and extended an arm as if to embrace me.

He smiled and acted calm — like I wouldn't remember the last similar attack — but he wasn't fooling me, not for an instant. I had already seen the club-like gold object he held in the other hand behind his back.

I stated coldly, "This treasure has poisoned your spirit."

Cristóbal smiled, "Come with me, we will..."

He swung, and just before he struck, I shot my arm forward and plunged a dark obsidian blade into his left shoulder — the injured one.

His thrust collapsed, and he howled in pain as I disappeared down the stairs and into the shadows.

# Chapter Thirty-three

Cristóbal exited the tunnel into the cave where the water dripped, dragging Yaotl's plunder-laden tunic behind him. His hoard contained not only golden masks, gems and coins but was topped by two wooden casks filled with gold dust. Together the gold and jewels weighed more than he did, but it represented a fortune.

There was enough wealth here for generations, he thought, so he put his back into it and slowly dragged the heavy load across the cave floor.

It was slow going. His leg injury from the tunnel trap still throbbed, and he relied mainly on the other leg; my attack on his already wounded shoulder made his left arm almost entirely useless. I watched him try to pull the tarp with his right arm only, and he couldn't.

He cursed me and grabbed the tarp with both hands, groaning.

When he neared the end of the tunnel, he could see that night had fallen outside, and the rain clouds now completely obscured the moon. The blackened stumps of the junipers in the entryway smoldered in the rain, and several were still burning strongly.

In the cave where the water dripped, he saw me, saturnine and defeated, sitting on the sand mound by the puddles. The rage that had gripped me in the dark chamber had departed, and I no longer felt compelled to stop him. He was just too strong. He wouldn't quit.

I sat there with my hands folded on my lap, waiting to see what he would do. The old metate next to me glowed softly.

He paused and for a moment his face softened. Despite the gray paint on my face, I could tell by his expression when he met my eyes that he was thinking of the young woman who saved him and sheltered him all those days.

But it was too late. I had no kindness left in me. If I could kill him, I would — anything to prevent him from leaving.

And I had another reason to live — one that screamed caution. My abdomen showed the beginning stages of pregnancy, and I could not remove my hand from it. Cristóbal stared at it and then gawked as the realization washed over him. He wondered if this was why I had been sick — and how it could be.

I said, "You remember what happened here? What you did?"

He was preparing to leave, but this question stopped Cristóbal in his tracks.

He answered, "*Si.* I remember."

I rubbed my tummy again, and Cristóbal stared at it.

"You are with child?" he asked, dumbfounded.

I indicated my abdomen and stated, "This is not your treasure."

He asked, "How?"

I said flatly, "Not your child."

Cristóbal flew into a rage. He shouted, "Then whose?"

I smiled as I remembered my embrace with Aditsan on the flat rock by the small pond. He had flicked water in my face, and I had forgotten where I was. In my daydream, I could see his eyes clearly.

I said to Cristóbal, "You leave a treasure far greater than the one you steal."

He shrieked, "Do not mock me!"

I pointed to the tunnel and said, "I did not tell you about the other cave because I knew it would be the end of you."

"You kept it from me!" he shouted angrily.

Cristóbal took out his pistol and checked it over.

He said, "You wanted it for yourself!"

I shook my head. "I have no use for it. It destroys men. I only brought you here because I have been so lonely. I should have known that you would not give up until you found it."

The rain continued to pour down, and the trees sheltered from it in the cave entrance billowed smoke into the evening. Above, lightning flashed in chained sheets across the sky.

Cristóbal turned away from me and walked into the box canyon.

I stared at the old metate, taking in its soft hypnotic glow. I listened to the water dripping as it mixed with the frantic rainfall outside. I smelled the faint scent of decay that always lived in the cave.

I closed my eyes... and then I saw my path.

I felt steady and relieved to suddenly know what I had to do.

I wet my finger and touched the orange powder that filled one of the bowls and then stuck it in my mouth.

I stood up and followed him.


The Spaniard limped forward, out of the cave, dragging the tunic. Once he had cleared the smoldering trees, he let go of his bundle and painfully straightened up. He surveyed the dark sky above with trepidation.

I passed through the smoke and took in the night as well. The nearly-full moon was trying to slide out from behind the inky clouds, and in its vague light, water cascaded down all around us. Down the middle of the box canyon, it formed a small stream that spilled into the exit chute.

I slowly glided around the Spaniard until I stood by the entrance to the chute. The rain rolled off my face like murky tears as it washed away the paint.

He hefted the tunic again and dragged it along the canyon floor while the thunder boomed around us.

Ten feet from me, he let go, seeing the exit at hand. He raised the pistol and said, "I am sorry it has to end this way."

A flash of resignation crossed my heart. "I can see you are haunted by this place."

Cristóbal pointed the gun at my heart and said, "I am."

I smiled at him.

He screamed, "Damn you!" and was on the verge of pulling the trigger when a bolt of lightning hit the gun and sent it flying. The bullet ricocheted off a far wall in the canyon.

Cristóbal's hand was red and blistered.

One of the smoldering trees collapsed on itself, engulfing the gun that had landed by its base. A shower of sparks rose high into the air.

Cristóbal was scared now. He gaped at his scorched hand in disbelief, then stared at me. "Witch," he whispered.

With shaky hands, he began to gather up the cloak again.

I said, "At first, I brought you here so you wouldn't kill Aditsan. I like the Listener. He did not deserve to die that day."

He kept his eyes away from me.

"But I always felt you might die here," I added. "It is what happens to men who enter the dark cavern — they lose themselves. But I thought I could keep it from you."

My heart was full of pain and sadness. Was I supposed to somehow kill him now? I didn't want to kill anyone.

"Cristóbal, please," I pleaded.

He took a step into the exit chute, which was running swiftly with rushing water, dragging his bundle with him while the water flowed over his feet.

Suddenly it was up to his shins, pushing him forward.

He grabbed a cask of gold dust from within the tarp and hefted it up onto his shoulder. He looked at me and said, "I am sorry."

The rain became torrential. A rapid stream now gushed through my canyon into the exit leading to Itzel Canyon, trying to sneak in from the three sides protected by stone walls.

\* \* \*

In Itzel canyon, Aditsan crouched by the exit to the chute that led to the box canyon. Water rushed down through the entrance to the box canyon, but above that gurgle he could hear the young woman.

The desperation in her voice filled him with panic.

But what enraged him were the shouts and curses coming from the Spaniard.

Kuruk had warned him that even a breath of air in the box canyon would spell his doom, but he couldn't stand by while the girl was in danger.

He filled his lungs with air and began climbing up the flooding chute.

\* \* \*

I stood by the chute, shaking with emotion. I felt the powder at work, and the wind and rain embraced me. I was not alone.

I stared at Cristóbal, knee-deep in the water now as he attempted to lift the second wooden cask of gold dust while balancing the first on his shoulder.

There is still a way, I thought. It doesn't have to end like this.

I filled my lungs with the wet night air, and then through the tumult of the rain and wind, I began to sing.

And even over the din of the storm, it stopped the Spaniard instantly. Cristóbal stared at me wide-eyed. The clouds parted, the rains eased up, and the bright moon shone forth. The soaked sandstone walls around us reflected the hoary light.

Silvery raindrops glittered mysteriously all around us.

And I could see in his eyes that time had altered. The moment I'd begun singing, it had slowed. The rain cascading around us now appeared suspended, and the moonlight reflected in each raindrop like a million stars.

I watched him take it all in, as did I. He smelled the blossoms of the cliffrose, and the soaked snakeweed, and the creeping, earthy smell of the rain.

And the wind sweeping down from the heights caressed his face, and I could see a softness coming over him, an awakening.

He smiled as he looked around.

He gave me a piercing look like he was seeing me for the first time. I saw regret flash in his eyes.

Cristóbal hesitated. He tried to move toward me again; his expression changed as if he grasped that he was leaving something that he may never attain again. Something sacred.

He stared at me like I was an angel, gaping open-mouthed.

I peered through the rain at him. "Stay."

He faltered and moved to set down the cask that he had shouldered, but the treasure-filled cloth was pushed forward by the current and shoved Cristóbal downstream. He stemmed himself against the tide but couldn't hold it for long.

He reached out his hand to me.

I smiled and choked down a sob when suddenly the raven landed on my shoulder. It stared at Cristóbal and cawed.

Then Aditsan emerged from the other side of the exit tunnel and seized Cristóbal by the shoulders. Cristóbal stared at him in disbelief.

He dropped the cask, and it exploded into a cloud of golden dust when it hit the sandstone under the rushing water, before being sucked away.

Cristóbal screamed as he lost his footing and was flushed through the chute by the mounting flood, together with his treasure.

Aditsan was taken with him.


I stood there frozen, and then my anger overtook me. I screamed out of rage and frustration and moved to the stone wall surrounding the three sides of the chute. I began pushing it all into the water—I wanted neither of them to enter the canyon again.

Some of Cristóbal's gold coins were still visible, as was much of the gold dust, but when the rocks began tumbling in, it was all buried. Soon the boulders restricted the flow enough that ash, leaves, and burnt branches completed the job of damming the chute.

In the blink of an eye, a small pond had formed where the chute ended, and water no longer escaped except in a slow trickle.

# Chapter Thirty-four

*T*en paces from the exit of the chute, Cristóbal lay on the ground choking and coughing. He looked around uneasily for the *indio* but saw no signs of him. He was sitting in a puddle. When he glanced up the chute, he was surprised to see it was now sealed with rocks, sticks, and mud.

"No!" he screamed as he pawed at the wall of rock.

He wanted to undo the plug, but the sky overhead was forbidding, and great bolts of lightning flashed from all directions. The canyon he was now in—the one Kamala called Itzel Canyon—was quickly becoming a river.

He stumbled down it, dropping and sliding along the way, assisted by an ever-heavier flow of water. Gushing streams plunged into the narrow canyon from the cliffs all around. The rain came down with an icy fury, dragging clumps of slush and snow with it.

At the bottom of Itzel Canyon, Cristóbal hoped to find reprieve. He didn't know where he was but could see clearly that he would drown if he didn't keep moving.

He had to make a quick getaway downstream. Scared for his life now, he started to run. But then he stopped and glanced back where he'd come from, up Itzel Canyon. Back toward her.

His eyes were wild with panic, but his mind raced with one thought—how do I get back here? How do I mark this place?

He took out his large knife and unbuttoned his shirt.

Teeth clenched, he touched the knife to his chest and drew it down; his scream was lost in the building wind.

A short way down the canyon, he passed another tributary to his side and carved another gash into his chest.

Lightning struck a tree near him, and he hurried to the next turn in the canyon and made his mark again.

Over and over, he cut into his flesh, making a map on his chest.

He continued in agony, the blood from his wound mixing with rainwater, coloring it red.

* * *

Alonso appeared on a bend of Oak Creek, riding his mule and leading the burros. In the night he'd heard a gunshot, and he was nervous.

A sudden storm had passed in the hours before sunrise, and now the sun was out and the forest steamed majestically.

He reached the fork where he had separated from his brother and gasped as he saw Cristóbal sprawled on the ground, pale and bloodied and battered.

Alonso slid off his mule and ran to him.

"Brother, what has become of you?" he demanded.

Cristóbal was weak but conscious.

He replied, "There is no time. Open my shirt."

Alonso did and was horrified at what he saw.

He asked, "Cristóbal, who did this?"

Cristóbal almost smiled at the question and then wincingly pulled a piece of soft leather from his belt. It was the one Kamala had painted a symbol on. When he opened it with shaking fingers, a gold coin fell to the ground.

Cristóbal looked at the symbol on the top of the piece of leather and then placed the leather over his chest and padded it down, moaning, his breathing heavy with pain.

He grabbed Alonso's shirt, panting, and pleaded, "You must go back for me, Alonso. I was a fool. Use the map."

Alonso was breathless, "What map? Tell me what you found!"

Before he could reply, the canyon filled with the faint sound of singing. They both froze. A gust of wind blew through, and then the singing was gone.

Alonso shook himself. "What is this witchcraft?"

Cristóbal moaned loudly and pulled his brother to him.

In a single, slow heartbeat, Cristóbal relived the moments he had shared in the canyon with Kamala.

While Alonso anxiously sat by his side, Cristóbal remembered her first appearance coming out of the log while he was hiding; her smiling with a flower in her hair. He recalled her joy about the adobe hut he had built up; saw her preparing him a bowl of soup while he was injured, and holding up a string of trout. And then, a pregnant Kamala appeared before his mind's eye. She was crying.

The memories became overwhelming as he heard Kamala's timid question, "Do you love me?"

He screamed. And then, with wild eyes, he whispered frantically about angels, and heaven, until suddenly he grabbed Alonso and shouted, "Kamala!" and then slumped back. Whether he had just lost consciousness or was dead, Alonso was not sure.

He leaned closer, trembling, and finally exhaled when he determined that Cristóbal was still breathing.

Alonso looked down at the gold coin. He picked it up and looked at his brother, unsure of what to do.

He then stared at the leather stuck to Cristóbal's chest.

Squeamishly, he lifted it and examined it. Nervously, he rubbed the back of his neck.

This was all a bit much for him. He rolled up the leather parchment and stuck it in his shirt.

# Chapter Thirty-five

$A$lonso cradled his brother's head while looking around fearfully. He pleaded, "Wake up, *Hermano*, I don't like it here."

Cristóbal stirred and opened his eyes.

"I was a fool," he said weakly.

He looked beyond Alonso, to the top of the sandstone ridge, and his eyes widened.

Suddenly an arrow came whizzing down from above and sank into Cristóbal's chest.

Alonso jumped backward, dropping the coin.

He screamed, "No!"

Another volley of arrows struck the animals. First, the burros sank to the ground, then the mule, which was bucking off, collapsed with a howl.

In horror, Alonso realized that Cristóbal was dead. He looked up at the top of the cliff and saw an *indio* standing there watching, a bow in his hand.

This was finally too much. He started ripping off his breastplate and armor. He flung his helmet to the ground.

Tearing open his shirt, he shouted at the cliff tops.

Over and over, he yelled, "Shoot me! Shoot me!"


High above Kuruk watched Alonso. He shook his head and backed away, moving to his small fire where he set down his bow and sat.

Across from him sat Aditsan, who was thoroughly drenched.

Kuruk said, "I would have let you kill him."

Aditsan was deep in thought and seemed unconcerned.

Finally, Aditsan said, "I never cared what would happen to either of them."

Alonso's screams could still be heard echoing up from below.

Kuruk said with a sigh, "Take the other before he drives us crazy."

Aditsan shook his head again.

Kuruk lifted his pipe. He took a long drag, slowly exhaled, and after setting down his pipe, he began to chant.


Below, Alonso stumbled down Oak Creek, empty-handed. He was still hysterical, and they could hear his screams echoing off the walls for some time.

He would never make it out of this horrid land. How could he hope to retrace their long journey back to the port of Guaymas? It would be better to die now.

He pleaded with the hills on either side of Oak Creek Canyon as he stumbled downstream, begging someone to kill him.

But the decision had been made. They were no longer concerned with him.

And then, finally, he was gone, too.

# Chapter Thirty-six

*F*all, the canyon was aflame in color. I munched on one trout after another, gorging with relish. I was now very pregnant and could no longer treat hunger casually.

The raven landed next to me.

I said, "I had to leave. It's worth leaving for fish."

It cawed loudly, objecting.

"I told you I wouldn't be long," I said.

I tossed a piece of fish to the raven, and it hopped forward to retrieve it.

Then I held up a leather bag with a red-tailed hawk feather dangling from the thong that tied it.

I said excitedly, "And, I have a new gift from Aditsan."

The raven hopped over to inspect it.

By my side was the Spanish helmet. It was set on a rock as if attending the meal. "He liked fish," I said, "you remember?"

The raven flew over to the helmet, hopped on top, defecated, and then cried out. "Awk!"

I laughed and began to sing.

\* \* \*

Not far away Kuruk sat by his fire. Aditsan approached and handed him a fur. A sharp wind was descending from the cliff tops, and he gratefully wrapped himself.

Once comfortable, he set out to light his pipe.

From a distance he heard a woman singing, and he paused. The melody echoed throughout the canyon.

Kuruk sat up and listened. The singing went on, coming and going like the wind, enchanting him, making him yearn for his youth and his long-dead wife, and then it stopped.

Aditsan looked in the direction of the singing and smiled.

Kuruk was glad for the boy. And he was happy for the girl as well.

# Chapter Thirty-seven

## Act I

### 1876
(April)

Jesse Jefferson Howard woke up choking, struggling against a dream in which he was drowning, flailing helplessly in dark water.

He lay on a thin blanket in the shade of a gnarled old tree.

He sat up, trying to control his breathing.

Looking down at his white knuckles, he saw he was clutching his gun: a worn Henry repeating rifle.

Fanned out before him were a dozen of his horses. They watched him curiously, startled by his sudden cries.

He wiped his mouth and leaned his gun against the tree.

A bouquet of colors painted the grass around him. Wildflowers, as far as the eye could see: a carpet of yellow laid down by the goldfields, the patches of deep orange of the golden poppies, and the purple stalks of the field lupines.

When his eyes swept over them, they teared up.

From the moment he first heard the rumor of the future reservoir, he'd been filled with unease. His ranch lay in a geographic depression near Ventura, California, which was booming and needed a dependable water source. His ranch would most likely be under water soon after twenty years of hard work.

For many of his fifty-nine years, he'd been tormented by nightmares, the images from his past mixing like the worthless rubble on the bottom of a gold pan. A lost love. Men dying in the mud. Others trying to kill him. Useless, bottomless holes in the ground. They all combined into one long tale of sorrow.

And then nightmares of drowning had followed.

He imagined his house on the bottom of a lake and shuttered. What will I do next? he wondered. He could still outwork men half his age, but it all seemed pointless.

Even if the water didn't come, it wouldn't matter with his wife.

He thought of the hope and promise from the early days of the ranch and pulled out a pocket watch. Flipping it open revealed a faded photo of a young woman — Nancy.

He looked at the horses. Beautiful animals, every last one of them. He had delivered each with his own hands.

He spat on the ground.

"Good riddance," he cursed.

Nancy was eighteen when they took the photo, he thought. Two years after they'd been married. Straight, soft blond hair, trimmed at the shoulders. Her eyes blue — in certain light green — and penetrating. She may have been small, but her heart contained an ocean of kindness.

He looked at the old photo again. She was trying to suppress a smile because he'd told her photographs were a serious business, and she should appear stern.

He sighed. What he would give to hear her laugh again.

When they had first settled at the ranch and Nancy became pregnant, he had dreamt of building a porch where he could sit on a rocker and watch the kids grow.

And do nothing — a sentiment that Nancy would laugh at.

"That rocker will be covered with dust before you ever use it," she'd say. And she had been right.

He lowered his head and choked back a sob.

He snapped the watch shut and put it back in his pocket.

She'd been dead fifteen years now, after only six together.

So, why does it still feel like it just happened? he asked himself. Why does my heart ache so much when I take in these spring flowers?

But he knew why. He had married Nancy Cline in 1855 on a beautiful spring morning. She was sixteen and he thirty-eight. She had marveled at the flowers, lambent morning sunlight warming her face, and said nature had provided for them.

"Better hurry and start the ceremony before they are gone," she had replied. "Nothin' lasts."

In their short time together, before she passed, she bore him two children: Jesse and Martha.

After Nancy's death, the children had been sent to the Santa Clara Mission, and for three years, he'd drifted around the ranch like a ghost.

When he got them back, he didn't let them out of his sight for a month, following them like a shadow. He taught them to cook and sew and do laundry, as well as ride and shoot.

He didn't stop until he felt they could survive on their own.

Nobody would ever take them away again.

Mattie—as Nancy had always called her—took to riding bareback on a black mare he gave her for her fourteenth birthday. She named her Shadow. And more than one person had told him his raven-haired daughter looked like an Injun when she raced by.

One afternoon two surveyors saw her charging past and were so taken that they named a nearby massif after her: Mattie Mountain.

Jesse was a pretty good shot and not a bad tracker. He was a quiet young lad who kept to himself. He didn't hunt with the anger that used to drive me, thought Howard, but that's good.

For a moment, his mind drifted back to the gold rush in forty-nine. He saw himself shirtless, covered in dirt and blood, a dead bear lying at his feet. A group of men stood in a circle around him, staring.

He shook his head to bring himself back to the present.

Now his kids were grown. They didn't need him anymore: Mattie was eighteen, and Jesse twenty.

He stood, taking a moment to extend himself to his full seven feet. Howard was a bear of a man with a full beard and unruly black hair. He slapped the dust off his pants, wrestled his black hat in place, and grabbed the rifle.

He surveyed the flowers again, one last time, before walking to the barn with a determined stride that was also long and graceful.

He saddled his horse, stowed a good supply of bacon, beans and dried meat in one saddlebag and coffee, pot and sugar in the other, and tied his bedroll on.

Then he climbed into the saddle.

The sun was low in the sky when he left his ranch. He aimed his horse east into the darkness.

His son Jesse would take care of things while he was away. Jesse had gotten used to his father's sudden disappearances, especially in the spring.

Mattie was more unforgiving. Like always, he hoped to sneak off without her noticing. "Where you runnin' to, Pa?" she would ask, demanding in a voice that left him feeling guilty

And what could he say? That he still missed their mother? That only the smell of danger from time to time made him forget her loss? His children were indeed the only important thing in his life, and yet, occasionally, he had to leave them.

He needed to taste that freedom that has no memory.

He knew he wouldn't make it far today. For now, he would take the old Spanish Trail east over the mountains, toward the Mojave Desert.

When the full moon rose in the sky ahead of him, he wasn't surprised. He hadn't been particularly aware of the moon's cycle, but now as he saw it greeting him, he knew he'd felt it.


Over the coming days, he pushed east. He wasn't sure of his destination. He just rode. Head down, always east.

It was April, and the Mojave was bursting forth in color from all the wildflowers. Howard knew this would be a short-lived springtime: the Mojave Desert was the driest in America, sitting in the rain shadow of the mountains he'd just passed through. After the spring rains, not much moisture made it here from the coast.

But the weather held out, and it didn't get too hot.

He followed the Whipple Trail, blazed by Captain Amiel Whipple in 1853. The trail was seldom used, and at times the track petered out, and he simply aimed at the rising sun each morning.

Fort Mojave came into view on a mesa ahead on day four, but he skirted it, dropping down into an arroyo.

He had no desire for company.

He enjoyed his solitude, and he continued to drift east, ascending the jagged peaks of the western wall of the Arizona Territory, until he stood beneath the mighty pines on the Colorado Plateau.

One night he camped beneath a towering ponderosa, on the edge of an alpine meadow, and woke to the ground shaking from a herd of elk thundering past.

He figured there had to be a hundred of them.

But he had plenty of food, so he just let them pass.

A day's ride further, he came across a few pioneer families trying to make a stand in the newly-named Flagstaff, but he still yearned for isolation, so he turned south until he reached the southern edge of the Colorado Plateau.

Here he stopped and set up camp on a spot that felt like the edge of the world. He exhaled and sat heavily to survey the stunning landscape at his feet: deep canyons of layered sandstone descending in faded reds and oranges and yellows, eventually bottoming out in a narrow valley.


Two tassel-eared squirrels were chasing each other up and down the red and black bark of an enormous pine tree. The early morning sun glinted off their fur as they tirelessly pursued each other.

Howard chuckled, almost spilling the coffee out of his tin cup.

Goodness, he thought, can't remember the last time I laughed.

He observed a stately, lone elk that passed by, the buck barely paying him any attention.

He enjoyed wandering around in this isolated land. The previous day, a short way along the plateau's edge, he had discovered the carcass of a mule deer that had perished during the winter.

The lonely impulse that had set him on the road was beginning to soften, and he was glad to be exploring — leaving a trail instead of following a path.

Nancy had always claimed that what was behind or ahead of us were small matters. What she thought important was what lay within us each day when we opened our eyes.

He leaned back and pondered her words. He didn't know if he could consider his past or future as tiny matters, but he would try to greet each day with fresh eyes. He took a deep breath and glanced around him.

The snow had only recently melted, and the forest lay in disarray: broken limbs and numerous small branches cluttered the ground, and damp, decaying leaves were fading into the soil.

An old raven perched on a branch above him and gurgled and clucked from time to time as he watched the valley below. The wind racing up the cliffs greeted the raven, ruffling his feathers.

Howard heard steps and reached for his gun, then an old prospector came into view, heading right towards him.

The man slowly ambled along, head down, limping slightly, following the ancient trail that skirted the rim. He led a burro loaded with picks, shovels and other mining gear.

Howard lowered the gun. The old-timer stopped and raised his head. They stared at each other. A gust of wind blew through.

"Howdy. Come sit," Howard eventually said. "Have a coffee."

The man nodded, a bit distrustful. "As a rule, I don't hanker to company," he said, then sniffed, "but that coffee sure do smell good."

Howard poured him some in a cup which the old guy handed over. The men silently sipped their coffees while watching the valley as the sun rose higher above the far rim. From below, the warm smell of sage floated up to them.

Howard asked, "Where you headin'?"

The old man shook his head. "I'm heading home, that's where—I'm done with this place."

Howard surveyed the landscape of vermillion buttes and mesas below and then the swaying pines towering above them.

"I kinda like it here," he said.

The man squinted at Howard, weighing him.

"You ever hear of Cliff Haines?" he asked.

Howard shook his head.

"Wish I hadn't," said the prospector. "He came across an old Spanish mine in this area about twenty years ago. The Lost Coconino, they called it. Worked it with a small crew for about five years before the Injuns killed 'em all."

The man stared at a pile of provisions that Howard had unloaded from his saddlebags.

"I'm on my way back to Tucson, but I'm out of supplies," he said. "If you set me up with a little jerky, I'll give you a lead."

Howard laughed sadly, glad he'd left the obsession for gold behind him. "No, I've got no use for mines."

He looked over the old prospector's emaciated frame and reached over to grab a wrapped bundle from the provisions pile.

"Take some bacon nonetheless," he said.

The old man snatched it, his hunger surfacing.

"Thank you kindly—that's about the only act of kindness I've seen in years."

After he had stowed it, the prospector stood to leave, but some internal code prevented him from just walking away.

"You might not care about that mine," he said, "but I feel bound to tell you about it. It sits in a box canyon, a good ways southeast of Williams, in this area. Two years ago, a guy named John Squires rediscovered it. He resumed operations there, but the next year everyone he'd left working the mine was killed by Injuns, except Squires, who died in a gunfight in Taos."

Howard chuckled. "Sounds like that mine's bad luck," he said. "And you're surprised I don't want to know about it?"

"You shouldn't shrug it off — there's a fortune in that mine."

"I'm not tryin' to be sardonic," interrupted Howard, "but like I said, I'm not interested."

"Wish I'd had that kind of smarts all those years ago," said the prospector, chuckling sadly. "I've wasted the last good years of my life searchin' for it and never came close. They say the box canyon has a hidden entrance, and I never could find it."

Howard gave him a blank stare, and the old miner shrugged.

"Anyways," he said as he painfully stood. "I gotta be on my way. Much obliged for the bacon."

Howard nodded and watched him shuffle along with his mule.


Several days later Howard decided to explore a deep ravine that had been carved into the plateau's edge to the east — Oak Creek Canyon, the old prospector had called it. There was still a chill in the air on the plateau, but once he descended, following a gentle brook, the weather seemed milder.

A footpath ran along the creek, and Howard casually followed it on his horse. Massive cliffs soon rose all around him, and the pines clustered close.

Down in Oak Creek Canyon, spring had already gained a foothold. Luxuriant green shoots were sprouting up in sunny patches along the creek, and there was a profound sense of life — new life! — returning.

The intoxicating scent of the earth, and the vegetation that clustered along the water, accompanied Howard and Shadow as they dropped even lower in elevation.

Birds sang out, and the wind — now gentle and soothing — swayed the branches of sycamores and cottonwoods.

He was irresolute; like he no longer controlled where he was going. The breeze and the swaying wildflowers he passed made him feel like he was floating along as he let the horse lead the way.

When they reached a lush clearing where the water lazily wove its way through the high grass, he dismounted and tied the horse's lead to a sapling. There was something about this place that gripped him.

Hundreds of small piles of rocks covered the ground. Some looked ancient, with thick moss obscuring them. Lizards clung to the rocks here and there, twitching their heads at him as he passed.

A handful of rainwater had gathered in a cavity on one of the larger rocks. In the shadows it was dark, and for a moment, Howard thought it was blood.

In the dirt he could see the heart-shaped hoofprints of a young deer, next to the fingerlike toes of a raccoon, but no human footprints.

Walking deeper into the quiet glade, he saw ahead there was a clearing where the water pooled around a large flat rock. The rock was moss-covered and could be reached by hopping across several stones protruding from the water.

Behind the flat rock stood a tall, flat-sided sandstone pillar with what looked like an ornament. Upon closer inspection, Howard found it to be a swirling petroglyph that had been etched into the stone. Moss covered the lower part of the rock and obscured some pictographs.

Howard stepped from rock to rock until he was standing on the flat rock in the middle of the pool. The water below seemed impossibly deep.

He took off his boots and socks and stuck his feet in the cool, clear water.

Nancy drifted through his mind, and he thought how much she would have loved the place. It was a question he asked himself often when he was out in the country. What would Nancy think of this?

And it always saddened him. If only she'd lived longer, and they could have spent more time together. The years since her passing had been difficult.

He thought of the burdens he carried with him — the fodder of his nightmares — and they suddenly seemed unsustainable.

The water swirled around his feet.

And he found himself crying, sobbing, choking on all the loss, the killing, the greed, the senseless destruction he'd experienced. In that quiet place, it all flowed out of him until all that was left was the husk of a man. A man who had once loved. A man who had once felt alive and vibrant.

And then a great calm overcame him.

A sense of acceptance.

He stared down into the water, its surface as smooth as a mirror. Something glowing seemed to be floating below him.

And then, without even realizing he had leaned forward, he plunged into the water and sank.

He didn't feel a need for air as he descended.

Just an acceptance.

And as he sank, water swirling around him, his mind filled with the sad sobs of a young woman crying.

In his mind, he could see her. She was dressed in buckskins and sat on that flat rock, her feet also in the water.

He didn't know why she cried, but her sorrow moved him, and his heart ached.

And then the woman's demeanor changed, and she began to sing.

His heart picked up with the song, stirring like it had suddenly found a lost current. In his vision, the forest around the singer responded, moving in unison to her melody.

Every single thing in this canyon, he thought, is conscious.

He opened his eyes, underwater still.

He glanced up at the sky above, eggshell blue. The sun's sharp rays plunged down at him, fragmenting into a million vibrant lights.

And then he felt the urgent need to breathe.

He flayed his arms and legs and ascended, gasping as he broke the water's surface.

A blue heron stood as still as marble twenty feet away, but its eyes watched him from across the lagoon.

The wind had stopped completely.

He sat in silence for a long time. Finally, he left the rock. He walked back to his horse, climbed into the saddle, and turned the mare upstream.

When they reached the plateau, Howard paused and looked over the canyon.

He could still feel that connection to the land that had flowed with the song. His body still breathed with it.

He was tempted to remain there for a few days, but he suddenly missed his kids. It had been long enough, and he decided to head back west.

Over the next few weeks, he slowly drifted back to California, but the entire time the crying woman's song played softly in his head.

# Chapter Thirty-eight

*A* line of six horses trod along Oak Creek, heading upstream. The brook trickled strongly with snowmelt coming off the plateau, and the cottonwood branches were tipped with light green buds.

The first riders were dressed in blue Union uniforms, the man in the lead sporting sergeant stripes, but the last was a civilian. They were rendezvousing with another group of men.

John James Thompson, the civilian, hailed from Londonderry, Ireland. He had left his home at age eleven and, within a year, had made his way to America. What was left of his youth he had spent in Texas. He was now thirty-four, with dark red hair and a scraggly beard.

Thompson sat astride a dun-colored mount, wondering if he'd been wise to accompany the soldiers. In a few hours they would be escorting a group of Apache prisoners to the reservation, leaving him alone in this wild place.

He had initially thought it a good opportunity to be one of the first settlers to see the land in the Arizona territory. Now that the last of the natives were being forcibly removed, the area was opening up.

Three years earlier, General George Crook had rounded up most of the Apache and Yavapai in the Verde Valley south of the plateau's rim and marched them to a reservation near Camp Verde. Now the bluecoats were about to collect the last renegade band in the area, a group of about twenty that had been captured a few days earlier.

The sergeant, a man with a handlebar mustache named Cush, had assured him that there would be no Apaches left in Oak Creek Canyon by the end of the day.

"We'll have them on their way to San Carlos before you know it," Cush had said. "Then you'll have all this to yourself — or at least your hundred-and-sixty acres if you manage to homestead it."

Thompson wasn't so sure. There were still plenty of savages out there, and raids were common elsewhere in the territory. His two decades in America had taught him that the lands west of the Mississippi could be dangerous.

He glanced above at the sky, which was a deep royal blue, dark and infinite, and then let his gaze fall on the high, color-banded crags that lined the creek.

Despite the assurance from Cush, he sensed that someone was watching him.

But the birds in the trees along the creek sang peacefully, and he wanted to shake the dread that lurked deep in his gut. He tried to take in his surroundings and wipe away the uneasiness.

It was mid-day. Bright patches of sunlight lit the sand along the brook, contrasting sharply with the deep green shadows that lurked under the manzanita and scrub oak.

In the brush along the way, a covey of quail crooned and clucked to one another.

A yellow butterfly floated past.

He exhaled and nudged his horse forward.

Beyond a tight bend through which they had to lead the horses, the trail swung to the right and ran through a grove of cottonwoods. Here they could ride side by side, and Cush reined back until he was next to Thompson.

Cush said, "That wily General Crook promised the Injuns that once they learnt the white man's ways, they could return — but mark my words, they won't make it back in a hundred years."

Thompson scratched his head. "What's to stop them from just sneaking back?" he asked. "Camp Verde isn't all that far away from here."

Cush looked away and shook his head. "They ain't in Camp Verde no more. Last winter, they was marched one-hundred-and-eighty miles to the southeast reservation."

Thompson could detect that Cush was holding something back and asked, "And how did that go?"

Cush spat out to get rid of the memory of that awful, bitter march. His mind was flooded with images of the freezing, stunned wretches, wrapped in thin blankets, barely aware of anything but their misery and a fierce determination to survive.

But all he said was, "There was about fifteen hundred Apache when they set out. 'Bout two hundred died on the way — mostly the very young and elderly."

The two men rode on in silence.

Thompson stole a glance at Cush's uniform. In '61, Thompson had joined the Southern Army when Texas had seceded from the Union, and although fifteen years had passed, he still hesitated at the sight of a bluecoat.

His military career had been a short one — all done before he'd turned twenty-one. A few months in, he'd been hospitalized in Georgia with a musket ball in his shoulder, and after that, he'd spent the remainder of the war in a prison camp in Illinois.

"So, these captives will be marched all that way, too?" asked Thompson. His mind swam with memories of his own forced marches: the poke of a bayonet in the small of his back, his cold, worn clothes hanging off him like rags, and the stale, half-rotten food that wasn't fit for animals.

Cush broke through his reverie.

"At least it's springtime," he said. "They won't have to deal with the cold."

No, thought Thompson, only with exile.


A little while later Cush pulled out his pistol and fired twice in the air. The repercussion shook the quiet canyon, echoing around the bend, and a dozen birds fled, flapping wildly.

"Let 'em know we're close," said Cush.

They came to a cleared area beside the creek. Here, a dozen soldiers surrounded a group of bound men who knelt in the dirt.

Beyond stood several wickiups and a small field with the withered stalks of last year's corn.

A captain saluted Cush and said, "We will all ride to Camp Verde together, and after, I can spare five men to accompany you to San Carlos."

"That'll be fine," said Cush.

Cush nodded at Thompson. "This here is Mr. J.J. Thompson — he's here to look at the land."

Thompson squirmed uncomfortably, realizing that this was his moment. Would he really be staying behind when everyone left?

He slid out of his saddle and looked around.

He glanced at the tall sycamores that lined the water and the bare red rock slopes that led to the distant rim of the canyon far ahead of them. The further you got from the creek, the more desolate the land became. It was now about noon. He sensed the heat and the silence and the glare as he gazed upon the clifflands.

Anything beyond the creek seemed to be a sinister wasteland.

Yet where he stood was lushness all around. There were tall trees and grass and plenty of shade. The drainages showed signs of recent rain, and the air tasted sweet. In the cool shadows where they were gathered, a trace of the morning mist lingered, and there was a general happiness that seemed to spawn from the fluttering of the numerous birds.

Thompson knew in his heart that he would stay.

Not because he found it perfect, but because this was both a place of intoxicating beauty and one of savage desolation.

It seemed to suit him, and the thought of living here fascinated him infinitely.

"So, you're certain this is the last of the Injuns?" asked Thompson while staring at the prisoners in the dirt. All were gazing at the ground and seemed resigned to their fate.

Thompson's heart went out to them, and in a heartbeat, he thought of all the friends he'd known and lost in that sad war. He'd seen too much killing and death — all at the hands of men wearing the same blue uniforms.

He shifted his eyes away, unable to bear the sight of the unfortunate Apaches.

But the bluecoats who surrounded him also looked worn down from their past. Most had begun their military career in the Civil War and witnessed too many battles.

The captain bore a scar on his neck — reputedly from Vicksburg. He seemed to take no pleasure in hunting the Apaches.

"Don't worry, sir," said the captain. "We've been up and down this canyon — it's empty. Hopefully, now, we can have some peace."

The captain nodded to a soldier who began rousing the captives. "Everybody up!" he shouted.

Their arms were bound, and they were tied to each other as they awkwardly stood.

The soldiers all mounted up, and the bulk of them started down the trail ahead of the captives. Then the Apaches too shuffled along, followed by a half-dozen soldiers, including Cush.

He whistled and waved as he rode off, shouting, "Good luck!" over his shoulder.


Thompson stood watching the soldiers depart until long after they'd gone from sight. He'd wished one of them had remained behind; a little conversation would lighten my mood, he thought.

Behind him he heard footsteps, and his blood ran cold. Turning swiftly, he saw nothing. He froze, opened his ears, and eventually discerned that the racket was caused by two little gray mice darting through the dead leaves.

His horse sensed his nervousness and stepped in place.

He calmed her. "Easy, girl," he said. "It's just you and me."

He began unloading his saddlebags. He only had supplies for a few days: a bedroll, some smoked meat, a few potatoes, one jug of water and another of whiskey.

He planned to go to the new settlement of Flagstaff for provisions if he approved of the land.

After tying the horse to a low limb of a cottonwood, he grabbed the jug of whiskey and walked toward the creek. On the way he passed the field where the Apaches had tended to their crops the previous fall. Withered vines of beans and squash twined around the corn stalks.

And then, in the soft soil, he saw footprints.

Instinct made him look up and survey the edges of his clearing. But he was alone.

He stared at the tracks again. So fresh. So recent.

He felt the presence of others.

He glanced at the wickiups. I should search them, he thought.

He paused at the entrance to one of the shelters, and his courage failed him there.

He backed away and instead took a strong pull off the jug.

All around him lay scattered evidence that he was in someone else's home. He inspected a smoldering fire by the creek and could see the remnants of their last meal and woven mats where they relaxed through the hot part of the day.

It seemed inconceivable that they were simply gone now.

In the back of his mind, he could hear sporadic gunshots and cannons bellowing thunder, but he knew they were not real sounds. Just echoes that flared up whenever he began to feel despair.

And the sight of the bound men had done just that.

He tilted the jug back again and drained a good amount.

The high cliffs around him began to spin.

"And why shouldn't I stay here!" he shouted at the crags around him. "Do I not get to be happy someday?"

His face flushed red as he took another swig.

The sounds of battle surrounded him now, no longer in the background.

He slid down the bank, over the slick unbroken sandstone, to the water's edge and took off his boots. The water flowing over his bare feet calmed him somewhat but didn't slow his drinking.

When the high cliffs eclipsed the sun and cast him in shadow, he glanced around furtively. He knew he should climb the bank and throw some wood on that fire.

But instead, he steadily drank and watched the gloom thicken.


Late in the night, Thompson woke. One leg lay immersed in the creek, and the rest of him was sprawled on a smooth red rock bank.

The jug of whiskey leaned against him—empty.

He dragged himself ashore.

He tried to stand and discovered he was still drunk.

The stars above tilted and slanted, and within seconds he fell to the ground again.

He lay on his side, staring at the creek that shimmered dimly in the starlight.

Sleep pulled him away, but just before he lost consciousness, his eyes focused, and he realized in the shadows across the creek, an old, white-haired Apache sat there watching him.

Thompson blinked twice, trying to see better, but then the world spun, and he passed out again.


Sharp rays of yellow sunshine woke him the next morning, filtering through the foliage, warming his body. It was mid-morning, and he guessed he'd somehow slept on the red-banded sandstone bank of the creek for just about twelve hours.

He was groggy and had a headache from all the whiskey, but his biggest difficulty was his vision.

At first, he lay there listening to the birds and the trickle of water, but when he tried to open his eyes, he found he could barely squint.

The world seemed awash in bright light that reflected like a million diamonds off the countless, tiny rapids in the water.

He focused his bleary vision on an olive cluster of mistletoe dangling from a branch of juniper next to him. When he managed to open one eye just a little, he looked upstream, where pale filaments of gossamer were ballooning over the creek—spiderwebs, riding the wind.

His mind felt overrun with cobwebs, and he tried to piece together the previous day: the ride up the canyon; the arrival and seeing the prisoners; the soldiers leaving and the solitude he was left with.

Suddenly, he remembered seeing the old Apache across the river. Whether it had been real, a dream, or a drunken hallucination, he didn't know.

He glanced in that direction and was startled to see four mule deer standing in the spot, watching him from the cool shadows.

They were all female, and two were smaller and looked to be only a few months old. They observed him, seemingly unafraid, bobbing their heads, the fawns wide-eyed and unblinking.

He sat up and took in every detail: the large black-tipped ears, the fur blowing in the breeze, the long sturdy legs and split-hooved feet.

And the black-tipped tails twitching behind them.

After the sudden surprise, they relaxed and eventually ignored him. They were surrounded on three sides by sugar sumac, and soon their delicate snouts were nibbling on the sweet leaves.

So intoxicating was the sight to Thompson that when the deer moved upstream, he followed them.

They seemed in no particular hurry as they browsed their way upriver, and Thompson was content to meander with them, splashing through the water when he had to.

Always twenty feet behind them, never much more.

He wondered why they showed no fear. Surely the Apaches must have hunted them.

After two hours, pangs of hunger alerted him that he was getting too far from his supplies. He'd been walking in a dream-like state, aware only of the animals among the beautiful flowing sandstone, and the stately sycamores, and the buffeting, pleasant breeze that accompanied the cascading waters.

And when he lifted his head to see where he was, he found the deer grazing in a grassy meadow where the water deepened, and a large flat rock sat in the middle.

Here, he crouched and listened to the forest around him.

And despite his hunger, he didn't walk back to his camp until the afternoon was half gone.

But when he finally turned to go, there was a new determination in his eyes.

He knew he would make this magical canyon his home.

# Chapter Thirty-nine

## 1878

*H*oward rode up to a small cabin about a mile from his ranch. His daughter, Mattie, sat on the porch with her one-year-old son, Emory, hugging him in a warm blanket. Accordion music drifted to the house from a shed that stood fifty feet away.

"Hey, Pa!" she shouted. "Come hold this little rascal for me."

Howard dismounted and tied his horse to a rail.

"Come here, son," he said and accepted the baby.

"You just sit here, Pa, and let me do a couple quick things."

The infant was just about asleep and didn't stir when handed over. In the house, Mattie scurried around, cleaned up a few dishes, tossed a log in the woodstove, and washed out a few diapers.

When she returned, Howard nodded at the shed.

"Seems like Stephen is chipper this morning," he said.

She frowned. Her husband, Stephen Purtymun, spent too much time in the shed these days. "Well, I'm guessin' he's got his new still up and runnin'. I won't let him hold Emory when he's been drinkin', so I'm glad you came by — 'cause I needed a break."

A half-mile off, a cloud of dust floated toward them. Mattie peered at it and saw a large herd of sheep moving south.

"Them Mexican sheepherders are takin' over more and more of this valley," she said. "What're we gonna do? Nobody seems to care that they're gobblin' up all the good grazin' land."

Howard shook his head. "Don't know."

Mattie seated herself and took the infant back.

When he was snuggled up close to her, she offered him a breast which he eagerly accepted.

And as they both settled down, she began to hum a melody.

Howard listened with a dumbfounded expression. He knew the tune. It sparked a deep memory. But he couldn't recollect how. It was like remembering being in love but not knowing with whom.

He stared at her for a full minute before he asked, "Where did you learn that song?"

Mattie giggled happily. "You taught it to me!"

"Me? "exclaimed Howard. "I don't think so—but it sure does sound familiar."

"Well, it should," she stated. "Remember when you came back from one of your jaunts about two years ago? I'm not sure where you went, but you were hummin' that song when you got back. You didn't teach it to me—guess I just picked it up."

The ride back from Oak Creek had seemed like a dream to Howard, and the memory of it was even more surreal. His heart had softened following his plunge in the deep pool at the peaceful clearing, and the easy-going glow that resided in his soul grew larger over the coming days.

He had been humming the melodious song of the crying woman without even noticing it, drifting across endless flat plains and through hills and canyons, never feeling the harsh sun or the bite of the wind.

His mind had surrendered to a golden glowing.

Apparently, he had continued to hum the melody after he'd returned. It didn't surprise him that his mind had clung to it. He would never forget the vision that had beset him while he floated in the quiet pool.

He thought sadly how over time, the lovely song of the canyon had faded from his mind, and in that distance, his nightmares had returned.

"I wish I could get back to that place," he said.

"I never asked at the time—but where'd you go?"

Howard glanced east. "I must'a ridden five hundred miles. Went all the way to Flagstaff, then down into a canyon south of there."

Then he told her about his journey — everything but the vision in the quiet lagoon. Still, there was a new light surfacing in Howard's eyes when he spoke of Oak Creek Canyon, and Mattie wanted to know more about it.

"Do you think you'll ever go back?" she asked.

He sighed and then met her eyes. "I sure would like to."

* * *

"Settle down," said Thompson, encouraging his horse to take it slower. He walked alongside her, holding her harness. He glanced back at a mule tethered behind her. Both animals were loaded with hay and firewood in what seemed to Thompson a herculean amount of work. If one of them tripped and broke a leg, all his efforts would have been in vain.

He was on his way to Camp Verde, on the other side of the valley. Despite trying to be frugal, the simple fact was he needed money if he were to build a cabin, and that meant venturing out of his canyon.

So, he'd taken a chance and invested the last of his cash in a mule to help deliver whatever he could harvest. He also had to clear the land so that he could build a shelter. Any trees unsuitable for a cabin he'd chopped into firewood, and he'd taken a scythe to the grass in several clearings and collected the hay to sell it.

When he delivered his first load of hay and firewood to Camp Verde, he discovered the soldiers there were unhappy with their meager diet. The creek was full of trout, he thought, and he decided to make a living off fishing as well.

Now that the snow had melted, the trout were hungry. There was still a chill in the canyon, a lingering taste of winter, and the insects hadn't emerged yet. At nearly every cast, a trout took his bait, and within several days he had the saddlebags filled with fish.

He had salted the fish but knew the heat would still spoil them if he didn't make good time crossing the valley. He was on the trail before sunrise, picking his way downstream, accompanied by a cacophony of bird song as the day began.

He was used to the solitude of his cabin and felt exposed when he emerged from the high walls of the canyon into the open desert.

He headed west with his horse and mule onto a plain where all the tall cottonwoods and sycamores disappeared. Instead, Thompson and his pack animals now wound their way through mesquite and creosote bushes amongst stunted piñon pines and junipers. The sun was on their backs, and their shadows wobbled ahead of them as they left the red rock canyons.

A roadrunner high-stepped ahead of them and disappeared into a thicket of catclaw. The grass was dried out and brittle, but underneath, green shoots were preparing to take over.

Prickly pear cactus thrived and sprawled all over.

The sun slowly crept higher, and early in the afternoon, they sighted Oak Creek again. It meandered southwest out of the canyon, rambling through the valley, and finally, they crossed paths again at a place called Page Springs.

Here they stopped for the night. Howard took off his boots and rubbed his tired feet. They had walked about fifteen miles — nearly half the distance to Camp Verde.

The flow of water relaxed him, and the openness of the land seemed refreshing. He checked the fish, and they appeared unspoiled. He set the panniers in the soft shade by the creek.

In the canyon, the high cliffs cut the sun from view long before the sky was swept with color. But here, he had a great open panorama. He sat on the bank of the creek, keeping to the shadows, and eventually watched the sky fill with vibrant reds and oranges and purples.

The magnificence of the sunset made him reminisce about his time on the Colorado River, where he'd often ended the day watching the setting sun reflecting in the water.

In 1868, when he was twenty-six, he'd left Texas on a cattle drive, heading for California. As fate would have it, they bumped into some Mormons in Utah who bought all their stock.

Here, Thompson heard stories about gold along the Colorado River. He set out to explore the waterway, covering hundreds of miles. Eventually, he built a raft and went into the ferry business, transporting people up and down the river.

During this time on the water, he met the James family.

Abraham James was a cattle rancher from Missouri. He was straight and tall with a dignified mustache and, as his name suggested, seemed like a character right out of the Bible.

He had a whole brood of children — seven in total.

When Abraham surveyed a landscape, he always acted like he was the first ever to see it, proclaiming the land's benefits and, more than likely, what it should be named. Thompson loved to hear him tell stories, especially around a fire late at night.

Over time, they became friends, and whenever he passed by, Abraham would insist he spend the night.

Abraham's youngest daughter, Margaret, was six at the time and developed a friendship with Thompson. Often, they would sit on the banks of the Colorado, telling stories, and speculating about the nature of the world around them. Their favorite game was identifying shapes in clouds.

Thompson lay back on the bank of Oak Creek and stared up at the dark blue sky and identified a fleet of sharp-edged clouds — cumulus ships — drifting through the cerulean sea.

One reminded him of young Margaret, sitting on a log.

On an impulse, he took out a pencil and piece of paper and started to write a letter. He wanted to tell the Jameses about the special place he had found.

It had been almost ten years since he had left the James family, and he wondered what Margaret was like now.

The next day, he reached the fort and sold his supplies. Before he left, he posted the letter to the James family.

Over the next year, Thompson made monthly trips to Camp Verde. Several mines had opened in Jerome, and he sold to the miners, too. On one of his trips to Camp Verde, he received a letter from Abraham James informing him that he would be coming to the area with his family to survey the land.

They arrived in the Spring of 1878.

He tried to talk Abraham into moving into Oak Creek Canyon, but the older man preferred open spaces. He settled along the creek in Page Springs, by the cool, clear water, where he liked to sit under the ancient sycamores and listen to the grackles frolicking in the reeds.

Abraham had married off his oldest four children but still had with him two boys, James and David, and Margaret.

For ten years now, Thompson had been missing trading stories with Abraham James. He yearned to reminisce about the old days on the Colorado and was thrilled the day had finally come when he rode up to the James family camp in the Verde Valley.

When I heard the rider approach, I went for father's rifle. All my life, I've worried about my safety. Father would trust anyone, and it fell on me to discern whom to let into our house — and whom to send packing. So I learned to shoot at a young age and soon after caught on that having a gun handy was also prudent.

I grabbed the Winchester, worked the lever-action to load a bullet in the chamber, and leveled the gun with the rider in the sights. "Hold it right there!" I shouted.

He stopped and raised his hands. Glanced around.

"I'm not looking for trouble," the man replied.

He sat astride his horse in the blaring sun, and he squinted at me as I was standing in the shade of a sycamore.

"I'm here to see Mr. Abraham James!" he yelled.

Suddenly, I recognized him. Jim Thompson. I lowered the gun and stepped into the light. "I bet you are."

He gave me a strange stare, a question on his lips as if he didn't dare assume I was the young girl he'd known ten years ago. And

I, in turn, wondered how accurate my assessment of him from a child's perspective had been. It seemed the days of our friendship were far in my past.

I stared back boldly, sizing him up. At first, I thought he looked the same — no older, except for some wrinkles around his eyes. But as I peered at him, sitting uncomfortably on his horse, I could see a weariness about him. Maybe it had always been there, and I'd just missed it as a young girl.

He nudged his horse toward me.

"Hi, Margaret," he whispered.

I grabbed the bridle when he was close and looked up at him.

"Hi, Jim," I said.

He sat there, speechless, his eyes meeting mine, drifting away, and then returning. I was used to men visiting father who hadn't seen a woman in a while and recognized the delayed speech — and an inability to meet my stare.

I teased him. "Well, are you gonna just sit there all day?"

He shook himself. Laughed. And slid out of the saddle and awkwardly shook my hand.

"Father is by the creek," I said and turned to lead him there.

But before we got there, I stopped and asked, "You been watching clouds without me, Jim?"

He blushed. "I saw your face in one just yesterday — although, to be honest, the face I imagined was much younger."

"No, sir," I said, a bit defiantly, "I am no longer that little girl."

We didn't talk much after that, but between us was now an unspoken acknowledgment that things had changed.


Abraham James and his wife watched the two. Margaret was close to marrying age, and there weren't many suitable bachelors in the Verde Valley. Thompson had been a good friend of the family when they lived on the Colorado River, and they were glad to be reacquainted.

After several months of these visits, it became apparent that Margaret and Thompson were in love. They agreed to be wed the

# Chapter Forty

## 1879

*H*oward hefted a jug of whiskey and took a long pull off it. He sat on a rise, lying against a flat rock while observing his horses below. On his lap, his rifle was ready.

A large flock of sheep was ambling towards him about a mile away, nibbling up the wildflowers in their path. The spring rains had kept the dust down, and Howard could see several Hispanic sheepherders walking behind the animals.

In the fresh morning air, he could hear their whistles.

And then the sadness overcame him once again. He cast his eyes over another field of blossoming spring flowers and remembered Nancy saying, "Nothin' lasts."

He took another swig of whiskey.

The sheepherders must've spotted him because they veered north, away from his property.

"And stay away," he muttered and downed another good gulp of whiskey. Soon he tilted his head back and eventually slipped into a dream.


And in the dream, he relived the rush of '49. He was thirty-two, digging and mucking in a dark hole, always armed, constantly checking over his shoulder. There were so many desperate men, and if any even suspected you'd struck pay dirt, they would jump your claim without hesitation.

He had only made it through because of his partner, Willie.

In the dream, Howard stood at the bottom of a shaft, covered with dirt, and Willie was staring down at him, grinning like a schoolboy. Willie had a mop of black hair and hailed from Dublin. He had a way of seeing the positive in every situation, no matter how bad.

"You look good, Bear," he said. "The dirt suits you."

Howard stood a solid foot higher than Willie, with a full beard and a shaggy black mane of hair. The moment they'd met, Willie had begun calling him 'Bear.' When he later learned that Howard had hunted bears, the nickname seemed all the more appropriate.

Both men were the same age and determined to make their fortunes in the California gold mines, but several years of hard work had shown no profit. And any money they had tucked away was now spent.

"You see China yet, Bear?" Willie asked Howard.

Howard cursed. "I bet I'm close," he said and tugged the rope, indicating another bucket was ready to be hauled up. Willie pulled it up while Howard climbed their rickety ladder.

Minutes later, Howard was squinting in the sunlight as both men dug through the pail. Initially, they'd found traces of gold and had sunk this shaft, hoping it was a good vein, but the last few weeks had shown little promise.

Willie poured some of the muck into a pan, added a little water, and swished the mix around until all that was left were the heavier rocks and pebbles.

The men inspected them closely.

Howard shook his head, and Willie tossed the rubble to the ground.

"Nothin'," said Howard. "I think we should give up on this hole. There ain't nothin' down there."

Willie sat and rubbed his stubbly chin. "Sure, Bear—I think we should be on our way. There are better ways to spend my life than muckin' out some dark hole. We need a new plan."

Howard sighed. "If I weren't so damn hungry, I'd just walk away."

Willie stared at the hills around them. "There's got to be a few deer out there. Why don't you hunt one for us?" he asked. "You said you hunt."

Howard nodded somberly. "I can. I should'a gone out before, but it seemed like we were hot on the tail of some gold."

Now Willie put on his best smile. "Then we're in business. You know how much they charge for a meal in the food tents? I think they'll pay you a lot of money for a deer."

Howard scratched his unruly hair, which was full of dust and clumps of mud. His beard needed a trim, too.

"I reckon if there are deer out there, I can find 'em."

Willie began rubbing his hands together. "Soon, we'll make our fortune — we're gonna be as happy as a schoolmarm at detention."

Over the coming week, Howard scoured the hills around them. Most of the game had been killed by other miners or had cleared out, and he was forced to search further and further away.

He did kill a raccoon and a porcupine, and as desperate as the miners were, they happily purchased what meager meat there was — but it only brought in a little money.

When he finally returned with a buck one day, Willie was ready with a butcher knife. Howard had gutted the deer but left it to Willie to skin and butcher it. Willie found it hard to contain his hunger, and the first thing he did was skewer a big strip of tenderloin and lay it suspended over the fire.

He offered the first bite to Howard, who refused.

"You take it, Willie," he said, "I ate a good portion of the liver yesterday after I gutted it."

Willie wrapped the choice cuts in brown paper and brought them straight to the food tents, where they were instantly purchased.

"I'm gonna sell everything I can," he said. "The rest I'll cook up in a stew."

"Good," said Howard, "don't take anything for granted 'cause game is scarce—it seems I'm not the first to try my hand at hunting around here."

"Wish we had a horse," said Willie, "then you could cover some distance and maybe find a place that isn't hunted out."

Howard smiled. "Don't you worry about that. I can walk a fair distance. Let's just fill our bellies and see where that takes us."

The next day Howard was out hunting again. Luck was on his side, and he bagged a doe within a mile of their camp.

Willie butchered the doe and quickly sold off the venison.

Hopeful, Howard rode out again the next morning. But this time, it seemed the game had just vanished.

"There are plenty of bear around," Howard told Willie, "but they're skittish. I've found their dens, but they roam far and sometimes don't return to a particular den for weeks."

Willie paced around. "Well, I can't do anything here while I'm waiting. Why don't you set me up in one of those dens, and I'll just wait for the bear?"

A dark sense of foreboding swept over Howard as he thought over Willie's plan. "I don't like it," he said. "You're no hunter."

Willie laughed. "These are black bear, not grizzlies—I think I can handle one if you leave me armed."


So when Howard headed for the hills again, Willie accompanied him. In a damp cave about five miles from their camp, Howard left Willie with a pistol—a Colt .45 with six rounds—and some dried jerky. The cave was small, ten feet square and four feet high.

"Don't light a fire, just wait," said Howard.

Then he walked away, feeling uncertain. It was no easy thing to just lie someplace, in the dark, waiting for a bear to come around.

The bear would most likely smell Willie, but he might get close enough for Willie to get off a shot. Howard was tempted to switch weapons and give his friend the rifle, but he knew he'd have little chance of hitting a deer at any distance with the pistol.

It wasn't until a few days later that Howard returned to the cave. Miles away, he'd killed a large buck, and he decided to butcher it and pack just the meat out rather than try to transport the carcass back.

"Right about now, a horse wouldn't be such a bad thing," he thought.

That night he'd smoked some of the venison, so he could fill his belly and have some jerky as provisions.

He now had sixty pounds of meat in his pack, and he grunted when he set it down outside the cave and called out. "Willie, you in there?"

An ominous silence greeted him.

He unslung his rifle, cocked it, and entered the cave.

Willie's body lay in the corner. The bear had torn him up. Howard moaned. There was a lot of blood. He wondered if Willie had gotten a shot off.

He checked the Colt, which Willie still gripped in his hand, and discovered the cylinder held all six bullets still.

He sat next to his friend and cried. He'd never felt so alone.

By the cave entrance, he could see the bear's tracks leading away. Howard glanced at the prints and said, "You may not be at fault here, but I'm gonna kill you anyway."

He sat Willie's body up in a corner of the cave.

"I'll be back real soon," he said, sobbing, "you sit tight until then."

He stepped outside, shouldered his pack, and hiked the five miles to the food tents. He sold all the meat he had—except the smoked jerky.

Then he grabbed a shovel and returned to the bear den.

Howard once again crouched by Willie's body, and now he was filled with rage. Earlier, the death of his friend had seemed unreal, but now the certainty had set in.

He was alone. His partner killed.

He thought of the bear.

It would return, eventually, of that he was sure.

He dragged Willie's body out of the cave and buried it about a half-mile away, then returned.

He laid down his one thin blanket, and then he waited.

Over the coming days, he barely moved.

He slowly chewed his smoked venison, and over time he took on the appearance of an animal.

He didn't think about days or hours or minutes.

At night he shivered but lit no fire.

When he eventually ran out of jerky, he simply ignored his hunger.

And when the bear finally did return, a part of Howard had all but forgotten about it. Like it was some mythical animal that he wasn't sure he still believed in.

He fumbled for his rifle in the dark.

The sun had set, and in the gloom of early evening, Howard could barely make out the creature as it stood in the entrance sniffing.

The bear was hesitant, and it swayed slightly.

And then it looked right at Howard and growled.

Slowly, Howard raised his gun and fired. But the bear moved, and the bullet hit its shoulder.

The animal roared in pain and charged at him.

Howard went to shoot again, but his rifle misfired.

He pulled out his knife as the bear was upon him, and they went down together with a thud.

Their cries mingled with the oncoming night.


The soft crooning of a mourning dove woke Howard the next morning. The bear lay against him, dead. Howard slid himself out from under it and examined his own body.

His left arm was caked in blood, and later when he washed it, he would realize it needed stitches.

His knife he found buried in the bear's heart. Lucky, he thought.

It took him a few days to gather enough energy to clean his arm and stitch it using some coarse black thread and a heavy needle.

And then another day to butcher the bear and pack the meat into town.


The miners he encountered on the path back to the camp gave him a wide berth. He hadn't thought about his appearance, but the eyes of those he passed were wary. Had he been more alert, he would have seen their hands were close to their guns.

He wouldn't have recognized himself if he'd glanced into a square of mirror. His face was smeared with dirt and dried blood — he didn't know if it was his or the bear's. His hair was clotted with mud and had grown into an unmanageable mess. His clothes were damp and dirty and hung loosely off his emaciated frame.

He didn't care. All he wanted now was to return to the woods.

Without Willie, he had no desire to dig for gold. But he simply couldn't focus his thoughts enough to leave.

Consequently, he hunted, at times venturing quite far from the mining camp but always returning. He came across very little game, but he was so persistent that he never returned empty-handed.

Any time he came across an active bear den, he would use it as a base and sleep there at night, waiting. Sometimes he would drift through the woods during the day, but always at night, he slept in a den.

Over the coming weeks, the miners and purveyors in the food tents began to talk about the tall, mud-covered hunter who dragged himself out of the woods from time to time, always returning with a pack full of meat, always looking like death — both someone who brought death and someone who was near it.


One day Howard twisted his ankle on his way back to the mining camp. He had a pack full of meat and made slow progress. He found a stout staff and hobbled along with its help, but it took him three days to cover five miles.

Still, he refused to leave the meat behind. It was all he had.

His time in the wilderness had left him skinny and sickly. His eyes had sunk into dark sockets, and his skin was crisscrossed with infected scrapes and cuts.

Within sight of one of the food tents, he collapsed in the mud.

He lost consciousness and didn't know how long he lay there.

Later he would discover someone had stolen his meat.


He woke in a wooden-floored wall tent, laying on a cot. A young woman tended to him. She seemed about sixteen and wore her soft, blond hair pulled back in a bun. Her dress was blue, like her eyes, and flowed around her legs as she moved.

"Oh, you're awake!" she said when she saw his eyes darting about.

Howard hadn't seen a woman in months.

When he tried to speak, all that came out was a scratchy rasp. The young woman chuckled and offered him some water.

"Drink this," she said.

He choked down the water and wanted to ask the woman who she was, but his exhaustion caught up with him, and he passed out.


He woke to the smell of beef stew floating through the tent. His hunger gave him the wherewithal to sit up. The bowl had been left by his head, on a wooden crate, with a spoon laid out beside it.

He finished the stew in minutes, and each bite helped restore his senses. It seemed he'd come back from a far-away place. He was just wiping his mouth when the woman returned.

"I can't pay for this," said Howard guiltily.

She laughed. "My dad runs a food tent, and he said he did business with your partner before he got killed."

"You knew Willie?" asked Howard.

She nodded. "My Pa did, and that's why he thought we should help you."

Howard was not used to generosity. He'd seen none since arriving in the goldfields. "That seems overly kind," he said.

"Not at all," she said. "It was the only Christian thing to do."

Now Howard blushed. "I'm afraid I'm not much of a church-goer."

"That's fine," she said, "I don't need you to go to church, but I could use a favor."

He stared at her for a minute until he realized she was waiting for him to reply. "Anything," he said.

She exhaled. "Good, 'cause you smell pretty terrible, and I'd really like you to get out of those clothes."

He felt his face flush red again. The young woman seemed so clean, pure and innocent that he felt guilty exposing her to his horribly unclean body.

"Here are some clothes you can wear while I wash yours," she said as she set down a shirt and pants.

Then she placed a basin filled with hot water on the wooden crate and said, "And why don't you wash up a little, too."

He nodded an agreement, but after she left, he found he was so weak he could barely get undressed. He sat naked on the chair, and for about thirty minutes, he struggled to wash himself.

The mud flowed off him and through the cracks of the rough-cut timber they'd used to floor the wall tent. Some scabs and scrapes managed to still cling to him, but he washed off most of the blood. There was something about removing the filth and grime that made him feel human again.

Eventually he crawled into the pants and lay back down on the cot. He was in the sweetest slumber when he heard someone bump the chair next to him.

He sat up on his elbow and asked, "Better?"

The woman gave a weak half-smile but then nodded at his head. "Well, I suppose you're as clean as soap and comb can make it, but you still need a shave and a haircut," she said.

He found it impossible to resist any request she made.

"Go ahead," he said.

The young woman surveyed his crazy mess of black hair and then lifted a large pair of scissors.

"I'm gonna start with the big shears," she laughed, "until I'm sure you're in there somewhere."

Howard surprised himself with a giggle and tilted his head back so that the hair could fall on the floor.

She cut off his hair a few inches from the scalp and took most of his beard with several well-placed cuts. Then she switched to a small pair of scissors and kept hacking away.

"You know how to work one of those?" asked Howard as he watched her sharpening a straight-edged blade.

She nodded. "Used to shave my Pa all the time."

He closed his eyes and enjoyed the feeling of the sharp razor gliding over his skin.

Suddenly, it dawned on him that he didn't even know the young woman's name.

"Nancy," she said demurely.

"I don't know how to thank you," he said.

"You just get better," said Nancy.

And over the coming days, he did heal up under her care.

"I think I'm done hunting for a while," Howard said to her one afternoon.

"Well, I'm done with this horrible gold rush," said Nancy. "I'm only here to help my dad, and except for tending to you, he rarely lets me leave the tent."

In the end they left together. They were married that spring and were soon settled down on his ranch.

Howard's dream continued, flowing through the years. Years filled at first with joy, and happiness, and new babies.

But then the dream turned darker. Nancy got sick and soon passed, and they took his kids away. He floundered through memories of mucking for gold again, desperate and hungry, and then found himself reliving a moment of the Mexican-American war, a charge against Santa Anna's men.

He was scrambling over a hill, chasing a man.

When he rounded the top, he discovered the guy had dropped and turned and was now aiming his gun at him.

There was no time to swing his gun around and get a shot off, and being as big as he was, he wasn't all too quick in his movements.

He turned, and the slug hit him in the back.

He fell to the ground, rolled, and raised his gun to fire...


Howard opened his eyes and saw the man, not twenty feet away. The late afternoon sun framed him with a bright halo. Howard squinted and could just barely make out the barrel of the man's rifle which he was slowly raising.

Groggily, he gripped his gun and fired at the man.

The repercussion pulled him completely from his sleep.

He looked up to see a brown-skinned sheepherder standing before him, gasping, and gaping at a red spot on his chest.

Before the man could utter a word, he collapsed, and within a minute, he was dead. By his side was a walking stick that Howard had mistaken for a gun.

\* \* \*

Thompson tied his mule to a post at the United Verde Copper Company supply store in Jerome. The mines were booming, and there were men everywhere, many covered with soot. His saddlebags were filled with trout, and the mule was also carrying some firewood he'd collected when passing by Page Springs.

The clerk stepped out and shook his hand.

"I'll take that firewood," he said. "But I hope you have more fish — the last batch got bought up right away."

"Sure do," said Thompson, patting the saddlebags.

The clerk helped him empty the panniers and bring in the fish, then Thompson untied the wood and stacked it.

Inside the store, the clerk counted the fish, figured in a little extra for the wood, and wrote a receipt.

"This gonna be cash or credit?" he asked.

"Little of both," said Thompson, "I need more ammo for my Colt, and I've got a few improvements to my place in mind."

"I'd a'thought you'd be done with your cabin by now," the clerk said. "You've been there a few years now."

Thompson grinned. "Four years," he said, "and it's fine for me, but next month I'm getting hitched — and I gotta spruce it up for my wife."

"Good for you," said the clerk. "Must be lonely up there in that canyon by yourself."

Thompson nodded. "I guess I can handle lonely, but there's a lot of work that really needs four hands."

The clerk nodded at a notice board with various letters and messages tacked to it. "Put up a note," he said. "Who knows, you might find someone who's lookin' for work."

Thompson borrowed a pencil, scribbled a message on a scrap of paper and tacked it up.

Then he turned back to the clerk. "Now how 'bout you set me up with some nails and a few small panes of glass."

Thompson eyed some blue ribbon. "And a few yards of that ribbon as well."

"Right on it," said the clerk with a smile.


Jim escorted my family from Page Springs to Oak Creek Canyon when father was ready for the spring move. Father had two sturdy horses pulling a wagon, and Jim had brought along his horse and mule.

The wagon was piled high, with father working the reins and mother sitting next to him. My eleven-year-old brother, David, sat on the back, sneaking a ride.

Jim walked along next to me. I felt radiant with a blue ribbon in my hair. His mule, tethered behind the wagon, was loaded high with all my possessions.

We proceeded very slowly, mother and I marveling at the wildflowers while the men scanned the cliffs around us.

My older brother James asked to use Jim's horse to scout ahead. I could tell Jim was worried that James might injure himself — or the horse — but he took a chance and let him because he wanted to please me.

The red rocks loomed closer, and at one point, we passed a short mesa on our right and a rugged mountain on the left.

"I reckon that there mountain looks like a crouching bear," said father in his proclamation voice. "I name thee Bear Mountain."

Jim smiled at me and raised an eyebrow.

At the mouth of Oak Creek Canyon, father again surveyed the vermillion cliffs. "And that one up there," he said, pointing to a limestone-rimmed formation, "that's Steamboat Rock — see, it's even got a railing running along the top."

Jim grinned at his soon-to-be father-in-law, amused by his penchant for naming things. "Works for me," he said.

That night we stayed at Indian Gardens — as Jim had decided to name his little homestead. Jim let my folks sleep in his bed for the night, and he bunked in a newly erected shed. He set me up in a back room and put my brothers in the barn loft.

The next day, we were married in a sweet ceremony by the gurgling creek. My father performed the ritual, and my family and countless butterflies and birds bore witness.

By mid-day, the James Family — minus me — were on their way up the creek, heading to Munds Park on the plateau. I was content to remain with my husband, where thoughts of my own future family danced in my head.

# *Chapter Forty-one*

$M$attie approached the jail slowly, riding Shadow. She was eight months pregnant, and her once lithe body was now cumbersome. The building was set on the edge of town, besides a small, gurgling brook. It had been recently made from rough-cut timber and smelled of pine. A dozen uncut boards still leaned against the wall.

It took some effort for her to slide out of the saddle.

She retrieved an apple pie from her saddlebag and entered the small structure, and a young deputy stood up and faced her.

"Can I help you, ma'am?" he asked.

Across the room, Howard lay on a cot in the only cell.

"I'm here to see my Pa," she said.

The deputy glanced at Howard. "I can let you in, but I have to lock the cell door behind you."

"That's fine," she shrugged.

Howard stood and put on his hat.

The deputy glanced at the pie. "I'm not supposed to let anyone give him anything."

Mattie's face flushed red. "Why? You think there's a file in it? Do I look like someone come to bust him out?"

Now it was the deputy's turn to blush. "No, ma'am, I guess you don't."

"Good," she nodded. "Then let me in. I need to talk to him alone. You can lock us in there together, but I'd like some privacy."

Reluctantly, the young man unlocked the jail cell, let Mattie in, and then bolted the door behind her. Then he grabbed his hat and went outside to sit by the brook.

In the cell, Mattie embraced Howard, who appeared old and beaten. "I'm here to break you out, Pa," she said in a whisper.

"Break me out?" asked Howard, trying to suppress a chuckle.

His daughter glared at him. "Yes, Pa, I won't let you do time. I know you didn't mean to kill that man, and you're too old to be locked away."

He scratched his head. "Where would I go?"

She smiled. "I don't know. Maybe back to that little canyon you're always talkin' 'bout."

He paused, seriously considering her words.

"It's tempting," he said, "but how would I do that?"

She handed him the pie. "There actually is a file on the bottom of the pie—use it to cut the bars."

Howard looked at the solid steel bars of his cell. They would take many hours to cut through.

"They're taking me away in the morning—there's no time."

She sighed. "Maybe I could get the jump on him," she said.

He laughed at the suggestion, which made Mattie's temper flare. "I may be big, but I can do it."

He shook his head. "No, I don't want you caught up in this."

Her eyes hardened.

"Deputy!" she called out. "Get me out of here."

The young man returned and opened the cell door. When she was out, he locked it again.

Mattie stormed outside and sat by the brook and cried. Her father had always been a bit wild, but he tried to steer clear of breaking the law when he could. She knew he wouldn't use the file.

She walked to several boards leaning against the building, pushed them over and screamed.

The deputy came running to the door with a worried look.

As soon as he stepped outside, there was a "thud."

Soon Mattie returned to Howard's cell with the keys in her hand.

"What did you do?" asked Howard nervously.

"I did what had to be done," she said flatly.

She unlocked the cell door, and he hurried outside to find the deputy unconscious with a swelling welt on his forehead.

"I didn't kill him, Pa," she said. "He'll be alright."

Howard looked at her nervously. "Sure, until he wakes up."

"Well, I'll take care of that—you get outta here," she whispered urgently. "Besides, I can't go with you in this condition—and even if I could, I'm not leaving my husband and baby behind."

Howard's eyes softened as he watched her.

"I can't let you take the blame for this," he said.

Mattie thought for a moment. "I'll say that he forgot to lock the cell when I left, and you came out and clubbed him. He's not gonna want to admit that a pregnant lady knocked him out."

Mattie pushed him toward her horse. "You take Shadow and get out of here."

While he reluctantly climbed into the saddle, Mattie ran back inside and grabbed the pie, which she managed to somehow fit in the saddlebag. Howard stared down at her unhappily.

"And when will I see you again?" he asked, tearing up.

"Don't you worry, Pa," she said, "when things settle down, we'll join you."

He nodded. She slapped Shadow's rump, and the horse started forward. "I love you, Pa," she said.

"I love you, too," he replied. "You just make sure this all falls on me!"

He headed east fast, with his head down and his collar pulled up high.

* * *

"My goodness, Jim," I exclaimed when I woke and saw the picnic basket next to me, "aren't you full of surprises!"

I peeked under the lid to see bread, jam, cheese and fruit, all packaged neatly. He had prepared it all while I slept.

He grinned. "Well, I reckon you'll love this place as much as I do, eventually. But I thought we should start with something fun—before we get to chores."

I sat up and rubbed my hands together.

"Okay, husband," I said and asked, "What are we gonna do?"

He put on his boots, which he'd kept off to keep the noise down. "I'm taking you to a special place — you're going to love it. But it's at least six miles upstream, so put on your best footwear."

I beamed. "You got yourself a date!"


Soon we were walking upstream, following the creek as it warmed to the first rays of the sun sneaking over the canyon rim. Jim carried the picnic basket in one hand and his rifle — a .44 caliber Spencer carbine — in the other. I wore a canvas backpack with a warm blanket stuffed inside. Into my hair, I had woven the blue ribbon.

The leaves were filling out, growing bigger and into darker shades of green, and with each day, the skeletal trunks and branches of the cottonwoods and alders along the creek retreated into the shadows. With them, hovering, was the last vestige of winter — that frigid coolness that has no recollection of summer.

But the snowmelt was over — even up on the rim — and now the murmuring creek had no urgency to it. It meandered again.

For much of the way we walked up the middle of the creek, hopping over low, flooded sections without getting wet, but when we needed to avoid the water, there was always a trail along one bank or another.

Jim said, "Over the last few years, I've marveled at some of these trails created by the ancients. I imagine they used them for eons — long before the Apache arrived — even now, long after their absence, there's still a path."

We moved slowly, enjoying the morning, and Jim didn't act surprised at all when we came across a few mule deer foraging. There were five of them. All does. Two were young, born that year and only a few months old.

"Aren't they precious?" I asked.

Jim nodded happily. "I see a few does most every time I walk this stretch. They seem to love it here. And I've yet to figure out why they aren't afraid of people."

The deer hopped ahead of us, in no rush, white tails flagging. Suddenly, I locked eyes on the rifle.

"Jim?" I asked, hesitantly, "Are you aimin' to kill one of those beautiful creatures today?"

He glanced at the largest doe walking directly in front of them. "No, darlin'," he said, "but it wouldn't hurt to hunt something if the opportunity arises."

I bit my tongue as we walked along over smooth worn stretches of sandstone and through patches of lush green grass. Jim shadowed me, knowing I was unsettled, anxious not to let anything spoil our day.

The trail was lined with vegetation, briars and berry vines that climbed over everything, stretching heavenward, desperate to break the grip of the dead white husks of last year's crop.

A woodpecker knocked on a dead trunk around the next bend.

Finally, I asked, "Do you think you could leave them alone? The friendly does along this stretch?"

He sighed, eager to please me. "Of course," he said, "anything for you. I'll keep my gun pointed elsewhere."

I snuggled against him as we continued.


By the time we arrived at the gentle lagoon, we had not seen the deer for a while. But sure enough, there were several of them grazing just beyond the standing stone with a moss-covered petroglyph on it.

The wind whistled through the pines above us, building and swaying, until suddenly it was no more, replaced by the twirling and chattering of a thousand birds.

Cool, clear sunlight bathed the rippling water. Beneath the surface, trout swirled, suddenly snapping upstream or down whenever whim suggested.

A family of quail pecked their way to the water's edge. The chicks looked like little puffballs on legs.

I smiled. "This is wonderful," I said as I inhaled the lovely fresh air.

My gaze swept over the setting and settled on the large flat rock in the middle of the clearing. I walked that way but found my path obstructed by myriad piles of stones that hid in the dead grass.

"They're everywhere," I said.

"Just do your best," said Jim, as he picked his way to the water's edge.

I got there first, hopped to the rock and laid down our blanket. Jim joined me, and we set to eating the picnic he'd prepared.

As a special surprise, he'd brought along a small rhubarb pie.

"I still had some stores in the root cellar," he said.

I shook my head happily. "I don't know when you found the time to do all that."

After we ate, we took a nap, and when we woke again, we undressed and made love on the flat rock.

Our only witnesses were the does nibbling fresh shoots nearby.


"I could just stay here all day," I exclaimed as I stretched luxuriantly in the sunshine. We were partially dressed—just our skivvies—on the blanket, lying on our backs again.

Side-by-side, we watched the ever-blue sky.

Eventually we got dressed, but neither felt compelled to get up.

"I remembered watching clouds with you on the bank of the Colorado," said Jim.

He looked up and saw one lone cloud floating by.

"I reckon that's a ship," he said.

"Nope," I giggled, "that's a duck."

We remained in that peaceful place for a small eternity. Neither of us kept track of time until Jim began thinking about dinner.

"You know," he said, "I could head upstream and see if there's any game about, and you could wait here."

"You gonna be gone long?" I asked.

"Couple hours," he said, and I nodded.

"I'll be fine," I said as he left, heading north upstream, carrying his gun and the empty backpack.

After an hour Thompson jumped a deer and even managed to get off a quick shot. He got lucky, and when he hurried to where the buck had been standing, he found blood splattered on the ground.

A lot of it.

He didn't think the animal could make it fár, and he began following the bloody spoor.

But the deer was stronger than he had anticipated and somehow made it a good way up onto the plateau. It finally collapsed on the other side of a slippery boulder field. When Thompson caught up with it, his heart sank. He didn't think he could carry the carcass out of here.

So instead, he butchered it where it had dropped, stuffing the pelt and the best cuts into his backpack.

He was so preoccupied with his task that it was already growing dark when he finally looked up, and on the far end of the valley, a full moon was peeking at him from the horizon.

Quickly, he shouldered his pack and hurried downstream.


When Jim left me, I hadn't a care in the world. The magical place he'd brought me to seemed so lovely, so perfect that I was happy to stay behind.

I lay there listening to the birds and the trickling water and before long fell asleep to this symphony.

My second nap that day!

When I awoke, it was dark. The silence disturbed me.

The crickets had not yet awoken from their winter slumber, and the birds had settled for the night.

I put my boots back on and wrapped the blanket around me.

I kept glancing upstream but saw no sign of my husband.

"Jim!" I called out, my thin voice barely penetrating the night.

And then the full moon slid over the rim of the canyon and shone down on me. It lit the lagoon, and the forest clustered around it and bathed everything in silver.

I felt like I was in a dream.

And then I heard singing.

It came from downstream, the melody floating over the water.

It was the most beautiful thing I'd ever heard.

Suddenly my only concern was to get closer.

I dropped the blanket and walked toward the song, all thoughts of my husband and the eerie canyon night forgotten.

I simply followed the melody down the canyon.

When I passed the West Fork, I deemed the source must be here, and I turned in that direction. I seemed to be floating along like a leaf on a river.


Thompson reached the lagoon covered in sweat. The calm night should have helped him stay cool, but in his panic, all it did was chill him. He'd expected to see Margaret waiting on the rock but found only the blanket and the remnants of their picnic.

Something was wrong.

He set down the backpack.

Her boot prints stood out clearly in the mud along the creek, and he followed them with rifle in hand. At first, he had hoped something had prompted her to return to their little cabin, but when he saw her tracks turn up the West Fork, a cold chill ran down his spine.

Why would she go in there?

After a few miles the hard sandstone prevented all prints. He'd never ventured into this canyon and didn't like the way its walls closed in on him.

He was about to turn back when he found a blue ribbon lying in the dirt.

He kept going. His heart pounded.

Moonlight lit the way, and he felt compelled to follow it further.

Out of the silver glow, a thunderous roar echoed through the canyons. Thompson's blood froze. He couldn't tell if it came from man or beast. It was different from anything he'd ever heard. If it hadn't been for Margaret, he would have fled there and then.

The sky darkened, eclipsing the moon, and suddenly it began to hail. A layer of cold mist floated above the ground.

Within a minute it was over, and the silence in the wake of the pounding hail felt unnatural.

Ghoulish white pellets now covered the canyon floor.

Thompson came to a long, confined section where the walls closed to within twenty feet of each other. From the shadows at the other end, he could hear something moving his way.

The clouds blew away, and the moonlight returned.

Something big was ahead. Running. Panting. Snapping dead twigs with its thundering steps. He stopped and held his breath, trying to hear better. Could this be the wind thrashing about dead limbs? Could that sound be natural?

A large crash resounded through the canyon ahead, echoing.

He hastily unslung his rifle and put a bullet in the chamber, leaving six more in reserve. It was getting closer now, whatever it was, and he could hear it breathing as it lumbered toward him in the eerie moonlit evening.

And then, from sixty feet away, he saw an enormous grizzly.

The bear didn't see him yet. He watched it breathlessly through the sight of his gun. The beast was silver in the moon's glow, and as it closed on him, he could see a long scar on its snout. Its hoary pelt didn't seem of this earth.

And then the bear sighted him.

It roared and shook its head. Then it charged, closing the distance quickly. Thompson aimed for the heart and squeezed the trigger.

The bullet hit high in the bear's shoulder and threw the beast to the side. It bellowed in pain but didn't slow.

This is the end, Thompson thought.

The bear smashed into him and launched him into the canyon wall. Then it kept going, charging past him with a limp until it rounded a curve and disappeared.

For one moment, he was washed over by a wave of relief, and then he thought of his wife.

What if she hadn't come up here at all but had turned back to the lagoon or the confluence of the West Fork?

Then the wounded, angry bear would be heading right for her.

"Margaret!" he screamed. He turned and ran after the bear.

It was late in the evening by the time he made it back to the lagoon. He glanced around. No sign of Margaret. He was about to anxiously return to their cabin when he saw the bear again.

It was moving through the high grass on the other side of the clearing. It was limping heavily, and it growled low, in pain.

Thompson inched closer, trying to get a clear shot. A large log blocked his way, and he ducked low to crawl under it. When he came up on the other side, the bear was gone.

He spun in a circle, checking the clearing through his sights.

And then the bear was before him.

He tried to raise his rifle and get a shot off, but the bear's paw swiped down and knocked him into a tree.

He crumpled there, and the world went black.

When he awoke, the sun was streaming down through the forest canopy. At first, he didn't know where he was, but the pain brought things back in focus.

His arm was bruised and tender where the bear had struck him, but he didn't think it was broken. His head was caked with blood — he must have slammed it into the tree.

When he stood, it was on shaky legs. He scanned the clearing and finally exhaled when he saw no bear sign.

He looked at the rock in the middle of the lagoon, and suddenly his heart stopped. There, lying on the rock, was his wife.

"Margaret!" he screamed and ran to her.

She was unconscious; her clothes were filthy, torn, and covered with mud. He tried to lift her, and she winced. Her left shoulder was bleeding. As she slowly opened her eyes, relief flooded over him.

"I'm gonna get you home," he said as he helped her to her feet.

They limped along slowly, her arms around his neck. Thompson didn't dare mention what he had seen on the way back, and Margaret didn't offer a word either.

# Chapter Forty-two

*I*t took Howard a month to get to Flagstaff. Being a bent old man of sixty-three, he didn't think the sheriff would waste a posse trying to track him down, but he may have printed "wanted" posters, so he thought it best to lay low and avoid towns.

He had found some dried meat in Shadow's saddlebags — along with a flint and a small Carborundum stone for sharpening his knife — and between that and Mattie's pie, he went for a while without worrying about food. Mattie had also strapped his rifle and a Colt pistol to the saddle and had packed ammunition for both.

He traveled slowly through the Transverse ranges, following ancient, well-worn trails up and into the San Gabriel Mountains. Shadow seemed to sense his mood and plodded along without complaint until they reached the desert.

Following a very short springtime, summer had descended upon the Mojave Desert that year with excruciating heat. The harsh sunlight seemed to penetrate to the farthest reaches of his mind, engaging his very soul to confront his guilt over the killing of the sheepherder.

He wondered if the man had a family. In the newspaper, he'd read his name: Ydeliomen Ustaun.

That's a strange name if I ever heard one, he thought.

His memory of the afternoon was vague and as angry as he'd been over the way the sheepherders were encroaching on his land, he never wanted to kill the man. It was that damn nightmare that confused everything.

Nancy might have helped him reconcile it in his mind, but she was gone.

"Didn't even mean to do it," he said out loud.

But the cruel sun wouldn't leave him alone, and he rode on, head bent, arms limp, while his mind was chanting the man's name, over and over: *Ydeliomen... Ydeliomen... Ydeliomen...*

His lower back started to ache. The slug from the gunshot in the Mexican-American war was still lodged there. Shot in the back, he thought sadly. The Joshua trees offered no shade, and it seemed he was always riding straight into the hot wind.

The rising sun burned in his eyes as he started east each morning. But he had to be on the lookout for rattlers — Mojave Greens — who possessed the deadliest venom in the southwest.

A couple of afternoons ago, he had almost been thrown off his horse when Shadow reared up in the face of an agitated snake with its rattle vibrating wildly. But he managed to stay in the saddle and back her away.

"There, there," he said to the horse to calm her down, stroking her neck.

When they were clear of the snake, he hopped down and inspected her feet to make sure she hadn't got bit. His heart ached when he thought of Mattie and how much she loved the horse she'd given him to escape.

"Those guys get grumpy when bothered," he told Shadow, "let's try to give 'em a wider berth."

They continued. A ghost on a tumbleweed, blowing east.

He barely remembered using the Whipple Trail, although later figured he must have. Or the climb up onto the Colorado Plateau. He arrived in Flagstaff dust-covered, with a sunburned face and bloodshot eyes.

The town was booming with the anticipated arrival of the Atlantic and Pacific railroads. Men were busy bricking up a new Brennan merchant building, some were leveling the proposed path of the tracks through town, and still, others were working in a new lumber mill that had been tasked with producing railroad ties.

Howard disliked the commotion. It reminded him of the gold rush in forty-nine: too many desperate men hoping that fast money would fix all their problems.

He thought of his old friend, Willie.

At the Brennan building, he talked to the foreman, a guy named Lockett, about employment. He hadn't spoken for so long that his voice was a hoarse whisper.

"Hello," he said, taking off his hat. He cleared his throat. "I need a job."

Lockett sized him up. "Well, you're big enough, but aren't you a tad old to be swinging a sledge?"

Howard still swaggered in the desert heat—sun-bitten. He wanted to tell the man he was stronger than most of the men he'd known, but he couldn't find the words.

Lockett noticed Howard's rifle.

"There're a lot of hungry men here," Lockett said, "I'd suggest hunting. Bring me some meat, and I'll pay cash for it."

"I'll do that," said Howard, nodding, but in his mind, he saw Willie's mangled body in the bear's den.

Lockett stuck out his hand and introduced himself, and Howard almost gave the man his real name.

"Howard," he said, then after a pause, he added, "Charley Smith Howard."

Lockett escorted him to the door. "Okay, Charley, I hope to see you soon."

And so Howard went back to hunting.

He set up camp at the mouth of the West Fork, just a short way downstream from the quiet lagoon he'd visited four years earlier when he'd plunged into the water. He began building a cabin there, and he hoped to have it completed before winter.

One morning he followed the creek downstream, about two-thirds of the way to the valley below, but stopped when he saw a small cabin by a recently plowed field.

The place looked well-tended with stacks of firewood, a smoke shed for drying meat, and even a few newly planted apple trees.

Clothes were hanging from a line in the back, and a closer glance confirmed that there were a woman's garments as well as a man's.

There was nobody home at the little place when he came through, and he was glad. The fact that another soul lived in the canyon bothered him and put him in a bad mood.

He quickly got out of there, heading back up the canyon.

Sitting on the plateau's rim, hot, black, porphyritic rock beneath him, Howard let his legs dangle over a drop of several hundred feet. A warm, dry wind rushed up at him, smelling of sagebrush and juniper.

He did most of his hunting on the plateau, amongst the whispering pines and the racing clouds, the snow-capped San Francisco Peaks in the distance. Lots of mule deer inhabited the area, and he'd come across several large herds of elk. When he killed an animal, it was easier to transport the meat to Flagstaff, too.

He liked it better up here: the air was clean and fresh, and he was alone with his thoughts. Moreover, he didn't have any neighbors, which pleased him more than anything.

Lockett was always glad to see him. He had started to call him "Bear" after a customer referred to Howard like that. The man had come from California with the railroad and remembered Howard from his days hunting for the forty-niners. He'd never known him personally but said he would never forget the sight of "Bear" Howard returning from the hills.

"That's a different guy," said Howard, hoping to keep his identity shrouded. But Lockett called him Bear, regardless, which only made him want to retreat deeper into the wilderness.

Through his explorations, Howard found a section of the plateau that extended to the east in a peninsula of land covering about ten square miles. It was bordered on the east by Oak Creek, on the south by the Verde Valley, and to the north by West Fork.

He called this his Kingdom.

It will be too cold to remain here year-round, he thought, but until winter is a bit closer, I won't worry about it. He stayed there as much as he could, sleeping in the open by a fire.

He tossed a pinecone into the abyss and wondered what others would think of his Kingdom. There were meadows up here and even a few alpine ponds, but it wasn't the idyllic pastures that most thought of when it came to conventionally beautiful landscapes.

Yet, he found the place magnificent. It was still wild. Mountain lions and bears, wolves and coyotes called this their home. Along with renegade Apaches and outlaws.

"Hope that keeps the civilized folks scared away," he said, chuckling.

Below him, the land fell away into intricately eroded red rock canyons, buttes and mesas. It was breathtakingly beautiful and also desolate once you veered away from the ribbon of light green around the creek, where the willows and cottonwoods were sticking close to the water.

Mostly he stayed put on the plateau, walking along the rim, staring down at the valley below.


From time to time, he returned to work on his cabin by the West Fork, but that required riding back toward Flagstaff for ten miles, cutting east to the escarpment into Oak Creek Canyon, and then riding down to the West Fork.

A journey of well over fifteen miles.

He started to scout for a shortcut. He thought about dropping straight into the West Fork from the rim but couldn't find an easy way down into the canyon that was suitable for Shadow.

A trail down into Oak Creek Canyon posed similar challenges. When he walked east, he could follow a path along the plateau that first gradually led down toward the creek but then slanted steeply. In just over a mile, the land dropped almost two thousand feet.

As he scouted this route, he decided that his horse could make it if he switched back and forth along the steep slopes. And from the trail's proposed terminus by the creek, he only had to walk a mile to his cabin.

Over the coming months, he worked on building this trail, edging it into the steep embankment where needed, and dragging dead wood and debris out of the way. In the end, he would build over thirty switchbacks to make the grade gentle enough for Shadow.

And once the trail was laid out, Howard had Shadow help him build it out. One afternoon he led her all the way down to the creek for the first time. She descended confidently, a basket with rope, a shovel and a pick strapped to her. When they reached the creek, they found a young man sitting in the shade of an ancient cottonwood.

"That's quite a trail you're building," said Thompson.

Howard eyed the young guy, a staid expression on his face. He could see the man had been in some kind of scrape, his face bruised and scabbed. "That your cabin down the creek?" he asked.

The man nodded. "It is—I'm Jim Thompson."

They stared at each other while the gurgling creek flowed by.

Howard didn't offer his name but eventually broke the silence, saying, "I guess that makes us neighbors."

Howard disliked the idea, but Thompson welcomed it.

"Well, I'm glad to have someone else around."

Shadow stood nearby and started to step nervously. Howard eyed the horse and said, "I guess I should be going."

"Don't go just yet," Thompson said, "I haven't talked to anyone besides my Margaret for a while."

He scratched his head. "Think you might come by for dinner some time? I know Margaret would like to meet you."

Howard shifted uneasily and glanced around, appearing about as restless as his horse. "I suppose I could."

Thompson extended his hand. "You come by anytime."

The thought of a social engagement made Howard antsy. He would rather face a mountain lion than be civil to strangers.

Whether it be a gold rush or a railroad, men seemed hell-bent willing to kill each other over stupid things — and he no longer wanted a part of their pernicious world.

He realized if he ever were to expect any peace from his neighbor, he'd have to find a back way into the West Fork. That way, I won´t run into him, he thought.

For a week, he traveled up and down the northern rim of his Kingdom. Below, the West Fork wound like a centipede, a labyrinth of red and yellow canyons.

He could descend near its source, far to the west, but that would make a long, twelve-mile walk to the mouth of the canyon, where it flowed into Oak Creek and his cabin lay.

But then he spotted a narrow canyon with promise.

From the rim, he could see that only the first few hundred feet of the canyon looked difficult; there, the land dropped steeply. After that, a smaller canyon descended more gradually, and where it merged with the West Fork was only six miles from his cabin.

Not bad, he thought. Now I must find a way down.

Howard lay on his belly, staring down into a canyon that ended abruptly, right below him, at a towering sandstone cliff. The sun and rain had worn down the rock, and there were few handholds. He was looking for a shelf to which he could descend because he didn't have enough rope to drop the total distance.

One side of the canyon was clad in tall pines. The walls were steep, but somehow the trees had found purchase.

He stood up and walked along the edge of the plateau. One step too close, and he would tumble into the abyss below his feet. He uncoiled his rope, found the middle, and looped it around a tree. Gripping the rope tightly, he leaned back over the edge and descended.

The pine needles made for slippery footing, and he scratched his way backward through thick clusters of dead limbs. Before he reached the end of the rope, he made sure he was wedged safely behind a pine trunk, then he retracted the rope and slung it around the next tree.

In this manner, he reached the upper end of the canyon. From there, he could easily descend. He coiled up his rope and had shouldered it when he noticed a small seep of water flowing out of a talus slope of loose rock.

The canyon wall rose sharply before him, but at his feet, broken rock and dirt had piled up into a long slope descending to the canyon floor. A large rectangular boulder stuck out directly in front of him, and beneath it, a dark circle marked the hillside.

Here, water seeped out and eventually trickled down the canyon. He inspected it closer, hoping there might be enough water for a drink.

There was indeed a small pool, but something unexpected caught his eye when Howard bent down to drink.

"I'll be damned!" he exclaimed.

It was gold. Just a few flecks, but enough to know there could be more.

He squatted in the shade of a juniper and looked at the dark patch where the water puddled, about twenty feet away.

"I've got no use for you," he said out loud to the gold flecks.

But still, he didn't leave.

And then two red-tailed hawks swooped over his head, so low he could hear their feathers rustling. They reached the bottom of the canyon, banked up and to the left, and then spiraled below him.

The sight made him think of his wife.

He walked over and stared at the gold again, then laughed and began his descent of the canyon — Itzel Canyon.

In a few hours, he reached his cabin.

* * *

I sat at our table and watched Jim, who cleared the dishes with a somber expression. My arm was in a sling, and there was a red spot on the bandage by my clavicle.

On a wood stove in the corner, the remnants of our dinner sat in a cast-iron skillet.

"That was mighty fine," said Jim, trying to lighten the mood. A few months ago, he wanted nothing more than to live out his days in the canyon with his new bride — me. But the event at the lagoon had changed him.

Still, it was good to see him trying.

I nodded, pleased he liked it, but I was still not entirely myself either.

Suddenly, I heard footsteps in the yard. The mule brayed.

"Who could that be?" I asked. I grabbed the rifle and cocked it with my good arm. Jim stuck his pistol in his belt, behind his back.

"Might be old man Howard," said Jim. "I mentioned I invited him by." I glanced out the window and scowled. "The one the merchant in Flag calls Bear?"

Jim nodded, and I added, "Bit late for visitors."

A knock on the door.

Jim answered it while I had my rifle pointed at the door.

A white-haired, full-bearded man stood in the dark, trying to peer into the cabin. It wasn't Howard.

"My name's Richard Wilson," said the stranger and extended his hand. He wore a vest made from bear fur and smelled ripe.

Jim nodded and backed up a half-step but didn't invite him in. "What can I do for you, Mr. Wilson?"

Wilson's eyes landed on me, and he looked me up and down. I kept the rifle pointed at him.

"Oh, my," he laughed. "I'm sorry if I disturbed you, ma'am."

"Not at all," I said, "You just tell us what you're doin' here."

Wilson held up a note and said, "I was passing through Camp Verde and saw that you needed a hand."

Jim nodded. "That was a while ago," he said, but he knew they could use help. "I've got crops that need planting, and I want to put on a new roof — are you handy?"

Wilson laughed. "I can do just about anything. My true calling is bear huntin', but I do what I can to stay afloat. And I hope to remain in this area for a while, so I'll take whatever work you got."

"Okay," said Jim. "I'll set you up in the shed."

"Come in," I said, and after he was seated, I closed the door.

While Jim collected a lamp and a blanket, I spooned some dinner onto a plate. "You must be hungry," I said

"Why thank you," he said. "I'm sorry we got off on the wrong foot—you can call me Bear."

I raised my hand to my mouth, attempting to cover the giggle that tried to sneak out. "I'm afraid I can't," I said. "We already got a Bear living in Oak Creek, and he's bigger than you."

I was, of course, referring to Mr. Howard, but Wilson took my meaning differently. "I know that beast," he said. "I saw it a few months ago when I was passing through here."

I slowly turned and faced him, and Jim froze in his attempt to light the lantern and listened.

Wilson scratched his unruly beard and pondered the memory.

He said, "I was camping south of the rim, hoping to reach Camp Verde the next day, when I was awoken in the middle of the night. I tried to get to my rifle, but before I could, a large bear tore right through my camp. He was running like the devil."

"Was it a Grizz?" I asked hesitantly.

Wilson nodded. "It sure was. But different from any I've ever seen. It was big and old and silver in the moonlight. And he had a big scar across his snout."

Jim returned with a lit kerosene lamp. "I've never seen a bear like that," he lied. "I bet it was just moving through."

"Well, I been chasin' bears all my life, and I'll tell you one thing—I'm not leaving until I kill that one."

Jim and I exchanged a glance. "Let me get you settled," he said to Wilson. When he opened the door, an owl's cry filled the night, and all the hair on the back of my neck stood on end.

# Chapter Forty-three

## Act II

### 1880
(May)

Jim and I lay on a blanket, a stone's throw from the creek. Butterflies fluttered about us in dappled splashes of sunshine. It was mid-day, and the coolness of the morning still clung to the quiet meadow we had set out to enjoy.

A little over a year had passed since the fateful picnic by the lagoon, but the echo of the events of that evening still resounded in each of us. I watched him, concerned.

After what I went through that night, you'd think that I'd be afraid of this place. But I'm not.

Now it's Jim I'm concerned about.

When I first met him, I was just a girl, but I could read people even then. Mother always said I had the gift.

He was young and full of dreams and plans, but even then, I could see he was damaged. During the years when he was adventuring on the Colorado, he seemed to have fended off his demons — for a while.

But when he witnessed the Apaches being marched out of Indian Gardens, old memories of his time as a prisoner in the war had been stirred up, and the latest events by the lagoon had plunged him even deeper into his internal turmoil.

I snuck a glance at him, lying by my side.

His skin was pale, his eyes sunken, and there was a nervousness about him as he watched the canyon walls.

I snuggled against him, hoping the news I was about to deliver would lighten his mood. Dragonflies and moths buzzed over us in ecstatic confusion.

The birds had returned with the spring. They chirped and twittered around us, chasing each other. I tried to engage Jim in a game of identifying them.

"Did you see that oriole?" I asked. The bird darted over us several times in a blur of orange, black and white.

He glanced up, not really looking; his thoughts turned inward.

Normally he would have smirked and shrugged.

"A bird's a bird," he would say, and then I would argue that they were each unique, and I would point out the ones that I could identify.

But today, he didn't take the bait.

All around us, the flowers and shrubs were blooming, the grass under our blanket was of the deepest green, but he didn't seem to notice any of this. Instead, he stared off, his eyes unfocused.

And how it broke my heart that he couldn't savor the beauty of the meadow blanketed in a golden yellow carpet. Goldfields, sunflowers, and desert marigolds lay in bright patches, and the snakeweed and brittlebush were tipped with tiny buttery flowers.

Interspersed were purple splashes from the verbena and owl clover and the orange-red stalks of the desert globemallow.

Not three feet from Jim's head, a hummingbird hovered by the bright red flowers of an Arizona firecracker. It was so close that I was sure Jim could feel the vibration of the wings.

"How 'bout that one?" I asked, knowing he knew what a hummingbird was.

But again, he gave it a bland stare.

I sighed. "Okay, sit up."

He did so, stiffly and reluctantly.

"Look around," I demanded, firmly but kindly.

The insects had returned from their winter slumber, and the fresh air was filled with commotion as flycatchers and swallows chased them. In a nearby juniper, filled with fat violet berries, a mockingbird called for its mate, and several mourning doves cooed softly from under the lower limbs.

And the trees around us swayed, bathing in the breeze and the soft sunshine. It was as if the meadow was breathing. The profusion of life that had returned to our little canyon was simply splendid, and if it hadn't been for the haunting, overwhelming memories of the night of the silver bear, we would have been quite content.

What I do recollect is like a dream. One moment I was waking up on the flat rock in the lagoon; the next, I was listening to a blissful wordless melody as I floated along the creek, chasing it.

And that song had stayed with me.

Even now, it soothes me while I observe the chaotic, crazy festival of life that is spring. It flows with me, and I with it.

I am not alone.

But Jim, my poor Jim, walked away with something different.

I didn't remember seeing him that night. I didn't remember being shot either.

But he was the only one there with a gun.

And later, one glance in his eyes told me I could never ask him about it. So, this ominous night existed in silence, and we never spoke of it.

But that only made it worse because now he didn't trust anything. The unknown had surfaced before us, and now to him, the whole world seemed to feel unpredictable.

He didn't think he could protect me.

He thought of himself as a failure. I could see it.

I stood and offered my hand. If only he knew that I could take care of myself.

He weakly gripped my fingers, stood, and allowed me to lead him across the meadow. I stopped before a large agave that had sent up a strong shoot. It looked like a giant stalk of asparagus.

"You know what this is?" I asked.

He nodded. "That's an agave."

I placed my hand on the shoot. It was only two feet tall, but there seemed some urgency to it like it was ready to burst upward.

"I'm told these can grow a foot a day this time of the year," I said. "And that if you put your hand on it, you can feel it grow."

He nodded but didn't move, so I took his hand and placed it on the compact green bud.

He gave me a weak smile, but then it slumped, and he said, "I can't feel it."

Then I took his hand and placed it on my belly.

"How about this?" I asked.

He glanced at me, confused, and then suddenly, there was a new light in his sad eyes. They teared up, and I could feel him trembling. "You're pregnant?" he asked.

I nodded. And he smiled again. But this was a genuine smile, and I soaked it up.


Howard ambled down the path, heading for the Thompson place. He'd promised Jim Thompson twice now that he would stop by.

He would have rather had a tooth yanked.

He didn't feel like being neighborly, but he'd shared the canyon with Thompson for a few years now and felt it was time.

About a mile from the cabin, he caught a flicker of movement and spied the young couple sitting on a blanket in a clearing along the creek.

He didn't want to intrude, but there was no point continuing to their cabin if they were here. He crossed the meadow, shouting, "Hello!"

Thompson sat up.

As Howard came closer, all the air rushed out of his lungs, and his heart began beating wildly. There, next to Jim Thompson on the blanket, sat his Nancy.

I watched the tall man stroll across the clearing. Unkempt beard, long, tangled black hair; there was a wildness about him. Something feral. He scanned both sides of the meadow as if he suspected an ambush.

Instinctively I reached for our pistol, which lay in Jim's holster by the edge of the blanket.

Jim touched my forearm. "It's okay," he said, "I know him."

The man called out, and Jim waved to him.

And then the man stopped a few paces away and gawked.

He stared at me, dumbfounded: a towering dark shadow that swayed with the wind.

I glanced back, unabashed. From his expression, I could tell he held me no ill will—but rather, that he thought I was someone he knew.

Someone he loved, I realized, the longer he was held speechless.

Jim tried to break the spell with an introduction.

"Honey," he said, "this is Mr. Howard. He's got that place by the mouth of the West Fork."

I knew, of course, whom he meant. We'd often talked about our elusive neighbor. Although he lived only a few miles up the creek from us, neither of us had set foot in the West Fork since the night at the lagoon. If he were home that night, we wouldn't have known, but from what I'd heard from the trader in Flagstaff, he spent most of his time up on the plateau anyway.

I knew Mr. Howard had to be in his sixties, and he stood like an old stovepipe, bent in weird angles in a few places. And yet, he radiated the strength of a much younger man.

He peered at me closely, and he looked like he was questioning his sanity.

"Mr. Howard," I said as I extended my hand up to him. "How nice to finally meet you."

In slow motion, he grasped my hand.

His eyes dropped to it, taking in every detail. Then they swept over my hair and my face and finally settled on my eyes.

"Ma'am," he managed to whisper.

"And this is Margaret," said Jim.

Mr. Howard nodded, then slowly shook his head.

"My, how you look like my Nancy," he said, softening.

I could feel his sadness seeping through his words.

"Is she passed?" I asked softly.

He nodded again. "Must be twenty years now. She was sixteen when we married, and me, thirty-four."

"Why, that's almost the same as Jim and I!" I said, standing, only to find I still had to look up at his face. He truly was a giant of a man.

Suddenly his eyes became dead serious.

He glared at Jim and said, "You take good care of her."

A bit defiantly, Jim replied, "I'll do my best."

I chanced a playful squeeze of Mr. Howard's arm and said, "He'd better — there's going to be three of us soon."

I patted my belly.

Mr. Howard's face melted into a crooked smile. "Well, that's about the best news I've heard in a long time. Congratulations!"

Jim blushed. "I just found out myself."

"Mr. Howard," said Jim and stood up, "I would like to show you around my place if you have a minute."

The older man began to protest, falling back on his reticence to socialize, but he conceded as soon as I spoke. "We're all going to have some fresh apple pie! I've kept this secret long enough. I want to celebrate! And I'd like you to join us."

"Okay, ma'am," he said. "I will join you for a bit. And if you need anything at all in the coming months, just let me know."

He was so different from what I'd expected. I glanced up at him. "Well, Mr. Howard, I hear you spend a lot of time on the plateau — do you ever venture near Munds Park?"

Howard scratched his beard thoughtfully. "I know where it is, but I don't have any need to go there directly," he said.

I must have frowned because he immediately asked, "Why are you interested in Munds Park if you don't mind my askin'?"

"My Pa is summerin' there, and I'd sleep better at night knowing someone checked in on him from time to time."

"That would be no problem at all," he said.

I felt emboldened by his compliance and couldn't stop the giggle that flowed out before I asked, "I hear you do not seek the company of other people much, Mr. Howard. Do you not like company?"

We began walking down the creek while he pondered my question. Soon he said, "In general, I don't mind most folks, but if you're being particular, I'd have to say I like some people and dislike others."

I couldn't help but pester him with another question. "And do you have any children?"

At this, his face broke into a smile, far deeper and more relaxed than his demeanor suggested he was capable of.

"Yes, I have two—and two grandbabies," he said, beaming, "I'm gonna bring them all out here one of these days."

We continued, our place just around the corner. With Jim ahead of me and Mr. Howard behind, I felt as safe as houses.

At Thompson's cabin, by the site where the old wickiups had stood, Richard Wilson rubbed salt into a wolf hide, preparing to stretch it. He looked up briefly and nodded curtly at Margaret and Jim Thompson and paused when he saw Howard.

"Howdy, folks," he said.

Margaret did the introductions and then said, "If you gentlemen will excuse me, I need to go warm up a pie."

Wilson went back to work, and the two other men sat down in the shade and watched him. Leaning against a tree was a Sharps

.50 caliber rifle. Howard eyed it for a minute, then extended his hand but stopped and looked at Wilson.

"May I?" he requested.

Wilson nodded a bit reluctantly.

Howard hefted it and stared down the sights and said, "I heard Billy Dixon used one of these at the battle of Adobe Walls and dropped an Injun at fifteen hundred yards."

Wilson was watching the man nervously; he let very few people handle his gun. Finally, Howard set the gun back down, and Wilson said, "Shoot today, kill tomorrow," then asked, "Have you seen battle?"

"Yes, I have. The Mexican War. I served under Sam Houston," said Howard. He rubbed his lower back. "Still got a Mexican slug in my back."

Thompson nodded. He said, "I took a bullet in Georgia when Sherman made his push for the sea. Got captured there, too."

"What did you do during the war, Mr. Wilson?" asked Howard.

Both men turned and looked at the old hunter.

Wilson had started poking holes in the hide and running leather strips through them.

"Well," he began and then paused. "Arkansas was far behind me when the war started—I'd already gone west. So, I guess I never really considered it *my* war."

Howard stared off, watching the creek, and Thompson nodded.

A gleam entered Wilson's eye, and suddenly he grinned.

"Don't get me wrong, I've done my share of killin'—just not blue or grey coats. Killed just 'bout every animal we got in the west and a few men if'n I'm bein' honest."

Howard held the man's eyes. "I suppose we've all done some killin'."

Wilson chuckled. "Well, I had my reasons. All I want now is to kill that big silver Grizz I saw a while back down in here—know anything about him?"

Howard raised an eyebrow. "Ain't seen many bear around here at all. Got some up on the plateau, but they're mostly black, no Grizz."

Wilson scratched his mop of white hair. "I ain't hunted much above the rim—maybe I should give that a shot."

Howard cleared his throat. "I'm here being neighborly, so I'll say this politely: I'd prefer if you hunted somewhere else."

Wilson's eyes narrowed and bore into Howard. "I suppose you don't want me venturing into the West Fork either."

Howard shrugged. "No, I reckon not. It's kinda my backyard."

Wilson sat back, several leather thongs still in his hand, his project only halfway finished.

He squinted. "Mr. Howard, I think you're hiding something."

Howard laughed. It was a deep, rich laugh that concealed nothing. "All I'm doing is protecting my privacy. What else would there be?" he asked.

But Wilson's eyes were alert, his demeanor edgy. "There's plenty you could be hidin'. You ever seen signs of the Lost Coconino?"

"That old mine?" asked Howard. "I heard of it but never saw nothin' that made me feel I found it."

"Nothin'? Really? You never came across any timber supports in a cave or telltale marks from a miner's pick on a wall?"

Howard laughed. "Nope. Wouldn't be interested even if I did—I'm done with gold."

Wilson shook his head. "I won't call you a liar, Mr. Howard, but I'm not sure if'n I believe you."

The hair on the back of Howard's neck stood on end, and he was about to rise and confront the man when Wilson turned his attention to Thompson.

"And I'd really like to know what you're hiding," he said.

"Me?" asked Thompson.

"Yes, you. I show up here a year ago, and your wife's been shot, clearly, but nobody will talk about it. And you both turn real pale whenever I mention that bear—but again, nobody's seen it."

267

Thompson stood and brushed his pants off. "I've got nothing to hide from you, Mr. Wilson. We've been over this."

Wilson looked at the ground. "Shit, I'm not tryin' to take anything from either of you—I'm just due for some good luck. For a break. And I'm gonna keep searchin' 'till I get one."

Later, Thompson and Howard stood by the path, not far from the cabin. The sunset was long past, and the sky peppered with brilliant stars. Several bats hunted above them.

"You know, I've been planning on building another cabin by the mouth of Oak Creek Canyon—down in the valley," said Thompson. "Now that Margaret is pregnant, I think I should get on it. There are a few other settlers there, and it might be helpful when the baby is born."

"Sounds prudent," said Howard.

Thompson was hoping not to offend his only neighbor. "And I reckon I'll leave Wilson here to watch over the place and tend to the crops."

Howard sighed. He turned and spat.

"You don't think much of Mr. Wilson, do you?" asked Thompson.

The tall man peered into the darkness.

Finally, he said, "I heard down in the valley you can get mail—could I possibly give your address to my Mattie?"

Thompson nodded. "You sure can."

"Good then," said Howard, placing a hand on Thompson's shoulder. "I'll be seeing you soon."

And then the old man headed up the mountain, using his steep burro trail, to his Kingdom on the plateau.

# Chapter Forty-four

## 1881

$A$ gentle breeze blew over the plateau, the pines swaying with it as if to music. The forests here were interspersed with numerous meadows, and many had secluded alpine ponds.

Howard pulled on a strand of barb wire until it was taught, connecting the trunks of two towering pines. Thick gloves protected his hands as he leaned back, putting his weight into it.

Satisfied, he wrapped the wire around a nail he'd already set in the stout tree. "That'll do," he said to himself. He took off his gloves and stretched his fingers, then surveyed the repair he'd just completed.

His fence now stretched from the south rim of the West Fork to the plateau's rim facing the Verde Valley. It was only a mile and a half long, but that little fence effectively staked out his Kingdom.

Ten square miles, he thought, and almost all of it protected by the steep canyon cliffs on three sides.

He was alone out here. The closest person was miles away. Even Shadow was absent—corralled in the West Fork for now.

Two black mules watched from an alpine pond, about fifty feet away. He would have preferred burros for his trail down into Oak Creek Canyon. Unfortunately, the mules were too large for that kind of work, and they were skittish around heights.

But they could pull a big load and were perfect for hauling a wagon on the dirt road to Flagstaff, and that's what he needed right now.

269

He continued along the fence, removing dead limbs that had fallen with the wind. The elk and mule deer could easily jump over the fence, but sometimes they didn't see it and smashed right through.

He found no other breaks but decided to get some fabric when he went to Flagstaff next and tie off strands where his fence crossed a deer run.

Near the rim, an old Indian trail followed the plateau, and here he had made a gate.

Just inside the gate, a large wagon sat parked in the shade. His rifle was propped against the wagon's only bench, next to his hat.

He sat on the bench and ate a lunch of jerky and bread.

He was about to lay down in the back of the wagon and take a nap when he caught a flicker of movement to the west. Beyond his fence, across a flat meadow, he glimpsed a dozen deer standing in the shade of a cluster of small pines.

He sat up and put on his hat.

"Time to go to work," he whispered to himself.

The first thing he did was swing open the gate.

He retrieved a bucket from the back of the wagon and filled it with a handful of grain from a burlap sack. Then he grabbed a bridle and horse blanket and walked toward the pond.

He shook the bucket and whistled.

The mules lifted their heads, as did the deer, but the only animal that moved was the mule missing an ear—Diggy. He took a few tentative steps toward Howard, who lowered the bucket and shook it again.

"That's right, boy," he said softly, "come on over."

Soon the mule was by Howard's side, nibbling grain from the bucket.

While Diggy was distracted, Howard put on the bridle and blanket, and as the mule was swiping up the last of the grain, Howard hopped on his back.

Howard leaned over and grabbed his rifle from the wagon as they passed through the open gate.

It didn't take him long to circle and get behind the deer. They seemed curious about Diggy but not alarmed.

When he was in place, Howard raised his rifle and sighted in on a large doe. He clenched his knees right before he fired to alert Diggy and to hold on in case the mule bolted.

A thunderous boom shook the forest.

Diggy jumped slightly like he'd been shocked but then remained still. The doe dropped as the other deer bounded off to the east.

Howard smiled as he watched them leap away, out of sight in three hops. They went straight into his Kingdom, some through the open gate, others over the fence.

He put another bullet in the chamber, pocketed the empty brass casing, and nudged Diggy toward the gate.

Over the next few hours, Howard and Diggy slowly pursued the deer. He used the rim to funnel them into dead ends, and he managed to shoot four more before they escaped across his fence to safety beyond.

When the shooting was done, he returned to the wagon. It took a little coaxing to get the other mule, Bagga, to come over, but eventually, he had both mules in the wagon's harness.

Now came the hard work.

He rode the wagon to each felled deer, gutted it, and then hoisted the carcass up into the wagon. He left the skins on for now because they'd keep the flies off for a while. He also kept the heart, kidneys and liver, letting them air-dry. Then he rubbed the innards with salt from several barrels on the wagon and packaged them with brown paper and twine.

The sun had set by the time he finished with the fifth deer.

In the descending coolness, he directed Diggy and Bagga north toward Flagstaff. He hoped to cover the twenty miles in the chill of the night and not have to worry about the meat spoiling.

Above him, a million stars glittered. Bats scurried about, chasing insects, and myriad fireflies lighted the meadows.

Abraham James was quite pleased with himself as he surveyed his summer camp on the plateau. The cool May weather on the highland suited him, and there was something grand about the ponderosa pines.

Elizabeth had gone to the pond to do laundry, dragging James and David with her and leaving him in a rare moment of solitude.

He imagined Page Springs would be nice about now. The prickly pear would be blossoming, with beautiful yellow and fuchsia flowers, and the grackles no doubt were still singing the sun up as it rose over the calm waters of the creek.

But it would grow warmer every day, and the older Abraham got, the more he hated the heat.

He was contemplating his day's chores when he saw the wagon approach. He recognized Bear Howard at the reins and waved him over. This was the third time Howard had come by since talking to Margaret at her cabin at Indian Gardens.

"Hello, sir!" shouted Abraham.

Howard pulled the mules to a stop and nodded. Diggy stood unconcerned while Bagga eyed a patch of green grass a few paces away.

"You coming or going?" asked Abraham.

"Goin'. Finished my business in Flag this morning, and now I'm on my way back to the rim."

"And when you going to see my girl again?" he asked.

Howard scratched his bearded chin. "I suppose I'll be down there in a day or two. You good here? Need anything?"

Abraham sighed. "I don't think so — but thank you for asking."

Howard raised his reins, preparing to go, when Abraham said, "Come to think of it, I could use one thing."

Howard stared expectantly until Abraham said, "I'd like to walk down to see Margaret from time to time, and I'd like to do it without my whole brood, but the valley is too far for me to walk in a day. And I noticed you're not often at your cabin on the West Fork. Do you think I could bed down there when I'm heading to the Thompson place?"

Howard didn't like company and tried to think of a way out of the request.

Abraham added, "When she was at Indian Gardens, I could make it, but the valley is another six miles downstream."

Howard thought of Margaret, and his Nancy floated before his eyes for a moment. Then, finally, he said, "Sure. I'm barely there. Treat it like it's your place."

Abraham reached into a bag by his side, pulled out a loaf of bread and handed it to Howard. "Take this. My wife baked it this morning."

Howard's sour mien mellowed a bit. "I enjoyed the last loaf. Thank you."

With that, he snapped the reins, and he was off.


Two western bluebirds chased a jay through the branches of a juniper, screeching playfully, until a terrifying cry burst through the window of a log cabin, shattering the morning.

Suddenly the birds were dead silent.

The cry came again, now rising to a wail.

My son, Frankie, wanted the entire world to know even six-month-olds had terrible days.

I emerged from the door of our cabin down in the valley, the infant clutched in my arms. We called the place Camp Kitchen. It sat at the mouth of Oak Creek Canyon on a rise that overlooked a bend in the creek.

I bounced the infant, trying my best to distract him.

"Come on, Frankie," I pleaded. "Be a good boy."

Jim exited the cabin and sat on a log, staring at the infant and me. He sighed, "Do you think we'll ever get a good night's sleep again?"

I was exhausted and red-eyed but entirely enamored with the little man.

I said, "I sure hope so—but he's such a little miracle that I'll go without sleep for now."

Jim moved to my side and snuggled against the boy. He smelled his head, and the baby's scent soothed him like no other. I don't know how, but from what I could see, the smell of his child and the sound of the baby's cries had banished his demons.

Jim no longer seemed to drift through echoes of the war or even of the dark night by the lagoon. Now he simply took in life through Frank's eyes—fresh eyes.

I spied Howard on the trail, heading our way.

"Your father sends greetings," he said to me when he got closer.

"Well, thank you for checking on him, Mr. Howard," I replied. "And we have a letter for you!"

"I'll get it," said Jim and disappeared into the cabin.

By the time he returned, Frankie had begun to cry again.

Howard gaped at the infant, aghast.

"I guess it's been a while since I been near a baby," he said.

"Ain't he precious?" I asked.

It seemed Mr. Howard thought it safest not to reply and open the letter from his daughter, Mattie Purtymun, instead.

Slowly, his face relaxed, and there was a tear on one cheek when he glanced up. "Looks like I'm a grandpa again," he said. "My Mattie had her third child—another boy! Named Albert!"

Jim stepped over and shook his hand, and I hugged him, which momentarily silenced the baby.

He read a little further and then beamed. "She also says as soon as she gets back on her feet, she'll be heading this way."

"That's great news!" said Jim. "If you want to write a reply, I'll post it when I go to Camp Verde next."

"Sooner the better," said Howard, full of rare smiles.

"And something else you'll be happy to hear," said Jim. "Wilson has moved on. It'll mean I'm split between Indian Gardens and Camp Kitchen, but I know he rubbed you wrong, so I'm letting you know."

Howard grinned. "Second best news I heard all day."

The next few weeks flew by for Howard. Hunting brought in enough cash to cover his few financial requirements, but he had no incentive to do more than he needed. He didn't like excessive killing. His trail from the rim into Oak Creek was complete, and the fence on his Kingdom only occasionally required repair, so he had some time on his hands.

His mules had grown fat from lack of activity, and Shadow was fidgety—ready for an adventure. Howard was restless, too. But, at sixty-four, he was still in great shape, so he decided to explore.

With a pack full of dried meat, rope, and a loaf of Abraham's bread, he set out to the remote corners of the plateau on Shadow's back.

They would wander into the countless ravines and draws for days, losing sight of the sun in the deep canyons. He followed the West Fork back to its source, twelve miles upstream from the confluence with Oak Creek.

From Jerome, where he sold venison, he explored Sycamore Canyon, where the Spanish supposedly once searched for riches.

On one of his explorations, he decided to return to Itzel Canyon. He had to tie up Shadow and lower himself from tree to tree, down the steep drop.

He returned to the dark spot where the water trickled out under a large boulder and stared at the flow.

His gaze fell upon a small gold nugget.

He picked it up. It was round and flat, like a coin, but if there ever had been any imprints on it, they had long been polished smooth. It felt warm to his touch. Tingling, almost.

He stuck it in his vest pocket and descended to the confluence with the West Fork.

# Chapter Forty-five

*T*he burning tingle had been subtle at first. But, from the moment Howard found the gold piece, he had developed a penchant for fondling it when he hiked. After a few days he noticed a red spot on his palm, and before the week was out, it had advanced into a rash—and soon it bloomed into a blister.

But still, he couldn't leave the piece of gold alone.

He toyed with it one morning as he rode along in his wagon, up on the plateau, after dropping off some venison in Flagstaff. The primitive road he followed wound its way through tall pines whose upper branches whispered in the wind. The meadows lining the track abounded in May flowers, and birds swooped low over the few alpine ponds he passed, hunting for insects.

He thought about how his worries had all faded away: His children would join him soon, he had found a new home here, and he was slowly concluding that nobody was looking for him—the mess in California forgotten.

Yet there was still a nagging in the back of his mind, and he suspected it came from the gold nugget. No matter where he explored, he felt a tug to go back to that place where he had picked it up.

He looped out of his way a bit—'bout an hour, he thought—to visit Abraham James and his wife, Elizabeth.

When he arrived at their summer camp, the two were sitting by a fire outside their wall tent. They stood formally and greeted him as he pulled the mules to a halt. Howard lifted several jars of honey and some ribbons.

"Hello folks," he said, "check this out. I'm getting stocked up for when Mattie arrives. I suppose she's a little old for ribbons, but I didn't know what else to get."

He shrugged, "The boys'll like the honey."

Abraham talked Howard off his wagon, and he sat on an unoccupied wooden chair by the fire while Elizabeth poured him a cup of coffee.

Howard nodded thanks.

Abraham tossed a small log on the fire. "The boys are off somewhere—they'll be sad they missed you."

Howard appeared lost in his coffee as he blew on it and then carefully took a sip. Eventually, he raised his head and glanced at Elizabeth. He said, "Ma'am, the only thing better'n your coffee is your bread."

Mrs. James smiled graciously. Abraham said, "And thank you for letting me use your cabin. It's come in handy twice now."

Howard bowed his head slightly and gazed into the fire. He caressed the gold piece in his hand, trying to keep it away from the raw blister in his palm.

"What's that?" asked Abraham.

Suddenly Howard became suspicious. Why? He didn't know. He had no reason to be wary of Abraham and hadn't thought much about the gold traces he had found in Itzel Canyon.

But suddenly, he didn't want to share what he did know.

"Just a relic from my gold rush days in California," he said.

"Can I see it?" asked Abraham.

Howard handed it over, reluctantly, but as soon as he did, he felt better—as if a weight had been taken off his chest. He thought of the nagging that had repeatedly encouraged him to return to the dark spot and was glad to be done with it.

"Keep it," he said.

Abraham's face lit up as he gazed at the gold. "I believe I will," he said.

A few days later, Howard left the Thompson place in the valley — Camp Kitchen — dragging his feet as he made his way upstream. He'd only visited for a few minutes. Upon arriving, Thompson immediately handed him a letter from Mattie, and Howard tore open the envelope right away.

"Oh, how I've waited for this letter," he called out.

But Mattie wrote that she would not be coming — at least not yet. "It seems she doesn't have the money to equip a wagon and make the journey," he said sadly. "And my older boy, Jesse, isn't any better off."

Howard sensed his years descend on him and felt old for the first time. He knew he could make money and now wished he'd been working to that end. Had he known she needed money, he would have been more industrious.

Thompson sat beside him. "That's too bad. Could we help?"

"I'll be fine," said Howard and said his goodbyes and headed out the door promptly.

Halfway to his place at the mouth of the West Fork, he came across Abraham, who was staring up at some of the towering rock spires along the creek. "You know," he said, "I used to look at these rocks, and a name would just pop into my head. Like it was pre-ordained. But now I don't hear the names anymore."

Howard scratched his beard. "Well, what do you hear?"

Howard noticed for the first time that the white-haired man was gaunt, and his gaze seemed unfocused.

Abraham spoke in a whisper. "It's like there's a place out there that's calling me. It beckons constantly."

Howard glanced at Abraham's clutched hand. "Maybe you should have one of your boys accompany you when you come down to visit," he said.

"Nonsense," said Abraham. "I'll be fine."


Over the next few days Howard roamed his Kingdom, checking fences and tending to his animals. But there came a day that he rose, grabbed a shovel and rope, and walked to the steep slope that descended into Itzel Canyon. Before long, he stood before the dark indentation where the water trickled out of the talus slope.

He stared long and hard, and eventually, he began to dig.

So busy was he that he didn't notice the sky darkening.

When the downpour hit, he decided to call it a day. He leaned the shovel against the hole for when he returned and descended.

At a small pond near the exit from Itzel Canyon, he washed his face and forearms. Then he drank deeply.

It was a six-mile walk to his cabin from here. He set out at a good pace. The sandstone was shimmering with small puddles from the rain, and the temperature had dropped sharply.

About halfway, he saw something on the canyon floor ahead. He approached closer and was horrified to discover a body lying face-down, half immersed in a puddle.

He hurriedly turned it over. It was Abraham. The man was pale and shivering, and unconscious. His hand was clasped tightly, and when Howard inspected it, he saw behind the pale white fingers, the entire palm was raw.

He tried to grab the gold piece, but even in his weak condition, Abraham wouldn't surrender it.

Howard hefted the old man over his shoulders and onto his back and slowly marched back to his cabin. He feared the man would die the entire way: Abraham James was in rough condition. He coughed and hacked, and his body burned with fever.

At his cabin, Howard stripped Abraham out of his wet clothes and helped him put on some dry garments. Then he heated some stew, fed him, and put him to bed.

Abraham's skin had a terrible pallor.

Once he had fallen asleep, Howard took the gold piece out of his grip and wrapped the blistered hand in a bandage. Then he quickly hopped on Shadow and hoofed it to Camp Kitchen.

Before the night was halfway over, Margaret and her husband were standing over Abraham.

But it did no good. For two days, Abraham shivered and coughed in feverish fits, and on the morning of the third day, he died.

# Chapter Forty-six

## 1882

*H*oward crouched before the dark hole in the wall. With a focused gaze, he attempted to bore through the rock with his eyes and see what he was up against. He hated that he again craved gold. But he needed money to help his children make the journey — otherwise, he might never see them again. Unfortunately, he was still a wanted man in California, so he couldn't go to them.

He'd dug in about five feet — enough to realize he was excavating a tunnel — and then dragged out what rubble he could. The shaft seemed to lead upward, naturally, at about a forty-five-degree angle.

It was messy work. Dark, dank mud and sticks and rocks had all cemented together into a conglomerate. Jagged slabs of rock tumbled between his legs as he pulled them free. Water trickled through the mix, making for slippery footwork.

He brought a candle in to see better, but the constant dripping soon extinguished the flame. Tight quarters also prevented using the long-handled shovel, so he scraped and clawed his way upward with bare hands.

There wasn't enough water leaking through to run a sluice, but he managed to collect a wooden bucket full and kept it at the tunnel entrance.

He peered up at the hole. "What's your story?" he called into the dark.

The debris he had unearthed lay piled by the shaft entrance. In the daylight, he could see it had a coating of gold dust. It might not look like much to someone unschooled in prospecting, but there was enough there that he wanted to run all of it through a sluice and filter out the gold.

But for that, he needed water.

He picked up a fist-sized boulder that he'd knocked free, dipped it in the bucket to wash off any dirt—or gold dust—and then inspected it.

Black. Porous. Round. River-worn. Basalt.

Not what he would have expected. Why would there be river-worn stones way up here? He dunked it underwater again to ensure no gold dust clung to it. And then tossed it down the canyon.

He repeated this process with a dozen other rocks: black basalt, flat, yellow slabs of sandstone, and chunks of white limestone. A small pile of mud and pebbles remained on the ground before the shaft, and Howard picked some of it up with the shovel, and in a few scoops, moved it all to a big mound about ten feet away.

This was his slag pile. And his real dilemma.

Ideally, he would process the pile right where it lay, creating a trough and using water to filter out the gold. Then, he could simply hike out with a bag of gold. But without water, he had to contend with what could amount to a lot of mud and rock.

Through spring and into summer, Howard worked on the shaft, slowly penetrating deeper. He hoped for a good monsoon season, which would begin in a month or so. His plan involved funneling rainwater from the rim into a wooden trough, and shoveling his slag pile into the channel while the water flowed, so the mud and lighter elements could be washed away.

He glanced up at the cliff behind him, at a black line of desert varnish stretched from a break in the basalt cap. The blackened sandstone indicated where water flowed a few times a year, and he proudly surveyed his wooden trough at its base.

Now all he had to do was wait for the rains.

But Howard wasn't good at waiting. So, he built a little cabin up on the rim, about a quarter-mile from his tunnel, to pass the time. It was small with a dirt floor, a wood stove and a single bunk.

He continued to hunt and used the proceeds to purchase more lumber and nails.

Above Itzel Canyon, he erected a platform with a strong pulley which he could use to lower down gear—and possibly haul up buckets of slag. He still had no easy way to get to the plateau from the tunnel. When he did place an object in the bucket, he had to wait until the next time he was up top, after ascending via his Oak Creek Canyon trail, to pull it up.

A journey of at least six hours.

He had ruled out using the West Fork, as tempting as it appeared. Itzel Canyon was too steep, so he would have to cart the slag down to the confluence first. His mules would never fit through the long, water-filled tunnel, either.

If he couldn't process the gold in Itzel Canyon, he would rather have the slag up in his Kingdom anyway. That way, he wouldn't have to worry about anyone coming upon the big pile of gold-bearing rock and mud before he processed it.

His best option was still using the rains to filter out the gold, and as July stretched into August, he did everything he could to be ready.

"Seems the monsoon rains are gonna just pass us by this year," said Lockett, a few weeks later, as he helped Howard unload an elk carcass from his wagon.

Howard raised his head and checked the sky.

"I suppose you're right," he sighed.

Howard caught Lockett's eye. "I need to drum up some cash, Lockett. Can you take any more venison?"

Lockett scratched his head. "Bear, I got a lot of hungry men here, and they need to eat—but the railway is moving on, and soon there'll be no more work. Already, half of the men here are idle."

Howard looked away. "Well, I got no work for them."

The merchant stepped around a small rail cart.

"Wish I could pay you in small gauge rail," he said, chuckling.

Howard eyed him. "What do you mean by that?"

Lockett nodded at the dock where several piles of the steel runners were stacked up. "When they first put a railway through, they run it in small gauge. Then when they catch up with the large rail, they tear the original rail up. I thought I was smart buying it all up cheap, but now I'm stuck with it."

As Lockett walked away, Howard stared at the pile of narrow-gauge rails for a good minute. Then he found Lockett by his register and made a proposition.

"I need three miles of narrow-gauge line and a crew to lay them down—say for five days. How many elk would that cost me?"

Lockett ran through the calculations in his mind. "I could use eight elk—four next week and four a week after that—but that would only cover the crew for four days."

Howard nodded. "That's fine. I'll cut and limb my own ties and have the path laid out when they arrive."

"I can get them there in three days," said Lockett, "that enough time?"

Howard grinned, life flowing through his veins again. He'd get his family out here one way or another.

"It's gonna have to be," he said and shook hands.

Locket kicked the cart. "I'll even throw in the little wagon here."

Howard had made his preparations by the time Lockett's men showed up.

"This way, boys!" he shouted when he saw their wagon.

Starting at his little cabin, he had plotted a course southwest through the meadows and clearings in the pines for a mile up to the rim overlooking the Verde Valley, and then east for two miles where it met up with his burro trail down into Oak Creek Canyon.

The last stretch followed the ancient path along the rim.

He told everyone involved he was planning on hauling timber.

He still wasn't sure if he would bring the slag down to Oak Creek, but between the rail line and his burro trail, if he wanted to, he now he had a way to do it.

# Chapter Forty-seven

## 1884

The dancing limbs of an ocotillo were waving at Howard as he ascended the trail up Itzel Canyon. On their tips, bright red flowers burst forth.

He stopped and took off his hat to wipe his brow.

A few cicadas were welcoming the warm temperatures, rapidly clicking their mating songs. The entire length of the high cliffs above rippled with heatwaves. There were ocotillos there, too, and tall, flowering agaves as well.

He glanced around the small canyon, realizing that spring had slipped into summer. He hadn't even noticed.

These days, he spent a lot of time inside the tunnel.

At the shaft entrance, he found his tools untouched. A small miner's pick. A lantern, this one protected from the water. One bucket to collect water, and another for rocks of interest.

His slag pile had grown ten feet high, and he agonized about whether to haul it up or wait some more for the rains to arrive.

They were overdue. Again.

Howard crouched to enter the tunnel and began climbing up. He had carved out a narrow passage of about twenty feet. At the end, he lay down on his side and tied the lantern to a tightly wedged limb.

Then he started to pry loose a few more rocks with the pick.

For the next hour, he dug and prodded his way forward and up another foot. His boots repeatedly slipped in the slick mud.

There seemed to be more water seeping through from above than usual.

He wrenched free another stone, then used his fingers to dig free the soil and pebbles.

And that's when he found another treasure.

A warm buzz spread on his fingertips as he rubbed the small flat disc.

He slid out of the shaft, fingers clutched around his find.

He dunked the object in the water bucket, then held it up to the light.

Gold. A coin, he thought, although one he'd never seen the likes of before. A skull was imprinted on one side, an eagle on the other.

He stared back at the shaft and asked, "What are you doing in there?"


Over the next few weeks he discovered more coins and collected them in a bucket. One afternoon he emerged from the tunnel with a whole handful. He washed them out and added them to the bucket.

He glanced at the sky and noticed the first thunderclouds of the season. Their rumbling black underbellies floated above him, menacing but full of promise.

A good downpour would be his chance to try the trough.

But the sky only threatened to break, then cleared, and soon he climbed back into the tunnel, taking his bucket of coins with him.

He climbed up into the shaft, now about twenty-five feet long, and tied off the lantern. In the dim light, a shiny black object reflected at him. He reached for it.

His fingers encountered a Mayan dagger.

Grabbing it tightly in both hands, he yanked it out.

The bottom half of the jade shaft was broken off, but the fluted edge was intact.

A giant thunderclap resounded through the canyon. It shook the plateau, and for a moment, he thought someone had set off dynamite.

The earth above him shifted.

He scrambled down the chute and into Itzel Canyon. Chain lightning was spread across the sky, and water dropped in massive sheets.

From all around a deluge descended. He had prayed for water, but not this much all at once.

As he watched, helplessly, a waterfall formed over his trough, and its growing torrent soon smashed the wooden construction to pieces.

He had started towards it, but a nearby crack of lightning had him scurrying for cover under a boulder. Within a minute, there was no trace of the trough.

The deluge was growing still, and Howard had to retreat into the tunnel. He crawled up into the dimly lit shaft.

He gripped the walls of the chute, scrambling as high as he could.

When he reached the lantern, he realized that he'd been tightly gripping the obsidian blade all this time, and it had cut deeply into his palm.

His blood mixed with the mud and water and flowed out below him.


The storm had washed everything away: the slag pile, the trough, even his tools by the mouth of the tunnel. All Howard had left was a bucket full of coins, a Mayan dagger, a lantern, and his miner's pick.

He grabbed a handful of coins and let them fall through his fingers. The familiar warmth radiated from them, and the flesh around his fingers began to ache.

He dropped them back in the bucket.

What to do with these? He asked himself. He glanced up the cliff and was relieved to see that the platform with the pulley seemed intact. The long rope was dangling at the cliff base where the trough had once lain.

He tied the bucket to the end of the rope but knew he'd have to wait until he was on top to haul it up.

He thought of the long walk it would take to get back to Oak Creek Canyon — via the West Fork — and then use his burro trail to get on top of the plateau. It was a journey of at least six hours. It bothered him. His gold would be sitting in the bucket, unguarded, the entire time.

He didn't like it. There was nobody around, but still. He didn't like it. He glanced at the steep, pine-clad slope which he occasionally descended. He'd left several permanent ropes attached but had never attempted to go up that way.

"No time like the present," he said and headed toward the slope.

Over the next hour, Howard scrambled and clawed his way, obliquely, to the top. The ropes helped, but his feet slid out from under him repeatedly on the slippery pine needles.

He crawled up the last fifty feet, scraped and angry.

At the platform, he hauled up the bucket.

When he held it in his hands, he stopped and surveyed the surrounding woods, slowly, suddenly paranoid as he walked the short distance to his little cabin.

He carried the bucket inside, and in the middle of the room, he dug down three feet and buried it. Then he refilled the hole, patted down the dirt and swept away any evidence.


Mr. Howard looked as nervous as a sheep on shearing day. He sat uncomfortably, almost jumping out of his chair when Frank — four years old by now — charged past him carrying a big stick.

"You give me that!" I shouted as I snatched the stick.

"Sticks stay outside," I added as I tossed it out the door.

Frank disappeared with a BANG as the screen door slammed.

Jim was making almost as much noise, pounding on a stovepipe that was sagging down from the roof.

I could tell it was all a little too much for old Bear, considering how reclusive he was. His eyes darted around the room as if he was looking for an avenue of escape.

I wished I could have offered him a reprieve, but I also needed to free up my hands.

"Could you please take Lizzie for a minute?" I asked.

He did. Still unable to refuse any request I made. Still unable to see anything but his beloved wife when he stared into my eyes.

It was a weakness I tried not to take advantage of, but I didn't think holding an infant was such a burden. In fact, I knew it was good for his soul.

"I'll be done with this in a minute, Bear," said Jim. Mr. Howard had tried to discourage the nickname, to no avail.

"I suppose I can handle this," said Howard, reluctantly. "But I'd rather help with the stovepipe."

"I'll take her back soon," I said when I passed him next. "I just wanted to add a few carrots to my stew."

There was a knock on the door, and Jim turned to Mr. Howard. "Heads up — Mr. Wilson is back. I know you don't like him much. I wish I could'a said no when he came searching for work, but the truth is I could use a hand with the new baby and all."

When the door opened, Mr. Howard grumbled and took in Wilson's white-haired visage. The man had aged some in the last few years, and he scowled when he entered the room.

"You still hidin' secrets up on your Kingdom?" he asked.

Howard glared back. "You sure do enjoy pestering people, Mr. Wilson. I'm surprised you're still alive."

Wilson smirked. "Well, the devil takes care of his own."

I didn't like the talk of the devil so close to the baby, and Mr. Howard handed him over the instant I glanced his way. I got a quick glimpse of his palms and said, "Oh, those look horrible — let me get a salve to put on them."

"Don't worry yourself," said Howard, covering them. Jim stepped over and handed Mr. Howard a letter. He said, "We got this yesterday — I was hoping you'd stop by soon."

Howard tore it open, and a moment later, shouted.

"She's done it! She's coming out!"

Jim slapped a hand on the taller man's broad shoulder and then shook his hand and said, "That's great news!"

Mr. Howard winced, and I grabbed his hand and raised it for a closer inspection. The palms and fingertips were all raw and blistered. "Father's hand was like that when he passed," I said. "I hope it's not a sign of sickness."

Wilson glanced at the blisters. "I suppose you got them blisters huntin' deer?"

Mr. Howard shook his head. "Nope, putting in fence posts."

Wilson scoffed, showing no doubt he didn't believe it.


Later the same day, Howard stood on the platform looking down into Itzel Canyon. He thought of all the work he'd done preparing to haul the slag pile up and away. All wasted effort.

At least he still had the gold coins. And there might be more.

But now he had Wilson to contend with, and he didn't think for a minute the man wouldn't come snooping around. The years hadn't treated the Arkansas bear hunter well, thought Howard. He looked desperate now. Hungrier.

He surveyed the platform. It seemed like a sign that was pointing straight down at his shaft. He grabbed a crowbar and began tearing it apart.

When he had removed all the nails and stacked up the boards, he hauled the wooden planks a quarter-mile to his little cabin, and there he stacked them against each other on the floor. Through the night, working by lanternlight, he continued. Howard eventually carried all the boards into the cabin, and before morning the structure sported a solid wooden floor.

He thought of the bucket of gold coins buried underneath, and when he finally walked away from the cabin the following day, he felt secure that they would be there when he needed them.

# Chapter Forty-eight

*T*he fear of Wilson stumbling upon his tunnel had Howard up early the next day. An hour after sunrise he was crawling up the chute, clutching his miner's pick.

In the back of his mind, he wondered if the gold dust from his slag pile may have found its way into pockets in the rocks during its flow toward the West Fork. Most likely, that flood had washed it halfway to Oak Creek, he thought with regret.

His fingers probed the darkness, nervously hoping they might encounter a coin or whatever else the mysterious shaft might contain.

And then he pulled a large stone out, and the tunnel shifted.

The ceiling above him dropped, rocks and boulders all falling at once on his legs and below him.

He tried to grab something for support, but it all fell away suddenly. He slid down, but rocks and gravel buried him, an unbearable weight pinning him down.

Suddenly a cold shock hit him. Water.

From above, enormous amounts of water began to flow through the chute, turning the gravel into mud. Everything was moving. He choked and gagged on the sludge, reliving the nightmare that had plagued him for years — since his days back in California on his horse ranch.

Just as he thought he was about to die, the flood of mud spat him out at the bottom of the chute. It washed him fifty feet down the canyon, where he now lay, choking and coughing.

It took him a while to regain his senses, and even then, he wasn't sure what had happened.

Eventually, he stood and stumbled up the canyon to the chute.

When he stared up into it, he saw a circle of blue light winking at him from the other end.


The water had punched a hole into the top of the chute and washed it clean, and he easily scrambled up it and into a small box canyon with high walls above. The canyon naturally funneled everything down toward the top of the chute, and around the new hole in the top, the ground was covered with algae and debris — like a bathtub ring.

A natural plug, he thought.

The water must have built up over the plugged chute until he finally excavated it away.

Howard looked around. The far end of the canyon ended at a steep cliff. Below, a pile of charred trunks hugged the wall.

To the left, a Sinaguan ruin lay tucked in a corner. Old bowls and pots stood along the wall by a circle of stones where the previous occupants likely kept their fire.

Against the wall by the ruin, a metal object caught Howard's attention.

He walked to it and picked up a Spanish helmet. He marveled at it for a moment, then noticed above it, tucked into an alcove where rain and sunshine couldn't reach it, was an old, leather-bound journal.

He carefully retrieved the book and opened it.

The spidery text written inside was in Spanish.

Howard read a few lines, then quickly shut the book.

He tucked it under his arm, took one last look around the canyon, then disappeared down into the chute.

# Chapter Forty-nine

## Act III

### 1885
(June)

*H*oward was napping by the creek's bank while his family prepared a meal. The river trickled by, dragonflies buzzing above its reflective, liquid-white surface. Islands of grass dotted the water, and on their shaded sides, swarms of newly hatched mosquitoes hovered.

The summer heat had arrived, and a drop in water level with it. The constant rumble of the cascading flow was still there, but it had mellowed, and Howard had mellowed along with it.

The highwater mark was visible in a line of debris: rotten leaves, spiderwebs, sticks and chunks of bark. Moss-covered rocks, usually submerged, now baked in the sun.

He slept like a baby, only occasionally waking long enough to hear the voices of the others. Then he would smile and drift off again, a part of him fearful that he was in a dream which would end. But it wasn't a dream. They were all there—his family—having safely completed the journey from California.

Mattie, now twenty-seven, and her husband, Stephen. And the boys—Emory, Jess and Albert—aged nine, six and four.

The assurance that the boys would know their grandfather coursed through his being, reviving him, and at the same time, washing away some of the pains of the past.

And his boy was here, too. Jesse. Grown, but still alone. With pride, he felt he could be a good influence on the young man.

He heard a shout and looked over to see Mattie leading her youngest, Albert, around on Shadow. The older boys were wrestling with their dad on a blanket where a picnic had been set out. Howard slowly began to sit up.

A few feet away, an agave had just finished its parabolic stretch upward, climbing to almost twice the height of a man, where it shot out tubular flowers of yellow and burnt red. A multitude of hummingbirds circled it, and Howard remembered Margaret's story of how she told Jim she was pregnant.

He glanced downstream and, as if on cue, saw the Thompsons heading his way.

They were expected.

Margaret was now twenty-one, and her kids were sprouting up, too. Frank was four, leaping ahead of them from rock to rock, while Jim chased after him. And she cradled Lizzie, who had just turned one and still didn't sleep through the night.

Howard was relieved to see that Richard Wilson was not with them. Wilson lived alone at Indian Gardens now, tending the crops in exchange for his rent. Thompson had asked Howard a few times if he'd seen him around, possibly up on the rim or inside the West Fork.

He got the feeling Wilson was slacking on his responsibilities.

Howard climbed to his feet and slowly walked over to the blanket, where he plopped down next to Stephen and the boys.

"Hey, grandpa!" they yelled and crawled over him and pushed and tugged until he lay on his back and surrendered.

Mattie cleared her throat to get everyone's attention.

"I want to thank my Pa for making all this possible," I said when the Thompsons had greeted everyone, and we were all seated. "I still can't believe we're all together."

A small feast was laid out before us: venison, rabbit stew, potatoes, greens from the garden, and corn on the cob with butter.

"Hear, hear!" shouted Jim Thompson.

I could tell our arrival in the canyon was the best thing that had happened that year as far as the Thompsons were concerned. Now there was another woman for Margaret to talk with and other boys that Frank could play with—and hopefully burn off some energy.

Margaret stood and walked to a soaproot yucca. She picked a dozen pure-white blossoms and returned to kneel by me.

"These are great mixed with a salad," she said. "Here, try one."

I nibbled on a petal and smiled. There was a slight tart aftertaste, but I thought they would make a great addition to a salad. "Delicious," I said.

Margaret giggled. "If you want delicious, wait until you taste Jim's rhubarb-brown sugar pie!"

We were celebrating the completion of a small cabin that would house us until we could build a larger, more permanent structure. My brother, Jesse, would need his own place soon, too.

But for now, we were so glad to have a roof over our heads after the long journey from California. Everyone had worked on the construction, even the Thompsons.

Pa had picked the location, about a mile downstream from his place at the mouth of the West Fork. It was, by no coincidence, I'm sure, located at the base of his trail up onto the plateau.

A place I'd yet to see.

Might as well have family watching my back, he had said.

Jim Thompson said, "I can't believe there are close to a dozen people living in Oak Creek Canyon—we're almost a town!"

Howard grabbed a piece of corn and pointed it at him, "I'm so happy to have everyone here, but let's not get carried away. You start calling it a town, and more people will come."

When the last corn cobs had been picked clean, Margaret uncovered her heated rhubarb pie, and Pa ate two slices. It had a soporific effect on him, and he slid into a second nap of the day.

The sun was hovering by the canyon's rim when Howard took his leave and walked the mile up the creek to his cabin. Mattie had asked him to stay overnight, but the quarters were tight with three adults and three kids.

He suspected Stephen and Jesse might sneak off for a drink, and he knew he was welcome, but he was ready for a little break.

The five children were so full of energy that watching them exhausted the older man. Their screams — especially once they retired indoors — set him on edge. It had been a great day, but he was happy when he reached his lonesome cabin just before darkness set in.

He lit a kerosene lantern, walked into the bedroom and opened a wooden chest. In the bottom, wrapped in cloth, was Cristóbal's leather-bound journal. A hundred and eighty years had stiffened and yellowed its pages.

Howard dragged a chair under the puddle of light cast by the lantern, sat down heavily, and opened the book.

His Spanish was a bit rusty, and the script was difficult to read, but slowly Howard followed along with the account of two Spanish brothers as they landed in the New World and made their way to the Verde Valley.

The entries were sparse, mostly logistical until they reached Oak Creek Canyon. Then they became barely legible, seemingly written by a shaking hand.

He held the book up to the light and translated the last line, written in a neat hand: *Today, we separate.*

After that entry, the writing became altered. Frantic. It took Howard some time to decipher the spidery text.

And the ink was somehow different, too.

Howard examined the page closely, then held the book away from his face with a puzzled expression. Had the Spaniard put down his last thoughts in his own blood?

*I believe a bear protects this canyon — or the treasure, I am not sure which, but I see his tracks in the morning.*

# *Chapter Fifty*

*I* turned in a dream while Stephen snored next to me, sated from the food and drink. In my dream, an old woman in buckskins sat on a rock in the creek and sang a wordless melody.

The woman had grey hair and a serene, wrinkled face. She moved slowly, and I realized she was fatigued as she sat there, feet in the water, singing.

The forest appeared to respond to her song. The trees and grass were swaying and breathing with her. And in my soft bed, by my husband, I also swayed, my whole body recalling the melody I had once heard on my father's lips.

And then the old woman sighed and slumped to her side.

She lay there, unmoving, and I didn't realize she was dead until the forest around her began to change.

Slowly, the leaves turned from green to brown and dropped, and then a wind came through and blew them over the woman's body, all but covering it.

By the time the bear showed up, her body had turned to bones.

The bear—an old brown grizzly—sniffed her bones and nudged them before ambling away.

And then they were covered with snow. First a dusting, but soon several feet of it, while the creek froze solid.

When the snow and ice melted, the water rose, and as I watched, the old woman´s bones were washed into the creek where they sank into the depths below the rock she had sat upon.

I floated in her dream, watching it all.

Eventually, I woke. I lay there, still; the world outside my window lit brilliantly by a pale full moon.

And then the hair on my arms began to rise as I heard the melody again.

I didn't think about what I did next, my body moving by its own volition. But soon, I found myself outside the cabin, following the beautiful melody upstream.

I recognized it, of course.

But the song I knew had been my father's rendition of it from years ago. What I was hearing now was all so much more.

The song made me feel that I was connected to the land.

Not a thought entered my mind about the hidden dangers in the canyon's night.

The song seemed to float over the water.

I reached the confluence with the West Fork and realized that Pa's cabin was just a short walk away.

I thought of sitting on his porch but stopped in my tracks when I saw a woman crouched on the side of the creek.

My first thought was I'd come across a ghost, but when I peered at her longer, I realized it was no spirit but Margaret.

"What're you doing here?" I asked.

She laughed. "I would guess the same thing as you."

I didn't understand. I asked, "Where did you learn that song?"

Again, she giggled. "That wasn't me singing."

I stared at her for a long moment. She was a few years younger than me, but no child. I believed her.

"Then who?" I asked.

Margaret slid down the bank to stand by me. She paused there and let her eyes drift over the silver forest. "I came here tonight because I knew you would, too," she said. "Since we arrived here a few years ago, I hear that singing nearly every full moon."

I peered deeper into the West Fork, where it had seemed to come from. "You ever follow it further?" I asked.

Margaret nodded, and then she began to tell me about the night of the silver bear and the lagoon. It seemed so farfetched that I didn't believe a word at first, but the more she talked, the more I sensed in my heart that she was relating what she thought to be true. At least most of it.

Eventually, I asked, "You expect me to believe that a necklace turned you into a bear?"

She looked at me defiantly. "Believe what you want—I'm just warning you never to go there. You ever hear that singing, just stay in bed."

"Okay," I said awkwardly, and we walked downstream together. Aside from the trickling of the creek, the night was quiet as the moon hung over us. After a few minutes I could hear the singing again, softer now, but we both pretended not to take notice.

* * *

The next day, late in the afternoon, Howard ascended Itzel Canyon. He was moving fast. A last-minute visit by his daughter had delayed his departure from his cabin on the West Fork, and he wanted to reach the hidden canyon before dark.

He crawled up the chute into the box canyon, his small backpack occasionally brushing the roof of the tunnel. It felt strange to scramble up what had been an obsession for the last few years—but now the chute was simply a way to get into the canyon.

The box canyon felt timeless. Like a clock wouldn't work here, even if you wound it every day.

He glanced at the old ruin, half-expecting someone to walk out of it. A ring of stones surrounding a firepit could have been placed there last week; in fact, ash was still present from the previous fire that had been lit here, who knows how long ago. Discarded pots, arrow shafts and baskets lined a shaded section of the wall.

But an uneasy feeling in his gut told him it had been a hundred years or more since anyone had been here.

Since he had read the Spanish journal, a strange new fear accompanied him when he came here. He slowly walked the perimeter of the small canyon, observing the high walls for another way in or out.

He cursed himself for not having gotten here earlier. In just a few minutes, the canyon would be cast in shadow. Already, the only direct sunlight was creeping up the eastern wall, soon to be a memory.

Suddenly he stopped dead.

Before him, in a patch of damp earth, he saw tracks.

Boot tracks. A large man. Recent.

He knew instantly they were Wilson's. It didn't surprise him that he had finally discovered his secret.

Howard walked back to the ruins and sat in the retreating sunlight. He opened his pack and took out the leather-bound journal, then flipped to the back and examined the last few entries.

He struggled with a word at the end of a sentence, but after repeating it several times, it came to him: Cave.

He translated the sentence: *She warns me not to enter the cave.*

What cave? He asked himself. He glanced toward the back of the canyon and a pile of debris against the wall. A shadowy darkness stared back at him from the base of the cliff, and he realized he had missed something when he'd stumbled around earlier.

He knew he would have to explore the cave. But he would do it tomorrow, with the sun on his back.

The sun had now passed beyond the high walls, and he was cast in shadow.

Before closing the journal, he focused on the last entry.

*"Bruja!"* Witch!

# Chapter Fifty-one

*J*im and Margaret Thompson were sitting on the porch of their Camp Kitchen cabin and watched Wilson approach, his rifle clutched in his hand. Usually, he would have come from the north, following the creek downstream, but today he came from the west, skirting Capitol Butte.

Margaret glanced up from a pair of pants she was mending and said, "Here comes a bad penny."

Indeed, Wilson looked like the type of company nobody wanted. His face was red and puffy, and his eyes darted all over the property as he approached, taking stock.

When he was a few paces away, Thompson said, "I had hoped you would be closer to Indian Gardens this time of year. The corn is just coming in, and unattended, the deer will gobble it all up."

Wilson stifled a grin. "Well, if'n it's so important to you, Jim, why don't you stay there for a while?"

Thompson stared back coldly. "Because that wasn't our arrangement."

Now Wilson let loose his grin, enjoying himself. "I'm thinking—maybe we needs a new deal. Maybe you should just sell that place to me. Why not do that?"

Margaret glanced up. "You don't have a pot to piss in, Mr. Wilson. How you aiming to buy Indian Gardens?"

He laughed. "Oh, I'm just messin'—but I do plan on having money someday."

Frank exited the cabin, slamming the screen door behind him.

"Hush, Frankie," said Margaret. "The baby is sleeping."

Thompson sat quietly for a moment, realizing he needed the old bear hunter. Then, in a friendlier tone, he said, "Mr. Wilson, I have to go to Prescott for a week, leaving in about an hour, and I could use a hand — both here and at Indian Gardens."

A wily mien crept over Wilson's face, and Margaret tried to cut Jim off. "I'm sure I'll be fine, Jim."

But Wilson said, "Oh, I'd be happy to help out."

Thompson sighed in relief. "Thanks, Mr. Wilson. I'll sleep easier knowing somebody is nearby in case Margaret and the kids need help."

Wilson smiled benevolently at Margaret.

"I'll check on 'em every few days."

Margaret was stewing mad as she prepared lunch for her husband before he set off. She didn't like Mr. Wilson and saw no benefit of his watchful eye. Being neighborly, she still made an extra plate for Wilson. But she wished the man would just leave. For some reason, he lingered.

His Sharps rifle was leaning against the cabin by the door.

Thompson glanced at it, "I see you got your bear gun out."

"Yes, sir," he nodded. "I do — and I'm plannin' on using it."

Margaret whispered, "On what?"

Wilson rose, lifted his rifle and peered through the sites. "On that silver Grizz."

Both Thompsons gave him a blank stare, and he guffawed. "Oh, how I love that expression! Everybody around here got secrets — if that ain't the truth. You got secrets, and old Bear Howard, he got secrets too!"

He looked directly at his hosts and added, "and I suppose if'n I'm being honest, I'd have to say I got a few secrets, too."

"You seen that bear again?" asked Thompson, his voice trembling.

Wilson shrugged. "No, but I seen his tracks."

"How can you tell it's the silver Grizz?" asked Margaret.

Wilson laughed. "Well, I suppose I can't say what color he is — but it's the only bear of that size I've seen since I first came here. Got to be him."

"Where'd you see the tracks?" asked Thompson.

Wilson eyed them both for a long moment before answering, "Deep into the West Fork, that's where."

Thompson turned pale and walked to the shed, and Margaret collected a few plates and disappeared into the kitchen.

Wilson stood up and brushed the crumbs out of his beard. He stepped off the porch and shouted, "I'm gonna use the outhouse before I hit the trail!"

When he was gone, Margaret came back out on the porch.

She stared at Wilson's gun, leaning against the cabin wall, then glanced at the outhouse.

She grabbed the gun and knocked its sight sharply against a rock in the cabin's foundation.

Then she quickly leaned it against the cabin again, but at a wider angle. When she entered the cabin she slammed the door, and outside, the gun fell to the ground with a clatter.

Wilson's shouts brought both Jim and Margaret to the porch. There they found Wilson staring at his gun in dismay. With an angry expression, he was examining the bent sight.

"How did this happen?" he growled.

Thompson looked around. Frank ran by again. "Seems like it fell over... maybe young Frank knocked it over by accident."

"Or it might have been me when I shut the door," added Margaret.

"Well, my bear gun is wrecked!" shouted Wilson.

Thompson nodded, thinking. He finally said, "Listen, I'll take it to Prescott with me and get it repaired — and I'll throw in a box of shells. Will that work?"

Wilson's face was beet red. "I guess it'll have to be."

Thompson went into the cabin and returned with a small, lever-action Winchester rifle in hand. "Take this while I'm gone," he said. "It's only a 32-30 caliber, but it's a good gun for birds and rabbits."

Wilson took the rifle but scoffed at it.

"This thing won't kill a squirrel."

Thompson shrugged. "It's all I got aside from the Colt pistol I'm leaving with Margaret."

Wilson spat on the ground and mumbled a curse. After casting an annoyed glance at young Frankie, he headed up the canyon to Indian Gardens with Thompson's rifle over his shoulder.

# *Chapter Fifty-two*

*T*he sun was beating down relentlessly as Howard hiked into the West Fork. He could make it to Itzel Canyon and up to the hidden canyon in less than two hours if he kept his head down, but in this heat, with the sun directly overhead, it would be slower going.

This was the hottest day of the year so far, and once again, he wished he'd set out earlier. Mattie had stopped by again, unannounced, and he wondered if she suspected that he was up to something. Maybe it hadn't been so smart building her a cabin less than a mile from his.

He had wondered all night what he might need to explore the cave and what he might find inside. He had prepared a pack with the journal, a lantern, stick matches, some rope, and some cloth and kerosene to make a torch if necessary.

The vegetation along the trail slumped, and the snake-like canyon undulated with heatwaves. He paused for a quick moment, took off his hat and wiped his brow, and looked around.

Only a few shaded bends in the West Fork still held water. In one, he spied a ripple in a deep pool caused by one of the few remaining trout. Had he been more relaxed, he might have dunked his shaggy black mop of hair in the water to cool off.

But despite the fact that his brain seemed to be baking, he was running late, so he re-seated his hat and stumbled ahead.

He saw no deer or birds. They knew better than to move about when the sun was directly above.

At the confluence of the West Fork and Itzel Canyon, he came upon a bear track in the soft clay along what had been a pool of water.

A good-sized bear, he thought—a Grizz.

He picked up his pace, loping his way up Itzel Canyon, and didn't stop until he was in the hidden box canyon.

Finally, he crouched before the cave entrance.


The ingress to the cave was concealed by the burnt husks of several blackened juniper trunks. Branches and leaves had clustered on top of that, hiding the cave.

Howard took off his hat and set it on the ground, then climbed through the debris and, stooping, entered the cave.

The cave had a low ceiling, and water dripped from it into puddles on the floor. Several large Sinaguan pots had been placed to collect the drops, which echoed hollowly every few moments.

A dank smell lingered in the cave, and Howard didn't like it at all.

To his left he noticed a dark recess. Enough light crept in through the doorway that he could make out a bear skull leaning against the wall. Above it, a bear claw necklace hung from a peg.

Otherwise, the recess was empty.

He glanced deeper into the main chamber. On a dry mound in the middle, he noticed a collection of bowls and offerings beside an old basalt mano and metate.

He inspected the items: a doll made from leather and a corn cob; a yellow drinking tube; several small bowls with colored powders; and another of tiny brown seeds.

Beyond the mound, the chamber ceiling slanted down toward what Howard could make out to be a tunnel. He took off his pack and set it down, knowing suddenly he wouldn't need the lantern as he stared into the tunnel.

It glowed dimly, with just enough light to see by.

He crept closer and peered into the passageway.

On the ground before him lay a pile of bones. They were tinted blue and covered with what appeared to be tiny mushrooms.

The walls were of basalt and looked like they had been cut by hand, long ago, as a luminescent lichen had since taken root in the cracks. He touched it, and a glowing powder rubbed off on his fingertips.

Howard stopped to collect his wits.

He thought of the journal. Was there anything he had read that might help him now? The author related that he had been warned to stay away from the cave, but not why.

Howard inched his way forward.

He thought he heard whispers. His heart was racing.

The dust on the floor glowed weakly.

Soon he came upon a small room with a large slab of stone on the ground with a hole in the middle.

He peered at it but could make nothing definitive out of it in the murky jade darkness. He was about to take another step when he noticed a boot print in the soft dust ahead of him.

He tried to check himself, but as he turned, someone moved behind him and clubbed him unconscious.


"You're not as smart as you think you are," said Wilson when he noticed Howard was stirring. Bear Howard lay sprawled on the ground, his face in the glowing dust a few feet from the hole in the floor.

Howard touched the back of his head and felt a thick, sticky liquid. He was bleeding, and a bit of blood had puddled in the dust. He thought he could hear someone whispering from the dark hole before him.

Wilson leaned over him, a sturdy wooden club in his hand. It was Aztec, and he admired a sharp ridge of embedded obsidian chips while slowly circling the man on the ground. He must have taken a fall, Howard thought as he glanced up at him because his face was covered with the glowing powder, too.

"You son of a bitch," snarled Howard weakly.

"I just saved you," continued Wilson. "If you'd taken one more step, you would have triggered a trap."

He looked to the shadows by the wall where a wooden structure lay partially concealed.

Wilson turned and stared down the tunnel, deeper into the cave. "Don't know why I did it," said Wilson. "You been keepin' secrets!" he added. "Big ones!"

Howard was barely conscious. His mind was spinning. He was uncertain of what was real and what wasn't.

Wilson's eyes were dilated, and his expression jubilant. He wore Thompson's small rifle over his shoulder and carried a compact leather backpack by the straps. Howard noticed it seemed to be filled with something heavy.

He set it down, untied the top flap, and began running his hands through its contents.

Howard groaned and tried to sit up. Wilson lifted a hand to show off several gold coins, letting them fall back into the pack one by one.

Under the coins, the old bear hunter's hands were red and blistering. "You really gonna tell me you didn't know about what's around the corner?" he asked with a truculent edge to his voice.

"You weren't going to share that?"

Howard managed to shake his head.

Wilson spat on the ground. "I reckon I don't believe you."

Wilson shook his head. "Well, you should'a shared it. Now it's too late. Now I got no room for any of ya."

Howard still couldn't speak, but he tried to stand up. The tunnel spun and stretched before his eyes when he tried to focus.

Wilson crouched before him and snorted.

"I don't believe you're gonna make it, Mr. Howard."

Then he stood up and brushed off his pants.

"With this fortune, I'm gonna buy up all of Oak Creek Canyon," snickered Wilson. "With you gone, your family will clear outta here, and by the time Thompson returns from Prescott, both his cabins will be burned to the ground."

Howard's eyes lit up anxiously, and Wilson chuckled.

"Oh, I forgot how much you admire young Margaret," said Wilson. "Maybe I'll just shoot Jim when he comes back and take her as my wife. She'll be more receptive with this fortune behind me."

Howard could take no more and once more tried to get to his feet. But his eyes lost focus, and he collapsed to the ground next to a crack in the slab through which his blood was seeping toward the hole in the floor.

Wilson laughed. "Good. Save me from havin' to kill ya."

He shouldered his small pack and headed down the tunnel toward the box canyon.

I stood by the door to Pa's cabin on the West Fork. Earlier in the day, I'd visited and felt sure he was up to something. He'd been in the middle of packing when I showed up but then denied having any plans.

But clearly, he did. He'd been gone for hours now.

So, I decided to find out for myself.

Margaret showed up at my cabin earlier, asking if she might stay the night with her two young'ns. I told her I had to do something and asked her to watch my children as well — which thankfully she obliged to.

Jesse and Stephen were building a still in a cave they'd discovered a mile downstream. I knew I might not see either of them for a few days — and then they'd be all hungover — so I was on my own.

It wasn't tough to figure where Pa had been going. A trail out the back door led straight into the West Fork, and clear as day, his fresh tracks aimed that way.

I hadn't reckoned he would go very far into the West Fork and was surprised that a few miles in, I was still following his tracks.

I walked silently, swept up in the beauty of the ever-constricting red walls.

But when the shadows began to lengthen, I started to worry. I had brought no supplies or even a lantern. Yet, I was unable to turn back. I felt in my core that something was dreadfully wrong.

When darkness overtook me, I, therefore, continued, even though I was no longer able to see Pa´s footsteps. I must´ve covered five or six miles when suddenly I heard the singing.

I stood at the confluence of the West Fork and a smaller, steeper canyon, listening.

At almost the same instant, an enormous full moon began to peek over the rim of the valley.

And I knew that song now. It pulled me along with its numinous tug. Margaret had warned me not to pursue it, but I had no willpower to resist.

Eventually, I found myself in a box canyon where the moonlight shone eerily right into a cave along the back wall. I drifted that way, like in a dream, still following the gentle melody.

By the cave´s entrance, Pa's hat lay on the ground. I picked it up and glanced around. Nothing. I was alone, except for whoever was singing. I set it back down and crept forward.

It was dark beyond the entrance, but deeper into the cave, I could make out a glow coming from what looked like a tunnel.

I found Pa's backpack on the ground there and crouched, shaking tremulously. I could sense a low hum seeping from the passageway, which frightened me.

I found a lantern in the pack and lit it using some wood matches stored with it. I felt better having a light, but as soon as the flame picked up, the singing stopped.

Then I thought I could hear sobbing or choking coming from deeper into the tunnel.

Someone was in there. I was sure of it now. Not too far away.

"Pa!" I shouted, and the darkness swallowed my cry without an echo.

Only silence, and the low hum, greeted me.

Despair swept over me like a cold fog.

Was the melody that had led me to this cave an instruction? Or was it a deceit? I didn't know.

I thought of Pa.

I gulped down a mouthful of air and began to sing the melody from memory as best I could.

Darkness swept over Howard in wretched waves of despair and regret. He seemed no longer in touch with his body. The room spun and pulsed around him, but he could make no sense of any of it.

For a moment he saw Nancy smiling before him, saying, "Nothin' lasts."

The room seemed to echo his thoughts, taunting, but he no longer resisted. When he opened his eyes a fraction, he could make out a man standing before him.

He knew it was Ydeliomen.

"Why shoot me, señor?" the man asked.

Howard clamped his eyes shut and screamed. Was he losing his mind? Was he dead? He shuddered as he asked himself if he was in hell.

"I wasn't a bad man, señor," continued Ydeliomen, "just a sheepherder."

Howard covered his eyes and whimpered. "I didn't mean to do it—I was confused. I didn't mean it."

He didn't dare open his eyes as he lay there trembling.

And then he heard the singing.

It was faint, but he recognized it.

And as he listened, his mind slowly came together.

He glanced around weakly. He was alone.

The singing seemed to grow somehow clearer, and then a surge pulsed through him when he realized it was Mattie singing this strange melody. And he somehow found the energy to flop over and begin crawling.

"Mattie?" he screeched weakly.

"I'm comin' for you, Pa!" she called, and he hoarsely yelled back, "No... Stay there!"

She hovered by the tunnel entrance, listening breathlessly as his stifled groans grew slowly closer. The pile of bones and chains horrified her, and she dared not think what else could be down that tunnel.

Eventually, he came within sight of her, and she rushed towards him and dragged him over the bones and into the chamber where the water dripped. She ripped a strip of cloth from her dress, wet it in one of the Sinaguan bowls, and dabbed his face with it.

"I got you, Pa," Mattie said.

Howard slumped in her arms. He was happy to be alive and out of the mad tunnel.

But then he suddenly remembered Wilson and his violent threats. "Where's Wilson?" he asked in a panic.

Mattie shook her head. "We're alone here, Pa."

"You gotta help Margaret and the children," said Howard, panic rising in his weak voice. "Don't let Wilson near them—he's gone mad. He'll kill 'em all if he gets a chance."

Mattie stood up and backed away. "What should I do?" she asked, but Howard was beyond exhaustion and collapsed, unconscious.

Mattie looked around, desperate.

In the dark recess, she spotted the bear claw necklace.

Outside, moonlight illuminated the box canyon.

Following an instinct, she grabbed the necklace, and when she emerged into the box canyon, she put it on.

# *Chapter Fifty-three*

$T$he straps of the leather backpack tugged sharply on Wilson's shoulders as he staggered through the West Fork, but he didn't dare take it off.

His mind still reeled as if drunk from the treasure, and he clutched the rifle in both hands as if he expected someone to jump in front of him at any moment.

He had stumbled out of Itzel Canyon half-mad, hell-bent on revenge, a sinister voice in his head repeatedly asking—how could they not have shared such a treasure? He now believed they'd all known about it, regardless of what Howard had told him in that dark tunnel.

The Thompsons, the Purtymuns, the Howards—they all had to go. He would never forgive them.

His pack contained a fortune. It had been difficult to take so little, but he knew he would return later and claim it all.

He'd come back better armed, with paid men whom he could trust.

In his hands he was clutching a handful of the coins, and he gripped them so tightly that his knuckles shone white.

He felt bewitched. At times, he was ebullient, overflowing with joy, and couldn't even remember what he was angry about. And then he would slip into a rage and shout at objects that seemed to melt before his very eyes. The land shifted and swayed as he stumbled down the West Fork.

And then Bear Howard's West Fork cabin was suddenly before him.

The sharp crack of glass breaking resounded in the West Fork. Richard Wilson was in Howard's cabin, stumbling around in the dark, smashing everything he could lay his hands on.

"Liar!" he screamed as he flipped over a wooden rocker.

He swigged on a jug of Howard's whiskey.

Outside, the moon lingered over the confluence of the West Fork and Oak Creek, but in here, the cabin was full of shadows.

"You got any more secrets for me, Bear?" he shouted.

Eventually, he found a lantern and lit it using some wooden matches he found by the woodstove.

A ghostly white light crept from the lantern.

Wilson glanced at himself in a small square of mirror, mounted to the wall, and was surprised to see he was covered with an orange powder.

He tried to shake it out of his hair, but the effort made him sneeze — and in the process, he inhaled much of it.

The cabin spun around him.

Wilson stepped outside and sat on a stump, where he had left Thompson's small rifle. From the murky shadows, he heard someone whisper — and then laughter.

He put a bullet in the chamber.

"Who's out there?" he shouted to the night.

He stared at the flickering flames of the lantern, and in them, he saw faces — terrors from his past that he'd prayed were forgotten.

He quickly looked away and tried to shake off the images by downing a large gulp of the whiskey, then tossed the near-empty bottle into the side of the cabin.

Wilson lifted himself laboriously from the stump and started down the trail, in the direction of the new Purtymun-Howard cabin. He stuck his arm through the handle of the lantern, letting it dangle from his elbow while keeping his finger on the rifle's trigger as he peered ahead.

Above, a full moon glowed down on the forest, and he realized he did not need the lantern, but its glow comforted him.

When he reached the Purtymun-Howard cabin, he fired two shots into the air and shouted, "Everyone out!"

Margaret answered the door, a Colt pistol in her hand.

"What do you want, Mr. Wilson?"

He was confused to meet her here.

"Where are the men? Where's Jesse and Stephen?"

"They're gone—it's just the children and me. It's the middle of the night—what do you want?"

"I want what's mine!" he shouted. "Now get out!"

Behind Margaret, the sleepy children crowded and whimpered, looking as nervous as horses before a storm. The older boys were timidly trying to see past her.

Suddenly, Wilson tossed the lantern against the side of the cabin, where it burst into flames.

"Obey me!" he shrieked.

Margaret lowered her gun and looked at him. "What have you done?"

"Fire!" she screamed at the children and began barking orders to get buckets and water while she grabbed a blanket and rushed towards the flames that were licking at the side of the cabin.

"Let it burn!" shouted Wilson, his crazed eyes reflecting the red flames as he slowly raised his gun, pointing it at her.

But then he caught a movement out of the side of his eye.

On the other side of the clearing, maybe a hundred yards away, a silver grizzly was staring him down

Wilson put a fresh round in the chamber, turned, and stared through the sites. Aiming for the heart, he focused, trembling as he perceived the size of the bear and its menacing and scarred body.

And only at the last minute did it dawn on him that he wasn't holding his Sharps.

The realization shook him. This was a much smaller gun.

Suddenly the bear charged, and Wilson fired prematurely, now panicked; the bullet sank into the bear's right shoulder, high and away from the heart.

The grizzly bellowed and roared but continued.

Wilson stepped away from the cabin, where Margaret and the children gawked, horrified, the buckets of water suspended.

By the time he jacked another bullet into the chamber, took a knee, and got off another shot, the bear had closed three-quarters of the distance.

This time the bear went down.

But a moment later, when it painfully got back on all fours and fixed its eyes on his tormentor, Wilson's courage failed.

He sensed in his heart that even with his Sharps, this bear could not be killed.

He turned and ran. And the bear limped after him, injured but full of fury.

They disappeared into the night.

Moments later, two more shots rang out.

And then the night was shattered by the scream of a man, drowned out by the roar of a bear.

# Chapter Fifty-four

Sunrise found me lying on a carpet of green moss, listening to the birds. I didn't even think about where I was until I heard the horse snort.

And then everything rushed back at once as I discovered I was sprawled on the rock in the lagoon, naked and severely injured.

Margaret rode up to the clearing; Shadow tethered behind her mount. She quickly slid out of the saddle and hurried to my side.

"Heavens," she said, "what happened to you?"

I tried to speak but could only moan as she tenderly rolled me on my side and examined my wounds.

"You've been shot—three times," she said. "Your calf, your thigh, and your shoulder."

I nodded, shaking, and she continued. "Small caliber, it seems. The bullets went clean through your leg. I don't know about the shoulder. I think we should get you down to Camp Kitchen so that I can fetch a doctor."

I closed my eyes in accordance. She retrieved a thin blanket from the saddlebag and covered me with it.

With her help, I limped over to Shadow and climbed up into the saddle. My faithful old friend watched me with his warm eyes, and his gait was soft as he carried me down the canyon trail.


When we approached the West Fork confluence, a shock went through me as I remembered Pa in the cave. I stared into the West Fork and tried to steer Shadow that way, but Margaret sidled up to me and grabbed the reins. "We'll get you sorted," said Margaret, "and then Jim will lead a search party to find your Pa."

But around the next bend, we came across him. He was lying on his side along the trail. My heart almost stopped for fear he was dead.

But then he sat up, and when he saw me, he lifted himself off the ground and stumbled toward Shadow. "I was tryin' to make it to your place," he mumbled. "Must'a fell asleep."

His hat was missing, and his hair was caked in dried blood and an orange powder.

He reached around my waist and hugged me, and I felt him sob. He was still out of it, and Margaret slid out of her saddle and persuaded Pa into riding.

She walked alongside us. We were moving slowly.


We passed our new cabin. One of the outside walls had been blackened by fire, but luckily someone had gotten a hand on it before it claimed the cabin.

Stephen and Jesse were cleaning up the mess, tearing away the bark that had blackened and stuffing fresh moss into the cracks between logs. They both looked a little guilty. When Stephen saw me, he rushed to my side.

"Will she be alright?" asked my husband in a worried tone.

"I think she's gonna be fine," said Margaret. "But she needs doctoring."

Frankie stepped close to Shadow, touching me tenderly. I saw my brother Jesse whisper to Stephen, who nodded.

Stephen quickly saddled two more horses, one for himself and another horse so Margaret could ride. He also handed Margaret some of my clothes.

It took a few painful minutes for Margaret to help me into the clothes, and the men looked away modestly until I once again sat in Shadow's saddle.

"I'll watch the kids," said Jesse, "and you can leave Frankie here for another night."

Margaret nodded thanks and clutched little Lizzie to her chest when they departed. "I'll be back for you soon, Frankie," she said, "you be a good boy."

When we were in sight of Camp Kitchen, I was surprised to see Mr. Thompson riding out to see us.

"I was halfway to Page Springs when I had a bad feeling about leaving you," he said. "Thought I was being superstitious until I got closer and saw the smoke."

"Well, I sure am glad you did," said Margaret.

The Thompsons helped get Pa and me inside their cabin, and then they looked after our wounds. Margaret heated some water and washed us, and then Jim did the stitching.

Jim used a sewing needle and coarse thread to run a few stitches through the back of Pa's head and then addressed the bullet holes in my legs.

He wouldn't close the shoulder wound for fear the slug was still there and dispatched Stephen to fetch a doctor that now resided in nearby Cottonwood.

Pa was restless after his head had been bandaged but wouldn't budge until the next day when Doc Smith pulled the slug out of me and stated I'd be fine.

Then he seemed desperate to find Wilson.

"That man is gonna pay for his deeds," he said bitterly.

I lay back, still puzzled. A profound tiredness came over me, and I drifted into a trouble-free sleep.

Four armed men set off the next day, on horseback, to find Wilson. They began at the Thompson-Purtymun cabin, where he was last seen. Jesse rode up and down the creek, looking for any tracks of either man or bear. Stephen checked on Bear's cabin and the mouth of the West Fork. And Thompson and Howard stopped by Indian Gardens, grabbed Wilson's hunting dog, and put scent to him.

Howard held one of Wilson's socks—a decrepit thing they found inside—in front of the bloodhound, and he immediately put his nose down and began running circles around the yard. Eventually, he picked up the trail, sounded off loudly, and darted down toward the valley.

The hound never slowed, the mixture of his owner's scent and that of a bear too much to resist, but the two men kept up easily on horseback.

Howard's head was bandaged with a white cloth which showed a red stain in the back. He seethed with anger. Margaret had tried to talk him into resting, but he wouldn't hear of it.

And Thompson was in a fury. He didn't know if he could control himself when they finally found Wilson.

The man had tried to torch the cabin while his wife and children were inside. He still had no idea what had happened between him and Mattie—but he would answer for it.

Soon the trail spilled onto a narrow little gorge that ran steeply into the plateau after a few rugged miles.

"That there canyon is a dead end," said Thompson.

Howard nodded gravely. The dog had gotten deep into the canyon, and before long, they had to dismount and proceed on foot.

It wouldn't stop barking during the thirty minutes it took them to access the steep shelf where he sounded from.

And then they found Wilson, face down in a puddle.

It appeared he had drowned.

But when they turned him over, they revealed a grueling fate. Claw and bite marks crisscrossed his face and chest, and his boots had just about been chewed off him.

Howard glanced at the scuffed ground and determined that Wilson had tried to climb a tree to get away. He nodded at a nearby juniper with a broken limb.

"Looks like he tried to get up that juniper, and the bear dragged him down by his boot."

At the base of the tree sat the compact leather pack that Wilson had worn in the tunnel.

"We should bury him here, under some rocks," Thompson said. "We can come back later with horses to haul him out."

Thompson was hefting a sandstone slab as Howard grabbed the pack and shouldered it. "I got something I need to do."

Thompson gave him a strange glance, then continued to dig a makeshift grave.

Howard spat on the ground near Wilson's body.

"Why bury him at all?" he asked coldly.

Thompson set down the rock he was carrying.

"I think it's the Christian thing to do. And it'll keep the scavengers away," he said.

"Seems a little late for that," Howard said and walked away.

Later that afternoon Howard stood in the cave once again, resting on the side of the dry mound with the offerings. He'd ridden Shadow as far as he could into the West Fork — all the way to the flooded tunnel — then tied her to a young cottonwood by the creek.

At the tunnel's entrance, he emptied the contents of the small backpack onto the pile of bones. He paused momentarily and picked up one of the gold coins, but as soon as he felt that familiar heat, he quickly dropped it.

Then he collected stones to wall up the tunnel. It seemed someone had done it before, seeing as there was a stack of rocks just to the side of the entrance.

He scrambled down to the base of the chute, and he grabbed a long-handled shovel that was still resting there from his earlier excavations.

Then he went back to the cave, and over the next hour, he slowly fortified the concealing barrier he had built with sand and dirt. When there was no trace of the tunnel visible, he began to relax.

But he wasn't done. He retreated to the circle of stones by the ruin and kindled a fire. When the flames were crackling, he opened his pack and took out the Spanish journal.

He flipped it open one last time, scanning the pages, but soon snapped it shut — and then tossed it on the fire.

As the yellowed pages took flame, he returned to the cave and walked into the small recess where the bear claw necklace hung on a peg. He took it down and returned to the fire.

He stared long at the necklace before dropping it on the flames as well.

When he left the exit chute to the hidden canyon, he knew he'd never return.

Within a few weeks, I was mostly healed and ready to return to my cabin, where my husband and children waited. I don't know if I'll ever explain what happened in that terrible cave.

Or how I ended up at the peaceful lagoon.

Maybe there are just some things beyond understanding.

But I know I still love this canyon — Oak Creek Canyon — even after the ineffable events of that evening.

And what family doesn't have a few secrets?

Our secret surfaces once a month under the full moon, when gentle singing accompanies the flow of water through the canyon.

None of us ever spoke about the events of that year. Pa tightened up and only got emotional if I ever mentioned the cave. Margaret hushed me and whispered, "I'm just glad we're done with all that."

And Stephen, my husband?

Well, I never did tell him either. He just thought old man Wilson went a little crazy.

I guess it's just as well. There are some things best left to the women.

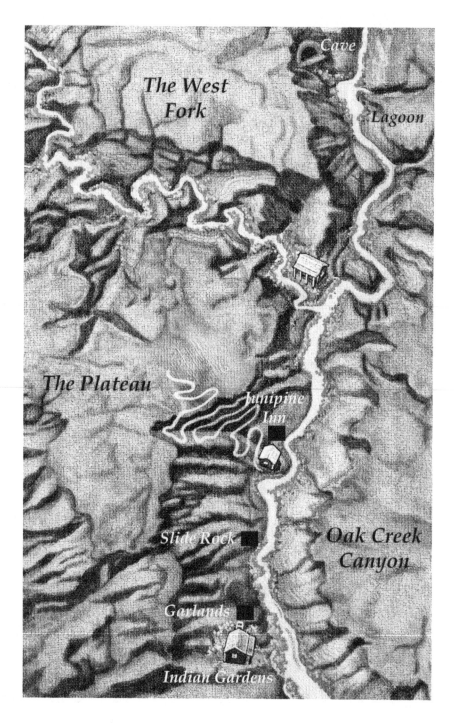

# Chapter Fifty-five

## Act I

### 1987
(July)

*I* love being up on the plateau in the summer. A cool, whispering breeze tumbles off the flanks of the San Francisco Peaks. It stirs up the stately ponderosa pines, swaying them gloriously and making the sweltering temps down in the valley seem like a distant memory.

Everything is out in the open. There are no secrets.

I try to get up here—Flagstaff—whenever I can, especially in the summer when the all-powerful sun seems to hover right over my house down in the valley in Rimrock. I'd been visiting friends in Flag when my editor, Tim, called and asked me to write about two lectures in Sedona.

I hated to leave the coolness, but I agreed to the assignments.

For four years, I attended Northern Arizona University in Flagstaff, graduating in 1981 with a degree in Journalism. I would have gladly stayed there if my great aunt, old Saan, hadn't left me her little cottage along Wet Beaver Creek in Rimrock—fifty miles away and three thousand feet lower in elevation.

It's not much, but the house is paid for, and it sits on the edge of the creek under the shade of a line of towering cottonwoods. A half-mile up the creek is a sinkhole surrounded by old ruins.

Over the last six years, I've tried my hands at a few things, but none of them stuck. At twenty-eight, I doubt I'm the young woman my mother Sarah wanted me to be. But she died so young—and her illness set in so quickly—that maybe she didn't have much time to think about how her half-breed daughter would fare in life after her passing.

All I know is I don't seem to fit in anywhere. I liked karate but dropped it after I got my purple belt—couldn't keep to the schedule. Tried painting, only to discover I was color-blind to red-green. And I've hiked just about every trail in the Verde Valley, only to find none ever led to where I wanted to go.

But journalism has somehow clung to me—I guess I'm lucky that my former classmate Tim works at the Red Rock News and likes me, or at least used to. He knows the type of stories I lean towards, too. I like sniffing out facts—searching for the truth. It's the one challenge my spirit seems to rise to. What's the story behind that myth? Or how could things have really happened like that?

Once, when I was drunk, I made the mistake of telling Tim that my mother used to call me Am Bear, a play on my name: Amber.

Since that day, that's all he's ever called me.

"Come on, Am Bear, just get me the story," he would say, and then add: "And please, leave your cynicism at home for this one. Our readers aren't all pessimists like you."

And I would snap back, "You can fluff it up as much as you want after I hand it in."


Now, as I leave Flagstaff, heading south to Oak Creek Canyon and Sedona, I watch the pure blue sky beyond the pines.

Not a cloud in sight.

No, that's not entirely true. To the southwest, I can see the first monsoon clouds building on the distant horizon. They're still a way off, but soon the rains will come, and the pine and juniper forests of the high desert and even the ponderosas on the plateau will sigh with relief.

I pass a hitchhiker sitting on the guardrail on the outskirts of town. He's hoping someone using the on-ramp will take him East on I-40. The kid looks skinny, about twenty-one, wearing faded tie-string pants and ratty sneakers. He's eating tuna fish out of a can with chopsticks.

I'm surprised he's not wearing a crystal necklace.

I give him a look, and I think to myself: This is what's wrong with Sedona these days. The NEW AGE—I'm sick of it. I didn't mind the spiritual aspect of it, but then the eclectic mix of beliefs grew to draw in astrologists, UFO enthusiasts, and others that channeled angels or "masters." Aargh!

At first, it was just a few psychics and tarot readers catering to tourists, but then the whole Harmonic Convergence thing began.

All this craziness started in 1971 when a guy named Tony Shearer wrote a book called *Lord of the Dawn.* In his book, he predicted that an exceptional alignment of the planets in our solar system—something called a *grand trine*—would lead to a massive shift in the earth's energy from warlike to peaceful.

So on August 16th and 17th, 1987, six planets—Mars, Venus, Mercury, Neptune, Jupiter and Uranus—as well as the sun and the moon, would come into alignment.

The Harmonic Convergence, a synchronized meditation event, was scheduled to happen simultaneously because Shearer was positive that the celestial line-up would inspire everyone to gather at sacred sites worldwide.

And it's all set to transpire now. Well, in less than two weeks, but to be honest, I'm more excited about the coming rain.

It's been damn hot down in the valley.

As I slowly wend my way through the switchbacks down from the rim into Oak Creek Canyon, I wish the psychics had never found Sedona. I think of old Saan and wonder what she would have thought of the New Age.

Most likely, she'd have laughed at the tourists coming to see psychics and get tarot card readings, all the while adhering to her own superstitions.

And yes, she had her share of secrets, too.

When I was young, she used to regale me with stories of hidden places and brave young women who fought legendary battles, but as I got older, she claimed she couldn't remember them.

I had a memory like an owl and pestered her for years for more details, but aside from cryptic hints, she remained silent.

She was Indeh, or Apache, as most know them — as was my mother. But she always swore her stories had nothing to do with her tribe. They were about places, not people.

"What matters most is where an event occurs, not when or who stumbles through the story," she would say.

Still, whenever she told a tale, I saw a tinge of pride in her eyes, and I felt the characters were kin. And as I grew, I developed a passion for local legends.

The creek trickles by alongside me as I drive. This late into summer, there's barely any water left, but it still calls invitingly through my open window.

I glance at the clock on the dash of my truck. I still have an hour until the lecture starts.

You may think my restlessness stems from my inability to find a place in society, but it's actually the opposite. I'm restless because I can't find a place — a location.

I pull over, park on the road shoulder. As I get out, I pat my truck. It's an old black Nissan with a cap over the back.

The truck is ten years old but dependable. I call him Heyduke, like the environmental vigilante from Ed Abbey's *Monkey Wrench Gang*. Sometimes I ask myself what Heyduke would do in modern Sedona. And then I smile as I envision him blowing up the Crystal Castle with a bundle of dynamite.

With all those psychics crowded into one building, you might think they would see it coming — but I bet they wouldn't.

Heyduke is irrepressible, like me. Plucky. Scrappy. Maybe a little bit angry. Always been there when I needed him. I've crawled into the back to sleep there countless times, and he never turned me away.


I'm parked about a mile north of the West Fork, in a quiet part of the canyon that tourists don't often visit. On the other side of the creek, I can see several caves a few hundred feet up the steep slope.

I've explored them too. I've hiked every inch of this valley.

My restlessness knows no limits.

I walk a few minutes along the creek, heading upstream. I can barely hear the gurgling water behind the cries of the cicadas.

They're desperate for the rain, too.

Soon I arrive at a peaceful lagoon with a flat rock set in the middle of the water, and behind it stands a patina-covered pillar with a spiral petroglyph on it. All around me lay piles of stones — cairns. Many have toppled, but a few, lichen-covered and ancient, have remained standing because they're away from the footpath.

From the creek's bank, I hop from one stone to the next to reach the flat rock in the water. It's covered with a soft layer of green moss.

I take off my shoes and submerge my feet in the water. The trees around me sway, like in one of Van Gogh's landscapes. His artwork alone was worth my venture into painting. When I stared at his images, I felt like I was seeing the very place that remained hidden to me all these years.

As strange as that sounds, it's one of my only clues.

I hum as the water flows over my toes. A forgotten melody dances on my tongue but will not surface.

A heron watches from across the lagoon.

Soon it's time to go. I reluctantly trudge back to Heyduke.

How quickly time can pass when you're in a timeless place.


I coast down the canyon, passing the crowded parking lot for the West Fork trailhead on the right and then Don Hoel's tourist cabins on the left. A few miles further, behind the Junipine Inn, I can see

331

old Bear Howard's trail—now called the AB Young trail—zig-zagging its way up the plateau.

Yup, I've hiked that one plenty of times, too.

Some cultures created paths leading to the mountaintops, believing the dead would use them to get to a site of power. And on that trail, I often wondered if I was walking alongside my mother.

More likely, it was old man Howard, who seemed to have spent half his life traveling up and down that track. Hiking enthusiasts act like they're exploring a new world, but all of us walk on paths that were laid down long before we were born.

Seeing it rise above the trees makes me want to hit the trail until I see the masses of tourists at Slide Rock State Park. They crowd around the small trickle that runs through the park, careful not to slip on the slick rock that lines the water.

A few miles down the road, I pull over and gas up at Garland´s. I run inside and grab a ham and cheese sandwich. My hunger has suddenly surfaced, and I know without sustenance, it'll gnaw at me throughout the lecture.

Across the street, a sign marks a historic location: *Indian Gardens,* where J.J. Thompson and his young wife, Margaret, built the first cabin in Oak Creek Canyon back in 1876.

I would give anything to go back in time to when they lived here. Less than a dozen people, no crystal crunchers, no tourists—sounds perfect.

Most people I know would much prefer to be led rather than explore. To be told where they can go and where they cannot. They'd rather have a clear path than a wilderness. And I think of those early settlers, more concerned with survival than paying the bills, and I envy them.


Back on the road, I think about the two lectures. Starting in about ten minutes, the first one is given by a National Geographic photographer, Martin Gray, on sacred sites.

I'm a skeptic by nature, but my mother once claimed to have visited a sacred site. For my mother's sake, I want to believe there are some special places out there.

The second lecture is scheduled for tomorrow. This Mexican Professor, Carlos DeNiza, believes he has located a lost Aztec treasure—here, in Sedona! The New Agers really attract a lot of wackos. Tim gives me these assignments even though he knows he'll have extra work damping down my cynicism.

I continue down the canyon, driving a little faster because my stop has made me late. On the way I gobble down my sandwich.

I wish I'd stayed in Flag. Or at the peaceful lagoon.

But Tim knows I need the cash. And so do I.


Martin Gray appeared beyond his years at thirty-four. Not that he looked old; it was quite the opposite. His short brown hair and mustache didn't set him apart from other men his age—it was his eyes.

A quick perusal of a bio Tim had given me outlined his vast experiences with so-called sacred sites. Gray had seen a lot of the world, and those experiences rippled through his soft brown eyes, and his expression, as he gazed over a crowd of about fifty.

He began his lecture on the minute, and I had barely sat down when he stuck the first slide into the projector.

The image showed a beautiful valley, with remarkable shafts of sunlight illuminating a gentle bend in the river.

"Throughout the world, ancient peoples discovered certain places of power, perhaps a spring, or a cave, or a mountain. These places had a mysterious power, a numinosity, a spirit," Gray said.

An image of a rock art panel followed. Gray looked up at his slide. "Sometimes, they marked them with petroglyphs, pictographs or piles of stones so that others might see them. There is a definite field of energy that saturates and surrounds these sacred places."

333

I thought of the quiet place I had just left and the small cairns stacked all around the lagoon. Interested, I perked up as Gray continued in a self-assured voice.

"Many of these sites are located at places with measurable geophysical anomalies — the so-called earth energies — such as localized magnetism, geothermal activity, and the presence of underground water.

"For reasons still not fully understood, these energies fluctuate in radiant intensity according to the cyclic influences of the sun and moon. Ancient peoples then used those periods for healing, spiritual and oracular purposes."

A man in the front row with shoulder-length black hair and round, black-rimmed glasses raised his hand. At Martin's nod, he stood up, revealing a lettered t-shirt that read: Rolfers Do It Deeper. He asked, "How do you feel man has affected these special places?"

Gray smiled. "Human intent," he said, making eye contact with the man and then turning to his audience.

"The force of human intention, and the effect that it has upon the amplification of the power of the sacred site, accumulates over time. The energy transference at the power places goes both ways: earth to human and human to earth."

The man nodded and sat down, apparently satisfied with the answer, but I was still mystified.

I raised my hand, and Gray glanced at me. "Yes, Miss?"

I asked, "What if a sacred site is lost, and all you have are legends? Can we know much about a sacred place through only old stories?"

He began, "The legends and myths of sacred sites are in fact metaphors, or messages, indicating the magical power of these places. These tales are extremely important because they function as indicators of the distinctive power of a place."

I pondered his answer, but before he could move on, I asked a follow-up question. "So, you're saying it's all about the places, not the characters in the legends?"

Gray's eyes sparkled as he considered my question.

"I'm not saying that," he replied. "What I'm proposing is that the legendary material associated with a place may show specific ways that certain power places will—or did—affect human beings."

I drifted into thought for a few minutes, weighing his words, and when I glanced up, Gray was thanking everyone for coming.

When the lecture was over, I snapped a few pictures of Gray answering last-minute questions and returned to my truck.

On the drive from Sedona to Rimrock, I watched the sun set on the far side of the Verde Valley, beyond Sycamore Canyon. The sky was still cloudless, and the sunset colors unexceptional for it, but it still soothed me.

Perched on the side of Mingus Mountain, Jerome winked at me in the twilight.

I followed route 179 until it ran into Interstate 17, where I drove south a few miles before taking the Rimrock exit.

Ten minutes later, I parked Heyduke at my place. Saan's old place.

Behind the house, Wet Beaver Creek trickled by.

Thick-trunked cottonwoods lined the creek and loomed over the house in the darkening gloom. I took in the freshness. Even at this time of the year there was a coolness about the yard.

I checked on the house, turned on the swamp cooler and opened a few windows.

Ten minutes later it was still too hot inside, so I grabbed some ice cubes, made a large glass of lemonade, and went behind the house to sit by the water.

There was no moon, and it didn't take long for the stars to show and brighten, bats cutting through the night before them.

The sacred sites lecture had my head spinning. It made me think about the past and my mother. I knew I wouldn't be able to sleep anytime soon, so I guzzled the last of my lemonade, grabbed a flashlight, and began walking up the creek.

Only a thin line of water flowed down the riverbed, and I proceeded at a casual pace by starlight, not even turning on the flashlight.

Eventually, I reached a bend where the water pooled, and I climbed the opposite bank. I was now on the Hobby Horse Ranch. I knew the owner, and she had no problem with me traversing her land, but I still crept along quietly, not wanting to rouse her dogs.

I walked across a small field that sloped gently toward the creek; at the high end, a massive, half-dead cottonwood stood defiantly. Water flowed at its base, having traveled by ancient aqueduct from Montezuma's Well — the forest service's name to the sinkhole.

In one of old Saan's childhood stories, she claimed that her grandmother had spoken of Apache dwellings — wickiups — that used to sit right where I was walking.

But there was no trace of them now.

I followed the aqueduct for about a mile, cutting through back yards and walking alongside the road. Eventually I reached Montezuma Well, proclaimed a National Monument by Theodore Roosevelt in 1906.

A sign by the entrance read: "The label, "Montezuma" is a misnomer – the Aztec emperor Montezuma had no connection to the site or the early indigenous people that occupied the area."

I grinned and thought of the lecture I would attend in the morning. Professor DeNiza was suggesting just the opposite: that Montezuma, or at least his treasure, did pass through here.


On the rim of the sinkhole, I sat staring down at the dark water. The monument had closed hours ago, and there was nobody around. The far side of the sinkhole was about four hundred feet away.

Below me, nothing moved. Because of the high level of arsenic in the water, not many species survived: water scorpions, leeches, and a few turtles.

I took a few breaths and then began to cry.

I always did when I came here at night.

The sinkhole was one of the last places I can remember visiting with my mother before we moved away — before she died. And as the evening breathed around me, I sat there remembering.

* * *

I was ten at the time, my mother twenty-eight. Although I'd come here many times over the years, this was the first time since I'd attained her age.

I cried again when I thought of how much more competent she seemed at this age.

There had been a full moon the night she asked me to take a little stroll from Saan's house.

"Come along, Am Bear," she said as she shook me from sleep.

I had followed along, barely awake, until we began moving alongside the channel of running water. Then the mellifluous gurgle of water brought me around.

I knew where we were going. But I had never been there at night.

My mother stopped only briefly at the rim of the sinkhole and then continued down into the well, following a series of cement steps.

At the bottom, we crouched by the entrance to some caves. Crumbling walls outlined several Sinaguan ruins that had been built into the alcove.

My mother's eyes glimmered in the ghostly moonlight, and I noticed they were dilated as she said, "Sometimes when I come here alone, I can hear a young girl crying."

I gave her a strange glance, unsure if she was telling me something I should fear or seek. My mother was everything to me, and I treasured this time alone with her. I thought I knew her well, but then she did something astonishing.

She sang a song.

Of course, I'd heard her sing before, but never a song like this.

The wordless melody bounced off the sinkhole walls and echoed into the night. But it wasn't just the melody that moved me: there was more to this song.

I looked out over the trees and bushes that grew down inside the sinkhole, and suddenly I felt they were conscious — watching me. Even the swaying flowers by my feet glanced at me shyly.

The stars above took on a new luminescence.

My mother caught my eye, and I could see her joy that I was growing to an age when she could start to share important things with me.

"When you get just a bit older," she said, "I'll teach you this song, and I'll take you to a sacred place — a secret place — that's hidden, and nobody else knows about."

I remember my heart filling with excitement at her words. I was overjoyed that she found me worthy of this secret and that we would share something "sacred." The world seemed filled with magic and possibilities.

But just as quickly, my world crumbled.

We moved away shortly after that night, and within a few years, my mother was dead.

# Chapter Fifty-six

*T*he moment I set eyes on Carlos DeNiza, I knew the lecture would be the polar opposite of the one on sacred sites. Same building — The Flicker Shack — same room, probably even the same slide projector, but this guy looked to be a whole different can of worms.

He strode into the lecture hall wearing an almost manic look of pride. Black hair, a neatly-trimmed goatee, Hispanic features — Carlos DeNiza looked well at thirty.

Tim had supplied me with his bio as well. DeNiza was an academic, not a field archaeologist or explorer. He came from a wealthy family, too, and looked like he was used to getting his way.

His eyes were full of confidence, but I sensed it came from something other than his good looks or his money.

He had a secret.

There were about twenty people in the room, chatting loudly. Somebody had joked about the treasures of *El Dorado*, and a shadow had crossed the professor's features — briefly. He would not allow unbelievers to dampen his mood.

He cleared his throat and turned on the projector.

"Attention, everyone, can I have your attention?"

He spoke English with precision and a note of bitterness.

"I want to thank you all for coming. Let us begin." He switched off the lights.

Half of us were still standing, and a grumble went through the room. Like a few others, I suddenly found myself scrambling to find a chair.

The professor showed the first slide, the projection of a Conquistador's helmet.

He smiled, showing perfect teeth, and pointed at it.

"Your pioneers were not the first ones to explore this area. It was the Spanish," said DeNiza. "They had a presence on these lands for hundreds of years."

The following slide was an old map of the Southwest.

"New Spain was south of here. They called this area *Tierra Incognita* — an unknown land."

The next few slides showed a series of Spanish explorers. DeNiza recited the names as each new slide appeared: "Tovar, Cárdenas, Oñate, Espejo — the list goes on. They risked their lives to come to a land of brutal savages and unforgiving terrain."

He then asked, "Can anyone tell me why they were so tenacious?"

DeNiza beamed. Nobody dared interrupt him.

He flipped a large gold coin into the air and smiled as he caught it. Everyone in the room stared at the coin, mesmerized.

"Gold!" said DeNiza.

"Not just a small amount of gold, mind you," he added. "This was a place of riches."

He inhaled slowly as he scanned the room. "It was a place with treasures that could drive weak men insane."

He turned back to the projector. The next few slides showed drawings and paintings of old mines and ruins.

"The seven cities of Cibola, where the streets were lined with gold," he said and clicked to the next slide. "The lost Coconino gold mine, the Lost Dutchman's mine. These are just a few, but if you live in Arizona, you are familiar with tales of lost treasure."

The following slide was of a painting that depicted two Spanish explorers. It was a powerful image, their faces full of emotion. They bore a strong resemblance to DeNiza.

"It was no different back then," declared DeNiza. "One of my ancestors — a man named Cristóbal — followed one of these tales of riches, and that's why I'm here today."

I scribbled a few notes, but I now watched the professor more closely than the slides.

He clicked the next slide in front of the projector: An image of a mound of Aztec gold, complete with gold masks, gold plates, and countless gold coins and chains.

DeNiza made a dramatic gesture and said, "Many of them were looking for this: Montezuma's gold."

A few in the crowd laughed.

He rubbed the back of his neck.

"You find this amusing?" He fidgeted nervously, then almost shouted, "It exists!"

He stared at the crowd, looking for a challenger.

He cleared his throat and continued, "You have my word. I believe..."

I ducked under the table, reaching for my bag, and my chair screeched loudly. I felt the room go silent.

I glanced up, knowing DeNiza was staring at me.

DeNiza raised his eyebrows at me and said, "I hope I'm not keeping you from anything, Miss."

"No. Sorry. Did I interrupt you?" I asked, putting on my best smile. I can be pretty charming when I have to be, but he wasn't buying it.

He scoffed. "My family has been waiting hundreds of years for this moment, and here I am about to finally locate this treasure. What will a few more minutes matter?"

"I told you I was sorry," I said again. "I was reaching for my camera. I write for the Red Rock News and wanted to take your picture. I just heard about your expedition."

I held up the camera like it was a press pass.

DeNiza smiled broadly. Placated. "I see. You are here to document my announcement of an imminent discovery."

"Oh?" I said, unable to quell the note of cynicism in my voice.

He gave me a hard stare. "Excuse me?"

I knew I was about to get in trouble—and I'd eventually get all kinds of grief from Tim—but I couldn't hold my tongue.

I said, "You can announce an expedition beforehand—but it seems silly to announce the discovery of a treasure before you actually found it."

DeNiza glared at me, indignant.

"I can," he said sharply, "because I will find it."

He grabbed the desk firmly and hissed, "It is my destiny!"

The crowd was quiet as they watched the show.

"Okay. Again, I'm sorry," I pleaded.

He looked past me and addressed the room. "Not only will I make this great discovery, but I will tell you the exact date."

The crowd erupted into nervous laughter.

I raised my camera and caught his eye. "So, what's the date?"

He inhaled and said, "August 16."

The crowd began to murmur skeptically.

"Yes!" he shouted. "On the harmonic convergence! This is no coincidence."

He was supremely confident, and that drew me in. I had to find out how much more there was to the story. I took a picture of him while the crowd settled down and then asked my next question.

"How can you be so certain you will find this fabled treasure and on this exact date?" I asked.

DeNiza fingered the remote, and we were shown an image of a map. It was strange map, like a stick-figured centipede with a circular symbol on the top center.

"Because I have a map," said DeNiza. "And this map is one of a kind. It will tell me where the treasure is."

He flipped his gold coin in the air again.

I found it strange that he was showing us his map but then realized it was just a bunch of thick black lines linked together—it could have been anywhere.

And then, my attention was riveted to the circular symbol on the top of the map.

I remained seated, but I could feel all the color leave my face.

I raised a slightly shaking hand.

"What's that symbol on the top?" I asked.

The symbol was split into two images. The left side contained a bear paw print under a necklace, or possibly just a heavy line indicating a cave. On the right, I recognized the symbol for a woman in childbirth, suspended over a rippled line of waves.

DeNiza offered his explanation slowly. "This is a symbol my ancestor used to indicate the treasure´s location."

I stared at it for a minute before saying, "I've seen it before."

DeNiza was condescending in his reply. "I would find that highly unlikely."

\* \* \*

In a dim, distant recess of my mind, I remembered our last night in Rimrock, at Saan's house along Wet Beaver Creek. I was ten. My parents were quarreling by the car — something they did all the time back then. My mother had married out of the tribe, a half-white Hopi named George Decker, so it was always "complicated," as she put it.

His father had been a minister — trying to missionize the Hopis in the fifties. But it turns out the only success he had in saving souls was in procreating one, knocking up my grandmother. He did marry her — and remained married to her for thirty years — but George, the only son they conceived, grew up ostracized.

At first, my mom was crazy in love with George, but things changed when he started drinking.

The drinking got George and my mother tossed out of the Hopi lands, but it was religion that forced him to leave the Verde Valley. Most folks didn't mind that he'd found the Christian God, but it made him unbearable when he combined his preaching with alcohol.

I happily avoided their fighting on that night and sat near the fire, wrapped in a warm blanket.

There were about twenty people at Saan's that evening; everyone seemed to know each other — and me. This turned out to be the last time I remembered, as a child, feeling safe and surrounded by friends.

When the sky darkened, someone threw several logs on the fire. Sparks danced all around. The heavens were full of stars.

Saan stepped out of the shadows, now dressed in a decorated buckskin jacket. She was white-haired, sixty-five years old, and seemed unaware of the large raven perched on her shoulder.

She shook a rattle as she walked, and a few of her friends chuckled. This wasn't a tribal ceremony, just old Saan telling a story.

But everyone there that night lived a stone's throw from the old sinkhole, and they all knew the creation myth that originated there.

"Before First Woman was born, our ancestors came up from the underworld. They lived in the bottom of the well because there was no water there then," said Saan.

My father returned from the car, red-faced, and Saan smiled at him as she walked around the fire. She seemed youthful as she chanted. Her step was light.

The fire roared to life.

My mother, too, had joined us by the fire and snuggled up next to me.

Saan continued, "They came up, and they lived in the sun. They were happy, they were."

Again, she circled the fire, but when she reappeared from behind the flames, the smile had left her face. She had mysteriously aged and now seemed angry.

"Then, there was a big flood," said Saan, "and many died. Many. Many."

She stared at everyone with a somber expression. "Do something wrong and the rains come."

My father looked away nervously as Saan stared at him for a silent moment. Then she continued, but now her tone was light again as if there was hope.

"But First Woman lived, she did," continued Saan. "She was the only one that lived 'cause she floated up in a hollow log."

She stopped and looked at me. "They sealed her up in it, they did."

I fidgeted under her stare.

"Don't worry, she wasn't alone," said Saan. "No. A bird helped her. And she also had with her a precious White Stone."

Saan looked around again, seriously. "Got that stone from the underground world, she did."

My father got up and walked away. He stepped quickly, but her words chased him.

"And she had a good hidin' spot," said Saan. "Now that's something everyone needs — a place where you can rest."

Saan smiled and circled the fire again, chanting as she went, a large, circular design on the back of her dress lit up by the flames.

The same symbol the professor was now pointing at.

A bear paw, and a woman in childbirth.

What was the story behind that? I wondered.

I would never find out from my mother. We moved the next day to go live back east, where George had relatives. For a while things were alright. I attended school, and mom found work waitressing.

I think my mother would have eventually brought me back to the Verde Valley, but she got sick. Cancer. And within a few months, she was gone.

\* \* \*

These memories had drained me of energy, and I sat quietly through the next few minutes while DeNiza rambled on. But his cocky comments and haughty attitude just rubbed me the wrong way.

I thought of my sensei in karate telling me to avoid the offensive whenever I could.

But then I couldn't resist.

DeNiza touched the symbol on the projection with his pointer and said, "This is where I will find my treasure — in this cave."

I hesitated for a second, then blurted out, "Why do you call it *your* treasure?"

DeNiza looked around the room.

"It belongs to my family. We have known of it for over three hundred years."

But I wasn't satisfied. "What about the symbol? It doesn't look Spanish to me."

DeNiza fought for self-control and then spoke in a voice heavy with mock patience, "Oh, are we back to that again?"

I stared at the floor and quietly replied, "It just seems odd."

He held up the gold coin again. "This is not just a piece of gold. This is an Aztec coin. It was found nearby, not in Mexico."

He stared at me and then everyone else.

Then he added defiantly, "I found it!"

I was angry that he had shrugged off my question about the symbol but flashed him a disarming smile.

I said, "Forgive me. I'm just trying to get everything straight for my article."

He nodded, straightened his shirt, and stood tall.

"I am an established professor of archaeology, specializing in Mesoamerican studies, not some amateur treasure hunter," said DeNiza, sweeping his eyes over the audience defiantly.

I thought: Obviously, a professional treasure hunter wouldn't give away so many details.

He stared at me, "And I think my years of research would surely trump your whimsical attachment to that symbol, wouldn't you? Miss...?"

The professor looked at me with raised eyebrows until I replied with my last name.

"Decker."

He took in my appearance, paused, and said, "Interesting. But Ms. Decker, we've wasted enough time with this chit-chat."

DeNiza pressed the control and returned to the slide of the two conquistadors. I noticed one had a string of scalps dangling from his saddle.

"I have dedicated my life to finding this treasure," he said. "Only a recent discovery made this possible."

All became silent as he held up the gold coin again.

He started to speak reverently, "Three hundred years ago, two of my ancestors searched for this treasure. They found something, but it cost one of them their lives, and the other told tales so outlandish that nobody believed him."

DeNiza stared at the gold coin and continued, almost to himself. "For generations, we have been ridiculed."

He set the gold coin down on the podium. Then he walked to the wall and flipped on the lights.

"I will restore my family's honor by rediscovering the treasure—you will see."

He stepped back to applause, his crazy confidence winning over a few in the crowd.

The two conquistadors continued to stare from the screen.


People were leaving the lecture hall. I lingered, under the pretense of taking a few more images and checking the spelling of his official title.

"I didn't mean to put you on the spot back there," I said apologetically.

He began to scoff at me but faltered when I smiled at him and fixed my hair. Men are so simple sometimes.

"I must have been mistaken about the symbol," I said. "You certainly seem to know what you're doing."

He was smitten and nodded graciously. "All my ancestors knew was the treasure was in the Arizona Territory. They had a map of a canyon, but there are many canyons here."

I looked at the gold coin sitting on the podium.

"And when you found that coin," I said. "You knew where to use the map."

DeNiza smiled broadly. "Precisely."

He picked up the coin and pocketed it. I caught a glance at the palm of his hand, which was strangely red.

For a moment he stared at me, hesitating, and finally pulled out a transparent sheet with the lines from the map drawn out.

He then laid out an unmarked copy of a topographical map and pointed to a canyon.

"This is where I found the coin," said DeNiza.

He took the transparent sheet and laid it over the topographical map. "You see how it lines up?" asked DeNiza.

I couldn't believe it. What had before looked like a crazy collection of lines suddenly matched perfectly with a modern map.

I also could not believe he was showing me exactly where he intended to search for his treasure.

I asked, "Who made this map?"

DeNiza stopped. He had a far-away look on his pale face, then he suddenly shuddered.

I grew impatient. "Professor, did the maker of this map find something?"

DeNiza stared at his map, and then without meeting my eyes, he looked at his shoes and said, "Yes, he most definitely did."

# Chapter Fifty-seven

*P*rofessor DeNiza drove a rented Jeep up State Route 89a north of Sedona, the top down, marveling at Oak Creek Canyon. The sky overhead was as blue as a Mexican tile as it peeked through the canopy of trees lining the creek. In little less than ten miles the road would top out on the plateau, and he knew he should slow and enjoy the ride, but destiny was calling.

He had four days left until the convergence.

It had been well over a week since his lecture, and during that time, he had secured all of his provisions. They were stuffed into two large canvas duffle bags in the back of his jeep: several coils of rope, flashlights and spare batteries, maps, a tent, a sleeping bag and food for a week. He also brought along a sterilized hazmat suit, chemical testing kits, and several reference books. He was ready.

He wasn't quite sure how he would carry it all, but he was ready. His stay at the Junipine Inn had been restful, and he'd departed after a leisurely breakfast in the garden.

Now, as he cruised along, he admired the beautiful forest that lined the creek. Sycamore leaves were quivering in the breeze, and the cottonwoods were shedding their fluffy seeds, which floated through the canyon like snowfall.

The summer heat had been oppressive, but as he went deeper into the canyon, it got cooler. He relished the patches of calm shadows that interspersed the sunlight.

Through the tops of the ponderosa pines on the slopes above, he saw colored limestone cliffs, yellowing as they rose and dotted with junipers.

Tourists were parked along the road taking photos, and inevitably causing traffic chaos.

DeNiza cursed them as he had to slow down again and again sharply.

He turned on the radio:

*"...who knows when the drought will break, but we could sure use those monsoon rains. With only scattered showers..."*

Once deep into the canyon, he pulled over to the left and parked near a sign that read: *West Fork Trailhead.*

DeNiza reached into the back seat and dragged out a cumbersome backpack. He shouldered it awkwardly and started to drag out the duffle bags.

A few yards away, I lay sunk low in my driver's seat. I was bored out of my mind, having waited here the previous day as well. When the professor finally pulled up, I really couldn't believe it and stopped chewing an apple in mid-chomp.

I knew he would come, of course. Any local could have picked out the West Fork when he showed me the map.

I spied on him through my window, which was open only a crack. He parked his car, awkwardly wiggled into a backpack, and then attempted to clamp a duffle bag under each arm. When that turned out to be too cumbersome, he endeavored to heft one of the bags up onto his shoulder. I watched, amazed.

He eventually settled on balancing one duffle bag on top of his backpack, behind his head, and carrying the other in front of him, clinging to it with one arm.

Before departing for the canyon, Carlos looked at his jeep, which still had the top down. He glanced at the sky, started to lower the duffle bags, then decided otherwise and turned to go. It was only a rental, after all.

We both noticed some boys tossing rocks at an old raven sitting on a low rail fence. The raven seemed ancient, but he easily dodged the rocks.

When I looked back around, DeNiza had started down the trail.


Just as DeNiza was about to enter a narrow canyon, a ranger approached him. The professor was so lost in thought that he simply tried to walk around him, but the man addressed him.

"I hope you're not planning on hiking in too far," said the ranger. A patch sewn onto his jacket identified him by name: O'Neil.

DeNiza was baffled. "What could you possibly mean?"

Ranger O'Neil rubbed his chin. "Well, this time of year, any rain might bring on a flash flood. Then that canyon can quickly become a death trap."

DeNiza set down the duffle bags. "I hadn't realized."

Ranger O'Neil glanced at the sky. "And we're due for rain."

DeNiza scanned the blue void overhead. "But it doesn't look like we'll be getting any today—I'll keep my eyes open for dark clouds. Anything else?"

The ranger shook his head. "You don't understand the weather here. It can be deadly."

DeNiza rubbed the back of his neck. "It'll take more than a little weather to stop me."

The ranger stood a bit taller. "These narrow canyons can be truly dangerous. Maybe you should consider doing something other than hiking a flash flood zone at the start of the monsoon season."

DeNiza flushed red. "No." Then he warned, "And I know important people who could force you to allow me."

The Ranger laughed, "Look. I'm just trying to keep you from getting killed."

DeNiza scratched his ear. "You're right. I'll find another trail."

He shrugged his shoulders. "I was foolish to be so persistent."

351

O'Neil wished him luck and walked off. When he was out of sight, DeNiza muscled one duffle bag up onto his shoulders again, grabbed the other one, and quickly headed up the trail.

I opened my door and stepped out when he was out of sight. I was wearing boots, shorts and t-shirt, and a red bandana. In my pack, I had stuffed a light-weight sleeping bag, a change of clothes, one heavy shirt, some trail mix, some freeze-dried soup and a bag of apples.

I shouldered my backpack, which had a one-person tent and a small tarp strapped to the outside.

Before I locked the door, I glanced at the sky and then reached around and rolled the window up tight.

"Adios, Heyduke," I said as I shut the door.

The boys were still teasing the raven.

I threw my apple core at one of them, hitting him in the back.

"Ouch!" he yelled. "What's up with that?"

I ordered, "Leave 'im alone."

The kid shrugged. "It's just a bird."

I picked up a rock and stared at him, "You want another one?"

His friend yelled over, "Let's get out of here, Bradshaw."

He stepped away. "Crazy bitch."

I raised the rock a little higher, and he stomped off with his buddies.

I stared at the old raven.

From my shirt pocket, I produced an old photo of me with my mother and Saan. I was six; my mother was wearing a buckskin dress decorated with beads. Everyone was smiling.

Saan was younger in the image, but you could still make out a seriousness behind her smile.

A large raven sat perched on Saan's shoulder. Its beak was near her ear as if he was telling her secrets. I stared at the photo for a moment and then carefully put it away.

\* \* \*

I started down the trail, moving at turtle speed because I didn't want to catch up with DeNiza. I'd hiked the West Fork many times, at least the first three or four miles before the official trail ends. It's a casual trail, and the biggest obstacle is crossing the mellow creek a half-dozen times in the first few miles.

While I dawdled, I remembered traveling with my father George to visit Saan when I was fifteen.

My mother had been dead for two years.

George's old station wagon sounded like it was about to die as we turned off the Interstate, and it continued to cough and sputter until we reached Saan's neighborhood.

About a block away, he stopped and cut the engine.

I had a distinct feeling that he was going to chicken out.

He no longer drank, but he had started dressing like some kind of missionary since my mother's death, and he never went anywhere without a bible.

He looked nervous, and a bit revolted as he surveyed Saan's house sitting darkly in the shade of the trees. He constantly fingered a cross hanging from his neck as he talked.

"This was a bad idea. We shouldn't have come," said George. "If we leave now, we'll have a good start on Montana."

I stared hard at him, "You promised mom you'd bring me here."

George was silent for a minute before he replied. "Your mother is no longer with us. I think we should, at the very least, move on first thing in the morning."

On the other side of the road, an old woman ambled by. She leaned heavily on a walking stick, and it was only after staring at her for a long moment that I realized it was Saan. I figured she had to be seventy, and she seemed to have aged quite a bit since I'd last seen her, five years ago.

"Here's your kin," said George. "Each year she looks more like an old raven."

Saan looked over and squinted at George.

As she crossed the street, heading in our direction, George turned to me. "I told your mother I'd do this," he said. "But now I don't know. I wish I had guidance."

He started the station wagon and glanced at the rear-view mirror like he was preparing to pull out into traffic.

I pleaded with him, "Dad, she's family, and you promised."

He corrected me. "Her blood may flow through your veins, but not mine." He met my eyes and added, "And I made that promise to your mother before I'd experienced salvation—before I'd found Jesus..."

Saan interrupted him by banging on the window with her walking stick, and George nearly jumped out of his skin.


George and Saan wasted no time greeting each other after he parked the car. The old woman walked into the house, gestured with her chin at a back bedroom with two twin beds, and exited the house by the back door.

I found her sitting in a plastic chair, looking down at the creek.

She patted an empty chair next to her and then put a wrinkled hand on my knee. "You can call me Auntie," she said. "It's been years since we last met—I'd guess about five. Do you remember me?"

I nodded meekly.

As I sat down, she added, "And of course, I knew your mother very well."

I stared at the water, watching a few ducks cruise by.

"I can't believe she's gone," I said. "She was so full of life."

Saan nodded and smiled.

She seemed to drift off, then spoke again, "When she was a young girl, she used to run through the woods like a deer. She had an old spirit, that one. We all grieved when she left us, we did."

I couldn't seem to find any words, but then I spat it all out at once. "Before my mother died, she made father promise to bring me back here, so I could get to know you again. He said he would, but now he's changed his mind and wants us to leave in the morning."

Saan seemed incredulous. "But we are your people. You come from here, and I've been looking forward to your visit for some time now."

I nodded while a tear rolled off my chin.

"I know," I stammered. "My mother loved you all so much, and she wanted me to come back here."

The old woman seemed to take this all rather hard. It took her a minute to compose herself.

She finally said, "My child, you are all we have left of her."

George was still in the house, so I steeled my nerves and asked the question that had been burning in my mind.

"Auntie Saan," I said, "my mother spoke of bringing me to a special place—someplace sacred, she said. Do you know where this place might be?

Saan eyed me for a minute, like a raven would, detached and distant. The coldness surprised me, and I didn't believe her when she said, "No, I have no idea."

I asked, "How do you know your stories are true, Auntie?"

Saan laughed. "Oh, they're true all right. You wouldn't question them if you'd been raised here, like your mother."

I nodded. "My dad's found Jesus. Do you believe in Jesus?"

She laughed again; it was almost a cackle. "I wish I could tell you it was all the same—Great Spirit or Jesus—but the truth is, I don't know about the white people. I don't know who they are or where they come from."

She reached for a bag by her feet, opened it and pulled out a handful of cracked corn, and tossed it on the bank for the ducks.

After a minute, Saan continued. "All I know is this is where your people come from—right here."

I remembered the creation myth she'd recounted. In it, the young woman had gone on to live in a hidden canyon and eventually been impregnated when a drop of water from the ceiling of a cave had dropped on her.

I pleaded with her, "But how could it be so? How can people be created from sun and water?"

Saan smiled and said, "It was not just sun and water, child. After First Woman floated to safety in the log, she was very lonely, so she climbed up the mountain to see the sun."

The old woman peered into my eyes. "But it frightened her, so she ran to the cave where the water always drips and hid there." She hesitated as she stirred the coals in the fire and then added, "When the water dripped on her, that's when she got pregnant."

I was confused, "But it doesn't make sense."

This answer amused Saan as well," It doesn't have to child. We don't always understand why things happen."

I insisted. "But where did this take place? Has anyone ever found this cave? Could it be the same place my mother talked about?"

Saan gave me a sly look, "Some may know, but they are quiet. For most, the cave remains hidden."

Saan shrugged her shoulders, "Maybe it was never meant to be found. Where there is light, there is darkness. Could be the elders had a reason to keep it hidden."

Then she laughed. "It must've been well hid if nobody ever found it."

I was crestfallen. At fifteen, the only thing that had gotten me through my mother's death was the hope that I could find the secret place she'd spoken of. I'd clung to it like to a life vest. Saan could see it in my eyes, it seemed. She watched me for a long time before speaking.

Finally, she said, "What I am about to tell you, I have been sworn never to repeat."

The somber look on her face scared me.

Saan patted my shoulder and nodded. "Once, when your mother was young, she disappeared for several days," she began her story. "We weren't worried because she was a child of the forest, and from time to time, she wandered, she did."

The ducks had eaten all the corn and now crowded around her feet, hungry for more. She tossed another handful on the bank.

"But when she returned that time, she was different," continued Saan. "She seemed to have grown wiser, and she didn't waste words—seemed to me that she had become a woman out there."

I was anxious to hear more. "What happened? Where had she been?"

Saan smiled. "Your mother had found a hidden box canyon, and in the back of it was a cave where water dripped. She said she had stayed there overnight."

"I knew it!" I yelled. "Did she tell you where it was?"

Saan shook her head. "No, she wouldn't. She made me swear I would never tell another soul. In all these years, you are the only one I've told."

"Do you think it was *the* cave?" I asked.

"Who could say," stated Saan.

I felt defeated once more. My heart sank. "So, it's lost again. Nobody knows where it is except my mother, and she's gone. And now my dad is going to take me away."

She put a hand on my shoulder and smiled sadly. Her wise eyes warmed me as she said, "All is not lost. The past is a well-worn trail that is always in use. Our ancestors walk alongside us every day. And even if all you have are scattered footprints, you can still reconstruct the truth from that if you are patient."

"But how?" I asked.

She sighed. "By not losing yourself. When you walk a trail, always do so with smoothness, resilience and steadiness."

"How will that help me?" I asked, growing desperate. I was fighting back tears. "Tell me one thing that is real!"

Saan's expression turned serious again, "I will tell you the name of the girl that lived in the cave."

"From your old stories?" I asked.

She nodded, and then she leaned forward and whispered something into my ear. I heard the word and repeated it to myself.

It was the last time I saw her.

# Chapter Fifty-eight

Carlos DeNiza had set off at a fast pace, for about a quarter-mile, until he'd convinced himself Ranger O'Neil was well behind him.

Then he started to slow down, stumbling.

He had way too much gear, it was heavy, and he was suddenly realizing that he was not in the great physical shape he'd believed. The Arizona heat was so dry that the sweat evaporated off him before it could cool him, and the pounding at the back of his head screamed that he was dehydrated.

He dropped the duffle bags, set his pack down, blurry-eyed, and leaned against the shaded, cool side of a massive slab of sandstone. When his vision cleared, he stumbled to the creek and splashed water on his face.

He took in the pleasant riparian smells of the creek, more of a mellow brook here. The tall pines were shading the trail ahead, and the wind whispered through them like a lullaby. If this wasn't such hard work, he thought, it would be a beautiful place.

He would have organized a porter, but there was no one he trusted. What if he simply couldn't carry his supplies all the way? He had planned to set up his first camp about six miles in, but now he was having trouble making the first mile. He rubbed his sore shoulders, hefted up the bags, and then continued down the trail.


Three hours later, he reached the end of the marked trail. He pulled out his map and saw with a sinking heart that he was only halfway.

Ahead of him, the canyon walls closed into a narrow gorge only thirty feet apart, and the flat sandstone floor was filled with water. There had been a few other hikers at the beginning of the trail, but now there was no one.

He moaned as he lifted his heavy gear onto his shoulders and waded through the cool water, soaking his new leather boots. Luckily, the summer heat had burned away much of the water, and even in the deepest sections, he wasn't in above his thighs.

A quarter-mile further into the canyon, the water dried up, and he could once again walk on the corrugated sandstone.

It was here, as he squished along in his wet boots, that he had a thought: Tourists have no reason to venture this deep into the canyon. Perhaps he should stash one of the bags and return later.

He paused, listening, just to make sure he was alone.

For a second, he heard splashing, but then it stopped.

He shouted, "Hello!" and it echoed through the canyon.

He smiled at his jumpy nerves and said, "Echoes."

But then, after he'd walked about five minutes, he heard footsteps again, this time sounding off the high walls.

He froze and sank. As the footsteps got closer, he turned pale and sat, sweating profusely.

Then they stopped.

Eventually, DeNiza could wait no longer and continued, slowly, constantly looking behind him.

The situation began to anger him, and after another five minutes, he finally summoned up the courage to wait and face his pursuer.

I didn't want to catch up with DeNiza as I hiked up the West Fork, so I took my time, strolling really, and thought of some of the legends I'd learned over the years. These tales stretched back to the dim antiquity of the ancestors of this place—not just the Sinagua and Apache, but other visitors too, like Mayans before them or the pioneers that came after.

I often wished life was as simple as depicted in these old tales.

It's not the stories of forgotten mines and buried treasure that spike my curiosity. Gold doesn't motivate me much—I've never striven for riches and doubt I ever will have any.

But stories of lost or unrequited love, or lost places, always drew me in.

One of my favorites is the Weeping Woman or *La Llorona*. They speak of a woman who cries for her lost children, or maybe it's a lost love, along a river. I've talked to people who claim to have seen her on Oak Creek, but I never have.

And the warnings in these fables are clear and straightforward, too. For example, a young child is cautioned not to take a shortcut and is told of a boy who didn't listen and was never found. From then on, whenever the child even thinks about the shortcut, he or she is reminded of the story.

I thought of Martin Gray's lecture on sacred sites and realized he was right: In these stories, the characters are reduced to archetypes, but the lessons stay highly relevant, and the setting is often specific. "Right there, on the top of that mountain, a young man died one night..." a typical story might begin.

Another reason I like the legends is they reinforce the belief that trails exist in both the physical world and the world of spirits: two different landscapes that, to many indigenous cultures, were inseparably entwined.

I walked along, happy with the thought that my mother may be walking alongside me.

Suddenly the day seemed gentler, and I felt my step lighten.

I inhaled deeply and smiled at the blue sky, high above me, reduced to a long narrow strip between the high walls of the canyon. I was drifting along when out of nowhere, a man jumped out from behind a rock.

I leaped back, lifted one leg in mid-air, and kicked the charging man in the ribs.

He staggered backward, red-faced and angry, and came at me again, gasping.

I retreated a half-step into a defensive pose, and only after I'd prepared myself did I realize it was DeNiza.

Recognition also lit up his face.

He shook his clenched fist at me and screamed, "You? How dare you follow me?"

I held up a hand. "Keep away from me."

He stopped, looking like a caged animal. His eyes seemed to dance around in his head as he contemplated how this would affect his plans.

Finally, he sat down heavily on his backpack.

"I should have known you were after my treasure," he hissed. "I should have seen it."

I pointed a finger at him and said, "I don't care about your stupid treasure."

He snorted in disbelief, "Then please, tell me why you are here?"

I turned away. "It's none of your business."

DeNiza looked at me incredulously. He said, "Of all the unmitigated gall—I could have you arrested."

I laughed, but he added, "I could have you thrown in jail."

I stopped. "Like it or not, Mr. DeNiza, this is a free country, and this is a public trail."

He rubbed his neck. "But you're not just hiking through, are you? You want to go where I'm going."

I nodded reluctantly, afraid of the calculating look in his eyes.

He said, "If you come with me, you give up all rights to the treasure—even to be named in the discovery of it."

I put on my most polite smile and said, "Fine."

But he wasn't through. "And you will assist me, both as a documentarian and in setting up a camp—and most importantly right now, in carrying gear."

I weighed my options and agreed, "Okay. Whatever. Let's get moving."

He smiled at me as he handed over one of the two duffle bags, and we continued up the trail together.

We put another mile behind us, and then DeNiza began to survey the canyon walls a bit more carefully.

He pulled out his map as we passed a small wash on his right. Taking a marker, he darkened the lowest right line on the map.

Again and again over the next hour, he stopped at any dry wash we passed, found it on his map, and darkened the corresponding line with the marker.

A few times, he took out the transparency and checked it against the map. I kept glancing at the symbol on the top.

He noticed and taunted me. "For someone who does not believe in my treasure," said DeNiza, "you seem to have a great interest in my map."

I laughed, "It's not that I don't believe in your treasure. I am just not interested in it."

DeNiza shook his head, "You really think I'll buy that?"

I tried to change the subject. "I just don't understand what you're doing!"

He impatiently stopped, pointed to one of the washes, and said, "This wash is dry, but when it rains, it would be a small river."

I looked at it. "Okay, so what?"

He held up his map and pointed. "When this map was made, it was raining, and all of these washes were flowing."

He indicated the map. "See, they are all shown clearly."

I looked around and said, "I don't know if you'd want to be here then."

I pointed at the map. "I've never seen a map like that. Where did you get it?"

DeNiza quickly rolled it up. "This is just a photocopy. The original is far too delicate to treat like this."

I leaned forward. "Will you let me see it?"

DeNiza moved to reply, then decided not to and walked off without a word. He wore a grave expression.

I laughed and ran after him. "Come on, let me see it."

He straightened his back and marched away.

"I do not think so."

But I continued to tease him, "Why not? Please? It's your map, isn't it? Do you have to ask permission from someone?"

He looked shocked. "It is my map—I can do with it what I please."

When the high walls cast us in shadow, DeNiza said it was time to set up camp. Even though my arms were tired from carrying his gear, I could have kept going, but he was done.

I set my tent up on a high bench on the side of the canyon. Warning bells had gone off in my head when I first set out because there was definitely a risk of a flash flood this time of year. I didn't want to be caught unaware in my tent if a sudden storm did hit.

The bench sat about thirty feet above the canyon floor, and it didn't surprise me when DeNiza followed suit.

I had my tent up in a few minutes, but it took him a half-hour to figure his out. I had the impression he didn't camp much.

The forest was as dry as tinder, and I'd left my stove behind to rely on the trail mix and apples. But I did have a couple of packets of dried soup in case the opportunity arose.

I'm sure DeNiza had a stove somewhere in his massive piles of supplies, but he seemed too tired to search it out. He stowed all of his belongings inside his tent after setting it up, crawled inside and fell asleep, leaving the tent screen unzipped.

I enjoyed watching the late afternoon pass.

The heat had stifled all movement during the afternoon hours, but the birds began to call out as the temperatures dropped.

I listened to them, trying to make out what their sweet calls might be trying to convey to each other.

Just before darkness fully set in, I heard DeNiza rustle. He sat up.

He appeared confused and stared at his knees.

I whistled, and when he looked my way, I tossed him an apple.

It landed on his sleeping bag. He grabbed it, softened a little, and nodded a thank you.

Over the next hour, he found a Coleman lantern, and I listened to it roar while he pawed through his supplies.

Under the glowing flame, I could see him examining his maps, and after he had caught me watching twice, he called me over.

I brought another peace offering in the form of some trail mix, which he hungrily devoured.

I sat down in the entrance of his tent, and he stared at me hard, like he was still trying to decide if he could trust me.

Finally, he sighed, picked up a plastic cylinder, and took the end off to slide out a rolled-up bundle. He unwrapped it and slowly revealed an aged piece of leather.

Drawn on it was the same tangle of lines I'd seen on the transparency, but they were dark red and cracked. I leaned forward, and as I looked closer, I realized with disgust what I was looking at.

I whispered, "These lines seem like they were drawn in..."

"...blood," DeNiza finished my sentence.

"That's right," he said. "The symbol on the top was painted, but the lines contain the blood of my ancestors—a man named Cristóbal. It came from his wounds."

I was confused and asked, wide-eyed. "What wounds?"

DeNiza began: "Cristóbal was running from something, of that I'm sure. But he was also leaving something. Something he planned to return for. It was a thing he could not live without. So, he needed a map to get back to the place he was escaping from."

I paled a little. "And?" I asked softly.

"Well, he didn't have a pen or a compass, so he used what he had on him—a knife."

"And he used his chest as a canvas?" I asked, shocked.

DeNiza nodded somberly.

The map was creeping me out, and I was happy to return to my tent when DeNiza rolled it up and put it back in the cylinder. But when I tried to sleep, the image of its creation kept me awake.

In the middle of the night, DeNiza started screaming. His eyes were still wide when I stood outside his tent and tried to calm him. He finally relaxed a bit, sat up and unzipped his tent, and tried to compose himself.

"I am sorry," he said. "I have always been troubled by nightmares. They will not let me be."

I looked at him squarely. "Is it always the same dream?"

He nodded. "In my dream I am running," he began. "And I am terrified as I stumble, exhausted. I am bleeding from numerous cuts, and there is a nasty gouge above one of my eyes."

His gaze was filled with fear.

I handed him some water. "It sounds like something that happened to your ancestor—you said his name was Cristóbal?"

DeNiza nodded. "But that is not the worst part. In the dream, I look behind me and see a wall of water emerge, rising as the canyon narrows as if to grab me."

He stared at me. "As it crashes, I wake up."

He had put away the map, but the transparency was still out. I picked it up and stared at all the lines traced on it. Then I shook my head. "It's no wonder you have nightmares with a map made from your ancestor's blood. Look at all these lines! It must have nearly killed him!"

DeNiza agreed. "Well, it almost did."

I set the map down and looked at DeNiza. "What could be worth doing that to your body?"

DeNiza suddenly looked more surprised than scared.

"My treasure. Are you blind? That's why he gave his brother, Alonso, the map. And before he passed, he whispered the secret to him."

"Come on, Carlos, do you think he did that all for some gold?" I asked. "What would drive a man to that extreme."

DeNiza laughed. "Are you insinuating that there could be something of more value than gold?" He arched his eyebrows.

I didn't reply, but I thought, "We'll see."

# Chapter Fifty-nine

*I* woke the following day to a sublime sunrise over light-capped spires. From the dark crevice where I'd slept, I had to peer way up to the rim of the escarpment, where the first rays of pristine light glinted off the white Toroweap sandstone.

Gradually the sunlight slid over the terra-cotta rocks until it hit the pink and vermillion layers, and then it burst forth in a profusion of color.

I smiled and said, "Good morning."

DeNiza eventually snorted himself awake.

I broke camp and ate an apple by the water while I waited about an hour for him to get his stuff together.

DeNiza did not mind the casual pace he had set that morning until we rounded a bend beyond where the high walls merged into each other, blocking our way.

A dark hole at the cliff base turned out to be a long, low tunnel that allowed access to the next section.

The passageway was filled with dark, motionless water. A tiny bright light marked the exit on the other side about fifty feet beyond the entrance.

DeNiza unbuttoned his shirt. "We will have to wade through. Carry the gear over your head."

I pulled off my t-shirt — I had on a bathing suit top underneath. My shorts would dry, especially in this heat. I did take off my boots and grabbed my Tevas from my pack. The rugged sandals could handle getting wet.

I stepped into the cold water, trying my best to hold my pack and the professor's duffle bag above my head.

The cold water in the tunnel quickly got waist-deep, and it didn't take me long to realize I should have taken two trips.

DeNiza entered the water. He was gasping as he trudged behind me.

Soon the light faded, and it was comforting when DeNiza turned on a flashlight. But he had a hard time pointing it while he carried his pack and a duffle bag over his head. He finally clutched the light between his teeth.

We passed a small recess in the passageway ceiling, and DeNiza pointed the beam up into it. The ceiling was covered with bats. There were also symbols scratched into the wall, and he moved to get a closer look.

Amazed, he took the flashlight from his mouth and said, "Well, look at this..."

I was left in the dark, and I called for him to shine me some light. Feeling unduly distracted from his discovery, DeNiza shouted, "SILENCE!"

Suddenly the entire cave was filled with motion. Bats flew everywhere.

Instinctively, we shielded our faces, and several splashes marked our belongings dropping into the water.

We frantically gathered them up and waded toward the light of the exit.


The professor's day went downhill after that. He hauled his gear on the shore and began unpacking it all. Over the next few hours, he laid everything out to dry and then slowly repacked it.

He was in a foul mood. He grumbled and complained about the delay all of this was causing.

I lay against a flat rock and waited.

My gear—including my sleeping bag—was all stowed in plastic bags. Only my pack was wet.

The sun was high overhead when we set out again.

But within a mile, DeNiza stopped once more.

I figured he'd developed a blister, or his shoulders were aching, but he actually wanted to consult his map.

He smiled as he held up the transparency.

"We've done well!" he said emphatically. "But we should stop and make camp."

We were deep in the West Fork, at a confluence where a steeper canyon joined from the left. The water had pooled in a glittering pond, and a flat rock along its bank seemed to beckon me over.

I lay down on my back on the flat rock and said, "I can stay here as long as you want."

DeNiza chuckled and nodded at the steep canyon. "Don't get too comfortable—in the morning, we're going up there."

I followed his glance, and for the first time since I'd started this journey, a feeling of foreboding crept over me. Up until this point, I was only searching for a lost canyon that my mother had talked about.

But when I stared at that canyon, something about it scared me.


That night DeNiza lit a fire and sat close to it. I tried to discourage him, knowing we could burn down the whole canyon if he wasn't careful, but he was determined to dry his damp clothes.

I sat across from him, watching every spark with trepidation—even chased down a few that drifted away. After a while, we had a low-banked flame contained by a ring of stones, and I relaxed.

DeNiza was shivering, despite almost leaning into the flame. It was July, but after the sunset, it got cool—not really cold, but his wet clothes were chilling him to the bone. The soaking seemed to have humbled him.

I couldn't resist throwing a barb at him. "So, Carlos," I asked, "Is this how you envisioned your great discovery?"

He laughed. "Not exactly, but I do have a contingency plan."

He pulled a bottle of brandy from his backpack and took a swig. He gestured to me. "*Quieres?* It will warm you up."

A vision of George hefting a bottle floated before me, and I declined.

He shrugged. "You seem pretty comfortable here," he said. "Has your family been in Arizona long?"

I smiled at the question. "My mom was a local," I said. "She was Apache—her people claim to have been created here."

"How risible. I'm sorry to disappoint you," said DeNiza. "But your ancestors came from Asia, and before that Mesopotamia. They were not created here, regardless of what apocryphal stories they tell."

I stared at the fire for a minute before replying.

"Well, even if they weren't created here, they took their identity from this place."

DeNiza gave me a disdainful sigh.

"Those are two very different things," he said.

He laughed and added, "Well, it's good to know I've got an Indian guide. A pathfinder! Even if she does believe in fairy tales."

As he lifted the bottle to his lips again, I asked, "So how is it that you have this map but don't know where the treasure is?"

He choked and struggled to quench a cough.

# *Chapter Sixty*

**W**e explored the steep canyon the next morning with a clear, bright sun shining directly on it. It looked less intimidating in the daylight, although it was clear to me from the start that we would never summit the plateau this way.

I expected us to have to scramble a lot and to get bluffed early, but the way was surprisingly open. Over the years, logs had fallen off the rim and dropped into the canyon, and other rocks had dislodged and tumbled down, but regardless, we had no difficulties.

About a third of the way in, DeNiza stopped and examined the sandstone we were climbing over. "Look at this!" he exclaimed excitedly. "These steps were carved."

I glanced over at the rock, which was directly in our path and seemed to have broken off at a ninety-degree angle, but I hardly thought it had been carved.

"Wishful thinking," I said and received a sour stare.

But then, ten minutes later, we came across a section that a fallen tree had sheltered, and on it were five seemingly-carved steps.

I stared at them, speechless.

DeNiza scoffed at me. "Not full of sarcasm now, are you?"

We continued to the top of the gorge but found no way to continue. DeNiza unpacked his maps and a compass and spent the next two hours poring over it all. By the time he looked up from his task, the shadows were lengthening.

"We won't find anything now," he said, "but there's still enough light to move camp."

I sighed. The hike up here had been relatively easy, after all, but I wasn't looking forward to descending and then climbing back up with my stuff — and his.

I followed the professor down the canyon, heading back to our camp by the small pond. On the way, I stepped close behind him and asked, "So, you don't know what he found?"

DeNiza flashed me a mouth full of perfect teeth and asked, "Cristóbal? Is it not obvious?"

I didn't reply.

"He had an Aztec coin on him," said DeNiza, laconically. "Possibly the very coin I found three hundred years later."

He shook his head in disbelief.

I was still skeptical. "Possibly," I repeated. "What did he actually say?"

"What did who say?" asked DeNiza.

"What did Cristóbal say to his brother right before he passed out?" I asked. "You said he whispered something."

DeNiza missed a step and almost fell.

"I didn't say he whispered anything," he mumbled defensively. "His brother told him to go back for the treasure."

I glared at him, "You're lying."

He puffed up. "You have no right to any information leading to my treasure."

"You're an idiot," I said. "And you know where you can stick your treasure."

I stepped swiftly past him and took the lead, which seemed to annoy DeNiza, judging by his exhalation. But when we got back to our camp, I stuck to his plan and broke down my tent.

An hour later, I was at the highest accessible point in the steep canyon, and I set up my tent on a limestone shelf.

It took DeNiza another hour to do the same, and he did so lethargically and in silence.

Before it was fully dark, he was in his tent, sleeping, with the screen unzipped. I could hear him twitching and thrashing around, reliving his nightmare once again.

I shouted over, "Hey, Professor! Zip up the tent."

He didn't move. I got up, walked over and bent to zip it up. On the top of his open backpack, I could see an automatic pistol.

I let him be—he could deal with the mosquito bites in the morning.

I crawled into my sleeping bag and listened to the evening while I tried to sleep. An owl called to the waxing moon, and the conversation lulled me to sleep.

Robert Louis DeMayo

# Chapter Sixty-one

### Act II

### 1987
(August)

*B*lackbird singing in the dead of night. No, not a blackbird — most likely a nighthawk or a nightjar. But it's something that's feeding on insects under the starlight.

And they're not bats; I can hear feathers ruffling above my tent when they buzz by. Such a soft sound to awaken to.

One of the birds calls out, "Poor will... poor will".

Crickets and cicadas cry out loudly too, it's a beautiful night, but beneath their chorus, I hear scuffling outside the tent. I sit up.

I unzip my tent enough to peek out and see three sets of luminous yellow eyes staring back at me.

They're perched by the entrance to the professor's tent.

I blink my eyes, questioning my sanity.

And then I realize they are ringtails. As my eyes adjust to the darkness, I see pointed ears floating over a small body — no bigger than a housecat. They look like a cross between a fox and a raccoon.

One of their long black and white tails unexpectedly pops up and waves at me.

I smile — they're like desert lemurs. And as I grasp they are munching on DeNiza's supplies, a slight giggle slips out.

When I climb out of the tent, they scatter, their black and white tails bobbing like glow sticks.

A waning moon has crept into the sky, rising long after sunset, but only now is it gazing down into our canyon — Itzel canyon.

I step into its glow to be bathed in a thin layer of silver moonlight.

Far off, a family of coyotes sings to the night, or maybe to the moon. There is a longing in their cries that I identify with.

Suddenly, something buzzes past my head — scaring the wits out of me for a quick second — and lands a few feet away. A large raven stands looking at me, defiantly.

"I remember you," I say, trying to catch my breath. "You owe me for the parking lot."

It hops around, making strange gurgling noises, and gives me another blank stare.

I eye it for a minute and then say, "Don't plan on getting any treats from me if you scare me again."

It tilts its head sideways, and finally flaps its way to the side of the canyon — about thirty feet away. It seems strange that the raven would be moving after sunset, and I follow.

I find the bird on the slope of the canyon wall, by the base of a large rock, hopping around.

It disappears into a shadow and doesn't return.

I wait a solid minute, then scramble up a scree of loose rock to reach the shadow, and when I do, I see a narrow chute leading upward.

It looks about thirty feet long, and the other end is flooded with soft moonshine.

I take in a long breath of the cool night air, trying to calm my nerves, and ascend.


I emerged into a box canyon, aglow in spectral moonlight. I felt like I must certainly be in a dream. There was no wind; it was dead silent, and time seemed to have stopped. Only the moonbeams flowed, casting disturbing shadows everywhere.

A glimmer reflected off something metallic by the wall, and I headed that way toward an old adobe ruin and a firepit. Each of my steps echoed loudly off the high walls.

By the crumbling ruin sat a Spanish helmet. It was set on a large flat rock as if on display. I reached to touch it but stopped mid-way when I heard a woman singing.

I froze, completely motionless. My heart was pounding. I was barely breathing.

The song held me in a trance. I tried in vain to determine where it came from.

It was my mother's song. I recognized the melody, and hearing it now made me remember aspects of it that I'd forgotten.

Like the sense of peace that filled me as I listened. I felt my mother's love and the life that thrived in the little box canyon. A nearby stand of cliff rose was blossoming, and the white petals gathered in what, to me, suddenly were communities.

Their sweet, heavy scent made me dizzy from twenty feet away.

Even the stars seemed conscious—looking down at me—as they pulsed on the firmament.

We were all one.

And then it was gone. The singing stopped.

"No!" I shouted, the loudness of my voice jolting me.

I quickly left the ruin and walked further back into the box canyon. It lay in heavy shadow, the moonlight eclipsed by the high walls. I took a few tentative steps into the gloom, and a dark chill crept over me.

Someone was standing there.

At the base of the cliff, I could make out what looked like a withered man with one arm stretched above him in a writhing gesture of agony, or perhaps warning. I blinked my eyes and stared hard until I realized I was looking at the twisted remains of a charred juniper. Old Saan would have called that one a medicine tree, and she would probably have claimed that a powerful spirit must reside within it.

I've always prided myself on the fact that I didn't fear many things. Throughout my life, I was calm when many of my friends wanted to run. It was curiosity that drove me more than courage. If someone told me there was a monster in a cave or a ghost in an abandoned house, I would have to check it out.

And it always turned out that the truth wasn't something to fear. I never once found a monster or a ghost.

But this specter of a twisted dying man, crafted from burnt and sand-worn juniper in the moonlit-shadowed canyon, spooked me to the core. I didn't think I could explore any further without the light of day on my side.

As I climbed back down through the tunnel, my eyes never left the canyon. Part of me felt if I turned away, the twisted juniper man would uproot and follow me.

When I got back to my tent, I zipped it up tight and silently crawled deep into my sleeping bag.

And only when my heart had slowed, and my breathing was back to normal, did I again think about the song, and who — or what — the singer may have been.


A scream shattered the tranquility of the next morning. I sat up just in time to see DeNiza bursting through the half-zipped entrance of his tent like he was escaping from a horde of hellish demons.

I figured it was just another nightmare until he kicked free of his sleeping bag and started pointing.

"There's something in my bag," he shrieked. He shook his leg and then touched his calf.

"I think it bit me," he added.

I lifted the sleeping bag and shook it.

A rattlesnake hit the ground and slithered away.

DeNiza cried, "There, I told you."

I grabbed my pack and fetched a small medical kit.

"How many times do I have to tell you to zip up your tent at night?" I calmly asked.

I pointed at his leg. "Take off your pants. Let me look." DeNiza took them off; there was a single perforation.

"There is only one puncture," I said, "it looks like it was a glancing blow." I handed him his pants. "You might get lucky, but we should start back right away, regardless."

"That's ridiculous," DeNiza snapped. "I am not going anywhere. My treasure is here! I can feel it."

I sighed. "You stupid man. If you got bit, this expedition is over. If you can't walk, you're stranded. I can't carry you back."

He started shouting. "I am not leaving! Go if you want—I don't need your help!"

I said, "There's nothing here for you."

DeNiza stared at me for a long minute. Then he narrowed his eyes and said, "You're hiding something."

I said nothing. I tried to control my eyes, but still, my gaze momentarily turned toward the scree and the tunnel.

DeNiza noticed it.

He started heading in that direction.

When he reached the talus slope, he could see a set of fresh footprints that led to and then from the tunnel.

He turned. "Is this why you want me to leave?"

He took a step toward me, his face contorted in anger.

"You found something!" he screamed and raised his arm as if to strike. But something stopped him.

He quickly glanced at his tent—at the open backpack.

Instead, he angrily jabbed his finger at me.

"You have no right to it!" he hissed. "You abnegated any at the start."

Then he stumbled up the hill and under the rock.

I waited a few seconds and followed.

# *Chapter Sixty-two*

*B*y the time I emerged into the box canyon, DeNiza had forgotten his anger—at least temporarily—and was staring around in awe. "This is it," he said reverently as he surveyed the box canyon.

"My treasure is here. I have done it!"

I looked around suspiciously, lost in my own world. Was this my mother's place? I kept asking myself.

Aside from the ruined adobe structure and a bunch of old pots, there wasn't much else in the canyon. I stared at the twisted juniper that had scared me the night before and found it far less daunting in the stark and honest light of day.

At the far end of the canyon—the area obscured by shadow the night before—a lifeless pine had dropped off the plateau. Beneath it, a mass of rotted logs, branches and leaves had piled against the cliff.

It appeared to be a dead end as the walls all ran straight up.

DeNiza approached the ruins and spotted the Spanish helmet. He picked it up and displayed it to me. He had that manic look of pride on his face again.

"My ancestor," he whispered, his face pale and clammy.

He quickly searched the ruin, then he walked the small canyon's perimeter, peering into cracks and crevices in the walls. A mortared wall with a cracked door indicated a Sinaguan grainery, and he stuck his head inside the gap, then pulled it out with a grimace. After he'd completed two loops, he began to limp.

He was heaving when I convinced him to sit down.

He glared at me, "You knew it was here!"

I ignored his words, "You're gonna need a doctor."

DeNiza sneered at me, "You just want me to leave so you can get my treasure."

I looked around but didn't say anything.

"I don't trust you," he snarled.

"Yeah, you made that clear," I said, but he remained quiet as I approached him.

"Lie back," I said and nodded at a gold ring he wore on his right hand. "Take that off before your hands swell up."

He did, still watching me, his eyes cold and focused.

"There's snakeweed here," I said. "If it turns out you were envenomated, I can make a poultice to put on the bite. That might help."

He was sarcastic in his reply. "Look who's suddenly an Indian. Did your mother raise you as a medicine woman? Wouldn't have been your father — not with a white name like Decker."

I stood up and walked away a few steps.

"Let it rot off," I retorted. "I don't care."

"That's what I thought," replied DeNiza. "You would like me to die so you can have it all. Finally, you are speaking veridically."

I was annoyed with him and said, "How much treasure can you carry out with one leg anyway?"

DeNiza became serious. "Maybe you should make the poultice."

I shook my head. "It would be pointless — if you are snake-bit, this expedition is about to become epic. If you weren't envenomated, then you'll be fine. We just need to wait."


DeNiza sat with his back to the wall and watched me set my tent up. I'd made two trips down into Itzel Canyon to retrieve my gear and was now going to wait until I was convinced he was okay.

Unfortunately, he seemed to be okay. Two hours had passed since he'd kicked the snake out of his bag, and aside from being slightly hysterical, he wasn´t showing any symptoms.

But he fidgeted constantly.

"Relax, Carlos," I said, "you're still a day ahead of schedule. Tomorrow is August fifteenth. Wasn't that your big plan? To rediscover the treasure on the harmonic convergence?"

He snickered, "I do not give a damn about this convergence — my quest is far more ancient."

I laughed. "Really? Oh, please do tell."

My tent was up, and I began throwing my gear inside.

He glared at me but couldn't resist having an audience.

"According to Shearer's interpretation of Aztec cosmology," he began, "the day Hernán Cortés landed in Mexico, April 22, 1519, was the beginning of nine hell cycles, each of 52 years."

I stood and grinned. "Oh, this just keeps getting better — nine hell cycles, really?"

He nodded. "And guess when nine cycles of 52 end if you began in 1519?"

He stared at me until I finally muttered, "That would be 1987."

His confidence returned and swept his features as he said, "Precisely."

"And is that when we begin a new era?" I asked cynically. "Another Age of Aquarius or something like that?"

He scoffed. "Shearer would have you believe it would lead to the end of evils in the modern world — no more materialism, war, oppression or injustice."

I gave him a hard stare. "And what do you think?"

He rubbed the back of his neck. "From 1987, there is still another twenty-five years left in the Mayan Long Count calendar, which ends in 2012. And when it terminates, no one knows if the Mayans thought it would be the end of so-called history, or if it might simply be the beginning of another 5,125-year cycle."

"You sound as skeptical as me," I said. "Why treat these dates so importantly?"

He gave me a grin. "Because it was important to the Aztecs."


DeNiza, it turned out, was doing fine. But the heat was taking a toll. By ten, the temperatures were in the nineties, and before noon it had to be over a hundred. DeNiza returned to Itzel Canyon, broke down his tent, then hauled it up the chute with his oversized backpack.

He'd unpacked the duffle bags the night before, and it took him several more trips to carry the loose gear up into the box canyon. I didn't help with any of it, and it pissed him off.

Instead, I got a low fire going in the pit by the ruins.

Above us, I saw monsoon clouds hovering. A few had long strains of virga trailing, but the rain evaporated long before it reached the ground.

DeNiza set a bag of provisions by the fire, and when I spotted tea in the mix, I boiled water in an old Sinaguan vessel. I made a cup for each of us, and when he saw that, he relaxed a little.

He grabbed an avocado and knife from his stores and sat near me, with his back to the shaded wall. He cut the avocado in two and gave me half.

I accepted it, and he smiled. "The word avocado comes from an Aztec word, *ahuácatl*, which means testicle."

"Not the high-brow humor I would have expected from you, Professor," I said.

He shrugged. "Then you do not want to know what guacamole means."

A rare laugh escaped my lips, and I sat against the wall next to him. The strip of coolness along the wall was the only place to hide from the brutal heat. Storm clouds occasionally floated over us, rumbling but casting no rain.

DeNiza stumbled around the canyon every hour or so, but it only took a few minutes in the glaring sunlight to force him back against the wall.

He glanced at a fence lizard clinging to the rock. "I feel like one of these creatures," he said. "Hiding from the sun."

He sat down with a huff and focused his attention on the wall opposite us. He was quiet for a few minutes when suddenly he jumped up and shouted, "Do you see that?"

I looked up expectantly. "See what?"

DeNiza leaned forward awkwardly, peering through the heat to the other side of the box canyon. He walked straight to the wall and pointed. "Here! Look! There is a vertical line of holes drilled into this rock face."

I was skeptical. "Are you sure they're man-made?"

DeNiza was rapidly losing patience with me and snapped, "Of course they are. Look at the precision."

Each hole was about an inch wide, deeper than a finger, and two feet above the last.

He proudly pointed to the holes. "This is a ladder."

I laughed. "Are you high? Where would it go to?"

DeNiza replied indignantly, "No, I am not high. I do not do drugs." Then he nodded at the holes and added, "The ladder goes up. They must have put the treasure up there."

We both looked up the wall, but fifty vertical feet were all we could see from the ground. Further up, the cliff slanted back and out of sight.

De Niza started to walk in circles, mumbling as he made his plan.

"We will make pegs," he said, "and place them in the holes and climb."

I walked over to the wall, examined the holes, and then glanced up. "You're on your own, Carlos."

He rolled his eyes. "You are a coward."

I shook my head, "I don't think the treasure is up there, and I'm not going near your so-called ladder."

He shrugged it off. "I do not need your help. You have no rights to this treasure anyway."

I sighed and replied, "You're gonna break your damn neck."

DeNiza stormed off, searching for sticks.

When he had collected an armful, he grabbed a sharp knife from his pack, sat against the wall, and started making pegs.

He was pretty worked up and made it a point of focusing his frustration on me. "You could have been famous," said DeNiza.

He chopped a long stick in half and added, "You could have been part of restoring my family honor."

He hacked at another stick.

I looked at the distance up the cliff again. I didn't bother to mention that nowhere in this expedition had he ever offered me to be part of it—other than as a porter.

It was fine by me. I wanted no part of his plans.

"No, I'd rather just watch this," I said.

DeNiza stopped working and looked at me for a long time.

"Yes, I can see this now," stated DeNiza. "Family honor doesn't mean anything to you."

I stared at the ground.

DeNiza continued, "You have nothing to say? Why aren't you telling me how proud you are of your people? Or your family? How about your tribe? No cute little stories about kin?"

I snapped back, "What's so great about people, Carlos? Or family, for that matter?"

DeNiza smiled and pointed at me with his knife. "That's right. You don't know them. You don't know your ancestors, either."

I got up and walked away. "Go to hell."

He gave me an evil grin as he drove his point home. "That is why you do not know yourself." He stuck the knife in a log and walked to the wall.

DeNiza placed one of his foot-long pegs in a hole and stood on it, testing its strength. Then he inserted another in the next hole.

In this manner, he began to climb the cliff face.

The large raven returned, suddenly swooping in and perching itself on top of a dried-out stalk of agave where it could watch the show.

"You see, it is so simple," called DeNiza. He moved up a step and said, "Because you could not conceive it, you shall not share in my great discovery."

I replied, "Why not let me worry about what I conceive."

To this, DeNiza laughed. It was a snort, really.

He said, "One like you is not worthy of my noble bloodline."

I leaned against the wall to watch, "Keep climbing, Carlos. This is gonna be good."

Soon he was thirty feet above the ground, but there seemed to be no end to the ascent. The rock face above remained vertical for another twenty feet before slanting back, out of sight.

As he moved to place another peg, a sudden "crack" echoed through the canyon. A nervous expression crossed his face. He tried to descend, but the peg he was standing on snapped, and he began to fall.

Frantically he reached for the passing pegs and managed to grab one long enough to slow his momentum, but then it broke as well and sent him crashing through the remainder of the pegs.

He hit the ground hard.

I watched with a satisfied grin as he limped to the fire.

The raven cawed and flew off. As it ascended above the section the professor was climbing, it got a bird's overview of everything. On the flat surface of the wall, out of sight from the box canyon, a huge Aztec glyph was carved into the rock.

And a light breeze blew over the image, tumbling grains of sand and whispering, "*Xibalba...*"

# Chapter Sixty-three

The distant sun crept over the rim of the West Fork, like a spider, shining yellow and black as it squeezed around the spires of rock. And its first intrepid rays shot into the box canyon, illuminating the entrance to a cave.

DeNiza leapt to his feet. He had hardly slept, and for the last few shivering hours, he'd simply waited for the sunrise. But when it had instantly shone under a dead tree and lit up the cave entrance, he was barely ready for it.

"Come on!" he shouted to me. He was excited, like a boy.

I followed him to the back of the canyon, where he grabbed the old pine that had obscured the entrance, and with a lot of grunting and moaning, he dragged it out of the way.

The pile of logs and debris left was rotted and covered with charcoal. Behind the rubble, I could see into a low cave.

DeNiza tore at the clutter that blocked the cave entrance, stirring fine powdered dust. In a few minutes, a way was cleared.

He was covered with soot, and he was grinning.

He held up a charred stump and said, "Looks like there was a fire here once." He stared up and saw how the overhanging cliff would have sheltered it from the rain.

As he moved one of the crumbling logs out of the way, an odd man-made object was exposed. DeNiza grabbed it and brushed off the accumulated ash and soot, and an ancient black-powder pistol was revealed. The wooden handgrip had been mostly burned away. He raised it reverently and mused, "Perhaps my ancestor died defending this treasure."

I said, "More likely trying to steal it."

DeNiza stared at me. "What makes you think my ancestor was such a bad person?"

We gazed at the dark entrance to the cave. It seemed the passing wind got sucked right into it. I asked, "What makes you think he was good? He carved up his chest, he scalped Indians, and he was ruthless."

DeNiza nodded. "He was a man of power in a brutal world. I think you cannot fathom the sacrifices he made in the name of a greater good."

"No, that's not it," I replied, "I've never had much money, but I can't see how a treasure could drive you to do what he did to his body."

DeNiza scoffed at me and shook his head.

We crouched as we entered the main chamber, which was lit up by the light from outside. Inside the cave, the air was stale. It faintly smelled of death in here.

The sound of dripping water filled the silence.

I paused on a mound in the middle of several puddles while DeNiza quickly walked the perimeter. Under several of the constant drips, the ancients had placed large clay vessels to catch the water. They were overflowing, and the dark water rippled with each drop.

DeNiza passed a dark recess by the entrance and glanced in, but without a flashlight, he could see nothing.

From my perch, I looked over the various pictographs that adorned the walls. Closer to me, on the mound, I noticed an assortment of offerings: several bowls containing different colored powders, a yellow drinking tube, some ancient dried seeds and a doll. There were also three river-rounded stones that were covered with an orange lichen, next to an old metate with a basalt mano.

The doll was made from a corn cob wrapped in a soft piece of leather. I held it up.

"Look at this," I said. "It has to be hundreds of years old."

DeNiza took it briefly, paused only long enough to confirm it wasn't made of gold, then tossed it on the ground. He sniffed one of the containers of grey powder with disgust.

"I'm surprised that stuff has not decomposed," he said.

He glanced at the dark recess again and said, "I'm going for a flashlight—don't touch anything."

I didn't move. Not because DeNiza had commanded it, but because I sensed something special about the place. The water dripping down into the clear pools echoed throughout the cave.

I looked around, taking it all in.

Beyond the dripping, I heard the voice of old Saan, saying, "She was scared, child, very scared. So, she ran to the cave where the water drips and hid there."

I looked around with fresh eyes, my hands exploring the sand mound, feeling the soft impression on the top. It looked as if someone had once lain on this very spot.

I remembered Saan also said, "When the water hit her, that's when she got pregnant."

I ran my hands under the sand, letting it sift through my fingers. And then I heard Saan again, saying, "Your mother said she found that place once."

I whispered, "What really happened here, Saan?"

Then my hand encountered an object: one that was solid and heavy.

I extracted an ancient leather bundle from the sand mound and gaped at it for a moment. A leather cord held it closed.

I was about to pull the cord when I heard DeNiza returning.

Quickly, I reburied it.


Over the next few hours, DeNiza scoured the cave. True to his word, he had brought everything he would need. He began by setting up a large, battery-powered floodlight, and then photographed the chamber and the various pictographs.

The dark recess by the entrance contained a partial bear skull, and he withdrew from it in disappointment.

But he was in his element, taking notes and doing fieldwork. Without even asking me for help, he carried his equipment into the cave, storing it all in the small recess.

The cave had become an archaeological site, and he sectioned it off in a grid-like pattern, using a small collapsible shovel, string, a hammer and stakes. Every few minutes, he scribbled something in a small notebook.

He stepped into a hazmat suit, apparently to test the various powders. It was a flimsy white outfit with a hood and a clear plastic face. "You look like an astronaut," I said. He blushed a little at that, apparently enjoying the comparison.

"Go ahead," he said, "laugh at me, but I will not have this expedition tainted because of contamination or incompetence."

He had given me specific instructions not to touch anything and only observe from the mound. I sat there on my perch in the sand, almost next to him; no hazard suit for me.

"Well, I hope there's nothing here that could mess me up," I said.

He relaxed. "No, most likely not. I would guess the powders are a mix of pigment made from natural sources, plus pollen, and maybe a psychedelic."

I lit up at that. I had done psychedelics — mushrooms in my case — at a Grateful Dead show in Oakland the year before.

He pointed at one of the bowls — the one filled with seeds.

"I believe these are seeds of the morning glory plant. The Aztecs called them *ololiuqui,* and they consumed them regularly because they contained a hallucinogen very much like LSD."

"Really?" I asked. "Why would they do drugs like that?"

He sat back and stared at me.

"You have no idea what this is all about, do you?"

I gazed back at him and had to admit to myself I really didn't.

"Okay," he began in his most patient voice. "In Mesoamerica, they held beliefs that the dead lived in the earth and mountains. Caves were sacred because they were a direct connection to that underworld.

"By going deep into caves, the Mayans and Aztecs supposed they could contact the dead. To them, a cave was basically a church, and by leaving offerings and conducting rituals, they could petition their ancestors for favor and protection."

"The underworld..." I teased. "That's pretty heavy."

He frowned at me. "It is my belief that the Aztecs thought this cave to be a door to the afterworld, and by leaving a sufficient offering, they might control who entered – and who returned."

"The power of life over death?" I asked.

He shrugged and gave a weak smile. "Who knows?"

"What about the psychedelics?"

DeNiza nodded. "The Aztecs believed when you ingested these substances – hallucinatory mushrooms or seeds – you were transported directly into the spirit world."

I fidgeted on the mound, pondering his words.

He continued, "Aztec warriors would take mushroom enemas before they went into battle."

"What the fuck, Carlos?" I said, shocked. "That's messed up."

He gave me a rare smile. "Yes, it truly is. But they believed once the hallucinogens were in their system, they were in the spirit world, amongst the gods – so any price was worth paying."


I woke in the dead of night, just like the previous night. I quietly slipped out of my sleeping bag and exited the tent.

What was left of the waning moon had slid across the sky hours before, and it was very dark. After a moment my eyes adjusted, and I moved away from the campsite and the adobe ruin.

From the back of the canyon, I could hear something that sounded like a chant. The further back in the box canyon I walked, the clearer the sound became.

This was not my mother's song, and something about it terrified me, but I had to follow.

As soon as I entered the dark cave, the chanting stopped.

DeNiza had turned off his floodlights, and I squinted in the dark. Then I saw that the far end of the cave had a slight glow. The basalt stones on the mound glowed softly, too. It was just enough for me to get my bearings in the dark and not trip on one of the survey strings.

I walked the perimeter of the cave.

And then, from the low end of the cave—where the glow was strongest—I could hear a voice.

It was very faint as it called out.

All the hair on my arms and neck stood on end. The voice was whispering my name. "Amber... Amber..."

This was not my mother's voice. I shivered and somehow found the nerve to crawl forward.

At the far end of the cave, I could see a small opening: air whistled through it. On the other side, I could dimly make out an open space. When I got closer, the whispering stopped.

I inched my head nearer to the opening, and suddenly the chanting started again—the same as the night before. But this time, it wasn't faint and distant—this time, the voice was only a few feet away.

I jumped backward, and the darkness smothered me and my courage, and I fled the cave.

Not twenty feet from the entrance, I almost ran into DeNiza, who was standing there. I shrieked and jumped.

He hissed furiously, "What are you doing here?"

I still hadn't caught my breath. "You bastard, you scared me."

He didn't care. "I asked you what you are doing here?"

"Will you relax?" I said. "I left my sweater on the mound, and I had to go to the bathroom. What's wrong with you?"

He seemed charged, like a thunderstorm.

I gave him a stare. "Can't I get a little privacy?"

DeNiza looked around suspiciously. He glanced at the entrance to the cave, only a few paces away.

He said, "I don't trust you. You're being deceitful—again."

"Lighten up, Carlos," I replied. "I just have to take a leak."

He stood staring at me. "I will have this treasure."

I unbuttoned my jeans. "Do you mind?" I asked.
He turned and walked away.

# Chapter Sixty-four

The bruises on DeNiza's chest and ribs had yellowed to almost the same color as the sandstone walls. He stood with his shirt off, leaning against the cliff wall, a short way from the fire. He was unshaven, hadn't slept a wink, and his polished, professional veneer was fading away.

I was heating a pot of water over the fire and looked busy, but from the corner of my eyes I kept a close watch on him as he showed a tension that promised trouble.

He walked to his tent, grabbed a fresh shirt, and began to button it up. He was red-faced and twitchy. It was taking a visible effort to look calm.

He caught my eye and chuckled to himself, then smiled broadly and said, "I can tell when you´re hiding something."

He wagged his finger at me. "I'm not sure why you would not want me to find my treasure," DeNiza continued. "I'm not even sure if *you* want to find it."

He picked up the Spanish helmet and stared at it. "But you know something, and you don't want to share."

I took the pot off the fire and added one of my freeze-dried soups: mushroom. I ignored him while I stirred the soup.

DeNiza said, "You can trust me. I'm in this for good reasons: family honor. Plus, I'm a respected professor. I have tenure."

I remained silent.

Exasperated, he turned his palms up and pleaded, "Please, where is my treasure? What are you hiding?"

I handed him a bowl of soup.

He took it, lifted the spoon to his mouth, and pretended to taste it. "Why won't you just tell me?" he asked.

He was starting to twitch with frustration.

I stood directly in front of him and demanded, "Tell me what Cristóbal said to Alonso just before he died."

DeNiza smashed the bowl of soup against the cliff wall. He seemed to grow in size as he stomped around and angrily yelled at me, "Why can't you just answer a simple question? Are you so afraid of trusting someone?"

I tried to speak but couldn't find the words. Finally, I spat out, "Screw it. You want to know what I know?"

DeNiza said, "I do," as he stepped forward in anticipation.

I met his eyes, "Once you find your treasure, will you tell me everything?"

DeNiza hesitated, scratched his ear, and then smiled and said, "Of course."

I pointed to the far end of the box canyon. I said, "On the other side of the chamber where the water drips, there's another room."

He pointed an accusing finger at me, "I knew you were hiding something!"

I shook my head. "You're the one that's hiding something."


DeNiza crawled to the back of the cave and pointed his floodlight directly into the small hole in the wall. I sat on the mound, watching him.

He said, "It seems like there's a chamber or tunnel here, but it has been walled off. I left my flashlight in the tent."

He paused at the entrance and warned me, "Stay where you are until I return."

I replied, "Just relax, Carlos."


At first, there was only a gap of a few inches between the opening in the wall and the ceiling, but soon DeNiza began shoveling away the dirt piled in front of it. It was not graceful to watch: the collapsible shovel was very small, and the professor was clearly inexperienced in manual labor.

But he was ecstatic. Sweat poured off him.

He'd had the foresight to wiggle out of his hazard suit first, whose pure factory white was already tinted pink. He wasn't so much afraid that he would get it dirty as that he might puncture the suit while digging.

After a few minutes the outline of a stone doorway became visible. DeNiza proudly pointed at his discovery, "You see this? These are not natural stones — this was built."

The stones that filled the entrance were a mismatched collection of sandstone, limestone and basalt.

"And these stones were added much later," he said and began taking them out, one by one, and placing them to the side.

Some of the stones — the black basalt — had an orange lichen clinging to them, which glowed slightly. But DeNiza barely noticed it when his eyes fell on what the wall concealed.

His jaw dropped, and he moved in slow motion as he removed the last few stones. His silence got my attention, and I crept closer, breaking his rule and moving off the mound.

Before him lay a pile of blue-tinted bones, chains and Aztec weapons, and interspersed were hundreds of gold coins. Small brown mushrooms had spread over everything.

DeNiza lifted one of the coins and gazed at it reverently.

But then a look of panic crept over his face when he felt the familiar warmth. He dropped the coin and then quickly scrambled into his hazard suit again.

He turned to call me closer and actually looked pleased to see me nearby already.

With the tip of one gloved finger, he nudged a mushroom cap and said, "These are *Psilocybe Mexicana*. The Aztecs called them *Teōnanācatl*. The Spanish believed this mushroom allowed the Aztecs to communicate with devils."

DeNiza lifted an Aztec club, only slightly, to show me a few of the mushrooms clinging to it. The weapon was made of wood, about four feet long, flat like a cricket bat, and had edges that had been lined with sharp chips of obsidian.

He noticed me observing the weapon and said, "It is called a *macuahuitl*. Only one example of this weapon survived the Spanish Conquest of Mexico, but sadly it was destroyed in a fire in 1884."

We both looked at the mound of bones and weapons and could make out at least a dozen more armaments.

"What a collection this treasure will make," he said.

I glanced beyond the pile and only now saw that there was a tunnel, not just a room. "And what about down there?" I asked.

DeNiza looked away from the tunnel nervously. In fact, I noticed then that he would not even glance in that direction. I would have charged down it in a heartbeat—but I could see now that he was afraid even to enter it.

"One step at a time," he said. "We must document this before we move on."

# Chapter Sixty-five

The *macuahuitl* truly was a work of art. DeNiza separated it from the pile, reverently, and several gold coins spilled off. He ran a gloved hand over the obsidian flakes embedded in the side of the weapon.

Under the hood, I could hear his muffled laughter.

"Still so sharp," he said.

He tenderly carried the club over to the light to see it better. He was talking to himself, mumbling something about filling his own museum. I noticed artifacts in the cave glowed slightly, but under the harsh light of the spotlight, they were covered with an orange powder.

When he turned away, I grabbed several mushroom caps and quickly stuck them in my pocket.

Since I'd set my eyes on them, my mind was racing.

I remembered ingesting mushrooms at the Grateful Dead show. We ate them an hour before the show began, and on our way to the Coliseum, had stopped at a rest area by a lake.

While my friends shuffled into the bathroom, I'd walked down to the water. And as my nervous system absorbed the psilocybin, my mind embraced the beautiful natural setting.

Suddenly the lake and trees around me took on a pastel sheen, and the grass and trees swayed in unison. And when I examined the trees closer, I had the overwhelming sense that they were conscious. Each individual tree now seemed aware of me, and I felt blessed to be in their presence.

Eventually, my friends returned and dragged me off to the concert. And that was fun, too. Magical, even. But what stayed with me was the connected feeling that had possessed me by the lake.

And when I heard my mother's song two nights earlier, I'd been overcome with the same sensation. Connected. Alive.

I didn't know how a song could convey a feeling like that. Couldn't fathom it. But my mushroom experience was my connection, and I had to explore that possibility.

So, while DeNiza tinkered in the cave, I heated some water in a Sinaguan bowl I found by the firepit and eventually dropped the mushroom caps into it. I let it steep for a few minutes, then drank the tea — eating the caps when the liquid was gone.

I had picked a dramatic day for my experiment. Dark-bellied clouds raced overhead, and an erratic wind blew through our canyon. It dawned on me that we were within the harmonic convergence, and I imagined the planets all lining up in my mind.

The canyon walls reflected the sun with a shimmer, rippling golden waves like they were a giant set of quaking lungs. And the sounds of birds and insects and creaking trees all merged into a chorus of conversations that I felt I understood. Dragonflies and butterflies spiraled past me, leaving contrails.

The raven landed next to me. Light reflected halo-like off its dark feathers. It stared at me knowingly.

"Hello, Auntie..." I said. My voice sounded like it came from another body.

I let my eyes drift over the Sinaguan pictographs that lined the walls. An image of a bear paw, and then one of a woman in childbirth, leaped out at me. Even after I closed my eyes, those images still ran before me.

I lay back and tried to control my breathing.

Keeping my eyes shut did make things easier.

While the gentle sounds of the canyon washed over me, I emptied my mind and waited to see what would fill the void.

Soon I saw the entrance to the cave. But it was different than now.

In my vision, several large alligator-bark junipers were flanking the ingress and clinging to one of them, a young girl of around ten stole glances into the cave.

She appeared terrified, more so as time went by until soon she began to sing nervously. It was my mother's song, and I swayed with it as I watched.

And then, from within the cave, from the shadows near the back, I could see two women crawling from a tunnel. When they reached the open air, the three embraced and cried.

With their tears, I cried my own. Not knowing why or who they were.

Before I could ponder this scene, I was swept away by the sun arching over me. I kept my eyes closed, but still, I watched it pass by — day after day — in a dizzying blur.

When the blinking light stopped, I was once again watching a young woman, maybe sixteen, and I observed her slowly wall up the tunnel.

It was tedious work, and by the time she was done, she sat in the dark, surrounded by several basalt rocks that had earlier been inside the tunnel. In the murky gloom, they glowed.

Time stretched then, and the woman drifted in and out of the cave until one day she returned and sat next to a metate. She placed a few dried ears of corn on the flat stone, grabbed one of the basalt stones, and, using it as a mano, began to grind the corn.

In the process, the lichen clinging to the rock was ground free and mixed with the milled corn.

The next morning, the woman ate a meal and waited for the sun. Over the next few minutes she began to look around strangely, and not long after, she began to sing.

And the song stayed with me while the sun spun overhead once more.

Visions danced before my eyes, some not making sense at all.

I noticed some of the women ground the lichen-covered mano into the metate to collect the orange powder and then store it in one bowl.

Time continued to spin and morph. I saw a young woman being marched in front of a ruthless Aztec lord—a man with filed teeth. Then I watched her in the cave as she put on a bear claw necklace and suddenly transformed into a bear.

And then another young woman screamed at a Spaniard who stared at her in confused adoration. He also appeared to gaze at the trees and shrubs as if they were something sacred.

It seemed these women were all within me. They were spinning and twirling through the years. I could hear their voices, and even though they spoke in different languages, their message was clear: Do not go into the dark chamber. Do not go into the dark chamber.

And the visions were always accompanied by the song, which sometimes held a magical power and at other times was just a song.

Over time the women changed until several appeared who were white. But, strangely, they also knew the song.

And the melody swept me along. Timelessly. Until eventually, I realized I'd been lying by the firepit, awake, for quite some time.

The sun had lowered itself over the far wall of the canyon, and I was in shadow.

I sat up and brushed myself off.

I was still a bit shaky when I finally stood up.

DeNiza hadn't left the cave, it seemed. I could see his floodlight pooling by the entrance.

I walked to him.

# Chapter Sixty-six

*I* paused at the entrance to the cave and observed the professor. He was still hunched in the corner, bent over the pile. Behind him, a tarp was laid out with an assortment of weapons and bones that he'd separated from the heap.

By his side, a plastic tray was filled with gold coins.

He kept digging into the pile, now and then turning to scribble down a line in his notebook.

As I approached him, I noticed a small tear in the back of his hazmat suit.

When he turned around, I was surprised to see him grinning euphorically, humming a tune. He smiled broadly and affably exclaimed, "Look who has returned!"

He had the hazmat suit hood pulled over his head, and his excited breath kept fogging the faceplate.

I smiled sheepishly, still partially under the subtle influence of the mushrooms. "Couldn't stay away," I said and sat down on the low mound by the bowls of powder and the metate.

And I couldn't stay away. The visions I'd just had made me want to explore the cave myself and see what truths might be concealed there — and maybe finally unravel the mystery of my mother's song.

The faces from my vision stayed with me — noetically — as did some of their actions. My eyes drifted to the metate and mano. I picked up the yellow drinking tube, examined it, then stuck the end in the bowl containing the orange powder, stirring it.

I thought of old Saan and my mother and wondered about their connection to the box canyon.

They had felt close to me when I was in the cave, and I wanted to embrace that feeling. It warmed me. DeNiza watched my every move — still smiling.

I said, "My Auntie used to talk about a place like this."

DeNiza sat back and pulled off the hazmat hood. He arched his neck and rubbed it vigorously with his gloved left hand. He inhaled some dust and sneezed.

He didn't move for almost a full minute while he stared at his gloved hands, and during this time, his mood slowly darkened. He pretended to acknowledge my words, almost as an afterthought, as he painfully stood as much as the low chamber would allow.

"Really?" he asked. "What did she say about it?"

I lowered my gaze. "She said it was a place where men weren't allowed."

The professor jerked and banged his head on the low ceiling. He staggered backward, and his jolly mood had now transformed to irritation. "Are you telling me you think I have no right to be here?" he snapped.

He lifted one of the Aztec weapons — a shorter, bone-handled club — and asked, "You think maybe I should step outside?"

He tested the club's weight by thumping his other gloved hand with it. His face had turned a dark red.

His voice rose. "That maybe this place is sacred to someone whom I might offend?"

I realized I should have kept quiet. "I didn't say any of that."

He seemed disoriented, "*Bueno*, because it is pretty damn sacred to me."

He stopped suddenly and stared directly at me.

Slowly he smiled. "Now I see your plan — your little game," said DeNiza. "You think if you can link this to your people, that they can claim this as their treasure?"

I shook my head. "I told you, I'm not in this for the treasure."

DeNiza grabbed me roughly. "Then tell me what you are really looking for, Amber?"

"I want the truth!" I screamed as he squeezed my arms.

He had caught me off guard, my mind still fuzzy from the mushrooms. Before I could react, he pushed me down, and when I moved to stand again, he backhanded me with force.

A drop of blood flew off my lip and landed in the sand, and suddenly the sky outside the entrance flickered with lightning.

The pain brought me around, but as I crept into a defensive stance with my feet planted, DeNiza pulled out his pistol and pointed it at me.

He loomed over me, menacing, daring me to advance until I stepped back submissively. A crazed look in his eyes made me fear him for the first time. I raised my hands defensively and said, "My father always said that this cave never existed, that it was just a story."

I looked around and sighed, "He was wrong."

DeNiza laughed, "I see no connection between this cave and your people. Do you think this is the only cave in Arizona with water dripping in it?"

"But it's clear Indians lived here," I said. "Look at the pictographs and pottery. And what about that symbol on your map?"

He gave me a pathetic look. "Yes, I will concede that Native Americans used the box canyon, and maybe even this cave—but there is no connection between them and the hoard in the tunnel. And the symbols you refer to on my map are Sinaguan, not Apache. They predate the arrival of your people in this valley."

I paused and then said, "My mother claimed that she found this cave years ago." My reply seemed to baffle DeNiza, and then he shouted, "No! Enough!"

He stood before me, belligerent. His hands were shaking as he raised the gun. Suddenly I had no doubt what his truculent behavior would lead to.

He was shouting now. "Do you think your mother's people would have left this tunnel unexplored? That they would not have burned with curiosity about what lies beyond?"

I shook my head. "Maybe they didn't know about the tunnel, at least not in modern times," I said.

He disagreed, "That is not realistic. Not if they were living here. Someone would know."

I suggested, "Maybe the women knew, but they kept it a secret to protect the men."

At this he started to laugh. "So that is why your mother never told anyone about it, right? And now you are carrying on the tradition. *Bastante!*"

He became serious again. "I am tired of your pathetic stories."

He was a stranger to firearms, and when he turned his gaze to the pistol to cock it, I reached behind me and grabbed the yellow drinking tube. He turned back to me, and I was ready.

I had raised the yellow straw to point at his eyes and quickly blew through it. A cloud of orange powder hit him in the face, momentarily blinding him.

He screamed, and I fled the cave, remaining outside in the shadows by the entrance. In the last moments of light, the dark monsoonal clouds shone orange and red overhead.

DeNiza grabbed a handkerchief from a pocket and wiped his face. "How amusing," he said. "You best stay outside. If you follow me, I will kill you."

He entered the tunnel, stepping over the remaining bones and weapons. In a few strides, he was out of sight. I listened to his steps fade, and then I heard a whipping sound, followed by a thud.

DeNiza emitted a piercing scream. Then, all was silent.


I stood as still as an egret, holding my breath and listening with my whole body. The silence that greeted me was formidable and hung in the air like a mist.

After a few long moments, I began to relax. I re-entered the cave and sat down heavily on the dry mound.

I had a bloody nose and a fat lip. As I wiped the gore off my face, I looked up and saw a bloody handprint on the ceiling. I gazed at my red hand. Then I lay back and stared at the ceiling.

After a moment, a drop of water let loose and hit me on the forehead.

# Chapter Sixty-seven

## Act III

### 1987
(September)

*I* tried to control my breathing, but my mind was racing, and the cave spun around me. The muffled smell of death skulked in the still air and seemed to move toward me despite no trace of a breeze.

I could hear a rasping ethereal whisper from within the tunnel and beyond that a low hum.

I glanced through the cave entrance at the now dark red-black sky outside.

It saddened me that my quest to find my mother's place – an obsession that at one time had shone like a clear flame lighting the way – had led me to such a seemingly-evil place.

The box canyon outside, the cliffs, the gentle pines – even the blood-colored sky above – had once been part of what I called home.

But not anymore. Now, this wilderness felt pitiless – as if it had turned against me – and my quest, pointless. All I had ever truly yearned for was a connection with my mother. And still, I didn't know if this was even the place she had talked about visiting all those years ago.

I wiped my brow and noticed my hand was covered with orange powder.

I gave it the smallest of tastes, trying to unravel its mystery. In my vision, I'd seen the women harvesting the powder for a mysterious use.

A red-tailed hawk screeched outside. The shrill cry pierced the still air of the canyon, found me sitting in the cave, and like a sharp arrow, seemed to fly straight into me.

I felt bewitched. The pictographs lining the walls appeared to be moving, as did the ceiling above them. And anywhere my eyes swept, they seemed to trail my vision.

Suddenly it dawned on me: The powder was a psychedelic. An intolerable weight pressed on my chest, and I could barely breathe. I must have ingested some when I blew it in DeNiza's face.

My gaze dropped low until it focused on the mound.

I heard the whispering stronger now.

The Apache say that the land stalks them; and I truly felt pursued. But they also believe the land forces them to live right, and I wondered how that could be. Were these whispers warning me away or leading me on? I didn't know.

I sighed, feeling lost.

I picked up the corncob doll. DeNiza had handled it roughly, and I straightened the leather covering before leaning it against the wall, behind the metate, in a place of honor.

"That's better," I said.

I reached into my pocket and took out the photograph of my mother and Saan. I decided that if my mother had found the box canyon and this cave, she had never ventured down the dark tunnel.

After staring at the picture for a minute, I placed it with the doll and said, "I think you both would have liked this."

I looked around the low cave. The rhythmic dripping of water was soothing. I added, "To be here."

I exhaled and wiped the blood and sweat from my face. My upper lip throbbed from where DeNiza had smacked me.

In a weak voice, I said, "Where there is lightness, there is darkness."

Looking up, I stared at the bloody handprint again—and then into the tunnel.

I boiled inside with rage when I thought of DeNiza and shouted, "Treasures that drive weak men insane? Isn't that what you said, Carlos?"

I looked around the cave and then outside.

I shouted again, "Got nothing to say? Is that really what Cristóbal died for—for a treasure?"

I squinted my eyes, peering into the tunnel, and listened.

And then I remembered the leather-bound bundle I'd discovered earlier. I dug into the mound and lifted it. Opening the thong and leather cover revealed a white stone with a gold band.

The sight of it took my breath away. I reached out my trembling hand to touch it. When the polished stone came into contact with my bloody fingers, it began to glow, and I sensed a soothing warmth rush through my body—a lightness.

I stared in awe for a solid minute, the low radiance lighting up the chamber. Could this be real? I asked myself. Or is it the drug? The whispers around me intensified, and I sensed if I listened long enough, they might tell me the secrets I was longing to learn.

I remembered old Saan speaking of recreating the past, claiming it was "a well-worn trail that is always in use." And oh, how I'd clung to her words when she added, "Even if all you have are scattered footprints, you can still reconstruct the truth from that if you are patient."

"But how?" I had queried.

And she had replied, "By not losing yourself."

I surveyed the cave where the water drips again. The tunnel that DeNiza had disappeared into remained silent but was never far from my thoughts. I was scared—and more than a little curious—about what might lay on the other end, and I found myself being inexorably drawn to it.

I stood and faced the tunnel. I didn't know if I was meant to explore it or not, but I decided if I proceeded, it would not be in a panic. Instead, I would do so as old Saan had suggested: with smoothness, resilience and steadiness.

I reluctantly re-wrapped the white stone in the leather bundle and buried it in the sand. Its secrets would have to wait.

Then I stood and brushed the dirt off my clothes.

I felt disconnected from my body as I forced myself to take deliberate, almost measured, steps toward the ominous tunnel.

\* \* \*

DeNiza regained consciousness to find a log holding him against the wall. His face was still covered with the glowing powder, and there was a radiance around his field of vision. He tried to move, and a piercing pain in his left thigh alerted him to an injury.

A light green glow filled the tunnel, and in that murky illumination, he discovered he had fallen victim to an ancient trap.

A stake at the end of the log had embedded itself in his outer thigh. A dark puddle was pooling under him.

"*Madre de Dios!*" he whispered.

His words echoed strangely in the chamber. And then he heard voices coming from the shadows around him. *Your treasure waits for you... Tesoro... it is yours for the taking.*

They lulled him. Enticing him. If only he could get free.

He wanted to shout for help but found himself mesmerized by the sight of his blood dripping into the puddle on the floor. Even the echo of the drops was enchanting. The fluid seemed to move of its own volition as it drained into a carved channel, eventually disappearing into a hole in the middle of a large capstone.

Instantly, the glowing lichen in the tunnel began to pulse.

This yanked him out of his awed stupor.

He twisted and screamed, and the decrepit wooden structure collapsed, ripping the stake out of his leg with a wrenching pain as the log fell to the ground.

The hazmat suit prevented him from seeing how badly he was injured, and he painfully crawled out of it. When he glanced at his leg, he almost passed out. His khakis had been torn away to reveal a nasty gash with a strip of dangling flesh.

He tore the sleeve off the flimsy hazmat suit and wrapped it around the wound as tightly as he could to stop the bleeding.

His leg ached when he put pressure on it, but he knew this would not deter him. Not when he was this close.

He examined the opening in the tunnel where the trap lay.

He spied his gun lying in the dirt and picked it up.

The glow poured out strongly from the hole before him, and with it the stale stench of death, rushing at him like the fetid exhalation of a carnivore. DeNiza could sense the effluvium had a source far greater than the bones he had passed at the entrance to the tunnel. It made him shiver and suddenly retch.

He bent forward to control his breathing and stayed that way for a few minutes, fighting the urge to flee but failing to muster the courage to continue.

Suddenly, like one of the undead, he stumbled and limped toward the exit of the tunnel. There, he glimpsed a vast domed chamber. Dark water flooded the floor of the cavern.

He took a step closer, blood dripping in his wake, and in the pulsing green light, he could now make out a causeway to an island with a large, pyramid-shaped structure.

Even from a distance he could see gold sparkling on the top of the pyramid. The room glowed and pulsed, and his fear dissipated. "Three hundred years!" he shouted effusively, grinning madly.

He listened to his echo and then added, "For three hundred years, we DeNizas have waited!"

Slowly he limped to the causeway. He was light-headed and disorientated and would suddenly stop and not move for minutes at a time.

He finally crossed the causeway and ascended the pyramid, slipping and staggering a few times. Every scuff of his boots echoed loudly.

Finally, he shook himself, and when his eyes fell on what lay spilled all over the upper stairs and platform, he burst into tears.

Golden coins, masks, and precious gems littered the floor, and an ornate throne sat amidst it all.

"This is the greatest discovery in the history of the Anthropocene!" he said, gawking at the unfathomable wealth.

Breathing heavily, with tears in his eyes, he said, "I claim this treasure in the name of the DeNiza family!"

He swayed and took a knee next to a pile of blue-tinted bones and chains. He said, "I claim it for Cristóbal and Alonso."

Then he started digging into the collapsing wooden chests and containers, and with each treasure he touched, his face seemed to glow brighter. He examined a golden goblet with precious stones inlaid.

His eyes were glossy as he said, "Mine."

He began to stuff some of the finer items in his backpack: a golden mask with a mosaic of garnets; a carved figurine with what looked like diamonds for eyes; and a thick chain of solid gold all made it into his collection.

He mumbled over and over, "Must have proof!"

And that's when DeNiza saw him.

On the golden throne, about twenty feet away, a man sat watching him. The figure leaned back languidly, but his eyes burned like hot coals, emitting a relentless fire.

The man was Aztec. His garb marked him as a warrior of the highest rank.

When the man saw that he had DeNiza's attention, he grinned slightly; and DeNiza sucked in his breath when he saw the filed, pointed teeth.

DeNiza sank to his knees and whimpered.

# Chapter Sixty-eight

*I* crept along the tunnel unsteadily, my nerves trembling. The lichen in the cracks of the black basalt pulsated with a sinister green light as if they were arteries, and their glow outshone the eons-old powder that covered the floor. I gawked at it, bewildered, my faculties temporarily in abeyance.

Soon I came upon an opening where emerald light poured hypnotically out of a hole in the floor.

I inched closer and noticed a puddle of blood trickling into it.

The hole was bored into the center of a heavy stone set into the basalt. When I could peer into it, I discovered it had sealed a room below.

As the light pulsed again, I glimpsed a scene of horror.

Below me, a bound man, a jaguar, a snake, and an eagle all stared up at me. The green light burned for only a few seconds, and in that heartbeat, the man pleaded desperately for help in words I could not understand.

Before the light faded, the jaguar snarled, and the tunnel was suddenly filled with the shrill piercing scream of the eagle.

And then all was silent again.

I gasped for air, and all the hair on my arms stood on end.

When the light pulsed next, I fearfully glanced into the hole again. But it was empty, except for a pile of bones.

I continued down the tunnel, its terminus only a few paces away, and I wondered what new aberration — what fresh hell — I would find when I finally reached the heart of this darkness.

Soon I was standing in an opening to a large cavern.

It was as silent as a crypt. Even sounds I made—my short breaths and the shuffling of my feet—seemed to be snuffed out and absorbed instantly. The air felt as if it hadn't been disturbed in centuries, but this stillness did not bear any semblance of peace.

The cavern rose into a dome where the lichen also thrived, and the entire ceiling was lined with glowing green veins of light.

Immediately before me, cold black water covered the floor, showing not a ripple.

A shout drew my attention to an island in the water, and I made out a large pyramid on it, rising into the green haze. I recognized DeNiza's voice. It carried a note of hysterical terror.

But then the whispering around me tuned it out as it grew more persistent. I could not understand the message until suddenly it screamed at me like a hundred voices: Do not go into the dark cavern!

A recognition swept over me: It was what the women had chanted during my vision from the mushrooms.

As if controlled by another, I spun around, and then everything faded to black.

* * *

Yaotl rose from the throne like a vapor exhaled by the earth. His eyes burned with a smoldering intensity that contained the eons throughout which he had waited for this moment.

He appeared to be savoring this as he slowly drifted toward DeNiza.

The professor could not believe his eyes and blinked them repeatedly. He spat out a high-pitched laugh and shook his head.

"How can this be?" he whispered.

The Aztec lord passed the pile of blue-tinted bones and smirked. He kicked one of the skulls—his own skull—out of the way.

Then he narrowed his gaze and focused his soul's tempestuous anguish on DeNiza again.

414

"You seek Xibalba," he stated gravely in a voice that was resonant and commanded respect.

DeNiza was thunderstruck that he could understand him. The man spoke Nahuatl, the language of the Aztecs, in which the professor was fluent. He had studied the ancient language for a decade.

DeNiza stood up and studied Yaotl's attire. He was seduced into something akin to admiration.

Yaotl said, "Nine hell cycles of fifty-two years each."

"Yes," stammered DeNiza. "That is correct."

Yaotl let his tongue slide over his pointed teeth while he surveyed the room. Then he solemnly added, "Four hundred and sixty-eight years."

DeNiza had regained some self-control and enthusiastically agreed, "Yes, yes… it is Nineteen eighty-seven."

The Aztec brought his gaze back on DeNiza, who trembled anew under Yaotl's gaze. "And how are my people?"

DeNiza shifted uneasily. "Most of the great cities were swallowed by the jungle, left to the monkeys and birds."

He swallowed dryly and added, "Your time has passed."

At this, Yaotl let out a booming laugh that reverberated off the walls of the cavern. Its echoes were still chattering when he shouted, "My time has just begun!"

DeNiza staggered backward, collapsing to his knees tremulously. He bowed, whimpering.

"Do you think I can return to the nothingness?" asked Yaotl incredulously. "That I can again submit to that impalpable greyness that obscures all? Where there is no victory? Or defeat?"

He faced DeNiza and gave him a cold, heavy stare. "I will not."

He stomped his foot angrily. "You have no idea what Xibalba is."

Trembling, DeNiza asked, "And what do you want?"

Yaotl's mien was fierce. "I want it all."

The Aztec took two strides toward DeNiza, grabbing a bone-handled club by his feet and raising it as he approached. "And I don't need you!" he shouted, swinging down.

Suddenly, a thunderous repercussion sounded.

DeNiza had his pistol pointed at Yaotl and had pulled the trigger.

Yaotl looked down at the hole in his chest, which quickly turned to vapor and blew away with the rest of him, leaving DeNiza standing alone.

The professor gave a hysterical little giggle and looked around.

He lowered his gun, and the trailing, acrid smoke made him sneeze. Again, he silently surveyed the room.

"Well then," he sighed after a moment. He shook the appearance of the Aztec off like a bad dream as if it had been a mere hallucination. "I guess I best get back to work."

And he returned to filling his backpack with various gold items and priceless artifacts of jade and silver and gold.

In the end he could barely lift the backpack onto his shoulders. He staggered down the pyramid under its weight, his injured leg threatening to buckle on each step.

At the bottom, he stopped and shrieked.

Yaotl was silently blocking his way.

"I told you, your time is over!" screamed DeNiza, grabbed his gun and shot at the man again.

As before, Yaotl faded away.

But yet he appeared again. DeNiza had to fire his gun twice more before reaching the end of the tunnel.

# Chapter Sixty-nine

DeNiza staggered through the tunnel, red-faced and covered with sweat, dirt and glowing powder. His face wore a crazed expression that somehow combined elation and pain.

He was bent from the weight of the treasure-filled backpack, breathing heavily, and limping from his leg injury.

He was jittery and kept glancing behind him.

He straightened, painfully, when he finally reached the cave where the water dripped, but then a sound from the tunnel made him look back.

He shouted and fired directly into the tunnel. "Enough!" he screamed, "it is mine!"

The repercussion shook the cave as if he'd fired a cannon, and outside, thunder rumbled like an echo.

DeNiza turned away from the tunnel and then stiffened when he saw Amber sitting on the mound with the metate and the offerings.

"Stealing artifacts for your court case?" he asked.

She had her back to him and somehow didn't seem aware of his arrival.

He approached the mound and said, "The world will not believe what I have rediscovered! But you will not be a part of it."

He reached forward, grabbed her by the shoulder and spun her around. His jaw dropped, and he stepped back in shock, and he raised his gun.

Amber had covered her face with grey paint, but that was the smallest part of her transformation. Her eyes were different altogether; they now contained an unswerving steadiness that bore into him.

And despite the fact that he had a gun pointed at her, her gaze held not even the faintest trace of fear.

What was even more disconcerting was the sense that he wasn't even looking at Amber, but someone — or something — else.

He staggered backward.

He glanced out of the cave but was unable to leave.

From the tunnel, he could hear whispering that warned him: *She will steal your treasure... She will claim it for her people.*

He pointed the pistol at her face.

Amber looked at him, unflinching, unafraid. Her strange composure made him falter, and he stood there with the gun shaking in his hand, unable to pull the trigger.

He tried to stoke his courage by taunting her.

"The truth is," he rasped nervously, "you're alone here. There's nobody to help you."

Amber's demeanor brightened suddenly. She covered her mouth to hide an almost girlish giggle. Her expressions now seemed more like that of a young girl.

Then the serious look returned to her face. She said confidently, "I am not alone."

DeNiza stared at her in confusion. "What?"

She continued, "There is somebody. Somebody hears me, and somebody watches over me. I am not alone."

DeNiza cried, "You have lost your mind."

Amber ignored him and moved to the cave exit into the box canyon where it was now raining. As she got close, the wind caught her hair and blew it everywhere.

DeNiza called after her, "I will not let you steal this treasure!"

He raised the gun again and sighted it on the back of her head. But Amber ignored him and stepped out into the box canyon, where it suddenly began to pour.

Without even turning, she said, "You should never have gone inside."

# Chapter Seventy

$S$uddenly I was standing in the rain, sheets of it cascading all around me. I didn't remember when it started or how I got to the box canyon. My last recollection was crouching before the dark cavern at the end of the tunnel.

Above me the sky rippled with lightning, and the walls of the box canyon shook with rolling thunderclaps. The monsoon had finally broken.

I was by the exit chute to the box canyon, where a small stream was now rushing by.

I felt something on my face and wiped it to discover I wore a layer of powdered paint.

I tilted my head up with my eyes closed and let the rain wash me clean.

A moment later, I nearly jumped out of my skin when DeNiza was suddenly beside me.

"What are you searching for, Amber?" he asked from just a few feet away.

His eyes swept the box canyon, then returned to the cave, about thirty feet behind us. "You think you can learn the secret of this place?"

I couldn't form words and just stared at him blankly.

I noticed he was wearing a heavy backpack and held his pistol in his right hand.

I was beginning to come around. Slowly, I remembered the orange powder and that we were both most likely under its influence.

"You've been drugged," I managed to mumble.

DeNiza faced me, water dripping off him. "You think this is all a hallucination? That I'm imagining it all?"

He laughed shrilly and turned to stare at the cave. "What I faced in that cave was no illusion — it was real."

"No," I said, "Psychedelic drugs can cause visions like that. They seem real."

He shook his head slowly, and in a tight voice, said, "Let's just get this over with."

He raised his gun and pointed it at me.

Lighting crashed into the far wall of the box canyon. The rain was coming down so hard I could barely see him. DeNiza looked at the exit chute out of the box canyon, which was now half-filled with whirling water.

"I'm sorry," he said. "But I can't leave you here to steal the treasure." He grabbed the pistol with both hands.

Another bolt of lightning shook the inky sky overhead, and he flinched. His eyes narrowed. "You think this was a place of safety? You think someone had a nice happy home here?"

I circled him slowly so that the exit chute was behind him.

He continued, "This place is a deathtrap — look around."

I did and saw that from all around, the rain funneled down into the drain. "If there's death here, it's because of you," I said. "What I sought was creation..., or love..., or life — something that would make it all make sense."

DeNiza tightened his grip on the pistol. "If you were not so obsessed with these fairy tales, you may have been part of my discovery."

I reminded him flatly, "I never cared about it."

He stared at me and said, "You're just a scared little girl."

I stood tall and steeled my nerves, preparing.

I said calmly, "I may have been once..."

As he returned his focus on the gun, I jumped in the air and kicked him squarely in the chest.

"Not anymore," I added as I swiftly set the foot back on the ground and steadied myself.

The power of the kick, combined with the weight of his pack, sent him backward into the water-filled chute, where he cannonballed upon impact.

For a moment he was visible, his body and the backpack blocking the flow of water. Then its force took hold of the whole bundle and flushed DeNiza and his pack through the chute.

I was left standing in the box canyon alone, looking at the chute, the water flowing into it, almost a river now.

\* \* \*

DeNiza had been flung down the talus slope. His backpack was torn wide open, the gold items scattered in the raging waters all around him.

He clawed at the precious items washing away and howled, "No! My treasure!"

He had rolled out of the stream and managed to pick up a few odd pieces. He stuck them in his shirt but cried out in frustration as he watched the rest disappear. "I must have proof!"

Downward he stumbled, chasing goblets and plates of gold as they were washed to the bottom of Itzel Canyon.

At the confluence with the West Fork, he stood and tried to regain his composure. He controlled his breathing and assessed his situation. Then a sound behind him made him look around.

From the dark sky above, a raven suddenly appeared flying directly at him. It hit him in the forehead with its claws extended, leaving a bloody gouge above his eyes.

DeNiza stood there, stunned, trying to see through the blood that was washing into his vision. He became suddenly aware that water was filling the narrow canyon. He realized if he didn't get out of there, he would drown.

A look of panic crossed his face.

In the back of his head he heard old Saan´s voice warning, "Do something wrong and the rains come."

DeNiza turned and started to run down the canyon.

# Chapter Seventy-one

*I* awoke the following day with yellow sunshine bathing me, letting me know the rain had stopped. I was curled up next to the old adobe ruin, near the fire pit, tight against the wall where the rain hadn't reached.

I moved unhurriedly as I sat up, as in a dream, not quite awake until a large raven landed by my head and cawed.

I stared at the bird. I still felt drugged.

Ten feet away, DeNiza's tent lay half-collapsed from the rain. My tent had fared better. I guessed I'd fallen asleep before I could crawl into it.

I spent a half-hour taking down my tent and packing my things in my small backpack. While I let the outer fly dry in the sun, I looked over DeNiza's gear.

I'm still not sure why, but I grabbed it all and stowed it in the small recess just inside the cave. For a long moment I stared at the weapons and gold coins laid out on the tarp, but in the end, I determined that I would have no part of the evil treasure.

I didn't like going inside the cave, and after two trips determined not to do so again. I stood by the egress and said a silent goodbye. I knew more time in the box canyon wouldn't bring me any answers.

When I exited the slippery chute leading from the box canyon, I stepped straight into a glittering world of sunshine and sparkling raindrops. They clung to the leaves and branches and flashed golden off the wet sheets of sandstone.

The strong scent of petrichor hung over the steep trail as I descended Itzel Canyon. I saw several gold coins on my way, lingering in the bottom of clear puddles.

I picked one up and then dropped it quickly when I felt the tingling warmth. I redoubled my effort not to take anything, convinced no good would come from that treasure.

There was a small river, no mere creek, flowing down the West Fork now, and I had to stay on the bank for much of the way. A few times, I waded waist-deep in the stream when the walls closed in and left no other option.

The drainages that I passed were all still running with rainwater, but the flow seemed to be slowing down. The trickling water was filled with soap suds from running over the roots of yucca plants.

I suddenly spotted the professor's destroyed backpack and called out, "Carlos!" hoping he was far away.

As I approached a turn in the canyon, I saw a large pile of logs and branches. Near the bottom, a flash of color caught my attention.

I hurried to the log pile and found DeNiza pinned under the debris.

It was a miracle that he was still alive, even if just barely. His head was just above the water that had piled up the logs and was still rushing under it.

He tried to smile and painfully asked, "This is how you imagined I would end up, isn't it?"

I denied it. "It isn't at all. I never wanted anything bad to happen to you."

He moaned and said in a strained voice, "No, I suppose you are telling the truth."

I tried to move a few logs, but DeNiza howled in pain.

"Stop!" he screamed in agony. It was hopeless.

A roaring sound upstream got our attention. Another rainstorm further up the creek had caused a surge of water; it was now coming crashing down the canyon.

It hit the bend and all but covered DeNiza.

I frantically tried to lift him out. He shrieked and coughed through the water. "It's no good. I'm dead anyway..."

"I cannot let it end like this," I said.

"Leave," said DeNiza. "Save yourself."

He stared at me for a moment and then said, "I have this coming to me."

I stood my ground. The water was rising. I asked, "Tell me what Cristóbal told Alonso right before he died."

DeNiza hesitated and then said, "It was nothing. He said only one word and then some gibberish."

I pleaded, "Tell me!"

Even now, DeNiza paused. He was having trouble breathing and struggled to raise his head a bit higher.

I held my breath in anticipation.

"He said: Kamala."

I remembered old Saan leaning forward and whispering the same name into my ear. I was awestruck.

"He made the map to get back to *her!*" I exclaimed, overwhelmed by the rush of conviction that swept through me.

Another surge of water headed toward DeNiza.

He blurted out, "Please, spare me your tales of unrequited love—this supposed madness of the heart. You think a woman was more important to him than that treasure?"

I replied, "He said 'Kamala'—and that's a woman's name."

DeNiza nodded weakly.

"And what was the gibberish?" I asked.

He gave a weak smile. "Cristóbal said that when she sang, he thought she was an angel."

I fell silent.

He finally asked, "You will still tell the world of my discovery?"

I shook my head. "Nobody's ever going to know, Carlos. It was never meant to be found."

Eyes filled with disbelief, DeNiza frantically tried to free himself. "What are you saying?" he asked, panting heavily.

I stepped back.

I said, "When I was young, I heard about the cave and the hidden canyon and was told they never existed."

DeNiza struggled to breathe.

I continued, "I don't care about the treasure. I never did. I just had to see for myself if the cave was real."

He was now exhausted from his efforts to keep his head above the rising water.

He coarsely asked, "Will you stop with these fantasies? The world must know of my discovery."

I shook my head again. "It's over, Carlos. I hope it stays hidden for a thousand years."

He howled and tried to wrench free, but it was no good.

Another surge of water came through and forced him to squeeze his eyes shut and hold his breath.

One last time he lifted his head out of the flood and looked at me. He said quickly, "I was a fool."

Then the water engulfed him, and he was gone.

I climbed a steep scree and scrambled to safety.

# Chapter Seventy-two

*T*oday is the fall equinox — when day and night mirror each other. From here on out, the nights will grow longer and the days shorter. After this day, life will begin to recede, and the vegetation in the canyon will start to die.

Yet today, there is no sign of decay as I wind my way up Oak Creek Canyon. The rains have passed, and almost all the vegetation holds some shade of green. Only the fruits of the prickly pear break away from the dominant hue; they've swollen and gone purple.

I believe Martin Gray would have told me that during these celestial events — equinoxes and solstices — energies or spirits are more present. Or at least, that's what the countless myths speak of.

And DeNiza might have bragged of the Mayans and Aztecs, and how very well they were aware of those dates.

But I shut him out.

I don't glance at the West Fork trailhead as I pass it.

For me, that is the past. I watched the headlines, waiting to see what might surface. I assumed somebody found DeNiza's rental jeep at the West Fork trailhead, and the Junipine Inn probably wondered what to do with his luggage, but nobody started a fuss.

I called Tim at the Red Rock News and casually inquired about missing hikers. Nothing.

At least in Sedona, he wasn't missed.

So, I moved on. I put Aunt Saan's place up for rent and began searching Flagstaff for a place to live.

I'm on my way now to look at a rental.

Me and Heyduke, on the road again. I think I mentioned how much I love my truck. I know if the rental doesn't work out, he'll still have me. I've got a new futon in the back, and I'm not afraid to use it.

I approach the switchbacks and see the first few trees with yellow leaves. None have dropped yet, and the forest seems particularly tidy without their clutter.

In Flagstaff I stop at Sprouts to get some food. No matter where I end up, I'm going to need to eat. The San Francisco Peaks stand proudly above the town, and I contemplate a hike before the snow sets in.

I grab a cart and begin loading it. I've been famished lately and can't seem to eat enough. Even now, as I shop, my stomach growls incessantly.

I step forward and reach for a loaf of bread on a top shelf, and bump right into a long-haired, bearded young guy with the sweetest smile I've ever seen on a man.

I drop my loaf of bread, and before I can move, he stoops and picks it up.

And we just stare at each other.

I'm speechless, and it appears he is too. But the silence that follows is comfortable, and soon we both chuckle.

"Hi," he says, extending his hand with my bread in it. "I'm sorry — but I'm starving and just want to get out of here and make a sandwich."

I accept the loaf, laughing. "Me too!"

I look into his eyes, and suddenly every other care I have melts away. Finally, I blurt out, "Would you care to go on a picnic?"

He smiles, and his eyes light up. "There's nothing I would rather do more. Let's get out of here."

# *Epilogue*

### 2019
(October)

*I*n the dream, a white-haired Mayan woman sits on a flat rock in a peaceful lagoon. She dangles her feet in the water, slides over the edge of the rock, and drops in.

Downward she plunges. And even though the size of the pond suggests the water can't be that deep, she is soon out of sight, obscured by the murky depths.

In a meadow not far away, a few does watch, wide-eyed. A light breeze blows through, shivering the leaves on the cottonwoods and sycamores. A raccoon skitters by on the far shore.

And then the woman resurfaces.

In her hand, she holds a round white stone with a gold band.

She hoists herself back onto the rock and smiles, her face flush from the exertion.

"We must remember to return it," she says.


I woke with a jolt, startling my sleeping husband. He grunted and rolled over, and I lay there quietly, trying in vain to return to sleep and back to the dream. Out the window, the horizon was tinged with gray and soft pink, and after a while, I decided to get up.

While making a coffee, I pondered the dream.

I recognized the white stone, even though it had been well over thirty years since I'd glimpsed it in the cave with DeNiza.

And I recognized the peaceful lagoon, too.

I hadn't been to Oak Creek in decades. Not that I was trying to avoid it, I just got swept up in life.

A few weeks after my incident in the box canyon, I literally bumped into a young man at a grocery store in Flagstaff. I'm not gonna tell you anything about him, other than that he's the love of my life, and I eventually followed him to New Mexico.

We had two children, a boy and a girl. They're grown now and not connected to this story in any way, so I won't tell you their names either. It's enough to say we're a good family, full of love and laughter—and grandbabies in the near future.

For thirty years it's been enough, but now, all I can think about is that white stone. Prior to this dream, nothing seemed to be missing from my life. I was happy. I had a family. I believed I was content.

Now I knew there was a task yet unfinished.

I sipped my coffee and remembered my past, and before the sun had fully risen, I was loading my car. Sadly, my pickup, Heyduke, had been retired, but the Elantra was only a year old and would complete the drive easily.

My husband gave me a strange look when I told him I had to go to Flagstaff to visit an old college friend. He was a bit nervous about me making the six-hour drive, but I assured him I'd be fine and be back the next evening.

In the driveway, he wished me a good journey and kissed me goodbye.


By mid-afternoon I was approaching Flagstaff. However, a detour forced me to use I-17 south to route 179, and I came into Sedona from the west through the Village of Oak Creek, passing Bell Rock and then heading up Oak Creek Canyon.

The town had twice as many residents since I'd lived there in the eighties and seemed to be booming. A banner advertised the *Illuminate Film Festival*, and another, *P.K. Gregory* at the *Page Springs Winery's Fall Harvest*. There were touring jeeps everywhere, a fair amount of traffic, and a whole lot of roundabouts that nobody seemed to know how to use.

Uptown appeared to have gone through several enhancements, with streetlights and new sidewalks.

I headed up the canyon and soon passed over Midgley Bridge, which spanned Wilson Canyon—named after an Arkansas bear hunter who got killed there by a grizzly in 1885.

Continuing north, I skirted the Rainbow Trout Farm on the right and then pulled into Garlands on the left. I ordered lunch, impressed by their new gourmet menu. I ordered the "Bear Howard" sandwich—roast beef and gouda—and stuffed it in my daypack.

Memories flowed over me as I drove north. I was surprised to see the Dairy Queen was still there, the parking lot filled with Navajo women selling jewelry. And Slide Rock State Park appeared just as crowded as ever.

When I glanced at the Junipine Inn, I suddenly heard DeNiza, in the back of my mind, bragging about the delicious breakfast he had in the garden back in eighty-seven. It was the first time I'd thought about him in years.

Don Hoel's cabins appeared unchanged. I wondered if I would need a room for the night. I hadn't entirely planned things out—or maybe I just hadn't admitted to myself what I was gonna do.

But I parked at the West Fork trailhead, shouldered my small pack, and started walking. Fall was upon the canyon, and the oaks and cottonwoods flashed yellow in the sun.

The first three or four miles were easy, and I stepped along in the company of dozens of tourists. Tall pines lining vertical cliffs engulfed us, and a determined breeze whispered through their needles.

Three-and-a-half miles in, my fellow tourists stopped to stare at the long, flooded section ahead, then turned back to the parking lot.

I waited until I was alone, then took off my boots and waded into the water. Luckily, the monsoon had passed, and not much precipitation had come down since then. At the deepest point, the water didn't go above my knees.

Back in Santa Fe, I kept in shape through yoga and hiking, but I was fifty-nine now, and deep down, I feared this expedition might be slightly beyond my capabilities. My nervousness kept me walking, though, and before long, I passed through the long tunnel — only a little water there — and eventually reached the confluence of the West Fork and Itzel Canyon.

The way up that canyon was surprisingly easy like someone had prepared it for me, sweeping everything out of my way. And I found no obstructions in the chute that lead to the canyon, either. I wondered if anyone had stumbled upon it over the years — it seemed easy enough to find.

I paused before ascending to catch my breath and calm my nerves, and then I once more climbed the chute into the box canyon.

It was as if time stood motionless in the quiet canyon. The crumbling ruin in the corner was still surrounded by old Sinaguan pots, and the fire ring still held its ash. Propped on a rock, the old Spanish helmet faced the chute — its top covered in bird droppings.

In the cave, water continued to drip randomly. DeNiza's gear was where I had left it piled in the small recess three decades ago, and the ground was still crisscrossed with his archaeological guide strings.

I tried not to look at the dark tunnel and instead focused on the mound with the offerings. It was growing dusky outside as the late afternoon sun cast the box canyon in shadow, and I noticed three lichen-covered basalt manos and the metate all glowing at me.

I half-expected to hear my mother's voice in the cave, but I didn't. On the mound, behind the bowls of colored powder, I saw the old photo of my mother and Saan. I picked it up and stared through the gloom at the image.

After a moment, I sighed and set it back down.

I dug into the mound and immediately came across the bundle of leather. I opened it and looked at the white stone. While I gazed at it, the years flowed around me, and I might have lingered longer had not a foul stench of decay floated toward me out of the tunnel.

Quickly, I stuffed the stone in my daypack and backed out of the cave. And then, with only one fearful glance over my shoulder, I crossed the box canyon and scurried down the chute.


I hurried along the trail. It was growing dark, and even though I carried a flashlight, I didn't look forward to the long walk back alone.

But now that I was out of the box canyon, the fear was leaving me. I felt safe as I walked along as if the narrow canyon and lofty pines I walked through supported my endeavor.

As if my mother were alongside me. Protecting me.

Before I even reached the flooded tunnel, I was immersed in darkness, but when I stepped out on the other side, I was greeted by a brilliant hunter's moon.

It escorted me all the way back to my car, where a ravenous hunger overtook me, and only now did I remember that I had a sandwich with me.

It was an unexpected pleasure. I'd anticipated a simple meat and cheese sandwich, but the sweet taste of caramelized onions and peppadew jam, topped with a bite of horseradish, jolted my mouth awake.

"Way to go, Garlands," I said, licking my lips.

I drove a mile up the road and pulled over north of Cave Springs campground. I settled the white stone snugly in the bottom of my daypack, shouldered it, and began walking upstream. Only as I approached the quiet lagoon did the moon wink goodbye and disappear over the western rim of Oak Creek Canyon.

I sat on the flat rock in the lagoon, my naked feet dangling in the creek. The moon was gone, the night dark. I felt alone. I was exhausted, and my limbs shook. A sadness came over me.

It was so dark you could get lost in it, and I imagined all sorts of things moving in the shadows. I could barely make out the stone pillar with the spiral petroglyph behind me, but at its base, several lichen-covered pieces of basalt glowed softly.

I began to sob as I remembered my mother's song, and my mission to explain it.

It was a quest that had failed. I had failed. I had found a hidden box canyon, which may have been the one my mother found all those years ago. Or it may have just been a canyon with a dark secret. I never found a direct connection between the cave and her.

And although DeNiza and I did uncover a sinister treasure, it wasn't what I'd been looking for. Even now, after years of marriage, and bills, and occasional hard times, I never once thought of returning for the treasure. When I went back for the stone, I never considered going through the tunnel again.

It was dark as ink, and there was a chill in the air. I took the white stone out of my pack and held it in my lap. The water was cold and whispered as it ran swiftly among the reeds that lined the shore. I stripped down naked and slid into the lagoon, taking the white stone with me.

I sank under, and in the murky gloom, I could see little. It seemed I dove down far deeper than should have been possible. Soon I reached the bottom of the large flat-topped stone I'd been sitting on and felt that under it was an open space.

It glowed slightly, just enough to see by, and I took the stone and placed it as far under the rock as I could reach. I lingered by it for just a moment before ascending.

Back on the flat rock, I lay down and caught my breath. I was shaking from adrenaline as much as from the cold. I dried myself with a sarong and then got dressed again, leaving my shoes off.

I rolled onto my side, intending only to rest a moment, but sleep quickly stole me away. And I lay there unmoving. Not cold. Not scared. Just sleeping like the dead until a soft dream sprang up.

And in this dream, I listened to my mother's song, and her love washed over me like a warm summer breeze.

I woke with the sun streaming down on my face and found in daylight, the place was a bit of a letdown. The lagoon didn't seem as big or as ancient in the bright light of day. The water still trickled by melodically, and in the first hours after the sunrise, the sky was pink, birds twittered about, and small critters scurried in the brush — but it was different.

Well-worn paths suggested it now saw a lot of traffic.

I hoped it was possibly the onslaught of fall that I sensed.

A large tree must have died, leaving a gaping hole in the canopy, for sunlight streamed directly onto the flat rock I sat on. I remembered this rock had once been covered with moss, but in the harsh sunlight, the moss could not survive.

The patinated rock with the spiral petroglyph had also been sun-bleached, and the moss that had once grown on the rock's bottom had died and was falling away.

I remembered the new state campground that now flanked the lagoon and knew tourists would be showing up before long.

I moved to the edge of the flat rock and let my feet hang in the water again. With the moss now gone, I noticed several round depressions in the rock where long ago, people must have ground food or medicine. My fingers traced their outlines.

A heron swooped down on the other side of the lagoon and watched me.

I heard a few shouts from the camping area as people began to stir. I sat silently, feeling closer to the mystery but still shy of an answer. Having heard the song recently—in my dream—its loss hurt me even more.

When the sun rose higher, I looked at the spiral petroglyph again. And then below it, I noticed two partially obscured pictographs. They must have been hidden under the moss all these years.

I stood and hopped from rock to rock until I was crouching before the pillar. Gently, I rubbed at what was left of the moss covering the ancient designs, and it crumbled to my touch.

Underneath it, a circular image was revealed. It had been cut through the middle by a crack in the rock. On one side of the crack, a bear print appeared with what looked like a bear claw necklace suspended above it. On the other side, a woman in childbirth squatted over several lines that seemed to represent water.

I knew deep in my gut that somehow this was connected to the story of the cave in the box canyon. But how?

I gazed at the three stones lying at the base of the pillar and remembered how they had glowed the night before—just like the basalt manos by the metate on the mound.

In the vision I'd had under the influence of the Aztec mushrooms, I'd seen women grinding them, harvesting the lichen—a lichen I now knew was a potent hallucinogen.

I glanced at the depressions on the flat rock in the lagoon. I stared at the three basalt stones. "You were brought here," I said.

I picked up one of the stones and carried it back to the flat rock. I knelt and ground the stone into the depression. When I lifted it again, a smattering of orange powder covered the indentation.

I wet my finger, touched the powder, and stuck it in my mouth.

And then I sat and faced the water, letting my feet soak, wiggling my toes. And after a few timeless moments, my perception began to alter.

Suddenly, the trees seemed to expand and grow, as did the clearing. Suddenly, the place felt ancient again, and with a shocking shift, I sensed the trees and plants were all watching me.

It was just as when I'd heard my mother's song all those years ago in the sinkhole.

My breath quickened as I glanced around me. I closed my eyes, and time seemed to stretch, and I slid to my side.

I sat up groggily when I heard several tourists chatting. I glanced around and noted at least a dozen people here, some taking in the quiet glade, others hiking through. By the base of a large sycamore, a young couple in their late teens was having a picnic, and an older girl of around twenty was setting up a slackline across the creek.

Closer to me, an older couple with a young daughter were skipping rocks across the lagoon. The dad looked about fifty, with a white streak in his hair — probably, I thought, from stressing out at some east coast job. And the wife, pretty, early forties, smiled as she took in the peaceful setting.

Their young girl was engaged in a cartwheel contest along the shore, counting off each one. "Forty-four, forty-five..."

The dad said, "I'd really like to hike that West Fork trail today."

The mom shrugged, "Well, don't forget my treatment at Uptown Massage at three-thirty."

The girl crumbled to the ground. "Forty-six!"

Soon the parents drifted downstream, slowly following the shore. But their daughter, a girl of nine or ten, was now hopping along the rocks in the creek, and with a quick glance to her parents, jumped to my rock and sat next to me.

"Hi," she said, not shy at all.

I smiled back, and the brightness in her eyes reminded me of myself when I was young. In fact, she was about the same age as I'd been when my mother took me to the sinkhole and let me hear the song.

And I let my mind linger on that memory, remembering my mother and how she sang for me that night. Her song swept over me, and as the trees around me watched and waited, I steadied my nerves, and then I began to sing.

The young girl looked at me strangely, and then she began staring at the trees around us. My heart skipped a beat as I realized my song was making her see the forest differently—just as I had when my mother sang it.

We smiled at each other and continued to gawk at the sycamores and cottonwoods swaying around us. They were sentient, ancient and peaceful.

As I sang, I felt loved and like I was sharing love.

I looked down at the young child and thought, "I could teach this—I could share it."

A rush ran through me as I thought of how differently people might treat each other if everyone could look at life from this perspective. It could change the world.

And then the young girl's parents called for her and came closer again, and as they heard my song, they also began to look around, peering closely at the ferns and shrubs along the creek. They, too, were suddenly looking at life differently.

The young couple having a picnic held hands, and each placed their free hand on the trunk of an old sycamore. The young man glanced at me and then whispered to his girlfriend, and she nodded back.

Further downstream, the young woman on the slackline had paused in a graceful split over the water—suspended in a stillness that even the great heron would admire. She appeared to hold her pose effortlessly as she swayed with the wind and the murmuring creek.

I wondered if placing the white stone under the rock had changed things. Whether it was because of the location, or the melody—or maybe the orange powder that had my mind tingling—I didn't know, but I knew it was my mother's song, and I was singing it.

And the people around me were feeling it.

*I didn't know what the lady was doing on the rock. It looked like a nice spot, and when my parents moved along the creek, I snuck out beside her.*

*She looked like an Indian, although I didn't know, having never met one before. But I liked how she smiled at me.*

*And when she began to sing, the whole forest woke up. I'd never seen anything like it. The tall trees, the flowers, and even the moss-covered rocks seemed aware of me now.*

*And I was aware of them.*

*A yellow butterfly drifted by my face, caressing me with its wings. In the water, I spied trout looking up at me too.*

*And as her song washed over me, I felt overflowing with happiness and joy.*

*I stuck my feet in the water next to her, and then I also began to sing.*

# *Postscript*

## 2020
(November)

Ruins revealed by Arizona's Slide fire tell the story of early settlers and now a greater mystery. **November 21, 2020.**

The 2014 Slide fire burned 21,000 acres between Flagstaff and Sedona, opening an unobstructed door to remote corners of the world's largest Ponderosa pine forest. The blaze also uncovered the ruins of a cabin at least a century old.

Local historians speculate that the cabin belonged to an early settler named Bear Howard. Howard had built a cabin at the front of the 13-mile long West Fork, so it seems likely that he would have made a cabin at the other end. The remnants of this cabin were sparse, with only the corner of one wall still standing.

Subsequent archaeological work at the site has unearthed the remains of a wooden bucket, buried under the cabin, that contained a small hoard of gold coins and a Mayan dagger. To complicate the mystery, the coins are highly radioactive.

Resident geologist Jeff Goebel noted that the gravel surrounding the coins in the bucket was local, and next month the forest service will begin an extensive survey of the area. "With a little luck, we might just find a mine, or cave, where these incredible items came from."

# *Pioneer Lineage*

### Jesse Jefferson "Bear" Howard (1817-1921) & Nancy Cline (1839-61)

Their children:
1856 – Jesse Jackson Howard
1858 – Martha "Mattie" Howard


### Stephen Purtymun (1855-1929) & Mattie Howard (1858-1947)

Their children:
1876 – Emory Purtymun
1879 – Jess Purtymun
1881 – Albert Purtymun


### John James Thompson (1842-17)
### & Margaret James Thompson (1864-1936)

Their children (eventually they had 10):
1881 – Frank Thompson
1884 – Margaret "Lizzie" Thompson


### Abraham James (1823-82) & Elizabeth James (1828-1900)

Their children:
1847 – Louisa
1849 – William
1851 – Augustus
1854 – Mary Jane
1861 – James
1864 – **Margaret**
1868 – David

# *Sirens*

**Kayah** (age 40) – Sinaguan – 800 A.D.
** *Her name means: Elder Sister.*

**Totsi** (*age 10*) – Sinaguan – 800 A.D.
** *Her name means: Moccasin.*

**Cocheta** (*age 16*) – Apache – 1395
** *Her name means: The Unknown.*

**Imala** (*age 18*) – Apache – 1521
** *Her name means: The Enforcer.*

**Kamala** (*age 20*) – Apache – 1705
** *We don't know her name.*

**Margaret Thompson** (*age 15*) – Pioneer – 1876.

**Martha Howard** (*age 27*) – Pioneer – 1885.
** *Nickname: Mattie.*

**Amber** (*age 28 & 59*) – Apache/white/Hopi – 1987 & 2019.
** *Nickname: Am Bear.*

**Little Girl** (*age 10*) – A new generation learns the song.

# A note from Martin Gray

Millennia before the development of organized religions, humans sought insights regarding the mysteries of life through various shamanic methods. These methods included the ritual use of specific places (caves, springs, forest groves), mind-altering plant substances (cannabis, psilocybin, amanita), and music (rhythmic drumming and chanting). Each of these practices - particularly when used together - produced heightened states of spiritual awareness, precognitive visions, miraculous healings, and the revelatory perception of the natural world as being remarkably conscious.

Certain individuals, whether through innate capacities or because of long training, possessed the ability to function as shamans, guides or healers for other people. A primary way this shamanic ability was exercised was through ceremonial chanting, singing and drumming, wherein participants, the pilgrims, were guided into a hypnotic state in which the shaman's insights and healing powers were conveyed to and upon them.

In *the Sirens of Oak Creek*, the singers are often influenced by a psychedelic, which appears to open a deeper realm of meaning within them—and in those who hear the song. Under this new perspective, nature is suddenly sentient, and the listener is drawn to it. Many scholars and doctors believe the mystical experiences brought on by drugs like psilocybin have the potential to revolutionize how we treat addiction and depression, and countless patients have claimed a session under a psychedelic drug was the most meaningful and spiritually significant event of their lives. It is no wonder that Amber (from the story) felt the heightened sensitivity to nature brought on by the song might change the world—if only everyone could see it this way.

*The author, on Steamboat Rock, Sedona*

**Robert Louis DeMayo** is a native of Hollis, N.H., but has lived in many corners of the planet. He took up writing at the age of twenty when he left his job as a biomedical engineer to explore the world. His extensive journaling during his travels inspired four of his novels and far-reaching work for the travel section of *The Telegraph*, out of Nashua, NH, as well as the *Hollis Times*. He is a member of The Explorers Club and chair of its Southwest Chapter.

His undying hunger for exploration led to a job marketing for Eos Study Tours, a company that served as a travel office for six non-profit organizations and offered dives to the *Titanic* and the *Bismarck*, Antarctic voyages, African safaris and archaeological tours throughout the world.

For several years after that, Robert worked as a tour guide in Alaska and the Yukon during the summers and as a jeep guide in Arizona during the winter. He was made general manager of the jeep tour company but eventually left the guiding world to write full time.

DeMayo is the author of eight novels: "The Making of Theodore Roosevelt," a fictionalized account of Roosevelt's first acquaintance with wilderness living; "The Light Behind Blue Circles," a mystery thriller set in Africa; "The Wayward Traveler," a semi-autobiographical story following a young traveler on his adventures abroad; "The Legend of Everett Ruess," a fictionalized account of the life and times of the young solo traveler of the American West; "The Road to Sedona," the story of a young family that heads up to Alaska to find work in the wake of 9/11; and "The Sirens of Oak Creek," a historical mystery of Oak Creek Canyon, Arizona spanning twelve centuries. Collectively, his books have won eight national awards.

In 2021 he published *Pithecophilia*, a collection of stories of primate encounters around the world and how they filled him with hope. And in 2022 he will release *The King of the Coral Sea*, an historical fiction account of Michael Fomenko's epic sea journey in 1958 from Cairns, Australia to Dutch New Guinea.

Currently, he resides in Sedona, AZ, with his wife Diana and three daughters: Tavish Lee, Saydrin Scout, and Martika Louise.

*Other Books by Robert Louis DeMayo*

**The Making of Theodore Roosevelt**
(Historical Fiction)

**The Wayward Traveler**
(Memoir-based non-fiction)

**The Light Behind Blue Circles**
(Travel Fiction)

**The Legend of Everett Ruess**
(Historical Fiction)

**The Road to Sedona**
(Non-fiction Travel)

**Pithecophilia**
(Memoir-based non-Fiction)

## *Also by* Robert Louis DeMayo

*"Pithecophilia — the love of apes and monkeys — is a slightly dry and academic term that fails to hint at the charm of this book. I found Pithecophilia a blueprint for anyone dreaming of exploring the world without benefit of a trust fund. Such a deficit did not stop Robert Louis DeMayo, who odd-jobbed his way across five continents over several decades on budgets most people would blow in one visit to Yellowstone. This book would make an inspiring gift for any young person who is a fan of Steve Irwin, David Attenborough — or Indiana Jones.*

Jonathan Hanson
(Amazon review)

### PITHECOPHILIA

From the steep slopes of the Virunga Volcanoes to the steamy jungles of Sumatra, *Pithecophilia* explores author, Robert Louis DeMayo's life-changing search for ape encounters, as he discovers the secrets of their history, biology, and what they can tell us about ourselves. Touching on the efforts of the world's leading conservationists and scientific institutions, you'll also discover how the early exploration of Africa and Asia's untamed wilderness shaped our knowledge of apes and how their efforts to document our planet's wild animals eventually led to efforts to save them. Imbued with touching memories, humorous anecdotes, and over fifty years of wondrous, magical, and sometimes terrifying experiences, *Pithecophilia* paints a beautiful picture of how primates are, in many ways, windows into our own souls.

Non-fiction Travel-memoir.
Wayward Publishing.
Available in print & eBook.

447

Made in the USA
Monee, IL
06 November 2023